Also by
Sarah Morgan

Look for Sarah Morgan's next novel
The Summer Seekers
available soon from HQN.

For additional books by Sarah Morgan,
visit her website, www.sarahmorgan.com.

Sarah Morgan

A *Wedding in* December

HQN

MIX
Paper from
responsible sources
FSC® C021394
www.fsc.org

Recycling programs
for this product may
not exist in your area.

ISBN-13: 978-1-335-14798-1

A Wedding in December

HQN
22 Adelaide St. West, 40th Floor
Toronto, Ontario M5H 4E3, Canada
www.Harlequin.com

Printed in Lithuania

This book is dedicated to Manpreet Grewal,
an inspiration in every way.

A *Wedding in*
December

Maggie

WHEN HER PHONE rang at three in the morning, ripping her from a desperately needed sleep, Maggie's first thought was *bad news*.

Her mind raced through the possibilities, starting with the worst-case scenario. Death, or at least life-changing injury. Police. Ambulances.

Heart pounding, brain foggy, she grabbed her phone from the summit of her teetering pile of books. The name on the screen offered no reassurance.

Trouble stalked her youngest daughter.

"Rosie?" She fumbled for the light and sat up. The book she'd fallen asleep reading thudded to the floor, scattering the pile of Christmas cards she'd started to write the night before. She'd chosen a winter scene of snow-laden trees. They hadn't had a flake of snow in the village on Christmas Day for close to a decade. They often joked that it was a good thing their last name was White because it was the only way they were ever going to have a White Christmas.

She snuggled under the blanket with the phone. "Has something happened?" The physical distance between her and Rosie made her feel frustrated and helpless.

Everyone said global travel made the world smaller, but

it didn't seem smaller to Maggie. Why couldn't her daughter have continued her studies closer to home? Oxford, with its famous spires and ancient colleges, was only a few miles away. Rosie had done her undergraduate degree there, followed by a master's. Maggie had loved having her close by. They'd taken sunlit strolls along cobbled streets, past ancient honey-colored buildings and through Christchurch Meadows, golden with daffodils. They'd followed the slow meander of the river and cheered on the rowing crews. Maggie had hoped, privately, that her daughter might stay close by, but after Rosie had graduated she'd been offered a place in a US doctoral program, complete with full funding.

Can you believe it, Mum? The day she'd had the news she'd danced across the living room, hair flying around her face, twirling until she was dizzy and Maggie was dizzy watching her. *Are you proud of me?*

Maggie had been proud and dismayed in equal measure, although she'd hidden the dismayed part of course. That was what you did when you were a parent.

Even she could see it was too good an opportunity to turn down, but still a small part of her had wished Rosie *had* turned it down. That transatlantic flight from the nest left Maggie with email, Skype and social media, none of which felt entirely satisfactory. Even less so in the middle of the night. Had Rosie only been gone for four months? It felt like a lifetime since they'd delivered her to the airport on that sweltering summer's day.

"Is it your asthma? Are you in hospital?" What could she do if Rosie *was* in the hospital? Nothing. Anxiety was a constant companion, never more so than now.

If it had been her eldest daughter, Katie, who had moved to a different country she might have felt more relaxed.

Katie was reliable and sensible, but Rosie? Rosie had always been impulsive and adventurous.

"I'm not in hospital. Don't fuss!"

Only now did Maggie hear the noise in the background. Cheering, whooping.

"Do you have your inhaler with you? You sound breathless." The sound woke the memories. Rosie, eyes bulging, lips stained blue. The whistling sound as air struggled to squeeze through narrowed airways. Maggie making emergency calls with hands that shook almost too hard to hold the phone, the terror raw and brutal although she kept that hidden from her child. Calm, she'd learned, was important even if it was faked.

Even when Rosie had moved from child to adult there had been no reprieve.

Some children grew out of asthma. Not Rosie.

There had been a couple of occasions when Rosie was in college when she'd gone to parties without her inhaler. A few hours of dancing later and she'd been rushed to the emergency department. That had been a 3:00 a.m. phone call, too, and Maggie had raced through the night to be by her side. Those were the episodes Maggie knew about. She was sure there were plenty more that Rosie had kept to herself.

"I'm breathless because I'm excited. I'm twenty-two, Mum. When are you going to stop worrying?"

"That would be never. Your child is always your child, no matter how many candles are on the birthday cake. Where are you?"

"I'm with Dan's family in Aspen for Thanksgiving, and I have news." She broke off and Maggie heard the clink of glasses and Rosie's infectious laugh. It was impossible to hear that laugh and not want to smile, too. The sound contrasted with the silence of Maggie's bedroom.

A waft of cold air chilled her skin and she stood up and grabbed her robe from the back of the chair. Honeysuckle Cottage looked idyllic from the outside, but it was impossibly drafty. The ventilation was a relief in August but froze you to the bone in November. She really needed to do something about the insulation before she even thought about selling the place. Historic charm, climbing roses and a view of the village green couldn't compensate for frostbite.

Or maybe it wasn't the house that was cold. Maybe it was her.

Knocked flat by a wave of sadness and she struggled to right herself.

"What's happening? What news? It sounds like you're having a party."

"Dan proposed. *Literally* out of the blue. We were taking it in turns to say what we're thankful for and when it was his turn he gave me a funny look and then he got down on one knee and—Mum, we're getting married."

Maggie sat down hard on the edge of the bed, the freezing air forgotten. "Married? But you and Dan have only been together for a few weeks—"

"Eleven weeks, four days, six hours and fifteen minutes—oh wait, now it's sixteen, I mean seventeen—" She was laughing, and Maggie tried to laugh with her.

How should she handle this? "That's not very long, sweetheart." But completely in character for Rosie, who bounced from one impulse to another, powered by enthusiasm.

"It feels so right, I can't even tell you. And you'll understand because it was like that for you and Dad."

Maggie stared at the damp patch on the wall.

Tell her the truth.

Her mouth moved but she couldn't push the words out. This was the wrong time. She should have done it months ago, but she'd been too much of a coward.

And now it was too late. She didn't want to be the slayer of happy moments.

She couldn't even say *you're too young*, because she'd been the same age when she'd had Katie. Which basically made her a hypocrite. Or did it make her someone with experience?

"You just started your postgrad—"

"I'm not giving it up. I can be married and study. Plenty do it."

Maggie couldn't argue with that. "I'm happy for you." Did she sound happy? She tried harder. "Woohoo!"

She'd thought she'd white-knuckled her way through all the toughest parts of parenting, but it turned out there were still some surprises waiting for her. Rosie wasn't a child anymore. She had to be allowed to make her own decisions. And her own mistakes.

Rosie was talking again. "I know it's all a bit fast, but you're going to love Dan as much as I do. You said you thought he was great when you spoke to him."

But speaking to someone on a video call wasn't the same as meeting them in person, was it?

Maggie swallowed down all the words of warning that rose up inside her. She was *not* going to turn into her own mother and send clouds to darken every bright moment. "He seemed charming, and I'm thrilled for you. If I don't sound it, it's because it's the middle of the night here, and you know what I'm like when I've just woken up. When I saw your name pop up on the screen, I was worried it was your asthma."

"Haven't had an attack in ages. I'm sorry I woke you, but I wanted to share my news."

"I'm glad you woke me. Tell me everything." She closed her eyes and tried to pretend her daughter was in the room with her, and not thousands of miles away.

There was no reason to panic. It was an engagement, that was all. There was plenty of time for them to decide if this was the right thing for them. "We'll have a big celebration when you and your sister are here for Christmas. Would Dan like to join us? I can't wait to meet him. Maybe we'll throw a party. Invite the Baxters, and all your friends from college and school." Planning lifted Maggie's mood. Christmas was her favorite time of year, the one occasion the whole family gathered together. Even Katie, with her busy life as a doctor, usually managed to beg and barter a few days at Christmas in exchange for covering the busy New Year shift. Maggie was looking forward to spending time with her. She had a niggling suspicion her eldest daughter was avoiding her. Every time Maggie suggested meeting up, Katie made an excuse, which was unlike her because she rarely refused a free lunch.

Christmas would give her a chance to dig a little deeper.

In her opinion, Oxford was the perfect place to spend the festive season. True, there was unlikely to be snow, but what was better than a postlunch walk listening to the peal of bells on a crisp, cold winter's day?

It promised to be perfect, apart from one complication. Nick.

Maggie still hadn't figured out how she was going to handle that side of things.

Maybe an engagement was exactly what they needed to shift the focus of attention.

"Christmas is one of the things I need to talk to you

about." Rosie sounded hesitant. "I planned to come home, but since Dan proposed—well, we don't see the point in waiting. We've chosen the day. We're getting married on Christmas Eve."

Maggie frowned. "You mean next year?"

"No, this year."

She counted the days and her brain almost exploded. "You want to get married in less than four weeks? To a man you barely know?" Rosie had always been impulsive, but this wasn't a soft toy that would be abandoned after a few days, or a dress that would turn out to be not quite the right color. Marriage wasn't something that could be rectified with a refund. There was no reason for haste, unless—"Sweetie—"

"I know what you're thinking, and it isn't that. I'm not pregnant! We're getting married because we're in love. I adore him. I've never felt this way about anyone before."

You barely know him.

Maggie shifted, uncomfortably aware that knowing someone well didn't inoculate you against problems.

"I'm excited for you!" Turned out she could fake excitement as convincingly as she could fake calm. "But I could never arrange anything that quickly. Even a small wedding takes months of planning. When Jennifer Hill was married in the summer her mother told me they had to book the photographer more than a year in advance. And would everyone stay? It's Christmas. Everywhere will already be booked, and even if we managed to find something it would cost a fortune at this time of year."

How many could she accommodate in Honeysuckle Cottage? And what would Dan's family think of Rosie's home, with its slightly crooked walls and its antiquated heating system? Could English country charm compensate for frozen toes? In the summer the place was picture-perfect, with its walled garden and profusion of climbing roses, but living here in winter felt more like an exercise in survival. Still, Aspen was in the Rocky Mountains, and that had to be a pretty cold place in winter, too, surely?

Maybe she and Dan's mother would bond over the challenges of heating a property in cold weather.

"You wouldn't have to arrange anything," Rosie said. "We're getting married here, in Aspen. I feel terrible about not having our usual family gathering in the cottage but spending the holidays here will be magical. Remember all those years Katie and I used to stare out of the window hoping for snow? There's more snow here than you could ever imagine. Christmas in Colorado is going to be heaven. The scenery is incredible, and it will be a White Christmas in every way possible."

Christmas in Colorado.

Maggie stared at the dusky pink curtains that pooled on the dark oak floor. She'd made them during the long nights she'd spent watching over Rosie.

"You're not coming home for Christmas?" Why had she said that? She was not going to turn into one of those mothers who buried their children in guilt. "You must get married where and when you want, but I don't suppose Aspen will be any different from here in terms of arrangements. To arrange a wedding in under a month would take a miracle."

"We have a miracle. Catherine, Dan's mother, is a wedding planner. She's amazing. This only happened an hour ago and she's already made some calls and arranged the flowers and the cake. Usually she handles celebrities, so she has tons of contacts."

"Oh, well—super." Maggie felt as if she'd fallen in a

river and was being swept along, helpless and flailing. "She doesn't mind helping you?"

"She's excited. And she has flawless taste. Everything will be perfect."

Maggie thought of her own imperfect life and felt a rush of something she recognized as jealousy. How could she be jealous of someone she'd never met?

Maybe she was having a midlife crisis, but surely if that was the case then it should have happened years ago when Rosie had first left home? Why now? She was having delayed empty nest syndrome.

She blinked to clear her misty vision and wondered why she'd ever thought it would be easy to be a parent.

Focusing on the practical, she made a mental list of all the things she'd have to do to cancel Christmas. The cake would keep, as would the cranberry sauce, waiting in the freezer. She'd ordered a turkey from a local farmer, but maybe she could still cancel that.

The one thing not so easily canceled were her expectations.

The White family always gathered together at Christmas. They had their traditions, which probably would have seemed crazy to some, but Maggie cherished them. Decorating the tree, singing carols, doing a massive jigsaw, playing silly games. Being together. It didn't happen often now that her daughters were grown, and she'd been looking forward to it.

"Have you told your sister yet?"

"She is my next call. Not that she's likely to answer her phone. She's always working. I want her to be my maid of honor."

What would Katie's reaction be? "Your sister doesn't consider herself a romantic."

Maggie sometimes wondered if working in the emergency department for so long had distorted her elder daughter's view of humanity.

"I know," Rosie said, "but this isn't any old wedding. It's *my* wedding, and I know she'll do it for me."

"You're right, she will." Katie had always been a protective and loving older sister.

Maggie glanced at the photograph she kept on the table next to her bed. The two girls standing side by side, arms wrapped around each other, their cheeks pressed together as they faced the camera, smiles merging. It was one of her favorite photos.

"I know you hate flying, Mum, but you will come, won't you? I badly want you all to be there."

Flying. Rosie was right that she hated it.

In company when conversation turned to travel, she pretended she was protecting the planet by avoiding flying, but in reality she was protecting herself. The idea of being propelled through the air in a tin can horrified her. It all seemed out of her control. What if the pilot had drunk too much the night before? What if they collided with another plane? Everyone knew that airspace was ridiculously overcrowded. What about drones? Bird strikes?

When the children were young she and Nick had bundled them into the car and taken them to the beach. Once, they'd taken the ferry across to France and driven as far as Italy (*never again*, Nick had said, as they'd been bombarded with a chorus of *are we nearly there* all the way from Paris to Pisa).

And now she was expected to fly to the Rocky Mountains for Christmas.

And she would. Of course she would.

"We'll be there. Nothing would keep us away." Maggie

waved goodbye to her dreams of a family Christmas at the cottage. "But what about a venue? Will you be able to find something at such short notice?"

"We're going to have the wedding right here, at his home. Dan's family own Snowfall Lodge. It's this *amazing* boutique hotel just outside Aspen. I can't wait for you to see it. There are views of the forest and the mountains, and outdoor hot tubs—it's going to be the perfect place to spend Christmas. The perfect place to get married. I'm so excited!"

Honeysuckle Cottage was the perfect place to spend Christmas.

Maggie couldn't imagine spending it in a place she didn't know, with people she didn't know. Not only that, but *perfect* people she didn't know. Even the prospect of snow didn't make her feel better.

"It sounds as if you have it all covered. All we need to do is think about what to wear."

"Mm, I was going to mention that. It's pretty cold at this time of year. You're going to need to wear some serious layers."

"I was talking about *your* clothes. Your wedding dress."

"Catherine is taking me to her favorite boutique bridal store tomorrow. She's booked an appointment and they're closing the store for us and everything."

On the few occasions Maggie had thought about Rosie getting married, she'd imagined planning it together, poring over photographs in magazines, trying on dresses.

Never once had she pictured the whole thing happening without her.

Now she thought about it, very little of her life had turned out the way she'd planned.

She stared at the empty expanse of bed next to her.

"That's—kind of her."

"She *is* kind. She says I'm the daughter she never had. She's really spoiling me."

But Rosie was *her* daughter, Maggie thought. She should be the one doing the spoiling.

No matter how hard she tried, it was impossible not to be hurt and a little resentful.

Already she felt more like a guest than the mother of the bride.

No! She wasn't going to turn into that sort of mother. This was Rosie's special day, not hers. Her feelings didn't matter.

"What can I do to help?"

"Nothing. Get yourselves here. Catherine can't wait to meet you. I know you'll love her."

Maggie wondered what Rosie had said about her. *My mother works in academic publishing. She loves baking and gardening.* To a high-flying celebrity wedding planner, she probably sounded as exciting as yesterday's laundry.

"I'm looking forward to meeting her."

"Can I speak to Dad? I want to hear his voice."

Maggie gripped the phone. She hadn't anticipated this. "I—um—he's not here right now."

"It's the middle of the night. How can he not be there?"

Maggie searched frantically for a plausible explanation. She could hear Nick's voice, *for goodness' sake, Mags, this is absurd. It's time to tell the truth.*

But the truth was the last thing Rosie needed to hear on the day of her engagement.

She would not spoil her daughter's big moment.

"He's gone for a walk."

"A *walk?* At three in the morning? Have you guys finally bought a dog or something?"

"No. Your dad was working on a paper until late and couldn't sleep. But he should be back any minute." She was slightly shocked by her own creativity under pressure. She'd always raised the girls to tell the truth, and here she was lying like a pro.

"Get him to call me the moment he walks through the door."

"Won't you be asleep by then?"

There was a sound of glasses clinking together and Rosie giggled. "It's only eight o'clock in the evening here. Will you get him to call me back?"

Unable to think of an excuse, Maggie promised that Nick would call as soon as he came in, and after a few more excited words she ended the call.

She sat for a moment, then walked to the window. It was dark outside, but the moon sent a ghostly glow across the village green.

In the summer it was the venue for cricket, and in the winter the trees were decked with tiny fairy lights paid for by the village council. There had been an outcry at proposals to divert traffic through the center of the village.

Maggie guessed they didn't have those problems in Aspen. Nobody was likely to have to fight the demise of the local bus service, or the plan to only open the library two days a week.

Unable to see an alternative, she picked up the phone and dialed Nick's number.

It rang and rang, but Maggie persevered. Nick's ability to sleep through anything was something that she'd both resented and envied when the children were young. It had been Maggie who had dragged herself from the bed every half an hour when Rosie was tiny, and Maggie who had borne the brunt of the asthma attacks even when Nick was home between trips.

Eventually he picked up the phone with a grunt. "'lo."

"Nick?"

"Maggie?" His voice was rough with sleep and she could imagine him shaking himself awake like a bear waking from hibernation.

"You need to call Rosie."

"Now? In the middle of the night? What's wrong?" To give him his due, he was instantly concerned. "Is she in the hospital?"

"No. She has news." Should she tell him or leave Rosie to tell him herself? In the end she decided to tell him. Nick tended to be blunt in his responses and she didn't want him spoiling Rosie's moment. "She and Dan are getting married." She heard the tinkling of glass and Nick cursing fluently. "Are you all right?"

"Knocked a glass of water over."

Nick was a professor of Egyptology, ridiculously intelligent and endearingly clumsy with everyday items. At least, Maggie had found it endearing in the beginning. It had become less endearing as the years had passed and he'd broken half her favorite china. She used to joke that he was so used to dealing with pottery fragments he didn't know how to handle an entire piece.

"She and Dan are getting married in Colorado at Christmas."

"This Christmas? The one happening next month?"

"That's the one. Dan's family own a luxury resort. I've forgotten what it's called."

"Snowfall Lodge."

"How do you know that?"

"Rosie mentioned it when she told me about her plans

for Thanksgiving. Goodness. Married. I didn't see that one coming. Our little Rosie. Always doing the unexpected." There was a pause and she heard rustling in the background and the click of a light switch. "How do you feel?"

Sad. Lost. Confused. Anxious.

She wasn't sure how many of those feelings could be attributed to Rosie's news.

"I feel fine." That was as much of a lie as letting Rosie think Nick was in bed with her. "It's Rosie's life, and she should do what she wants to do."

"What about Christmas? I know how important it is to you."

"We'll still be having Christmas, just not at Honeysuckle Cottage. The wedding is planned for Christmas Eve." She didn't quite manage to keep the wobble from her voice.

"Are you going to go?"

"What sort of a question is that? You seriously think I wouldn't attend my daughter's wedding?"

"I hadn't given it any thought at all until two minutes ago when you first mentioned it. I know how you love Christmas at the cottage, and how much you hate flying. I know pretty much everything about you."

She thought about the file she'd left open on the kitchen table.

He didn't know everything.

"If my daughter is getting married in Aspen, then that's where I'll be, too."

"How? I've never managed to get you on a plane. Not even for our honeymoon."

"I'll find a way." She could do a fear of flying course, but that felt like a ridiculous waste of money. Alcohol would be cheaper. She didn't often drink, so a couple of gin and tonics should do it. "We can sort out details later. She wants you to call her back so that she can tell you in person."

There was a pause. "Where does she think I am? What did you tell her?"

"That you were out walking because you couldn't sleep."

His sigh echoed down the phone like an accusation. "This has gone on long enough. We should tell them, Mags." He sounded tired. "They're not children anymore. They deserve to know the truth."

"We'll tell them when the time is right, and that time isn't when your youngest daughter calls all excited to tell you she's getting married."

"All right, but we tell her before we arrive in Colorado. We'll call her together next week. We've been living apart for months now. It's time to tell both girls that it's over."

Over.

Maggie felt her throat thicken and her chest hurt.

It was because it was the middle of the night. Things always seemed worse at three in the morning.

"I'd rather tell Katie in person, but she's elusive at the moment. Have you heard from her lately?"

"No, but that isn't unusual. You two have this mother-daughter thing going on. You're the one she always calls."

But Katie hadn't called. She hadn't called in a while.

Did that mean she was busy, or that something was wrong?

"I'll try calling her again. She usually does nothing but sleep and eat over Christmas. Traveling to Aspen might be difficult for her."

Difficult for all of them.

A sister who didn't believe in marriage, and parents who were divorcing.

What sort of a wedding was this going to be?

Katie

"THAT'S IT, SALLY. All done." Katie removed her surgical gloves and stood up. The stitches were neat and she was satisfied she'd done the best possible job. There would be a scar, but Katie knew that with or without a scar Sally would never forget tonight. "Is there someone we can call for you?"

The woman shook her head. There was bruising and swelling on her left cheek and disillusionment in her eyes. "I never thought this would happen to me."

Katie sat down again. Her shoulder ached from sitting in one position for too long and she rolled it discreetly to try to ease the discomfort. "It can happen to anyone. It's not about you. It's about him. It's not your fault." It was important to say the words, even though she knew she probably wouldn't be believed.

"I feel stupid. I keep thinking I must have missed something. We've been together for two years. Married for four months. He's never done anything like this before. I love him. I thought he loved me. We met when I started a new job and he swept me off my feet. He seemed perfect."

Katie shivered. "Perfect" wasn't normal. What human being was perfect? "I'm sorry."

"There were no signs. No clues."

"Perfect" might have been a sign. Or maybe she was jaded.

Over the years she'd worked in the emergency department, she'd seen it all. Children who were abused. Women who were abused and, yes, men who were abused. She'd seen people who knifed each other, people who drove too fast and paid the price, people who drank and then climbed behind the wheel and took a life. There were plenty of regular accidents, too, of course, along with heart attacks, brain hemorrhages and any number of acute emergencies that required immediate attention. And then there were the hordes who decided the emergency department was the easiest place to access medical care of the most trivial kind. Each day she waded through a mixed soup of humanity, some good, some not so good.

"When we met, he was sweet and kind. Loving. Attentive." Sally wiped her cheek with the heel of her hand. "I'm trying not to cry, because crying hurts. The physical injuries are awful, but the worst thing is that it shakes your confidence in your own judgment. You must have seen it before. I can't believe I'm the first."

Katie handed her a tissue. "You're not the first."

"How do you handle it? Working here, you must see the worst of human behavior."

Katie's shoulder chose that moment to give an agonizing twinge. Yes, she saw the worst of human behavior. She had to remind herself that she also saw the best. She wondered what would happen to this woman. To this marriage. Would she forgive him? Would the cycle continue? "What will you do? Do you have a plan?"

"No. Until he threw me down the stairs I didn't realize I needed one." Sally blew her nose. "The house is mine, but I don't feel safe in it right now so I'll probably stay with my parents for a while. He wants to talk to me, and I suppose I should at least listen."

Katie wanted to tell her not to go back, but it wasn't her place to give advice. Her job was to fix the physical damage. Helping Sally deal with the emotional carnage and find some degree of empowerment was someone else's responsibility. "The police want to talk to you. Are you feeling up to it?"

"Not really, but it's important so I'll do it. This was going to be our first Christmas together." Sally tucked the tissue into her sleeve. "I had it all planned."

The time of year seemed to amplify her distress, but Katie knew from experience that tragedy didn't take a break for Christmas.

Someone opened the door. "Dr. White! We need you."

Saturday nights in the emergency department were not for the fainthearted, although these days it wasn't only Saturdays. Every night was insane.

"I'll be right there." She glanced at the nurse who had assisted. "Can you make sure Sally has all the information she needs?" She turned back to her patient. "When you're ready, there are people you can speak to. People who can help."

"But no one who can turn the clock back. No one who can turn him into the man I thought he was."

Katie wondered if Sally's worst injury was the damage to her belief system. How did you ever trust a man again? "I hope everything works out for you."

Katie was unlikely to find out, of course. The place was like a conveyor belt of trauma. She dealt with what came through the doors, and then she moved on. There was no long-term management here.

"You've been very kind. Your parents must be proud."

"Dr. White!"

Katie ground her teeth. The reality was that compassion had to be squashed into the shortest time possible. They were two doctors down and she had a queue of patients waiting for her attention, so she smiled at Sally again and left the room.

Would her parents be proud if they'd witnessed her life over the last few weeks? She didn't think so.

She was probably letting them down. She knew she was letting herself down.

She looked at the nurse who was hovering in the corridor. "Problem?"

"The guy coughing up blood—"

"Mr. Harris."

"Yes. Harris. How do you do that? How do you know everyone's name even though you only spoke to him for less than a minute?"

"I like to make an inhuman experience as human as possible. What about him?"

"His tests are back. Dr. Mitford saw him and says he needs to be admitted, but there is a bed crisis."

When wasn't there a bed crisis? You stood more chance of finding a unicorn in your Christmas stocking than you did a hospital bed. Demand exceeded supply. A patient she'd seen at the beginning of her shift was still waiting for a bed six hours later. Because there was always a risk of hospital-acquired infection, Katie sent people home whenever she was able to do so. "Did you manage to contact his daughter? Is she on her way?"

"Yes, and yes."

"Call me when she arrives. I'll talk to her. He might be better off at home if there is someone there to take care of him." And better for his dignity. She'd seen on the notes that he was a retired CEO. Once, he'd probably commanded a room. Now he was the victim of human frailty. No matter how busy she was, she tried to remember that landing in the emergency department was one of the most stressful moments of a person's life. What was routine to her was often terrifying for the patient.

She never forgot what it had been like for her mother being in the hospital with Rosie.

Katie saw three more patients in quick succession and was then hit by a wave of dizziness.

It had happened a few times over the past few weeks and she was starting to panic. She needed to bring her A game to work, and lately that wasn't happening.

"I'm going to grab a quick coffee before I keel over." She turned and bumped straight into her colleague.

"Hey, Katie." Mike Bannister had been in her year at med school and they'd remained friends.

"How was the honeymoon?"

"Let's put it this way, two weeks in the Caribbean wasn't enough. What are you doing at work? After what happened I thought—are you sure you should be here?"

"I'm fine."

"Did you take any time off?"

"I don't need time off." She forced herself to breathe slowly, hoping Mike would move on.

He glanced over his shoulder to check no one was listening. "You're stressed out and on the edge. I'm worried about you."

"You're imagining things." She was totally stressed out. "I probably have low blood sugar. I'm cranky when I'm hungry and I haven't had a break since I walked into this place seven hours ago. I'm about to fix that."

"You're allowed to be human, Katie." Mike's gaze settled on her face. "What happened was nasty. Scary. No one would blame you if—"

"Worry about the patients, not me. There are more than enough of them." Katie tried to ignore the pain in her shoulder and the rapid beating of her heart. She didn't want to think about it and she certainly didn't want to talk about it.

She'd once overheard her mother saying to someone, *Katie is solid as a rock.*

Up until a month ago she wouldn't have disagreed.

Now she felt anything but solid. She was falling apart, and it was becoming harder and harder to hide it from her colleagues. Even the thought of going to work brought her to the edge of a panic attack, and she'd never suffered from panic attacks.

Her mother kept calling suggesting lunch and she kept stalling because she was afraid she might break down.

"Sorry." A nurse bumped into her as he sprinted from one end of the department to another and the wail of an ambulance siren told her the workload wasn't going to ease any time soon.

"The paramedics are bringing in a nasty head injury. And that film crew are driving me insane," Mike said.

Katie had forgotten the film crew. They were filming a "fly on the wall" documentary. She suspected they were beginning to wish they'd chosen a different wall.

The cameraman had passed out on day one after witnessing the aftermath of a particularly nasty road accident. He'd hit his head on a trolley and she'd had to put eight stitches in his head. His colleagues had thought it hilarious that he'd ended up on the other side of the camera, but she could have done without the extra business.

"It's like a war zone," one of the journalists had observed earlier in the evening and given that he'd worked in an actual war zone at one point, no one was about to argue with him. "No wonder you're short-staffed. Aren't you ever tempted to ditch the whole thing and retrain in dermatology?"

Katie hadn't answered. She was tempted by a whole lot of things, and it was starting to unsettle her.

Medicine was her life. She'd decided to be a doctor the night Rosie had her first asthma attack. Their father had been away. Katie had been too young to be left alone, so she'd gone to the hospital, too.

She'd been fascinated by the beeping machines, the soft hiss of the oxygen and the skilled hands of the doctor whose ministrations had helped her little sister breathe again.

At eighteen she'd gone to medical school. More than a decade later, she was still working her way up the ladder as a doctor. She liked her colleagues, she loved the feeling that she was doing good, but lately that feeling didn't come as often as it once had. She wanted to do more for her patients, but time and resources were in short supply. She was becoming increasingly frustrated by the limitations of the job, and starting to question whether it was right for her.

The time to ask herself that question would have been twelve years ago, not now.

She turned away from Mike.

A junior doctor was hovering, waiting to discuss a case with her but before she could open her mouth the drunken head injury arrived. The man was covered in blood and bellowing like a wounded animal.

It was another hour before she was finally able to visit the break room, and she grabbed a protein bar and a cup of coffee while she checked her phone.

She had three missed calls from her sister. In the middle of the night?

She gulped down the last of the bar and dialed, calming herself with the knowledge that her sister was perfectly capable of calling in the middle of the night to say she'd taken up ballet or decided to run a marathon.

Please let that be all it is.

If something had happened to her sister, that would be the end of her.

"Rosie?" She tossed the wrapper in the bin. "Are you in hospital?"

"For crying out loud, can't a girl call her family without everyone assuming I'm in hospital? What is *wrong* with you people?"

Relief flooded through her. "If you're going to call your family at four in the morning then you can expect that kind of reaction." Katie decided to give her feet five minutes' rest and kicked off her shoes. "So is this a catch-up call?" She eyed the chair but decided that if she sat down in it she might never get up again.

"Not exactly. I called because I have big news, and something special to ask you."

"Big news?" Why, when her sister said those words, did they sound so terrifying? "You're throwing in your studies and you're going to travel in Peru?"

Rosie laughed, because there had been a time when she'd considered exactly that. "Guess again."

With Rosie it could be anything.

"You've taken up Irish dancing and you're moving in with a colony of leprechauns."

"Wrong again. I'm getting married!"

Katie spilled her coffee, and it splashed across her skirt and her legs. "Shit."

"I know you're not the world's biggest romantic, but I can't believe you actually said that."

"It was a reaction to the severe burn I just gave myself, not a reaction to your news." She never used to swear, but years working in the emergency department had changed that. "You were saying?" She grabbed paper towels and mopped the mess. "Married? Who to?"

"What do you mean 'who to'? To Dan, of course."

"Do I know about Dan?" Katie lost track of her sister's relationships. "Oh wait, I do remember you mentioning him. He's your latest."

"Not only my latest, but my last. He's The One."

Katie rolled her eyes, relieved it wasn't a video call. "You thought Callum Parish was 'The One,' too."

"He was my first. You always love your first."

Katie hadn't loved her first. Katie had never been in love. She was pretty sure that part of her was faulty.

"What's his problem?"

"What's that supposed to mean?"

"You always pick men who are going through a hard time. You like to save people."

"That is not true. And Dan doesn't have a problem, except perhaps that his future sister-in-law is insane."

Future sister-in-law? Katie struggled to get her head around it. "If he doesn't have a problem, why are you marrying him?"

"Because I'm in love!"

Love. A disease with an uncertain prognosis that often struck without warning.

"I'm checking you're not being pressured into something, that's all. It's important that you're doing it for the right reasons." Katie couldn't think of a single reason that made sense, but she was willing to accept her own limitations in that area. Rosie was right. She wasn't romantic. She didn't watch romantic movies. She didn't read romance.

She didn't dream of weddings. She lived a life drenched in reality. She saw plenty of endings, few of them happy.

"Can't you be pleased for me?"

"I'm your big sister. My job is to protect you."

"From what?"

"From anything and everything that might harm you. In this case, from yourself. You're impulsive and very free with your affections. You're gentle, and frankly adorable, and you're a target for every lame duck."

"Dan is not a lame duck."

"Maybe not, but then you don't see bad in anyone. And—how can I say this without offending you? You're not a great judge of men."

"You've offended me. And, by the way, 'adorable' makes me sound like a puppy that fell in a puddle. It's not a compliment for someone on track for an academic career. You *never* take me seriously. Maybe I'm not a high-flying doctor like you, but I'm at Harvard doing a PhD. Some people are impressed by that."

"I do take you seriously." Didn't she? "And it's possible to be cute and academic. I know some people are impressed, which is why it's my job to keep you grounded so that the whole Ivy League thing doesn't go to your head. And to that end we do need to remember here that you're studying fairy tales, which basically sums up your entire view of life." It was a long running family joke, but Katie felt a twinge of guilt as she said it. Maybe she'd made that joke a little too often.

"I'm studying Celtic languages, folklore and myth. *Not* fairy tales."

"I know, and I'm proud of you." Katie softened her tone. She *was* proud of her sister. "I also love you and want to protect you."

"I don't need protecting. I love him, Katie. Dan is—he's—incredible. He's funny, he's kind, he's so laid-back it's unbelievable frankly and he kisses like a god. I never thought I could feel this way."

"You can't marry a guy because he's good in bed." It had been so long since she'd been to bed with anyone, good or otherwise, that she probably wasn't the best judge of that either.

"That's all you heard from what I said? It's so much more than that. He's perfect for me."

After dealing with Sally, the alarm bells in Katie's head were deafening. "No one is perfect. If he seems perfect, it's either because he's working hard to hide something, or that you haven't been with him long enough to see his flaws. Remember Sam."

"I just told you I'm getting married, and you have to mention Sam? Do you really think it's good timing?"

"You adored Sam. And, by the way, you thought he was The One, right up until the point you discovered he'd slept with two of your friends."

"People sometimes behave badly. It's a fact of life."

"You're excusing him?"

"No, but we were at college. People go a little crazy at college."

"He hurt you, Rosie. You cried so hard it triggered the worst asthma attack you'd ever had. I will never forget that crazy drive to Oxford. And lying to Mum, because you begged me not to tell her." Her mother knew less than fifty percent of the things that had happened to Rosie since she'd left home. Sometimes Katie felt the burden of that. She saw the unfiltered version of Rosie's life.

"I didn't want to worry her. I've done more than enough of that in my lifetime."

"And then there was—what was his name? James. He insisted you paid whenever you were together."

"He didn't have much money."

"He was a leech." She'd had to lend Rosie money, but she didn't mention that. It wasn't about money. It was about judgment.

"Dan is different." Rosie was stubborn. "You'll see it the moment you meet him."

"Great. When can I meet him?" The sooner the better as far as she was concerned. Engagements could be broken, couldn't they? Relationships ended all the time, particularly Rosie's.

"That's why I'm phoning. We're getting married at Christmas, right here in Aspen. Can you think of anything more romantic? Blue skies and snow."

"*This* Christmas? The Christmas that is happening in less than a month? Are you kidding me?"

"Why is everyone so surprised?"

"Because generally you're given more than a few weeks notice for a wedding and you've only known him for a couple of months." An image of Sally's bruised, tear-drenched face slid into her brain. *There were no signs. No clues.* "Does Mum know?"

"I called her first. She was thrilled. So was Dad."

Katie was fairly sure her mother would have had an anxiety attack. "What's the hurry? Why not wait a while?"

"Because we don't want to wait! We want to do this as soon as possible. And I really want you to be there. But don't bring the doom and gloom."

"Sorry." Katie swallowed. The last thing she wanted was to hurt her sister. "It's been a tough few weeks at work, that's all. Ignore me. Of course I'll be at your wedding.

You're not only my sister, you're my best friend. I wouldn't miss it for anything. Forgive me."

"There's nothing to forgive. I know you're looking out for me." Rosie's voice was soft and warm and her generous response made Katie feel worse.

Her sister's capacity to forgive human frailty was both her strength and her weakness. It made her vulnerable to every loser and user that crossed her path.

Was Dan one of those?

"What's the plan? Do I have to book somewhere to stay?" The thought of making travel plans drained the last of her energy. "What about Mum and Dad?"

"They're coming, too, of course. And everything is arranged apart from your flight. Dan's family own this amazing place in the mountains. It will be the best vacation you've ever had."

Katie had been dreading Christmas. She'd been wondering how she was going to hold it together during all that family time. Usually she loved it. She loved sleeping late and eating her mother's amazing food. She loved catching up with her dad and hearing about his work. But everything was different now. Her life had changed forever on a dark, rainy night a few weeks before.

And now she felt exhausted. Could she honestly fly to Aspen and put on a happy face?

"When would you want us to fly out?"

"The wedding will be on Christmas Eve, so we thought you should all come a week before so you have time to get to know Dan and his family. Then you can stay over Christmas and fly back before the New Year, or whenever you like. Oh, Katie, I'm so excited! I can't decide between a horse-drawn sleigh and a husky ride for the guests."

"Well, don't ache your brain on my account. I'm perfectly happy walking."

"They have feet of snow here already. It's a winter wonderland. You might not find it so easy to walk."

"Walking is one of the few things I excel at. I've had years of practice."

"I want you to be my bridesmaid. Maid of honor. Call it whatever you like."

Katie didn't want to call it anything. Why couldn't her sister see that this wedding was a massive mistake?

"Are you sure? I'll probably leave a muddy footprint on your dress. I don't know much about weddings." She knew even less about the duties of a maid of honor, but presumably they didn't include being a killjoy.

"All you have to do is smile and help me out. You'll be able to resuscitate Mum if she has a panic attack on the plane. I feel bad that I'm ruining her family Christmas. You know how important it is to her to have everyone together. I miss you. We haven't spoken in ages. I was even starting to wonder if you were avoiding me."

"That's ridiculous. Busy, that's all."

Tell her what happened to you. Tell her that you feel as if the world is crumbling round you.

Rosie, she knew, would be horrified. Knowing her kindhearted sister, she'd probably jump on the first plane and fly over.

Katie blinked. She was the one who looked out for Rosie, not the other way around.

She was Rosie's rock and her support. And never had Rosie needed her support and counsel as much as now.

Right there and then she made a decision.

Forget Christmas. Forget relaxation. Forget figuring out her own issues.

Her first priority was to stop her little sister making a massive mistake that would end in misery.

"I wouldn't miss the wedding for anything." She needed to meet Dan in person and figure out a way to save her sister from herself. And if she managed it early on in the week, then they might still all be home in time to spend Christmas in Honeysuckle Cottage.

With luck, her mother would be too focused on Rosie to notice that anything was wrong with Katie. "I can't wait to be Bridesmaid of Honor, or whatever the correct title is. Don't dress me in purple polyester, that's all I ask. I don't want static shock. And don't spend too much money." *Because this wedding isn't happening.* She turned as the door opened and Mike walked into the room. "I need to go. I'm at work."

"I'm proud of you, Katie. I tell everyone my big sister is a doctor."

Big sister is falling apart.

She was a fraud. "Go. Have fun, but not so much fun you forget your inhalers."

"Katie—"

"I know. I'm the inhaler police. Party. Live life. I'll call you tomorrow." She ended the call and slid her feet back into her shoes.

Mike raised an eyebrow. "Nothing like giving out advice you don't take yourself. When did you last party and live life?"

"I'm partying in my mind. I'm at a virtual party right now."

"Does that come with a virtual hangover? Who is getting married?"

"My sister. In less than four weeks."

"This is the sister who is studying fairy tales?"

Katie winced. "I might have overdone that joke. She's studying Celtic languages, myth and folklore at a certain Ivy League college. She would claim it contributes to the understanding of the culture and beliefs of society. It has been the subject of many lively arguments round the dinner table. She really is super smart, but I still think of her as my little sister and I overdo the teasing." She rubbed her forehead with her fingers. "It feels like yesterday I was reading her board books."

"Big age difference?"

"Ten years. I think my parents had given up on having another child, and then Rosie arrived."

"And you were hit by a massive dose of sibling jealousy?"

"What?" Katie stared at him. "No. I adored her. Right from the first moment I saw her funny little hairless head." She thought about Rosie, an adorable toddler, following her everywhere. Rosie in her favorite dinosaur pajamas. *Rosie turning blue with an asthma attack.* "I confess I might be a tad overprotective, which is why I'm flying to Colorado to meet this guy."

"You haven't met him?"

"No. And don't look at me that way. I'm already freaked out. They've known each other a couple of months. What can you know about someone in a few months? What if he's a gambler, or a narcissist? He could be a psychopath. Maybe a serial killer."

He leaned against the door and folded his arms. "Dr. Doom. Always the optimist."

"I am not Dr. Doom. I am Dr. Reality, thanks to the years I've spent working here. Having the realities of life under your nose tends to cure optimism. There are no certainties in this life, we both know that."

"All the more reason to grab the happy moments that come your way."

"Did you honestly say that? If you get thrown out of medicine, you could write greeting cards." She finished her coffee and walked to the door.

"Katie—"

"What?" She turned and saw the concerned look on his face.

"Does your family know what happened to you?"

"No, and there's no reason to tell them."

"They could give you support."

"I don't need support. I'm my own support." Her parents had done enough supporting in their lives. It was time for them to enjoy their time together.

"Maybe a couple of weeks enjoying outdoor living and breathing in mountain air will be good for you."

"Maybe." Blocking out his concerned look, she let the door swing closed behind her.

She didn't care about outdoor living. She didn't care about mountain air. She didn't even care about a white Christmas.

She was flying to Colorado for one reason, and one reason only.

She was going to stop her sister's wedding.

Maggie

ARMED WITH A strong cup of coffee, Maggie typed Catherine's name into a search engine.

There were pictures of Dan's mother at a benefit in Manhattan, slender as a reed, blond hair swept up in a style befitting a red-carpet appearance.

Feeling gloomy, Maggie scrolled through a dozen more images.

Catherine, skiing a near-vertical slope in Aspen.

Catherine, fist in the air in a gesture of triumph as she stood on top of Mount Kilimanjaro, raising money for a charity researching heart disease.

Catherine, rushing to a meeting in a form-fitting black dress with a planner tucked under one arm.

Rosie had told her in an earlier conversation that Catherine's husband had died suddenly of a heart attack when Dan was in college. The family had been devastated by the loss, but Catherine had forced herself forward.

Maggie enlarged the photo. This woman didn't look broken. There were no signs of grief or anxiety. Not a frown line. Not a silver hair. How could someone survive such a life blow and look so together? A leading American magazine had run an article on her, entitled "From Tragedy to

Triumph." Maggie read it from beginning to end, learning that Catherine Reynolds had set up the wedding business after she was widowed, turning her skills as a hostess into a commercial venture.

Dan was twenty-eight, which meant that unless she was a medical freak, Catherine had to be at least late forties.

The woman smiling back at her from the screen didn't look forty.

Maggie fiddled with the ends of her hair. She'd had it cut at the same place for the past thirty years and had kept the style the same. In fact there was very little of her life that she'd changed.

While Catherine had been reinventing herself and starting over, filling her life with new challenges, Maggie's life had slowly emptied. First Katie had left home, and then Rosie. Her daily calendar, once filled with a whirl of school and sporting commitments, had big gaps. She'd carried on doing what she'd always done, working at her job and tending her garden. She'd been used to cooking for four, but that had turned to three, then two and then, after the life had drained from her marriage, one. Instead of building a new life as Catherine had obviously done, Maggie had carried on living a diluted version of the life she'd always had.

She pushed her laptop to one side and looked at the file that lay open on the table next to her. It was almost full. Soon she wouldn't be able to close it.

Reading about Catherine's determined fight to reinvent herself made her feel pathetic and useless. Catherine had lost her husband in a tragic way. Maggie had lost hers through carelessness. Or was it apathy? She didn't even know.

Maggie couldn't shake off the feeling that she'd somehow wasted her marriage.

Part of the reason she hadn't yet shared the news with the girls was that she hadn't managed to absorb it herself.

Should she and Nick have tried harder?

Conscious that she'd wasted an hour depressing herself, Maggie closed the file and tucked it into a drawer out of sight. She didn't want Nick to see it, or it would trigger a conversation she didn't want to have.

Next she closed her favorite Christmas recipe book that had been open on the table for the past week and slid it back into its slot on the shelf. She wasn't going to be needing it after all.

It was embarrassing to admit it, but she'd been planning Christmas in her mind since September and making lists since October. The first hint of winter in the air had her thinking of slow-cooked casseroles, hearty soups and roasted root vegetables. She'd been looking forward to the festive season for the comfort of its culinary rituals; stirring, simmering, baking in a warm cinnamon-scented fog. Most of all she'd been looking forward to the time she'd get to spend with her family.

She curled her hands around her mug and stared through the window into the garden while she sipped her coffee. Frost sparkled and shimmered on the lawn and a layer of mist added an ethereal touch. At this time of year the only splash of color in her garden came from the holly bush, its berries bloodred and plump. Maggie had been hoping the birds would leave enough for her to use as decoration around the house, but it no longer mattered.

She wasn't going to need berries. Nor was she going to need the mistletoe that grew in clusters on the ancient apple tree. She wasn't going to be here for Christmas.

She'd already had her last Christmas in Honeysuckle Cottage and hadn't even known.

She'd never been away for the holidays before. Never had a Christmas that she hadn't owned. She had friends who delighted in "escaping" at Christmas so that they could avoid the craziness, but Maggie loved the craziness. What would Christmas look like without that?

And why was she worrying about Christmas, when the real issue here was Rosie's wedding? What was *wrong* with her?

She checked the time.

Nick had said he'd be with her at eleven and it was now half past. Since he was invariably late for things, including their wedding, that wasn't a surprise. In the past it had infuriated her that he was fluent in Classical Greek but couldn't seem to communicate what time he would arrive home. He could read hieroglyphic but not, apparently, a watch or a simple text message.

To begin with it hadn't mattered. She'd loved his passion, and the fact that he was so focused on the things he loved. What he lacked in reliability, he made up for in spontaneity. One day he'd be brandishing two tickets to a concert at the Sheldonian Theatre, the next a picnic which they'd devoured by the river watching sunlight dance over the surface of the water. Nick had uncovered the fun side of Maggie. For her that was as much of a discovery as Tutankhamen's tomb. She was the child of older parents who took their responsibilities seriously and invested everything in her development and education. Earning their love had been exhausting, and it was an uncomfortable, stressful relationship. Having fun hadn't been part of her life until she'd met Nick in her first few weeks at Oxford.

He'd been studying Egyptology, and she English. His reputation and academic career had bloomed. They'd stayed in Oxford, and she'd taken a job with an academic publisher and spent her days editing textbooks. If it had ever crossed her mind that she didn't love her job the way Nick loved his, she ignored the thought.

And then Katie was born and the strength of her emotion and the power of the bond she'd felt had shocked her. Maggie had loved fiercely, and discovered that her passion was for her children, her husband, her family. For creating a home like the one she'd dreamed of living in herself.

Katie's arrival gave her the perfect excuse to reduce her working hours. She'd ended up taking responsibility for the childcare simply because she enjoyed it more than she enjoyed working.

When Katie had started school, Maggie returned to work for the same publisher but once Rosie arrived she'd taken a second career break. Her youngest daughter had been born premature, a tiny fragile being weighing less than a bag of sugar. As a baby Rosie had suffered endless coughs and colds, and then came her first asthma attack.

Maggie had never forgotten it. After that, they'd happened regularly, and life became a series of sleepless nights and panicked journeys to the hospital.

For the first decade of Rosie's life, Maggie had walked around in a fog of exhaustion.

They'd moved out of the center of Oxford and into Honeysuckle Cottage, hoping that the air pollution would be less than it was in the middle of the city. Tests showed dog hair to be a trigger which meant that they'd been unable to have the family dog that Nick had badly wanted.

Rosie's childhood had been a roundabout of canceled plans and terrifying sprints to the hospital. Then she hit the teenage years and it became harder to control. It wasn't "cool" to carry an inhaler, and denying her condition landed her in the hospital on far too many occasions. The tension

SARAH MORGAN 47

of it affected all of them, as did the general ignorance from their friends and acquaintances who had always thought of asthma as being something mild and benign.

Maggie remembered the day Katie had stomped into the kitchen and slammed her books down on the table.

I'm going to be a doctor, because then I can cure Rosie.

Maggie had often felt guilty that most of her time and attention was focused on her youngest daughter, but Katie hadn't seemed to be affected. She was a bright, fiercely determined child who had grown into a bright, fiercely determined adult. She'd set herself goals, and lists of things to do to achieve those goals. Unlike Nick and Rosie who made decisions based on impulse and emotion, Katie never did anything she hadn't thought through.

She'd gone from being a hardworking child to a hardworking adult. Now she was a dedicated and talented doctor and Maggie was proud of her.

Unlike Rosie, who veered from one thing to the next, Katie always knew exactly what she wanted and never wavered.

The sound of the doorbell cut through her thoughts and she walked to the door and opened it.

Nick stood there. His long wool coat was one he'd had for years. He wore it with the collar turned up and his favorite scarf wrapped round his neck. He gave her that same crooked smile that had snagged her attention all those years before and she felt a rush of sadness. Where had their love gone? There had been no great falling-out. No clandestine affairs or flirtations. She'd tried repeatedly to identify when her marriage had malfunctioned, but had been unable to pinpoint a specific event. She and Nick had lived parallel lives and then drifted apart so gradually neither of them had noticed, until one day they'd simply been unable to connect the way they once had.

Even their decision to part had been mutual and amicable.

Sometimes she wondered if they'd simply lost each other under the pressure of being a family.

Despite everything, she felt relief that he was here. She needed to talk to someone. Anyone. She opened the door wider. "You've lost your key again?"

"For once, no, but I didn't feel comfortable using it. This isn't my house anymore." He hesitated and then stepped over the threshold.

"It's still your house, Nick. We bought it together and when we sell it we'll share the proceeds. You have a right to walk in whenever you like." No part of her was screeching *change the locks*. Why would she?

"I don't want to intrude." He glanced at the stairs and she gave a half laugh as she realized he was respecting her privacy.

"You think there's a Christmas elf hiding under my bed? Santa? Some muscular young guy?"

Another serious relationship wasn't on her wish list. As for anything more superficial, well, the thought of an affair was ludicrous.

"It's cold in here." Nick touched the radiator closest to him. "Broken again?"

"It waits for the first hint of frost to malfunction." As usual she was wearing two sweaters, which made her look heavier than she was.

"Do you want me to call someone?" He didn't offer to look at it himself. Nick could hold a lecture hall spellbound, but he couldn't fix a dripping tap and was bemused by flat pack furniture.

"I've already done it. They're coming next Monday."

"You look tired."

"That generally happens when someone calls you at three in the morning." She knew Nick probably would have gone straight back to sleep. His ability to sleep, no matter what the crisis, had been a source of envy and frustration over the years. She would have given anything to be able to switch off and let someone else take responsibility for five minutes. Maybe it was because he knew she couldn't that he'd been able to switch off himself, soothed by the knowledge that she was in charge.

"Rosie shouldn't have called you in the middle of the night."

"She was excited. She wanted to share her news. And I'm pleased. She might be living miles away, but I still want to be part of her life."

"But middle of the night calls always scare you. I'm sure you answered in a panic, assuming she was having an attack. Not easy to go back to sleep after that." He gave her shoulder a squeeze. "Sit down. I'll make coffee and then we'll book flights."

"Oh." Her stomach gave a lurch. "What's the rush?"

"The wedding is happening in a little over three weeks. We'll be lucky to get seats as it is." Nick ground beans and made two cups. The machine had been their indulgence, a mutual gift that kept delivering when stress piled upon stress. Coffee had become a shared habit during those early, sleep-deprived years and it had stuck. They both drank it black, mostly because they'd been too tired to reach for the milk. "Then there's the fact that if I give you time to think about it, you'll find a reason not to do it."

She took the coffee gratefully, knowing he was right.

"I have to do it. I'm not going to miss Rosie's wedding."

"In that case, we need to book." He put the cup on the table and unwound his scarf.

The scarf had traveled the world with him. It had protected him from sandstorms and dust storms and he refused to be parted from it or have it replaced. It fascinated her that someone so clever could think a scarf could bring luck. She couldn't understand how someone with his brain could think there was something magical about a wool/cotton mix.

"I can't believe Rosie is getting married. She's so young." She was desperate to talk to someone about it. Nick might not have been her first choice, but as he was the only candidate for her confidences, he won.

"Twenty-two." He spooned sugar into his coffee. "If this were ancient Egypt, she would have been married a decade ago."

Comments like that, Maggie thought, *were why a woman needed girlfriends.*

Sometimes she wanted to lift up the nearest frying pan and clock his clever, but somehow still clueless, brain.

"This isn't ancient Egypt." Sometimes his head was so deep in his studies, she was convinced he'd forgotten that. "And we haven't even met him."

"Well, we're not the ones marrying him. As long as she likes him, that's all that matters."

"*Likes* him?" Sometimes she despaired. "They've barely spent any time together. And it's all been heady, romantic good times. That's not real. That's not what marriage is." Marriage was holding tightly to each other as you stumbled over rough ground. Marriage was never letting go.

She and Nick had let go.

He stirred his coffee slowly. "Maybe it should be. Maybe there should be more of those romantic good times."

What was that supposed to mean? Was it a dig at her? "Life happens, Nick. Someone has to handle it."

"Woah—" He sent her a startled look. "What did I say?"

"You were implying that I was so busy looking after the practical side, I forgot to be romantic."

"I wasn't implying anything." He put the spoon down. "You know I don't think that way. I don't go for hidden messages, or subtext or any of those other complex ways of communicating. I was simply saying that romantic, heady times can be real, too."

Was she overreacting? "All I'm saying is that they're still in the dizzy whirlwind stage. They're not arguing about who is going to change a lightbulb or cook dinner. They haven't had to cope with things going wrong. We both know there will be challenges. That's life. They barely know each other. I'm worried this is the wrong decision."

"If it's the wrong decision, then it's their wrong decision." He took a sip of coffee. "And people who know everything there is to know about each other can get divorced, too."

She felt herself flush. "I know that, obviously, but—oh, never mind."

This was often how a discussion between them ended, with her giving up. It hadn't always been that way. At the beginning, they'd talked about everything but somewhere along the way that had stopped. Conversations had gone from deep to shallow and practical.

Can you pick up Rosie's prescription on the way home?

At some point she'd stopped sharing with him and it occurred to her now that she had so many thoughts and emotions that he knew nothing about. She'd never told him she sometimes felt inferior next to him, even though she knew deep down that she wasn't. She felt, somehow, that she'd forgotten how to be her.

She remembered attending a parents' evening where the teacher had said *oh you're Katie and Rosie's mother* as if that somehow became an identity. At the time it hadn't bothered her because she *was* their mother. And she was Nick's wife.

Who else was she? Lately that question had started to trouble her.

Nick put his mug down on the table. "You're upset."

"A little, yes. I've been looking forward to Christmas for so long. I brought the decorations down from the attic last week, and the cake is made—" She finished her coffee. "Ignore me. Christmas is just a day. We can all get together some other time."

Nick frowned. "We'll all be together in Aspen, but we both know that's not why you're upset."

She put her cup on the counter. "What do you mean?"

"You're not upset because of Christmas. You're upset because our Rosie is marrying an American. You're thinking that she might choose to live there permanently. Have kids there. Grow old there."

Maggie felt as if someone had punched the air from her lungs.

She'd been trying *not* to think about that. She hadn't allowed herself to think about that part of the equation.

She'd kept her thinking short term. Christmas. That was about all she could handle. But Nick was right. Deep down that had been her fear from the moment Rosie had made her announcement.

Maybe he knew her better than she thought he did.

She felt a surge of emotion that felt almost like grief. When Rosie had moved to the US to study it had shaken her, but she'd told herself that it was only a short-term thing. Not for a moment had she considered the move might be permanent.

"I feel as if I've lost her." She wasn't going to cry. That would be ridiculous. All that mattered was Rosie's health and happiness. "You probably think I'm the most selfish mother on the planet, wishing she'd come home."

"I don't think you're selfish. I think you're a great mother, you always have been. Perhaps a little too good."

"What's that supposed to mean?"

"You put those girls ahead of everything else."

"You make it sound like a sacrifice, but it wasn't. I loved being there for our girls. If I had my time again I wouldn't change a thing." Some people had big dreams and big goals, but Maggie enjoyed the smaller things. The first buds appearing on the apple tree, the soft scratch of pen on paper as Katie had done her homework at the kitchen table, the scent of fresh laundry, the joy of the first cup of coffee of the day, and the sheer pleasure of a book that transported her to another life and another place.

But it was true that taking two career breaks had narrowed her choices. And then there was the fact that she'd built up goodwill with the publishing house where she worked. Because they trusted her to get her work done, they were flexible when she needed time off to care for Rosie. Worried that a new employer might not offer the same latitude, she'd felt it safer to stay where she was.

She looked closely at Nick and noticed the fine lines around his eyes. He looked tired.

"Have you eaten?"

She knew he sometimes forgot, and judging from the sheepish expression on his face this was one of those occasions.

"No. I forgot to shop, so I thought I'd grab something in college."

"I'll make you something if you have time to eat it."

"I always have time for anything you cook." He stood up. "What can I do to help?"

She gaped at him. "That's the first time you've ever said that."

"That's not true. I clean up after you. I am a champion cleaner-upper."

"But you don't usually help with the cooking part."

"Because you're so good at it. Also, you never let me near the kitchen."

Was that true? Probably. She'd wanted and needed something that was all hers. Something she could excel at and own.

Plenty of people would have rolled their eyes at her apparent lack of work ambition, but Maggie didn't care. She'd been there when the girls had taken their first steps. She'd taught them both to read. Never once had she felt that what she was doing was anything less than valuable.

It was only in the past couple of years that she'd started to feel dissatisfied.

She envied people whose life looked exactly the way they wanted it to look. People like Nick and Katie, who had a passion and followed it. Even Rosie seemed to know the path she wanted to take.

Maggie felt as if she'd strolled randomly through life with no map.

"If you want to help, you could fetch eggs from the fridge." She pulled a large bowl out of the cupboard and a whisk from the drawer.

When he put the eggs next to her she selected six and broke them into the bowl while he watched.

"The last omelet I made was crunchy."

She tried not to smile. "Generally, it's best not to include the shell."

"Ah, so that's the secret. I knew there had to be one."

She snipped fresh herbs from the pots she nurtured on her windowsill and added them to the mixture, then she poured half into the hot pan, waiting as it sizzled.

"It isn't only about me. I worry about her."

"You have to stop protecting her, Mags."

"The day I stop protecting my child is never going to come."

"You know what I mean. She knows she will always have our love and support, but we have to let her live her life the way she chooses to live it."

"Even if that life is a million miles away?"

"That's an exaggeration."

"It might as well be that far." She lifted the edges of the omelet and when she was satisfied she folded it perfectly. "Life can be tough, we both know that. You need family around you. What if she does settle there? What if they break up? What happens if they don't break up, and have babies? I'd want to be able to help, but I won't be close enough."

"Wait—you're worrying you might not be able to help with the baby they don't have yet? You expend a huge amount of energy worrying about things that haven't happened."

"I don't expect you to understand." She slid the omelet onto a plate, sprinkled it with a few chopped chives and handed it to him. "All I'm saying is that it will be tough to support them from here."

He put the plate on the table and sat down. "This looks

delicious, thanks." He picked up a fork. "And as for support, maybe they'll live close to Dan's mother."

Why didn't that make her feel better? Her mind raced ahead. Catherine was already arranging her daughter's wedding, and there was every chance she'd be the favored grandmother. Maggie would be the stranger they saw a few times a year.

Who's that, kids? No, it's not a stranger, it's your granny. Give her a hug and a kiss.

She imagined them recoiling, screwing up their faces as they tolerated a kiss from this semistranger.

A lump formed in her throat.

She wanted to tell Nick how it had made her feel, but she couldn't find a way to say it that didn't make her seem horribly small-minded. And maybe she was being ridiculous. Worrying about things that hadn't happened. She did that a lot.

She poured the rest of the egg mixture into the pan, even though she didn't have much of an appetite.

"Talking of tough stuff," Nick said, "we need to fix a time to tell the girls the truth about us."

"We can't tell them yet, Nick."

"Why not?" He took a forkful of fluffy omelet. "Neither of us has had an affair, we don't hate each other, we don't have any issues being in the same room. We'll still be able to meet up at family gatherings and it won't be awkward. Not much will change."

Was he serious?

"Everything will change. We're their parents, Nick! They see us as a unit. And maybe family gatherings will be amicable for a while, but in time you'll meet someone. Then you'll be bringing someone else and we'll have to take turns and—"

He put his fork down. "Maybe you'll be the one who meets someone."

Where? How? She almost asked the questions aloud and then realized how sad they made her sound. She needed to build a new life. One that didn't have Nick in it. She needed to join a choir, or learn Italian, or *something*. Anything.

After the wedding, she promised herself. After the wedding, she'd pull herself together. First she'd spruce up the house, then put it on the market and find somewhere smaller.

The idea of selling Honeysuckle Cottage made her feel physically ill. All the best parts of her life had happened here. Nick. Katie. Rosie. She still remembered the day they'd moved in. Nick, ducking his head to avoid the low beams. Fixing a gate across the stairs so that Rosie didn't tumble down them. And hours spent in the garden, shaping it into the tranquil haven it was now.

There had been tough times, but the place was full of laughter and memories. All those things would be erased when someone else moved in. They'd see a dent in the wall and think it needed fixing. They wouldn't smile, remembering that was where Rosie had ridden her bike into the wall on that Christmas morning when it had been raining too hard to go outdoors.

A new story would be written into these walls.

But that wasn't her immediate concern.

"Hear me out." She tipped her omelet onto a plate and grabbed a fork. "Whether it turns out to be a mistake or not, this is Rosie's big day. This is all about her and Dan. A celebration. What do you think it will do to the mood if we announce our divorce at the same time?"

"If we do it today, then it won't be at the same time. She'll have had time to get over it."

"This isn't flu, Nick. You don't 'get over it.' A divorce changes the landscape of our family. We all have to find a new way to be together. To fit. It's going to be a massive adjustment." Saying it aloud somehow made it all the more depressing. "And today she is going to choose her wedding dress. It wouldn't be appropriate to spoil her day."

"Divorce is part of life. Life happens. Wasn't that the point you were making earlier?"

"It doesn't have to happen before what is supposed to be one of the happiest days of our daughter's life." She forced down a mouthful of her breakfast and then put her plate down.

"So what are you suggesting?"

"That we act as if nothing has changed."

"You—" He broke off, bemused. "You want us to attend this wedding together as a couple? Pretending everything is fine?"

"Yes. We present a united front. There will be plenty of time to share our less-than-happy news once the wedding bells have stopped ringing and the snow has melted."

"To be clear about this, you're suggesting we 'act' married?"

"Well, technically we are married, Nick, so it shouldn't be much of a challenge to pretend for one week."

His gaze was steady. "You want us to travel together, share a hotel room—"

"Whatever it takes." She wasn't going to offer to relinquish the bed. Nick could sleep anywhere, whether it was a tent in a desert or the hard floor of a hotel room. Maggie could barely doze off if she was lying on a feather-filled mattress, so she didn't need to make things harder for herself. "It will be easy enough to keep up the pretense. It's not as if we argue all the time or anything."

He pushed his plate away. "It doesn't feel right to lie to them."

"We're not lying. We're withholding our news. We haven't told them we've been living apart for a while. What difference does it make to wait a few more weeks?"

"We haven't told them because we agreed it was better done face-to-face when we're all together."

"You seriously think the right time to announce a divorce is at our daughter's wedding?"

He sighed. "No, I don't think that." There was a long pause. "All right." The words were dragged from him. "But as soon as they're back from their honeymoon, we're telling them."

"Agreed." She felt a rush of relief which died as he reached across and dragged her laptop toward him.

"What's this?"

Why, oh why, hadn't she closed the browser? "I was finding out a bit about the family."

He lifted his gaze from the laptop to her face. "You mean you've been torturing yourself."

"I have no idea what you're talking about."

"You're the same before every college social event. You panic about what you're going to wear and what people will think of you."

"That's called being human."

"You're lovely, Maggie." His voice was rough. "I wish you had more confidence."

She was a soon-to-be-divorced mother of two grown children who didn't particularly like the way her life was looking. She thought about the file, safely tucked away in the drawer.

What did she have to feel confident about?

And if he thought she was so lovely, why were they getting divorced?

He tapped the keys and brought up airline details.

"How are we going to transport all the Christmas gifts?" She picked up her coffee and sat down next to him. "I won't be able to carry everything."

"Take a few key things, and they can have the rest next time they're here."

"I always make them a stocking. And I can't imagine a tree without all the decorations the girls made over the years. It's tradition."

"So pack them up and bring them." He glanced up from the screen, seemed about to say something and then changed his mind. "We'll pay for excess baggage if necessary."

Excess baggage. He could have been describing her.

"I can't pack our decorations. That would be ridiculous." She watched, anxious, as he keyed in dates and checked prices. "Is the flight overbooked?"

"I'm sure you'd like it to be but no, there are two seats left on the early flight. Business class." He dug into his pocket for his wallet.

"Nick, we can't fly business class."

"Why not? We deserve a treat."

Flying? A treat? The reality of strapping herself into a seat on an airplane and waiting for takeoff loomed in her brain. Her heart started to pound. "It's an extravagance."

"I know you're scared of flying, but if I don't book this now you won't be going to your daughter's wedding."

Maggie moaned and put her head on the table. "How did Christmas turn into this?"

"They give you free champagne in business. I'll pour

a bottle of that into you before we take off. You won't feel a thing."

Maggie lifted her head. "What did you say to Rosie?"

"Last night? I can't recall. You know me. I'm not as good at bouncing awake as you are. It takes me a while to surface. I hope I said the right things."

What were the right things? She wasn't sure. Should she have issued a warning or said congratulations? "She's so young."

"We were young."

She was tempted to say *and look at how that turned out*, but she stopped herself.

Even though it had ended, their marriage hadn't been a disaster. Believing that would mean the entire previous thirty-five years had been a mistake, and it hadn't been. They'd had many happy years which was, perhaps, why she felt so sad about everything. It was messy, but life was messy wasn't it? Full of good and bad, ups and downs, triumph and disappointment.

Part of her felt that somehow, they should have been able to make this work.

"Your mother tried to stop us getting married. She was very disapproving. She thought I was too serious."

"She'd never seen you after a bottle of sloe gin, and I've told you before that she never approved of any of the women I dated. She was afraid they'd take her little boy away." He stretched out his legs. "Yours wasn't much better."

"They wanted me to marry someone with a regular job. They were suspicious of your trips to Egypt, and the fact that your hair fell over your collar. It all seems so long ago, I can barely remember it although it was stressful at the time."

"We did what felt right for us. We didn't listen to our parents and Rosie and Dan won't listen to us either, so there's no point in wondering whether we should say something. We made our own decision, and now we should leave our daughter to make hers."

"That's very mature and rational." She topped up their mugs and sat down next to him. "Talking of mature and rational, I spoke to someone about selling the cottage last week. I was thinking we should put it on the market after Christmas, but their advice was to wait until spring. That would give us time to do some of the repairs, and make sure it's looking its best. The garden is always gorgeous in May." It should be. She'd spent hours on it. It was something that was all hers. Somewhere she felt calm. Whenever she was stressed, she went outdoors and tended the garden. The upside of her anxiety was that her garden looked fantastic.

Nick spooned sugar into his coffee and gave her a long look. "You're sure you want to sell the place?"

No, she didn't want to sell it. Selling it would break her heart. "It's too big for one person. I'm rattling around here. And not only me. The windows rattle. There's so much maintenance needed in an old place like this."

"Remember the first time we saw it? You said *this is it. This is the one.* We hadn't even taken a look inside."

"I knew. I knew right away." She glanced around the kitchen that had been the set for so many family dramas. "You thought a new build would be less work."

"It would have been less work, but also would have lacked character."

"I'm starting to think 'character' is a euphemism for 'old and in need of repair.' So you're happy for me to put it on the market whenever they feel the time is right?"

His gaze was veiled. "Whatever works for you."

They were so polite. Civilized. There was no awkwardness or animosity. They were simply two friends who had lost the chemistry. She stared hard at his jaw, at the curve between his neck and shoulder where she'd so often rested her head. When he'd come back from a long trip it had been like those early days of their relationship, the passion between them intense and all-consuming.

Where had those feelings gone?

She stood up suddenly, her chair scraping on the stone floor. "That's what I'll do, then. It's been a lovely home for us, but it's time to move on." Time for her to move on, too. This place was so full of memories they almost suffocated her.

"On to practical matters—" he finished his coffee "—I'll book a cab to the airport. All you need to do is pack a suitcase. This could be fun, Mags."

"The flight?"

"Christmas in Colorado."

Maybe she wasn't very adventurous, because all she really wanted was Christmas at home. She'd wanted one more year of lighting a fire in the hearth and decorating a large tree.

Next year she'd be living in a small apartment, or maybe a small Victorian terrace. Would Nick even join them, or would he have the girls on a different day? Whichever way it turned out, she knew that no Christmas gathering would ever be the same again.

"You should look at the website. Aspen looks beautiful. It's surrounded by forest and snowy mountains. When did we last have a proper white Christmas?"

Maggie thought about the Christmas cards half-written in her bedroom. "Snow might be nice."

"And for the first time ever you might be able to relax and enjoy yourself. You won't have to do the cooking."

Maggie loved cooking. She loved slicing and dicing, stirring and tasting. She loved the craziness and the chaos of the kitchen at Christmas. The sound of the fridge door opening and closing. The smell of toast as someone made a late-night snack.

It was the empty silence she hated most.

The knowledge that no one in the world really needed her anymore.

The girls loved her, she knew that, but they didn't need her. They were adults now, with their own lives.

Did she even have a purpose?

She still worked for the same publisher and she knew she was valued, so why didn't she get more satisfaction from her job?

Gloom descended on her and suddenly she wished Nick would leave. His life hadn't changed much. His days were still filled with work, lectures, students, research. The only thing that had altered for him was where he slept at night.

She became brisk and practical, as she always did when she was stressed. "We're agreed we'll delay telling them until after Christmas?"

"Yes, but I'm not much of an actor. What if they guess?"

"Then it's up to us to make sure they don't. We were married for more than three decades. I think we can manage to get through ten days."

She hoped she wasn't wrong about that. They could make it work, surely?

How hard was it to pretend to be in love?

They were both about to find out.

Rosie

WAS SHE MAKING an awful, dreadful, *hideous* mistake?

What if Katie was right?

Rosie stood in the fitting room of the expensive bridal boutique in downtown Aspen, clutching a dress she no longer wanted to try on.

It was true that none of her previous relationships had exactly been long lasting, but wasn't that part of being young and growing up? How were you supposed to know a relationship was right if you hadn't stumbled through a few wrong ones first?

But Katie was right that those relationships had all seemed right at the time.

You, she told her reflection in the mirror, *are impetuous, impulsive and a walking disaster.*

As a child she'd flitted from one passion to another like a bee searching for nectar. When she was eight, she'd wanted to be a ballerina. At nine, an astronaut. By the age of ten she'd turned to teaching and lined up her dolls in classroom style. And so it went on. She couldn't help it. She became wildly enthusiastic about something, and then moved on.

Her track record with boyfriends looked much the same.

And now there was Dan who she loved totally and absolutely. But it was true they hadn't known each other that long.

Did that matter?

She was beginning to wish she hadn't called her sister. But how could she not have called her?

"How does it look?" Catherine's excitement penetrated the door. "I think it might be the one. The moment I laid eyes on it, I knew it was perfect. I can't wait to see it on you, and I can't wait to see Dan's face when he sees you wearing it! Oh, I think this might be the best day of my life."

It was turning into the worst day of hers.

Rosie wanted to claw her way out of the room. "I'm still changing, Catherine."

"Do you need help, honey? I can—"

"I'm fine, but thank you." She closed her eyes and leaned back against the wall. What was she going to do? She needed to get her head back into the place it had been before that phone call. Either that or press pause on the whole thing. But how could she step off this runaway train without seriously injuring all those involved? This wasn't a night class (she'd switched from French to Italian after a term) where she could rethink her options.

Why did Katie's comments have so much influence on her?

She was old enough to make her own decisions, independent of her sister.

Catherine tapped on the door. "If you're worried about the price, don't be. This is my special gift to a special woman. It's not every day your precious only son gets married. I can't wait to welcome you officially to the Reynolds family. My Dan is a lucky, lucky young man."

Rosie pressed her hands to her ears to try to block out the sound of Katie's voice. She adored her older sister, but part of her was angry that she'd injected doubts. Why couldn't she have been happy and supportive?

She needed space to think, and she couldn't think while she was trying on a wedding dress.

She glanced around the fitting room for an escape hatch. Surely she couldn't be the first bride-to-be to wonder if she was making a mistake? Why didn't they cater for that type of thing? She slid her fingers down the edge of a mirror, hoping it was secretly a door, but all she saw was her own panicked reflection staring back at her.

When Dan had said all those things during Thanksgiving dinner, and then proposed in front of his whole family she'd been deliriously happy. She'd never felt about anyone the way she felt about Dan. The last few months had been the happiest of her life. She adored her family, but they still treated her as someone who needed protecting. Was she using her inhaler? Had she had an attack? Their anxiety had fueled *her* anxiety. Moving far away had been the best thing she'd ever done. Terrifying, of course, and to begin with she'd been homesick, but the freedom had more than compensated. She'd felt stronger. More capable and independent. She made decisions without everyone questioning her. And then she'd met Dan, who had made her feel stronger still. She'd been so sure of her feelings for him, it hadn't occurred to her to question whether saying yes to his proposal was a good idea. And then there was the love in his eyes and the fact that the fourteen people seated around the table had already made up their minds that this was a great idea.

Of course *she'll say yes*, his paternal grandmother had whispered to her sister, who had been in full agreement.

Who wouldn't want to marry our Dan?

It had seemed a reasonable question to Rosie.

Who wouldn't?

Their delight at the proposal simply endorsed her conviction that this was the right thing. And why wouldn't it be? Everyone thought Dan was wonderful. *She* thought Dan was wonderful. He was the best listener, and there were times when she felt closer to him than she did to her own family. She'd said things to him that she'd never said to them, including how hard it was to push herself to take risks when people were constantly telling her to be careful. And he'd talked to her about the loss of his father, and how deeply it had affected him. True, they didn't know the small details about each other's lives, but the small details were less important than the big things. She'd assumed they'd have plenty of time to learn more about each other, but then his mother had suggested a Christmas wedding and excitement levels had escalated.

Rosie felt as if she'd been picked up by an avalanche and swept down the mountain.

She'd wondered herself if Christmas might be a little soon, but only because the logistics of arranging something at such short notice blew her brain. Organization wasn't her strong point. She had nine thousand, four hundred and twenty emails sitting in her inbox because she never liked deleting anything and filing didn't come naturally to her. Her essays were often finished at the last minute, and doctor, dentist and hair appointments always ended up being an emergency.

She'd opened her mouth to tactfully confess that there was no way she could organize a wedding in such a short time frame, but Dan's family was already in deep planning mode. She'd half expected Catherine to leave the room and start whipping together a bouquet.

Rosie was already in love with Dan's family, particularly his great-aunt Eunice whose hearing was now challenged but who filled in gaps in sentences with her own active imagination.

Did she say she's feeling horny?

No, Great-Aunt Eunice, she said the table decoration was thorny.

And then Dan had kissed her and said how much he adored her and how this wedding was going to be magical and perfect and suddenly it was agreed that they were getting married in a month.

It had all seemed delightful, and then she'd called home and felt the waves of anxiety traveling across the Atlantic with the speed of light. Their doubt had penetrated the champagne cloud cushioning Rosie's brain.

And it wasn't only Katie. Her mother was worried, and Rosie hated worrying her mother.

She'd caused her family more than enough anxiety over the years, and she was uncomfortable with the idea that they all thought she was making a mistake. It made her question her own judgment. Gone was the confident woman she'd become over the past few months.

She was sure she loved Dan, but how did you actually *know*? It wasn't as if there was a blood test you could take. No one was going to sit across from her in a white coat and say *yes, you have high levels of love, so I can assure you you're going to be fine.*

Love was a feeling, and if Rosie had learned one thing during her time on the planet it was that feelings were unreliable. Hers certainly were. The fact that her life was filled with clothes she never wore, shoes too uncomfortable to walk in, and old boyfriends that she never called was proof of that.

What if her love for Dan turned out to be as transient as her love for Rollerblading?

Trying to pull herself together, she wriggled her way into the dress Catherine had chosen.

Ivory silk and beautifully cut, it fell in a simple sheath and pooled on the floor.

Rosie turned sideways and smoothed the fabric over her hips.

The woman had taste, there was no doubt about that. The dress looked incredible. So incredible that her doubts retreated. It was a good omen.

Nerves were natural, weren't they?

She tried to imagine her and Dan growing old together and Katie apologizing as she turned up to celebrate their golden wedding.

Look at the two of you! I was so wrong.

"Rosie?" There was another tap on the door. "Can we see you in it, honey?"

Rosie took a last look at her reflection and opened the door.

Catherine gasped and covered her mouth with her hand. "Oh my—"

The seamstress who had been standing ready to suggest alterations, gaped. "Oh *my*—"

Rosie did the obligatory twirl, the aftereffects of the previous night's champagne making her head spin. *Note to self—hangover pirouettes are not a good idea.*

"You're beautiful, honey." Catherine's eyes filled. "You can try on as many as you like, of course, but I honestly think this one is perfect. How about you? Are you having doubts?"

Rosie looked at herself. The dress was gorgeous. Classic. Flattering.

Definitely an omen.

"I love it." She wasn't having doubts about the dress. She was having doubts about the wedding, and those doubts were multiplying in her head like a virus.

Only last week he'd mentioned that he adored dogs and she'd thought *I'm allergic to dogs.* She hadn't said anything. There were plenty of small things they hadn't shared and it hadn't bothered her at all, until now. Now it was just one example of something he didn't know about her.

Tense, Rosie stood as the seamstress fussed around her, checking the fit. "The waist needs to be taken in a little. You're so slender. And December in Aspen is cold, so you might like to take a look at our range of faux fur wraps. Maybe a muff?" She stepped back and pressed her hand to her chest. "You're going to be a beautiful bride. I do love a Christmas wedding. It always feels like a double celebration."

Christmas.

When someone said that word, Rosie thought of Honeysuckle Cottage, the scent of cinnamon and pine, and her mother rustling up homemade treats from the kitchen. She thought about fleecy pajamas, mugs of steaming hot chocolate and long chats with her sister that went on until the early hours. There was always an enormous tree that smelled of the forest, decked with the usual decorations, all of which came with a story attached, and the annual gathering with the neighbors, when Mrs. Albert from next door always drank too much sherry and told stories of her time at Oxford during the war.

The reality of it sank in.

She'd planned on going home for Christmas, as she and Katie did every year. She'd already wrapped her gifts. Christmas was *always* spent at home with her family, and even though she'd lived away from home for four years, she'd been close enough to see her parents frequently. Honeysuckle Cottage still felt like home to Rosie. Student accommodation, however fun, couldn't compare with her cozy bed in the attic room that had been hers since childhood. When she snuggled under the covers and stared up at the stars through the skylight, she felt more relaxed than she did anywhere else.

Christmas Eve was her favorite time because her parents still insisted on making her a Christmas stocking and thanks to creaky floorboards she always heard them fiddling outside her bedroom in full Santa mode.

She'd been looking forward to it, but now it wasn't going to happen.

There would be no devouring her dad's scrambled eggs and smoked salmon for breakfast. No frosty walk on the village green, or lavish slices of her mother's unbeatable fruitcake. No staggering home from the village pub singing carols, substituting the usual lyrics with something definitely not PG.

She'd be spending Christmas in Aspen, with Dan's family. In fact they'd be *her* family, because she'd be married by Christmas Day.

Panic closed in on her. She and Dan hadn't thought through the detail.

Where were they going to live?

Dan was an only child. Would he expect them to have Christmas in Colorado every year? It was yet another subject they hadn't explored together. And what would Dan make of her home? He was tall. How would he handle Honeysuckle Cottage with its low ceilings and lethal beams? And then there was the blending of two families.

Catherine had been so kind and welcoming, but she

was always perfectly groomed and looking her best. Rosie didn't feel comfortable mooching around in her pajamas, so she'd been up, fully dressed and made-up for breakfast each morning. And Catherine was such a superwoman. She was always on her phone, solving people's wedding problems.

Rosie thought about her own mother, and the hours they'd spent chatting at the kitchen table. Maggie worked, but work didn't dominate her life in the way it did Catherine's. Would she and Catherine even get along?

Tension squirmed in her stomach.

She'd been excited about her family flying over, but now she wasn't so sure. What happened when two families didn't blend, but collided?

Was it going to be a happy family Christmas, or a recipe for disaster?

She took a deep breath and tried to calm herself.

If she needed evidence that a whirlwind romance could work, she had only to look at her parents. They'd married a few months after they'd met and were still happy together thirty-five years later. *Take that, Katie!*

The more she thought about that one simple fact, the better she felt.

Her parents' marriage was strong and indestructible. They were rock solid. Why shouldn't she and Dan be like them?

Her parents were a shiny example of what a marriage should look like.

She'd confess her worries to her mother, although she could already imagine what she'd say. *Your father and I met and married in a whirlwind, too, and we've done fine together for more than thirty years.*

Feeling better, Rosie smiled.

If anyone could put her doubts to rest about marriage, it would be her mother.

Katie

KATIE UNLOCKED THE DOOR of the small two-bedroom house she'd rented for the past decade and dropped her bag on the floor.

Vicky appeared in the doorway, wearing a thick red Christmas sweater over spotted pajama bottoms. "Who are you?"

"Very funny." Katie slid off her coat and hung it on the peg. It had been raining nonstop for a week and London was gloomy and cheerless. Her fingers were frozen, and her hair was lank. She'd never felt less festive in her life.

"I'm serious. I used to share this place with a friend, but I reported her missing weeks ago. The police are looking for a body."

"Great. If they find one, let me know. I'll swap it for the one I'm walking around in." Her shoulder throbbed. It kept her awake, not because of the pain, although it *was* painful, but because of the memories that came with it. She glanced at Vicky's feet. "You're wearing two pairs of socks. Did the heating break again? Please tell me we have hot water."

"You look like hell, Katie."

"Thanks a bunch."

"You're at work the whole time, you hardly ever go out,

and when you're home you're either Cactus Katie or you fall asleep in front of the TV."

"'Cactus Katie'?"

"Prickly. Dangerous to be close to."

"Oh. Well, if you're planning to water me, use vodka." She pushed her damp hair away from her face. "I admit I may be on a short fuse at times, but we have a staffing crisis."

"You've had a staffing crisis for the past few years. We used to manage to eat together at least once a week, and now I can't even get to speak to you on the phone. I'm worried about you."

"Don't be. I'm fine. Is the kettle hot? It's cold out there. If I don't warm up soon, I'll be treating myself for frostbite." She walked into the kitchen and put her phone on the table next to a take-out pizza box. "Any of that left?"

"One slice. If I'd known you'd be home, I would have saved more for you."

"A slice is enough." Katie pulled it out of the box, took one mouthful and pulled a face. "What *is* this?"

"Christmas pizza."

"That exists?"

"Apparently. I was trying to get in the mood."

"I'm not even going to ask what sort of mood. Turns out one slice is more than enough. I should warn my colleagues. It might be a new cause of death." Katie put the half-eaten slice back in the box. She couldn't remember when she'd last eaten a healthy meal. She should probably cook something, but by the time she arrived home she was too tired. "Sorry I haven't been around much." Her phone started to ring and she glanced at the screen. "How are you?"

"Better than you." Vicky put a cup of tea in front of her.

"Aren't you going to answer that? It's your mum. She might want something."

"I know what she wants. She wants to take me to lunch and talk weddings."

"Weddings?"

"Rosie is getting married at Christmas."

"*This* Christmas?"

"Yes. In Colorado. And before you ask, no, I won't be going home to Oxford. Somehow I have to get myself on an airplane and fly to Aspen and stop her doing something she's going to regret forever." She lowered her head onto her arms and closed her eyes. "It's a long flight. At least I can sleep all the way."

Although these days she didn't sleep. She collapsed into bed exhausted, but her mind refused to cooperate. Instead of shutting down it came alive, producing a slideshow of images she was trying to forget. There was no respite. She'd been on the *what if* and *if only* roundabout for so many weeks she was dizzy.

This wasn't like her. She had no idea how to handle it.

"Wait. You're intending to *stop* the wedding?"

"Absolutely." Katie lifted her head. "She's known him for a few months, Vick."

"So?"

"So I have cheese in the fridge that's older than their relationship. What can you possibly know about someone after a few months? It takes time for a person's worst traits to be revealed, but I intend to fast-track that part."

Vicky blinked. "To be clear about this—you're going to Aspen in order to dig up dirt on the man your sister is in love with?"

"*Thinks* she's in love with. I'm glad you understand. And I won't be digging as such. I'll be spending time with him.

I've had so much more experience than Rosie at seeing the bad side of people, and I'm not emotionally involved so I won't find it hard to ask the tough questions."

Vicky let out a long breath. "This could be your future brother-in-law."

"Not unless he passes the interview process."

Vicky shook her head. "I've suspected it for a while, but this confirms it. You need help."

"You mean Rosie needs help. I agree. That's why I'm doing this."

"No, I mean *you*. You're the one who needs help." She leaned forward. "Katie, I love you, we've been friends since the first day of medical school, but I'm telling you now this is not rational behavior. People don't fly across the Atlantic to stop a wedding. Normal is going as a guest. You buy a dress. Maybe a hat. Take a gift. Throw confetti. You don't ask tough questions of the groom and tell the bride you think she's making a mistake."

"I don't think it. She *is* making a mistake."

"If it's a mistake, then it's her mistake. This isn't your responsibility, Katie, and it isn't even your business. Do you want to know what I think? I think you should go to the wedding and relax for once. Stop trying to fix everything and everyone. Aspen is stunning. My parents took me skiing there when I was sixteen. If I had the money, I'd go again. Breathe in fresh air. Chill a little. A Christmas wedding in the snow sounds like fun."

Not to Katie, but nothing much seemed like fun at the moment.

Maybe Vicky was right. Maybe she needed help. Not because of her reaction to Rosie, which seemed entirely sane to her, but because of the way she felt generally.

Was she clinically depressed? She had no idea. These

days she didn't even have the energy to diagnose herself. "Are you not even the tiniest bit sympathetic that I have to drag myself on a fourteen-hour journey when even the half-hour commute almost finishes me off?"

"You're going to spend Christmas playing in the snow at a luxury mountain resort and you expect me to feel sorry for you? You're going to have to work harder."

Katie tried to smile, but her head was filled with everything serious. She'd forgotten how to laugh and have a lighthearted conversation. She was consumed by guilt, and doubt and—yes—anxiety. And now she had her sister to worry about, too. How was she going to get through a week with family without falling apart? She honestly had no clue.

She knew she wasn't good company either at work or at home.

Vicky sat down opposite her. "Are you going to tell me what happened?"

Katie lifted her head and looked at her friend. "I don't know what you're talking about."

"A few weeks ago you came home looking worse than you do now, if that's possible. You didn't want to talk about it and I respect that, but—you looked traumatized." Vicky reached across the table and took her hand. "I know something happened at work and I know it's eating away at you. I'm your best friend, Kat. We've known each other forever. You can talk to me."

"Not about this." Katie tried to pull her hand away but Vicky tightened her grip. "I'm handling it."

Vicky finally let her go. "If you don't want to talk to me, fine, but you have to talk to someone. You can't carry on like this. Even before that night, your life was ridiculous. You move from home to work and work to home."

"Plenty of people do the same."

"But do you even enjoy it? You used to be happy. You used to talk about how much you loved it, and the cases you saw. You were animated, but now you're..."

"I'm what?"

Vicky swallowed. "Like a robot or something."

"Thanks." Had she loved it? It was true that she had satisfaction from meeting goals. She'd always been the same. Work for an exam, pass with top marks. She'd worked hard at each step, enjoying the forward motion. Onward and upward. "I don't think anyone *enjoys* dragging people back from the brink of death every day." The pressure was so intense it felt like being squeezed by a nutcracker.

"But you used to find it satisfying. You loved making a difference."

Her heart beat faster. "Do you think we do make a difference?"

"Of course. Don't you?"

"Most of the time I feel like I'm trying to stop the *Titanic* from sinking by putting my fist in the hole. It's not working. We do what we can, but it never feels like enough."

And since that night she was questioning everything. She'd lost trust in herself. In her judgment.

You made a bad decision, Katie.

Bad call.

The blood pounded in her ears and her breathing grew shallow.

It didn't matter how many times people told her that it wasn't her fault, it felt like her fault.

"Well, if you have your fist in the *Titanic*, I can tell you that you're sinking with the ship, Kat. We do our best. That's all we can do. But you're giving too much. You're working at the expense of your social life. You're working at the expense of your health! When did you last kiss a guy?"

"There was that guy in the pub a few weeks ago."

"That was in June. And the fact that you remember it so clearly means you've had no action since. And by the way, one drunken kiss in a pub does *not* a relationship make."

"Is it my fault he didn't call?"

"I don't know, is it? *Karen.*"

Katie felt her cheeks burn. "It's very close to my real name. And he had my number."

"Not your whole number. You always change the last two digits."

"What can I say? It's easier than saying *I don't want to see you again.*"

"Have you ever given your real number to a man?"

"Yes. And I ended up having to get a new number when he wouldn't leave me alone. I prefer to keep things simple."

Vicky leaned forward. "What you're doing at the moment isn't living. You're existing."

What she was doing was trying not to lose her grip. If she kept busy, everything would be okay. She almost told Vicky then, but part of her was afraid that if she exposed that single pulled thread in the fabric of her life, the whole of her would unravel. "Maybe you're right. Maybe I need a break. I'll be fine when I've had time off."

"Will you?"

"I don't know." She pushed the pizza box away from her. "I feel as if I'm going crazy. Damn it, Vick—what's happening to me?"

Vicky stood up and put her arms around her. "You need professional help. Would you talk to someone?" The kindness and compassion in her voice almost tipped Katie over the edge.

She could barely force words past the lump in her throat. "I have you."

"But you're not talking to me, and all I have to offer is turkey pizza—you need someone with expertise."

"Your turkey pizza wasn't up to much. You're a lousy friend."

Vicky didn't smile. "Go to occupational health."

"And what?"

"I don't know. Maybe they'll sign you off sick."

"I have a holiday coming."

"Not long enough."

"Staff taking sick leave is one of the reasons it's so bad at the moment. If I go off, too, that would make things a thousand times worse for my colleagues."

"You can't be a good doctor, feeling the way you do. How are you supposed to make good decisions?"

She hadn't. She hadn't made good decisions.

She stood up abruptly. "I need to get to bed."

"So that you can get up and do the same tomorrow morning."

"That's right." She finished her tea and put the mug in the dishwasher. "Thanks for the tea and the listening ear. And the pizza. It was an experience."

"You're welcome. I hope you feel better in the morning. Oh, and, Katie—"

Katie paused with her hand on the door. "What?"

"Just so you know—from where I'm sitting, it doesn't look as if you're handling it."

THE FOLLOWING MORNING she didn't feel better, nor did she feel better for any of the twenty mornings that followed. She booked her flight on automatic, an open ticket because if things went the way she expected them to she'd be coming back after a couple of days. She approved Rosie's suggestion for her dress even though she'd barely glanced at it.

The conversation with Vicky played round and round in her head.

You can't be a good doctor if you're in a state yourself.

Katie had never failed at anything in her life. She badly wanted to be a good doctor, and that was how she found herself sitting in front of a doctor as a patient for once.

It felt enormous to be admitting that she wasn't doing well. If she said it aloud to a professional, then that would make it real. There would be no more pretending these feelings might blow over.

The occupational health doctor was brisk and to the point.

"I read your medical record, so I know what happened to you." She removed her glasses, her expression kind. "I'm wondering why it took you this long to come and talk to me."

"I didn't feel I needed to." Katie fidgeted. "I was doing fine. I haven't missed a day of work—"

"Why not?"

"Excuse me?"

Dr. Braithwaite glanced briefly at the notes. "After what happened I would have expected you to have time off. And perhaps counseling. Have you considered talking to a psychologist?"

"No." Her heart rate increased. She clasped her hands in her lap, hoping that the woman across from her couldn't see that she was sweating. "I don't want to spend what little free time I have talking about something I'm trying to forget. I prefer to deal with it my own way."

The doctor nodded. "But you're sitting in front of me now, which tells me that you're not finding that as easy as you thought."

Katie felt tears burn her eyes and blinked. "I think about it all the time. Flashbacks."

"To the attack?"

"Yes, but mostly to events leading up to it. I keep thinking what might have happened if I'd done something different. He—he said it was my fault—"

"And you believe him?"

"It *was* my fault. But we were so busy that night, I didn't give him the time he needed. It's about triage. Always about triage. What you don't realize is that risk is not always obvious. Sorry." She grabbed a tissue from the box on Dr. Braithwaite's desk. "I'm not normally like this."

"How are you normally?"

"A coper." She smiled through her tears. "I'm a coper. Never a day off sick. And a perfectionist. Never an exam I couldn't pass, or a problem I couldn't handle. You name it, I aced it."

Dr. Braithwaite nodded. "Do you see perfectionism as a good thing?"

"It is in medicine. In medicine you're expected to get it right every time."

"But how could you? Humans are flawed, are they not? Errors are inevitable, and of course we should do our best to avoid them when lives are at stake but there is a difference between setting high personal standards and perfectionism. One makes you strive to do the best you can and the other, being unobtainable, makes you self-critical and unhappy. It also makes people afraid to reveal anything that could be perceived as weakness and prevents a person taking risks because failure is not seen as an option."

Katie blew her nose. "Your advice is to go out there and fail?"

"I think you should consider the possibility that you can

make a mistake and still be a good doctor." Dr. Braithwaite pushed the box of tissues closer to her. "Admitting that you need help isn't a weakness."

"I've wanted to be a doctor since I was a child. Every exam I worked for has been leading me here. I have slogged and sacrificed, and now I'm questioning the whole thing."

"Because you believe you made a mistake?"

"Not only that. I think—" she swallowed "—I think maybe I don't want to do this anymore."

"And that scares you?"

"Of course." Because if she wasn't a doctor, who was she? Katie stared at the paperweight on the doctor's desk. "I've never felt like this before. I'm worried that I'm going to unravel and it's not going to be pretty."

"And what would happen if you did 'unravel'? Why would that matter?"

"Because people rely on me." She thought about her mother, and all the worry she'd had with Rosie. She'd be appalled if she knew how bad her elder daughter was feeling. "I don't want anyone to worry about me. I've got this. I need—" She slumped in her chair. "I don't know what I need. I don't suppose you have a magic potion?"

Dr. Braithwaite was thoughtful. "You didn't take a single day off after what happened?"

"I took a couple of hours while I was being stitched up, and I've had a couple of physio appointments since then which don't seem to make a difference. I had to talk to the police of course, but other than that, no." Katie shook her head. "I'm better keeping busy."

"Maybe not." Dr. Braithwaite reached for a notepad. "Are you working over Christmas?"

"No, I'm off from tomorrow and back to work on New Year's Eve."

"You won't be working New Year's Eve. I'm signing you off until the middle of January. That gives you a month."

Katie sat up with a gasp. "You—a *month?* I can't be away from work for a month. Even taking an hour out for this appointment has created extra work for my colleagues. We're already stretched to the breaking point in the department, and winter is coming, and—"

"Dr. White—Katie—" Her voice gentled. "Have you heard the phrase *physician, heal thyself*?"

"Yes, but there's nothing wrong with me. My shoulder has healed perfectly well and so has my head." Apart from the constant throbbing, and the nightmares.

"Those aren't the injuries that concern me." The doctor scribbled something. "I'd like you to talk to one of my colleagues. A psychologist who specializes in dealing with traumatic events. She's very good at what she does."

"I don't want to spend my time talking about something I want to forget."

"That's your decision, but I'm giving you her number anyway and I suggest you call her." Dr. Braithwaite tore the paper from the pad and handed it over. Then she tapped some keys on the computer and printed out a prescription. "I'm giving you a short course of antidepressants. I think they may help you handle this acute phase. Come back to me in the middle of January and we'll talk again."

Katie took the prescription, even though she knew it was going straight into a drawer. She didn't know what she needed, but she was pretty sure it wasn't antidepressants. "Thanks."

Dr. Braithwaite put her pen down. "Are you going away over Christmas? In my opinion you need a complete break, away from London. Time to recharge."

"As it happens I'm going to Colorado. I need to—" She

almost said *stop my sister getting married*, and then realized how that would sound to someone who didn't know her. It had sounded bad enough to Vicky who *did* know her. "My sister is getting married and I need to be there to support her." She expected the doctor to smile and say all the usual things about how exciting and what fun.

She didn't.

"So you'll be focusing on her, and her needs and your days will be busy again. I want you to focus on your own needs for once, Katie. You need time to think."

She didn't want time to think. "You want me to tell my little sister I can't go to her wedding?"

"No, but I want you to carve out some time for yourself. On reflection, maybe the Rockies in winter is exactly what you need." Dr. Braithwaite tapped her fingers on the desk as she studied Katie. "Mountains. Snow. Fresh air. It might be good for you."

Katie wasn't convinced. Having made a fool of herself and howled in front of Dr. Braithwaite who was a total stranger, how was she going to hold it together with her family?

Her mother would notice right away that something was wrong, which was why Katie had been avoiding her. Fortunately, she hadn't been able to book the same flight as them, so she was traveling separately a day later. She felt guilty about that, too, because her mother wasn't so much a nervous flyer as a terrified flyer and Katie probably should have been there to help, but it wasn't her fault that there were no seats.

She had a long flight to pull herself together and produce a convincing act.

And maybe she *did* need to give some thought to her

own approach to life. Maybe it was okay to fail in some circumstances, but not this circumstance.

She had a family to fool and a wedding to stop.

Rosie

ROSIE STOOD IN the arrivals hall of the airport, craning her neck to see her parents.

Dan stood behind her and wrapped his arms around her to stop her being jostled by the crowd. "Do you know that you always bite your lip when you're nervous or excited?"

"I do not bite my lip." She stopped biting her lip.

"You don't even know you're doing it. Also, you hug yourself and there's no need because you have me to hug you now." As if to prove it, Dan tightened his grip. "I haven't seen you this stressed. Is this what your family does to you?"

"Being around them always makes me a little anxious."

"I'd noticed. By the way, you might want to take off your earring."

She turned her head to look at him. "You don't like my earrings?"

"I love your earrings, but you're only wearing one of them." He gave her a wicked grin. "I suspect the other is back home somewhere in our bed."

She gasped and lifted her hand to her ear. It was bare. "It must have fallen out when we—"

He covered her lips with his fingers. "Small children within earshot."

"We were so late leaving, I didn't even check."

"We were a little distracted." He kissed her jaw. "Don't worry. At least you remembered pants."

She gave him a shove with one hand, and removed her one earring with the other. "I'm relieved you noticed. I'd rather not greet my parents looking as if I just climbed out of bed, thank you." She turned back to look at the throng of people. "Where *are* they?"

"Probably stuck in immigration. Or waiting for baggage. You need to chill."

She didn't know how to "chill." That word didn't appear in her vocabulary.

He should know that. He should know everything about her, surely? How else could he possibly be sure he wanted to spend the rest of his life with her?

A person should know what they were committing to. At what stage does what you know become enough?

Oh stop it, Rosie!

She was hearing the voices of her family even though they hadn't even arrived yet.

She wished she'd never talked to Katie. What if they embarrassed her in front of Dan?

She wished she could inject herself with something and kill all the little doubts that were multiplying in her mind. Right now, her focus should be on her parents. Her mother would probably be a nervous wreck after the flight, and that was assuming her father had managed to get her on the flight in the first place. What if he hadn't?

Maybe they were still in Heathrow.

Her imagination took a long-haul flight of its own with no stopovers. She pictured her mother collapsing at the departure gate and having to be sedated. Or, worse, being midair and trying to claw her way out of the plane.

"Can you open the door of a plane when it's in the air?"

"No, of course not."

"Why 'of course'?"

"Because the cabin is pressurized, and the internal pressure is higher than the external pressure. The differential air pressure would mean you're pulling over a thousand pounds—not possible. It's physics."

Rosie hated physics. "My area of expertise is folklore and mythology, so there is no reason why I should know that."

He let go of her and turned her around to face him. "Why are you asking? Does your mom have a habit of trying to open plane doors midflight?"

"No." But that was because her mother avoided flying whenever possible. "My mother hates flying."

"If she hated it that much, she wouldn't have come."

"You don't know my mother. There is nothing she wouldn't do for my sister and me." And Rosie was feeling increasingly guilty for dragging her mother away from home at Christmas. She loved Christmas and always made such a fuss of everyone. "She's always been there for us, no matter what."

"And this is your wedding! I'm sure she's happy and excited for you."

Rosie wasn't sure of that at all. She was starting to feel a little sick. What was it about her family that made her revert to child mode? "What if they never made the flight?"

"Then your dad would have called."

"Do you have to be so logical?"

He smiled. "Yes, it's part of who I am, you know that."

"I do know that." She said it firmly, to remind herself

that there were in fact plenty of things she knew about him. She knew he was passionate about health and fitness, having lost his dad to a heart attack when he was twenty. She knew he preferred reading nonfiction to fiction, that he absorbed facts like a sponge, and loved the outdoors. And she knew that being with him made her feel as if she could take on the world. He never questioned her competence or decisions. His belief in her had made her start to believe in herself.

"You're overthinking this. That creative brain of yours is working overtime." He cupped her face in his hands, his expression kind. "Are you sure this is about your parents? Nothing else? You've been getting more and more stressed the last couple of weeks."

"You're imagining things."

"I know you, Rosie."

Did he? Did he really?

"You can't arrange a wedding in under a month and not expect a little stress, Dan. That would be unrealistic."

"So it's the wedding?" He stroked a strand of hair away from her face. "Not that I'm an expert on weddings, this being my first and only one, but I thought it was supposed to be fun and exciting."

That was what she'd thought, too, but it turned out they were both wrong.

She didn't feel giddy with excitement; she had a tension headache.

"Let's talk about something other than weddings for five minutes."

"Hey—" he pulled her back into his arms "—it's going to be okay, I promise. Once your family arrives, you'll be more relaxed. You're probably stressed because your sister couldn't make it out on the same flight. I know you miss her."

Mmm. Right now she wanted to kill her sister.

Why were relationships so complicated?

"She emailed yesterday. She wants us to share for a few nights so that we can catch up. Is that okay with you? At Christmas we always end up sharing a room. It's kind of a tradition."

Dan grinned. "I'm assuming I'm not invited to this sisterly sleepover?"

"You're not invited, but it's going to feel weird being separated from you. I'm not sure how I feel about it to be honest."

Katie had said in her email that she desperately missed girlie gossip and that she wanted a few nights together like they always had at Christmas, but now Rosie was wondering if there was more to the request than an urge for sisterly bonding.

She'd tried calling, but her sister hadn't answered her phone.

Dan seemed relaxed about it. "It will be fun, and it's understandable. She hasn't seen you in ages. She wants to gossip with her little sister."

Rosie hoped that was all it was.

She almost told him then. She almost told him what Katie had said, and how she'd put doubts in her mind.

But how could she? She didn't even know if those doubts were real. She didn't know what she wanted. There was so much she could talk to him about, but not this.

"I hope you like her." *I hope my sister doesn't subject you to interrogation.* What if she did? What if Dan decided it was all too much? Rosie leaned her head against his chest, feeling detached despite the warmth of his arms. It was as if a barrier had somehow appeared between them. One of the things she'd loved about him from the start was how easy he was to talk to, but right now she couldn't find a way to say what needed to be said. She felt him stroke her hair.

"You've talked so much about her, I feel as if I know her already."

There had been a few things she'd left out. Like the fact that her sister hadn't sounded thrilled about the wedding. "It's been an insane few weeks."

He lifted her face to his. "Mom hasn't been too overwhelming?"

"Not at all. She's the kindest person and so generous. I love her." That was true, even though it was also true that Catherine's expectations about the wedding added another level of pressure.

"And she loves you." He smiled as he kissed her. "She told me that if she could have chosen a daughter, she would have chosen you."

And...more pressure.

Oh this was ridiculous. She needed to tell him about the conversation with Katie. But then he might be mad at Katie, and she couldn't bear that. She didn't want to begin a marriage with family tensions.

"Tell me something I don't know about you."

"You mean a really deep, dark secret?"

She swallowed. "Yes."

"Something no one else on the planet knows about me, not even Jordan?"

"Yes."

"Are you sure? Because I have some pretty serious stuff buried in my past."

Her heart started to pound. Maybe Katie was right.

Maybe there were things they didn't know about each other that really mattered.

"Tell me. You can tell me anything." And she should be able to tell him anything, shouldn't she? After he'd made his big confession, whatever that was, she'd tell him straight out about her doubts. Neither of them would be hiding anything.

"It's pretty shocking."

"Go *on*."

He took a deep breath. "When I was seven I found my Christmas presents under my parents' bed and opened them all."

Anxiety turned to relief. "That's it? Oh, you—" She pushed at his chest and he grinned.

"I told you it was shocking."

"I'm being serious."

"This was serious. I was grounded for two weeks. And no, I didn't get any other gifts that year. That was when I figured out Santa wasn't real, although I did wonder briefly if maybe he'd paid us an early visit and stored mine under the bed."

"That's your deep, dark secret?"

"Yes." He lowered his head and kissed her briefly. "I don't have deep, dark secrets, Rosie. I'm pretty straightforward."

"I know, and I love that about you." Her heart was still knocking against her ribs. She'd braced herself to hear something awful, and she should have known it would be a joke. He loved to tease her, and most of the time she loved his brand of teasing. "Here's something about me that you don't know—I'm allergic to dogs. And cats."

He raised his eyebrows. "Seriously?"

"Seriously. My worst asthma attack ever happened when

I was staying with a friend who owned a dog. Which basically means I can't ever own a pet."

"Damn." He ran his hand over his face. "Then we're done. We're over. Better call Mom and cancel the wedding."

Her heart almost stopped. "Are you—" she swallowed "—are you serious?"

"No, of course I'm not serious. You should know that." His expression was midway between amused and exasperated. "What's wrong with you today?"

"I don't know. I'm worried you're going to change your mind, I suppose."

"I love you, Rosie. You. All of you. No, I didn't know you were allergic to animals but never mind. We'll work with it. Do I like dogs? Sure. But I like you more. If marrying you means I have to get my furry animal fix outside the home, then that's what I'll do."

He made everything sound so simple.

"That's—" she swallowed "—good. Because I thought maybe that if you'd always imagined a family home with a pet, then—"

"I can live without a pet, Rosie."

"Right. You—you don't see obstacles, do you?"

He frowned. "That wasn't an obstacle."

"It might be, to some people, but that's what I mean— you don't see them." And she loved that about him. "I thought there might be things we don't know about each other, that's all."

"I'm sure there are. But not because we're keeping secrets. Not because there's something dark we need to hide. It's finding out those small things that are going to add to the fun."

He was so sure of everything. So confident.

It made her feel a little better.

He lowered his head and his lips brushed hers, teasing, seductive, a reminder of what they'd shared the night before and the night before that.

She felt a punch of desire and wrapped her arms around his neck. The sounds of the airport faded into the background and her world was filled with nothing but Dan, his mouth, the sudden blast of heat as his arms locked around her. Her head spun.

When he finally released her, she kept her hand on his shoulder for extra support.

Someone strolling past them muttered *get a room*, and Dan grinned.

"That's not a bad idea. How about we check into an airport hotel and I'll show you how much I love you? We'll tell your parents we were stuck in the snow."

Even though it was a ridiculous idea, she was almost tempted. Her legs still felt like liquid and her body throbbed with need. The chemistry between them was off the scale. When they were naked and in bed she never had any doubts at all.

"Dan, I've been wondering—" *Say it, Rosie, say it!* "I'm wondering if we should have taken more time over this, that's all. It's happening very fast and that's a lot of pressure."

"You are so thoughtful, but don't worry about it. Mom is a champion last-minute organizer. She has never met a crisis she hasn't defeated. Frankly she thrives on it. Everything will be fine. It's given her something to focus on. I haven't seen her this happy since Dad died."

And still more pressure.

Everything he said made it harder for her to speak up.

"Dan—"

"Wait—is that them?" Dan peered over her shoulder and she turned, searching the flow of people.

They ranged from the very young to the very old, many of them arriving to celebrate the holidays with loved ones. They surged around her wearing scarves, hats and eager expressions while juggling suitcases and parcels.

She saw a family placating a fractious toddler, an exhausted mother soothing a baby.

She didn't see her parents.

"It's not them."

"You're right, they are taking a long time." Dan frowned at the last trickle of people. "Your dad would have called if there was an issue, right?"

"I hope so." Unless he'd forgotten to charge his phone, a habit of his that drove all of them crazy. She rose on tiptoe to study a new bunch of people emerging through the doors.

Not her parents.

She was about to text again when she spotted her father's head above the crowd.

"There he is! He's the one with the windswept hair and the glasses." She gave a wave. She was relieved to see them.

"I see him. And is that your mom? Is she okay, do you think? She looks a little—unsteady on her feet. Oh." Dan gave an awkward laugh. "I guess she is okay. She's really into your dad, right? Do they always kiss like that in public? That's pretty cute. Maybe we should have got that room after all. They could have used it." Because he was taller than her he had a better view, but as the people in front of her parted she saw her parents locked in a passionate embrace.

Rosie was aghast. *What the—?*

"They're not normally like that. I mean, they have a great marriage obviously because they've been together forever, but they're not usually that demonstrative." She was thoroughly mortified while next to her, Dan was dying with laughter.

"I think it's cool, and I can promise you that I'll still be kissing you like that when we've been together for thirty years. Maybe your mom is glad to be alive after the flight. Nothing boosts your gratitude levels like a near-death experience, right?"

"Right." When she'd worried that her family might embarrass her, this wasn't the scenario she'd had in mind.

She saw her dad unpeel her mother's arms from his neck.

They were still too far away for her to hear what was being said, but she saw her mother straighten her clothing and slide her arm through her husband's.

It seemed like a gesture born of necessity rather than affection. Studying her closely, Rosie thought it looked as if her mother was leaning on her father.

Was she sick or something?

Anxious, she let go of Dan's hand, ran to her parents and hugged them. First her mother, then her father. "I was starting to worry. How was your flight?"

"It went in a flash," her mother said. "The cheap seats were full by the time we booked, so Dad treated us to business class seats in the middle row. We were able to hold hands and watch movies. It was like dating again. It made us realize how much in love we still are."

Rosie froze. Was this really her mother? Her sensible, practical, steady mother? "Er, Mum—"

"What sweetie? I love your father, that's all. I want you to know that. We are so happy together. Happy, happy, happy. Everything is fine, you don't have to worry about a thing. Did I mention how happy we are?"

What wouldn't be fine? What shouldn't she be worrying about?

When someone told you not to worry it generally meant there was something to worry about.

She glanced at her father for clues and he gave a tired smile.

"It's been a long flight, and you know flying isn't your mother's idea of entertainment."

"Oh but it *was* entertaining and after the first few glasses of champagne I wasn't nervous at all!" Her mother sounded joyful. "That lovely man kept topping my glass up—"

"Lovely man?"

"One of the cabin crew. And Dad was talking and flirting outrageously with me. I was laughing so hard I didn't even realize we'd taken off until the seat belt sign went ping."

Rosie had seen her father hold a lecture hall in thrall, debate issues vigorously at the dinner table and eviscerate intellectual snobs, but she'd never seen him flirt.

The fact that she couldn't imagine it was fine with her.

She admired and was grateful for her parents' steady relationship, but that didn't mean she wanted to dwell on the details.

"I'm glad the flight was bearable."

"It was more than bearable. It felt as if we were going on our honeymoon. If it had been a night flight we might even have—"

"Mum!" Was her mother *drunk*?

Her father patted her shoulder. "Sorry we kept you waiting, Rosie. We're last out of the door because they've lost your mother's suitcase, including her wedding outfit."

"Oh no, that's terrible." Was that an omen? No, of course it wasn't an omen. On the other hand if she was going to believe in good omens, she also had to believe in bad ones. *Stop it, Rosie!* "What do we do?"

"We've been told to go to wherever we're staying and wait for her case to be delivered."

"And when will that be?"

"They don't know. Hopefully soon."

"I'm more worried about the presents I packed. They were only small things, but I chose them carefully. We don't need clothes." Her mother rested her head on his shoulder, unconcerned. "It will be like our first Christmas together. Remember that? It snowed, and we didn't bother leaving the bed. We couldn't afford heating, so we relied on body warmth. We didn't get dressed for days."

Rosie wanted to cover her mother's mouth with her hand. "Too much information, Mum." Had neither of them noticed Dan standing behind her? How much had he heard?

This was a nightmare. The first time she was introducing her parents to her fiancé and her mother was nothing like herself.

Her father didn't seem like himself either. Usually he was the most laid-back person she knew, but today he looked tense. Perhaps that wasn't surprising given the stressful flight he'd had with her mother.

"I want you to meet Dan." Hardly the best timing, but what choice did she have? She grabbed him by the arm and tugged him forward.

"Great to finally meet you in person." Dan stepped toward them, a smile on his face and hand outstretched, enviably comfortable with people. He'd told her it came from being an only child and having to look outside the family for playmates, but she suspected it was part of his personality.

He shook her mother's hand, then her father's and he was so warm and welcoming that Rosie relaxed a little.

Maybe he hadn't noticed that her mother appeared to have consumed a little too much alcohol on the plane.

And then her mother let go of her dad's arm and teetered toward him.

"Oh, Rosie, he's *gorgeous*. No wonder you want to marry him quickly." She closed her hands over Dan's biceps and squeezed. "So strong. Yummy. And those eyes and that *smile*."

"Mum, please—"

Sadly her mother wasn't done. "You obviously work out, Dan."

Kill me now. "Dan is a personal trainer. That's how we met, remember? I decided I had to stop being a couch potato, so I joined a gym. I'm sure I told you."

Why had she been worrying about the future of their relationship? After this, their relationship probably had no future. She should give the ring back right now and save Dan the trouble of asking for it.

She sent him an agonized look and was relieved when he winked at her.

The fact that he was struggling not to laugh made her feel a little better. Somehow, he always managed to find humor in situations she found stressful.

She loved him. She really did love him.

And she was so grateful she managed a weak smile in return. "I think my mother likes you."

"Which is good news all around as I'm soon to be joining the family. It's been a long journey for your parents," he said calmly. "Let's get them home."

His kindness was another thing she loved about him.

Katie was right that most of Rosie's past boyfriends had treated her carelessly. Dan was always thoughtful.

Oh what was *wrong* with her? She should be dancing with joy that she was marrying him. She should be relieved they were doing it quickly before he had a chance to discover what a flaky person she was.

Already he was chatting comfortably with her parents. "The weather can be pretty changeable at this time of year, so we're pleased to have blue skies to welcome you today. And don't worry about the luggage. I'm sure my mother will be able to help you out with some emergency clothing."

"I doubt it," Maggie said. "Unless she went through a seriously fat stage at some point. Did she keep her pregnancy clothes?"

"Mum! You're not fat and you don't need anyone's pregnancy clothes." Since when had her mother been insecure? She'd never been one of those women who had obsessed over appearance. She took care of herself and liked to look her best, but that was as far as it went. "I think we should get out of here so that we can do most of the journey while it's light."

Dan seemed to agree because he scooped the luggage that hadn't been lost and they all trooped to the car.

"Do you want to sit in the front with Dan, Dad?" At least that way she could silence her mother if necessary. Rosie opened the door for her father, but her mother grabbed his hand.

"This is our first trip together in a long time. We want to sit together, don't we, Nick?"

Rosie saw her father pause.

"Maybe that would be the best idea." He squeezed Rosie's shoulder and nudged her into the front seat next to Dan. "She'll be fine, don't worry. My fault. I should have taken her glass away but I was so relieved that she wasn't screaming in terror, I let her carry on."

Rosie slid into the passenger seat and prayed the journey would pass quickly. The thought of four hours trapped in a car with her drunk mother didn't thrill her. With luck she'd fall asleep and wake up entirely sober.

Catherine had invited them to join them up at the lodge for a family dinner that evening, but Rosie was already planning to postpone that event.

She'd arrange room service and tell Dan's mother that they were jet-lagged and feeling the effects of the flight. That was true, if you counted alcohol poisoning as one of the effects of a flight.

Hopefully after an early night, her mother would be recovered.

There was still the issue of the missing suitcase of course, but Rosie would fix that problem tomorrow.

"You've lived in the area long, Dan?" Her father shifted the conversation onto safe ground.

"I was raised in Boston, but my parents came out here to ski when they were first married, fell in love with the place and that was it. My dad bought a plot of land before it became unaffordable, developed it and the rest is history. They love the outdoor lifestyle and the culture. When he died, my mother built up the wedding business." Dan glanced in his mirror. "You guys live in Oxford. All that history right there on your doorstep. I've always wanted to visit."

"It's a wonderful place," Maggie said happily. "We live in a pretty cottage with roses and honeysuckle round the door."

Dan smiled. "Sounds charming."

"It is. And you don't need to worry that you won't see it, because I will *not* be selling it. I've made up my mind.

I know it's too big for one, but I love it too much to ever leave."

Too big for one? Rosie frowned. What was her mother talking about?

"Two of you live there," she said patiently. "You and Dad. That's two, not one."

"Oh yes. The thing is, I see us as one. Isn't that right, Nick? After so many years together, we've blended into one being."

Her mother had totally lost it.

Dan reached across and squeezed Rosie's hand, then glanced in the mirror at her mother. "It's your family home. My family feel the same about Snowfall Lodge. My mom always says she'd have to be dragged away from the place. I think when you've lived somewhere a long time, it becomes part of you. I understand why you wouldn't want to sell your home. That makes sense to me."

It made no sense to Rosie because the question of selling Honeysuckle Cottage had never arisen.

Her parents adored the place. It was the only home Rosie had ever known. They'd never mentioned selling.

"Aspen was originally a mining town, and then the market for silver collapsed." Dan eased into the flow of traffic leaving the airport. "Fortunately skiing became a thing, and the town developed from there. The position is great. We're right by the Roaring Fork River, and we've got Red Mountain to the North, Smuggler Mountain to the East and Aspen Mountain to the South."

"The Roaring Fork River," Maggie murmured. "That sounds romantic. We have the Thames and the Cherwell."

"It's a tributary of the Colorado River. You guys should come back here in the summer." The traffic eased and Dan put his foot down. "The drive over Independence Pass is stunning."

"We can't take that route now?"

"Closed in the winter. We're forced to take the long route."

Rosie glanced over her shoulder. "It snowed yesterday. It's so pretty. I can't wait to show you, although it will be dark when we arrive of course, so you won't see it properly until tomorrow."

Dan adjusted the heating. "So far we've had above-average snowfall for the season. And Rosie is right—the place is a winter wonderland. Snowfall Lodge is busy. We're booked right through until March. I'm pleased for my mother. She's put all her energy into this since my father died."

"So the lodge is a hotel?"

"Of sorts, but not one of those sterile impersonal places where no one knows or cares who you are. Our guests tend to be on the fussier end of the spectrum, and we pride ourselves on personal service. My mother used to handle it all herself, but as she became more involved in the wedding side of things, she hired a manager. Every guest has a file. If you're allergic to feathers and you don't eat meat—it will be right there in your file so that next time you stay everything will be exactly as you like it. And for those guests who need extra privacy, we have our tree houses. They're built high up in the tree canopy and offer a unique opportunity to stay deep in the forest. The views are incredible. You'll be staying in one of those. My mother insisted."

"A tree house?" Maggie frowned. "They're actually built into the trees?"

"On stilts," Dan said. "Don't panic. They're more ritzy than rustic. They've won several architectural and environmental awards. You're going to love staying there. The tree houses are made of wood, so they blend into the forest and the local wildlife sometimes visit. They're always popular with honeymooners. Where else can you sip champagne in the hot tub under a midnight sky? It should be perfect for you."

Rosie shrank in her seat. She didn't want to think of her parents as honeymooners.

Worried that her mother might be tempted to make some quip about being naked again, Rosie dived into the conversation. "How is Katie? I've barely heard from her the last couple of weeks." After that phone call, all they'd exchanged were a few emails covering practical issues like her dress and flight arrangements. Unsettled by their previous conversation, Rosie had been nervous of calling her sister again and Katie hadn't called her, either.

"You know your sister," her father said. "She's busy saving lives."

"Let's hope that's all it is." Maggie leaned her head on his shoulder. "If you ask me, there's something going on. Every time I suggest lunch, she makes excuses. That's not like her. Normally she snatches every opportunity to be fed. She's avoiding me."

Rosie felt a shimmer of unease. She'd had the same feeling about her sister, but had assumed it was because she'd upset her. She and Katie had their disagreements of course, as sisters did, but never anything serious and nothing long lasting. Their clashes were no more than sisterly sniping over small everyday things.

It's your turn to clear the kitchen.

Did you borrow my shoes?

This time felt different. As if Katie was keeping her at a distance.

"She's probably busy." That's what she'd been telling herself. She hoped she was right.

"It's a shame you guys couldn't fly out together, but those Christmas flights are always a nightmare. As well as the tourists, everyone wants to be home for the holidays."

"Family is important at this time of year. I love you," Maggie told Nick. "Have I told you today how much I love you?"

"Many times," Nick said dryly, and Rosie closed her eyes.

She'd never seen her mother this demonstrative. Normally it was the odd look, or touch that proclaimed them as a couple. A quiet togetherness. Today her mother was behaving as if this was their last day on earth and she was determined to make the most of it. It had to be the alcohol, but even that was strange because she'd never known her mother to drink much, not even at Christmas.

She was never going to persuade her mother to fly again if this was what happened.

"How about some music?"

She could see Dan was trying not to laugh. "This is nowhere near as embarrassing as the first time you met my aunt Elizabeth," he murmured in an undertone. "Remember that?"

The shared memory made her smile, but it was only when she glanced behind her again and saw that her mother was asleep on her father's shoulder that she allowed herself to relax.

The scenery grew more spectacular as they approached Aspen. The sky was a pale, arctic blue, the winter sun bouncing a soft, shimmering light over the snow-laden peaks.

As someone who had spent most of her life in a small

English village where a few flakes of snow created wild excitement for the children and a ridiculous degree of disruption for the adults, the mountains never failed to thrill her and having snow at Christmas appealed to the romantic side of her nature.

Feeling a little better, she stretched out her legs. "Do you ever get used to the view?"

Dan shook his head. "Never."

"It's beautiful." Her mother woke, groggy and enchanted at the same time. "Nick, look!"

"I'm looking."

"Now the flight is behind me, I'm excited. It's wonderful to be here, isn't it? We've never been away for Christmas. And we'll be staying in a tree house, just the two of us. It really *is* a second honeymoon." There was a pause, and then a sound of rustling as her mother shifted closer to Rosie's father. "You're still handsome, Nick. Have I told you that lately?"

Rosie wished her mother would go back to sleep. Unfortunately, the short nap seemed to have invigorated her and she maintained a running commentary.

"I've never seen mountains this high. And the snow is so smooth and perfect on that field over there it reminds me of my Christmas cake."

Rosie felt a wave of nostalgia. She wouldn't be eating her mother's Christmas cake this year. And what about next year? She didn't know. That was one of the details she and Dan still needed to work out together. That and so many others.

She stared out the window as Dan took the sharp turn that led up the wide tree-lined driveway leading to Snowfall Lodge. Snow lay in soft mounds, blurring the edges of the road.

"Rosie tells me you work in academic publishing, Maggie." Dan slowed. "That must be interesting. Do you enjoy it?"

"No. If you want the truth, I find it intensely boring," her mother said. "I work in a quiet office, with quiet people, doing the same quiet thing I've done forever. I hate it."

There was silence.

Rosie turned her head and saw a deep furrow appear on her father's brow. He seemed as shocked as she was.

Even Dan, something of a conversational expert, seemed to struggle with a suitable response.

Rosie felt as if her world had shifted a little. "You hate your job, Mum? Really?"

"Why is that so surprising? Not everyone is lucky enough to do a job they're passionate about. Sometimes you fall into something and before you know it you're still there twenty years later."

"I—I thought you loved your work."

"It's been perfectly fine. Ideal in many ways, because they were flexible about letting me work from home whenever you were sick which was important. It was a practical choice. I'm not the first woman in the world to make a practical choice."

The practical choice sounded depressingly uninspiring. Rosie felt a twinge of guilt.

Was this her fault? She knew that her constant emergency trips to the hospital had put pressure on the whole family but she'd never considered that her mother might have stayed in the job because it made it easier to care for a sick child.

"Why haven't you talked about this before?"

"I don't think anyone ever asked. Dan's the first. His

emotional intelligence is clearly as well developed as his muscles."

Of *course* they'd asked about her job. For years when she'd been living at home, Rosie had asked *how was your day?*

But how had her mother answered? She couldn't remember.

She was sure she'd never heard her say that she hated her job, but maybe there had been subtle hints that she'd missed. Maybe she'd heard a polite response and not recognized it as that. She hadn't looked deeper, but that was because it had never occurred to her that her mother didn't like her job. Why would it? If you didn't like something, you said so. Her mother never complained about anything. In the absence of evidence to the contrary, Rosie had assumed she loved her life.

Growing up, all her friends had envied Rosie her mother. Maggie was always there to greet her after school with hugs and fresh wholesome food. She adjusted her hours to fit around whatever family crisis—usually of Rosie's making—happened to assail the inhabitants of Honeysuckle Cottage at any point in time.

When Katie had developed flu a few days before her exams for medical school, it was their mother who had taken time off and driven her to the exam, plied her full of medication, and picked her up afterward. It was their mother who had slept in a chair by Rosie's side when she was in the hospital, and her mother who had encouraged her from the sidelines when she played sports.

Rosie realized she'd never seen her father do any of that, and until this moment that had never even struck her as odd.

Her father had always seemed like an exciting figure to her. He was energetic, passionate and often elusive, disappearing from their lives for weeks and sometimes months at a time and then reappearing with exotic gifts and stories of sandstorms and badly behaved camels. This being before mobile phones, they often wouldn't receive more than a single postcard during the time he was away.

Rosie recalled admiring her mini-Sphinx bookends, while her mother patiently fed the washing machine with clothes that seemed to contain more sand than the desert.

Their family had expanded and contracted as he came and went and her mother was the one responsible for that easy elasticity. She'd held everything together in his absence, and then welcomed his presence as if he'd never been away.

There had been no criticism that Rosie could remember. No resentment as he'd packed his passport and she'd packed lunches for the girls.

What must it have taken to be that flexible?

Compromise.

A whole lot of compromise on her mother's part, and little on the part of her father.

Rosie realized with a flash of shame that she really only ever thought of her mother in relation to her role in the family, not as an individual. Her mother was her rock. The person she always turned to when she had a problem. When had she ever asked her mother if she was happy? Never. She'd made an assumption. Her mother had always been there for her, one hundred percent dependable, no matter what. Who was there for her mother? The answer was her father, of course, except judging from the look on his face that wasn't the case. He looked as shocked as she felt.

Had he ever thought about the sacrifice Maggie had made for them all?

Rosie decided, right there and then, that she wasn't going

to burden her mother with her current crisis. She was going to make sure her mother had a relaxing holiday because no one deserved it more than she did.

"I'm taking you straight to your tree house so you can settle in." Dan raised a hand in greeting as they passed some of the staff who worked at the resort. "Then I'll talk to my mother about getting you some emergency clothing."

He pulled up outside the tree house. "We're here. The path should have been cleared, but it does get icy so be careful."

The tree house sat high in the tree canopy, blending with its surroundings.

"We're actually *in* the forest. It's like something out of a fairy tale. Magical." Maggie climbed out of the car, and slid her arm through Nick's to steady herself. "Can you smell the trees?"

"My mother is a keen gardener. She loves trees," Rosie muttered, grabbing her mother's coat from the seat.

"And stars." Maggie tipped her head back. "I love stars, too. Do you see them, Nick?"

"I see them. Are you going to be able to make it up those stairs, Mags?"

"Why? Would you like to carry me?"

Struggling not to smile, Dan unloaded Nick's suitcase. "We have the best night sky. When I was young, my father and I used to hike at night to take photographs. We'd go through the forest and up to the lake."

Maggie glanced around her. "The air is so clean and the trees—it smells of Christmas. Is that Douglas fir?"

"We have a mixture of fir, pine and aspen here."

"It's the most romantic place I've ever seen. Don't worry about finding me spare clothes, Dan. We won't need any out here."

Rosie ushered her toward the stairs that wound upward to the deck and the front door. "The cabin is equipped with robes and toiletries. Why don't you settle in, get a good night's sleep, and I'll come over and see you in the morning. I'll bring clothes with me."

Dan frowned. "But my mother was—"

"It's fine, Dan." She sent him a meaningful look. "My parents are tired. I think they need to sleep off the journey," *and the drink,* "and hopefully they'll be fresh to enjoy the day tomorrow."

"Thank you." Her father stepped forward and gave her a hug. "Don't worry about your mother, Rosie. Everything is going to be fine."

Why did they keep saying that?

What was she missing?

Insisting that Dan wait outside, she picked up the suitcase and helped her father guide her mother through the door of the tree house.

"This is charming." Maggie stopped in the entrance. "Nick, isn't this charming?"

"It is." He nudged her forward so that he could close the door on the bitterly cold night.

Rosie loved the tree houses, particularly this one. All of them had the same basic design: cedar-clad walls, exposed beams and floor-to-ceiling windows with incredible views in every direction. Directly outside was a small pond and a stream, and deer and elk often came exploring. It was the ultimate cozy retreat.

Rosie had spent a couple of nights in one the first time she'd visited, but now she was staying in Dan's room in the apartment above Snowfall Lodge that was home to the Reynolds family.

Maggie stepped toward the dining table at the back of

the room. "It's an antler chandelier! Is that—" she swallowed "—did the animal die?"

Her mother couldn't bear the thought of any creature being hurt.

"No, they're naturally shed at the end of the mating season, so you can switch the lights on without having to worry about your conscience. The bathroom is through to your right, and the bedroom is up the stairs." She gave her father a quick guided tour. "Does Mum need nightclothes?"

Her father patted her shoulder. "She can wear one of my shirts. She'll be fine."

"I don't need anything," her mother called from the bedroom. "Naked is fine. The bed is huge. What size is it? It's bigger than king or queen—more like a whole monarchy."

Rosie backed toward the door. "Is she safe on those stairs?"

"Probably not. I'll handle it."

"I think they provide a stair gate if you need one." She hesitated. "Dad, is everything okay?"

"Why wouldn't it be okay?"

"I don't know. I—" She shrugged, not sure whether it was a good idea to voice her feelings. She wanted it to all be in her imagination. "Ignore me. I'm sure you're right, it's the stress of the flight, that's all. The fridge should be stocked, so if you're hungry—"

"We'll have an early night and see you in the morning."

"Okay. If you're sure." She could hear her mother humming a song about a lonesome pine and made a hasty retreat.

Dan was leaning against the railing that surrounded the deck, his eyes amused. "You remind me of a zookeeper who just managed to cage a dangerous wild animal without losing a limb. Everything okay in there?"

"Yes." If you ignored the fact that her mother was about to run around the cabin naked. And was apparently deeply unhappy with her life. "I think we should go. Your mum is probably waiting and I should tell her that my parents won't be joining us."

"There's no rush. I already called her. She's totally cool with it all. Do your parents have everything they need? Why did you stop me coming in?"

"Because there's only so much embarrassment a girl can stand in one day, and I already hit my quota."

"Why are you embarrassed?"

"You're seriously asking me that?" She trudged past him toward the car. "If I'd known my mother would be drunk, I wouldn't have asked you to come with me to the airport."

"I wouldn't have let you do that drive alone."

She stopped and turned. "Are you being sexist?"

"No, I'm being caring." He caught up with her. "You don't know these roads the way I do. I've been coming here summer and winter almost all my life. And you're used to driving on the wrong side of the road."

"It's not the wrong side where I come from. And I'm a great driver."

"You are a great driver, apart from those moments when you forget which side of the road you're supposed to drive on."

"That happened twice, and on both occasions I saw a car coming at me in my lane and swerved back in plenty of time."

"That was when I took up drinking." He looped his arm around her shoulders. "I'm kidding. You're a great driver, but it's a long journey and two people makes it easier. And now you need to relax. Your mom was terrified of flying, so she had a drink. Don't overthink it."

"It's not the drinking, it's all the things she said. My mother basically told us that she hates her life."

"People don't always say what they mean when they've had a few drinks."

"And sometimes they say exactly what they mean." Was there something else her mother would have wanted to do? "My mother took the job in publishing when she graduated, and she's worked there ever since. I assumed it was what she wanted to do. I mean, if someone is doing something, you assume it's what they want, don't you?"

"Maybe, although I'm sure most of the population don't end up doing their dream job."

They crunched through fresh snow on their way back to the car. The air was bitterly cold and flavored with wood smoke and the smell of pine.

She felt the weight of his arm resting on her shoulders. "Did your mother always want to be a wedding planner?"

"No, but looking back on it the clues were always there. She organized her own birthday party at six years old. It was themed and she hand made the invitations."

"How do you know that?"

"Great-Aunt Eunice told me. Also, there are photographs. My mother has been arranging parties ever since. She organized four of her friends' weddings." He stooped and picked up a pine cone. "Moving here permanently from our home in Boston, and setting up the wedding business was a way of processing the loss of my father, but it turned out to be the best thing she could have done. She loves this place, and she loves the work."

"Right." So his mother was living the dream, while hers—she frowned. Did her mother even have dreams? "My mother was an only child, and my grandparents died before I was born so I don't have any stories like that. All of a sudden I feel as if I don't know her."

"Of course you know her. It's probably not something you think about much, that's all. We never do when it's our parents. What does she do in her spare time?"

"I don't think she had much spare time when we were growing up. Since we left home—I don't know. Our house is pretty old and takes up a lot of time. There's always something wrong, or a room that needs decorating. She does it herself. She's good at that kind of thing. And the garden. She loves the garden."

"There you go. You do know what her passion is. Not everyone makes a job from what they love, but it doesn't mean they don't have passions in their spare time." He handed her the pine cone and opened the car door.

She didn't move. "What if she really has spent her whole life doing a job she doesn't love?"

"Then that was her decision. And before you lie awake all night worrying, why don't you wait and see how she is tomorrow? It's possible she didn't mean any of it."

"What makes you think I'd lie awake all night?"

"Because I know you."

"Right. Yes, you're right. We know each other." She breathed. "And I do overthink things. I'm sorry I'm tense but it's the first time you've met any of my family and forgive me I would have rather it hadn't been when my mother was drunk and slobbering all over my dad. It was all a bit horrifying."

He laughed and pulled her into a hug. "I love your parents. And your mother reminds me a little of you."

"Drunk?"

"Open. Friendly." He kissed her. "Forget it. And don't worry about your mom. She'll be fine in the morning."

Maggie

MAGGIE WOKE FEELING as if an entire construction project was taking place in her head.

For a moment she couldn't remember where she was, or how she'd ended up in this much pain. She remembered Nick handing her a drink in the departure lounge, and she remembered not confessing that she'd already had two gin-with-very-little-tonics before leaving home, so as not to cause raised eyebrows at her alcohol consumption while in midair. The rest of the journey had been a blur.

She wasn't a big drinker at the best of times. On top of that, she'd been starving herself for three weeks in order to be able to look better in her clothes. The combination of gin, champagne and an empty stomach hadn't been good.

She groaned and buried her face in the pillow. It was the softest, fluffiest pillow she'd ever laid her head on and the duvet folded around her like a cloud. She didn't want to move, but she knew she needed water. And painkillers. Also, very possibly a doctor and access to an intensive care unit.

This couldn't possibly be the alcohol, surely? Maybe she'd caught flu on the plane.

She felt as if she had hours to live.

"Good morning." Nick appeared in the doorway, a glass of water in one hand and a mug in the other. The aroma of fresh coffee was enough to persuade her to lift her head from the pillow.

The movement was agonizing.

He set the mug down next to her. "How are you feeling?"

"Do you mind not shouting?" Even the comfort of the pillow couldn't neutralize the pain in her head.

"That bad?"

"Worse. I think maybe I need a doctor. And a lawyer so I can write my will."

He sat down on the edge of the bed and held out the glass of water. "What you need," he said, "is fluid, and then breakfast."

Her insides churned. "My stomach disagrees."

"Trust me, it's the best thing. I'll make it while you take a shower."

Was she capable of walking to the shower?

Gingerly, she sat up. And realized she was naked.

With a squeak of embarrassment, she pulled the duvet across her breasts. "Why am I naked?"

"You insisted that was how you wanted to sleep. You said it made you feel sexy and at one with nature."

"What?" She never slept naked. She favored snuggly pajamas that kept out the winter chill. "How did I get to bed?"

"I put you there."

"Oh this is *bad*." She took the glass in both hands and took a mouthful. Why did it feel awkward that he'd seen her naked, when they'd been together for more than thirty years? "Did I—I remember that we met Dan."

"Yes. And you liked him. You liked him a lot."

She stared at him. "What's that supposed to mean?"

"Nothing."

"Don't 'nothing' me. Was I rude to Dan?"

"No, you were very—affectionate and welcoming."

"I don't like the sound of that. And what about us?" A horrid thought struck her. "Did they guess that we're getting a divorce? Did I say something? I intended to show them how much in love we are."

"You definitely did that." Humor flickered in Nick's eyes. He put his hand in his pocket and pulled out two painkillers. "I thought you might need these."

She swallowed them without arguing. "Was I embarrassing?"

"*Entertaining* would be the word I'd use. I've ordered a crate of champagne from Dan's mother. We're having a bottle a night for the rest of our stay."

How could he joke about it? And how could he look so disgustingly good after that long flight? He obviously hadn't drunk as much as she had.

He was wearing a navy cable-knit sweater and a pair of heavy-duty hiking pants that had survived the rigors of his job. No matter where he was, Nick always looked at home in his surroundings.

She handed back the glass. "You'll be drinking it by yourself. I am never, ever drinking again as long as I live."

After a few sips of coffee, she felt a little more human. Human enough to take in her surroundings. She was in a tree house. An actual tree house. The bedroom was suspended high above the living area, the open aspect allowing access to the same forest and mountain views through the floor-to-ceiling windows. The remaining three walls were made of glass. They were enclosed by jagged peaks, and all around them was forest, trees stretching high, branches bending under the weight of snow. As she watched, the snow tumbled off a branch and drifted past the window in a gentle avalanche of white.

Everything in the room blended with the surroundings, from the carved wooden bed frame to the luxurious cream throw draped over the bottom of the bed. It was the feather-soft bedding that had presumably kept her warm while she'd slept naked.

"This place is incredible." She glanced at Nick and noticed now that his eyes were tired and he hadn't shaved. "Where did you sleep?"

"On the couch. Luxury compared to some of the places I've slept in my time." He stood up. "The bathroom is downstairs."

"Thank you. Where's my suitcase?"

He paused. "You don't remember?"

"What am I supposed to remember?"

"The airline lost your suitcase."

"What? No! The presents. My gifts for the girls were in there." And not only the gifts. Maggie thought about all the shopping trips she'd endured trying to find exactly the right dress to wear at the wedding. She didn't love what she'd found, but it was the best of all the options she'd tried. And now it was gone, and if it didn't turn up she was going to have to start again. Not only that, but her research had told her that anything she bought here in Aspen was going to cost her a fortune.

But it wasn't only her dress that was the problem. Apart from the ones she'd worn for the journey, all her clothes had been in that suitcase. Her favorite red sweater that she always wore at Christmas. Her pajamas.

"I've left a shirt and a sweater in the bathroom for you. Put those on for now, and we'll make a plan to replace your luggage later."

"Replace it? Why can't we wait for it to arrive?"

He hesitated. "I called the airline an hour ago. At the moment they haven't managed to locate your case."

"How is that possible? I thought everything was electronic these days. Can't they track it?"

"Something went wrong with the tracking. We don't know if, or when, it will arrive."

Some women loved shopping. Maggie loathed it. The thought of doing it all again, and in an unfamiliar place like Aspen, almost made her slide back under the covers. "What am I supposed to wear to go and buy new clothes?"

"Rosie is coming by in a minute with some things she hopes will fit. She and Dan have a meeting with the florist this morning, so Catherine has offered to take you shopping and out for lunch."

"Catherine? Are you coming, too?"

He gave a half smile. "I'm not invited. Apparently, it's a girls' trip."

This day was getting worse by the minute. She wasn't a girl. She hadn't been a girl for a few decades. And shopping with someone as poised and elegant as Catherine was going to do very little for her fragile self-esteem. "What are you going to do?"

"Dan's uncle is taking me on a snowmobile around some of the trails that lead from Snowfall Lodge into the forest."

"How come you get to do the fun stuff? Can we swap? A snowmobile ride sounds so much more fun than shopping."

He raised an eyebrow. "Even with your current headache?"

She imagined bumping over frozen ground. "Maybe not. But shopping doesn't go well with a headache, either." But she couldn't think of an excuse. And she did need clothes. "I suppose I can't get out of it?"

"Why would you want to? It's the perfect excuse to spend time with Dan's mother before the wedding."

"Seriously? I thought you said you knew me."

He frowned. "I do know you."

"Then how do you not know that the *last* thing I want to do is meet Dan's mother when I'm hungover and without clothes?"

"The hangover will pass, and we're going to lend you clothes."

"Clothes I won't look good in."

"Well—" he floundered. "As long as they fit, I'm sure you'll look fine. And since when did you need clothes for confidence?"

"Since my daughter's mother-in-law turned out to be this super successful, slim, elegant, perfect person." Somehow her thoughts came out of her mouth. "And if you truly knew me then you'd know I'm intimidated by successful people! How do you not know that, Nick? *How do you not know?*"

She rarely saw Nick lost for words, but he was lost for words now.

"But—" He raked his fingers through his hair. "You're a successful person, Mags."

"Me? How am I successful? I don't run my own business. I'm not a world-renowned university professor. I haven't rebuilt my life from the ground up having lost my husband. I haven't re-evaluated my life after a minor trauma, let alone a major one. I'm not a doctor like Katie, or a student at Harvard like Rosie. I—I don't know what I am. I'm someone who trundles along, wiping dust off the same surfaces, sitting at the same desk I've sat in for most of my working life, doing the same job that frankly anyone could do. And I'm not even thin." As she hurled that final sentence into the air she saw a wild look of panic appear in Nick's eyes. He had the look of a man who suddenly realized he was holding an unstable, volatile substance.

"I happen to like the way you look."

"We're getting divorced, Nick. So you can't like it that much." She flopped back against the pillows and then wished she hadn't opted for a movement so violent. Or a conversation like this one. She was never drinking again. "Forget it. Forget I said anything."

He rubbed his hand over the back of his neck. "Not easy to forget."

"Well, try. And now if you'd leave me alone, I'd like to take a shower."

He didn't move. "You're saying you're intimidated by Dan's mother?"

"Goodbye, Nick."

"But you haven't met her. She's a human being, probably struggling like the rest of us."

Maggie sat up. "You don't get it, do you? I'm the type of woman that makes someone like Catherine Reynolds roll her eyes."

"Why would she roll her eyes?"

"Because I've spent most of my life building a home. I make curtains and grow vegetables. I know a hundred different ways to cook with carrots. Do you honestly think that will impress her? She'll think I've sold out the female sex by not having a glittery career with an upward trajectory."

He blinked. "You don't think you're being a little hard on yourself here?"

"No, I don't. Because these days women are supposed to be able to do all of it providing they are goal focused and own a great planner."

He gave a choked laugh. "Mags—what the hell is going on?"

"Nothing is going on. Probably because I've never been a planner type of person. Maybe, if I'd had a planner, I would have been able to cram more into my life."

"Is that the goal?" He looked bemused. "To cram more in? Is this about work? I thought you loved creating a home. You said you wanted the kids to grow up in a different environment than you."

"I did. I do." So why, suddenly, was she questioning it all? Why did she feel lost and—irrelevant? If Catherine had managed to reinvent her life, why couldn't she?

"If you love it, then it can't be wrong."

"You just don't get it."

"No, you're right. I don't." He sounded exasperated. "Why do you need to impress her anyway?"

"Only a man would ask that question."

"At least wait until you've met her to start making judgments. You might like her."

But would Catherine like *her*?

"Could you leave the room?"

"Why?"

"Because I'd like to get dressed now."

"I've seen you without clothes before."

"Not for a very long time."

"Well, you don't appear to have changed significantly."

"What's changed is that we're not together anymore." She knew it was ridiculous for it to feel awkward, but it did. A part of her had pulled away. For protection. Clothes were protection, which made it all the more unfortunate that she didn't currently appear to own any.

He shook his head, muttered something under his breath that she didn't quite catch but was sure wasn't flattering, then left the room.

Maggie waited until she heard him clattering around

in the kitchen and slid gingerly from the bed. She took the stairs carefully, holding tightly to the curved wooden rail that appeared to have been carved from the branch of a tree. If she'd trusted her legs not to give way under her, she might have taken the time to admire it.

She stepped into the bathroom, purring as the underfloor heating warmed her bare feet. So much better than Honeysuckle Cottage where a nighttime trip to the bathroom came with a risk of frostbite.

There was a large tub and a walk-in steam shower enclosed in glass.

By the time she emerged ten minutes later, she was deeply regretting her outburst.

Wrapped in a soft white robe, she found Nick in the kitchen. "I don't suppose I can wear this for the rest of our stay?"

"It might raise eyebrows. On the other hand I've always believed in the importance of expressing one's individuality." Nick was frying bacon and the sizzle and smell made her realize how hungry she was.

When had she last eaten? On the plane, presumably.

He tipped it onto a plate, added slices of toasted sourdough and scrambled eggs. "Eat."

She sat on the stool at the kitchen counter and picked up a fork. "I'm sorry."

"For what?"

"For the things I said. Ignore me."

"I'm not going to do that, but the rest of the conversation will have to be postponed because Rosie texted to say she's on her way."

She'd already said more than she wanted to. She took a mouthful of food. "This bacon tastes so good."

"Maple cured locally according to the packaging."

She cleared her plate and realized he was looking at her. "What's wrong?"

"I'm thinking you look twenty in that robe with wet hair." He drank his coffee. "Where did the years go, Mags?"

Was that a literal question? How was she supposed to answer?

"Don't get sentimental. I can't handle it with a hangover. Is there any more toast?" She hadn't eaten carbs for three weeks and she was so hungry she was willing to eat anything that wasn't nailed down.

He sliced the loaf. "Next time we're on our own and not about to be disturbed, I also want to talk about what happened in the car yesterday—"

"We agreed we were going to pretend to be in love. Don't panic, I wasn't trying to seduce you." Was it possible to seduce someone you'd been married to for three decades?

"I wasn't talking about the flirting." He put the toast in front of her, along with a slab of creamy butter and a pot of homemade plum jam. "I was talking about the fact that you don't like your job."

Maggie stuck the spoon in the jam. Had she said that? Her feelings about her job weren't something she usually voiced aloud.

"You should know better than to believe the ranting of an inebriated woman."

"That's what I said to myself, until you said all those things this morning."

"You shouldn't believe the ranting of a woman with a hangover, either."

He topped up his coffee. "So you don't hate your job?"

She took a bite of toast. Chewed. "It's fine."

"That doesn't sound like a ringing endorsement. If you don't like it, why haven't you moved on?"

She put her toast down. "Because it suited our lifestyle. One of us had to be there for the girls. Your job involved so much traveling. You weren't always there for the school run, parent-teacher meetings and those middle-of-the-night emergency runs."

"But Rosie left home four years ago. If you wanted to do something different, you could have done it."

She pressed at the toast crumbs with her forefinger. Should she tell him? "I applied for a job a month before she left. I thought it would do me good to be occupied with something."

He stared at her. "You applied for a job? Why didn't you tell me?"

Maggie shrugged. "Because I was afraid I wouldn't get it. And I didn't."

"But you didn't even tell me you were going for it. Why?"

"Why do you think?" She fiddled with the crust of her toast. "I was protecting myself from humiliation."

"We're married, Mags. I love you. Why would it be humiliating to tell me about it?"

She decided not to point out that he'd said *I love you*, when what he'd meant to say was *I used to love you*.

"Because you always succeed at everything. You get every promotion and every job you apply for."

"But—" He looked flummoxed. "What was the job? Was it another publishing role?"

"No. I applied to be a garden designer." It sounded ridiculous now. How had she ever thought she'd stand a chance getting a job with no qualifications? And yet she'd felt so hopeful when she'd applied. She'd put together a portfolio of photos of her garden, and friends' gardens she'd worked on, sure she'd be able to prove herself in an interview. But she hadn't been offered an interview. Instead she'd received an impersonal email telling her that she didn't have the experience they were looking for.

She'd printed out the email and put it in her file. And never mentioned it to anyone until today.

"I know you love the garden. You've transformed Honeysuckle Cottage. Do you remember when we moved in? It was a wilderness."

She remembered. And she remembered her excitement at the gradual transformation from wilderness to a dream garden. "A hobby doesn't qualify you to do a paid job."

"Very few people get the first job they apply for. These days people apply for multiple jobs."

She pushed her plate away from her. "I applied for multiple jobs."

"What? I can't believe you didn't tell me this."

She shrugged. "There was nothing to tell. I didn't get a single interview, let alone a job. Maybe I don't sound like the type of person who uses a planner."

"I didn't know you were unhappy with your life."

"I wasn't, but my life has changed, Nick. It changed after Rosie left home. I needed something else, but it isn't as easy as it looks in the movies. That isn't how real life works." Her head throbbed. Which of them had started this conversation?

"I hadn't thought about the sacrifice you made until last night in the car."

"Staying at home wasn't a sacrifice, it was a choice. And you're right, I loved being there for our girls."

"But it makes you feel inferior. And I don't understand why it would."

"Think about it, Nick! Do you ever read a feature praising a woman whose life is to care for her disabled child or parent with Alzheimer's? No, you don't. When someone talks about 'achievement' they're talking about salary and status, not the fact that you actually managed to take a shower and change your clothes after being in the hospital with your child for two nights straight even though, believe me, *that's* an achievement. You read about hedge fund managers who get up at three in the morning so they can get their workout done, use the gym, clear their emails and make a healthy breakfast for the whole family before putting in a full day of work in the city and returning home in time to read bedtime stories and then do another few hours of work before having perfect sex, three hours undisturbed REM sleep and waking up and starting again. You read about women who were at home with children and suddenly realized that if they started charging for all the cupcakes they made for their children's friends and school events, they could turn their baking skills into a profitable business. And, by the way, the woman I read about didn't look as if she'd ever baked a cupcake in her life and she certainly hadn't eaten one. What you *never* read about is the millions of normal women who are struggling to hold it all together and don't own a planner because we don't exactly know what we'd write in one!"

"Maggie, breathe!"

She breathed, and realized he was looking at her as if she were a stranger. "Sorry. Might have got a little carried away there."

"A little?"

"Ignore me. I'm feeling a little bruised by all the rejections, that's all. My file is full."

"You keep a file? Where?"

"It doesn't matter. I've accepted that a new direction isn't as easy as it looks. Or I thought I'd accepted it, and then I read about Catherine who makes it look easy." She finished her toast and lifted her mug of coffee. "Don't look so traumatized. Maybe I don't have a job I love, but I adore my family. Life is always a compromise."

"But you're the one who made the compromises." His voice was rough. "I flew around the world, leaving you to hold the fort."

"And you missed out on being with the girls. You weren't there when Rosie took her first steps, or the first time Katie read a whole page of her book and realized that words linked together. That was magical." She put her coffee down, remembering. "If I could have my time again, I'd do the same." But maybe she could have worked a little harder to find a different job. She'd played it safe, staying in the same place where they accommodated her family pressures. Maybe she should have looked a little harder to find the one thing she would have loved to do. But she wasn't like Nick, who had excavated his parents' garden aged five and written to the director of the British Museum when he was nine. She didn't have one overriding passion.

He was frowning at her. "What you said earlier—I don't always succeed at everything."

"You do, and that's okay. I'm proud of you, Nick. I always have been."

"You're talking about my work."

"It's more than your work. It's your passion. It's the most important thing to you, we all know that."

"Family is important, too. I didn't succeed at that." His voice was rough. "I didn't succeed at our marriage."

She lifted her head and looked at him. There was a long silence.

He started to speak but then paused and his gaze shifted to a point over her shoulder.

"Rosie is here. Bad timing. Looks as if she has some clothes for you."

Maybe it was good timing. The conversation had gone from uncomfortable to confusing.

And then Maggie realized that she'd forgotten the part they were playing. "The sofa—"

"I cleared the bedding away, don't worry." He threw another glance at the door. "Mags, are you sure we shouldn't—"

"Yes, I'm sure." She didn't let him finish the sentence. "We're here for a wedding, Nick. You don't discuss divorce at a wedding. Even the most emotionally insensitive person should be able to see that."

"Are you saying I'm emotionally insensitive?"

"I wasn't, but if you genuinely think this is the right time to tell her then maybe you are." She walked to the door as quickly as her headache would allow. Rosie stood there, looking sleek and chic in a tailored ski jacket, her jeans tucked into snow boots.

Maggie's heart filled with love. Why didn't people see that not all people were motivated by money and status? Some were motivated by love. The choices she'd made had been driven by love.

Even now, Rosie still seemed vulnerable to her. Perhaps because she'd been by her side for all those difficult moments when she'd struggled. It was hard to see beyond the young girl she'd once been. Or maybe it was because Rosie was so open to life and all it had to offer. She put up no barriers, and that was both a good thing and a bad thing.

Maggie opened the door and gulped as a blast of freezing air rushed toward her. "Good morning, sweetheart. Come in out of the cold."

Rosie stepped inside and gave her an anxious look. Her

long hair flowed from under her wool hat, and her cheeks were pink from the cold. "How are you feeling?"

"I'm fine, and I'm sorry if I embarrassed you. Next time I'll go for a general anesthetic to get me through the flight, not alcohol." She hugged her daughter. "Forgive me?"

"Nothing to forgive." Rosie kissed her and then tugged off her boots, scattering snow everywhere. "It snowed again in the night. Another couple of inches. Dan and Jordan went out early to get first tracks." She saw her mother's blank look. "First run of the day. Fresh powder. They'll be down before the hordes of tourists finish breakfast and head out for the day."

Maggie couldn't imagine choosing the icy slopes of a mountain over her snug, warm bed. "Who is Jordan?"

"Dan's closest friend. They met when they spent summers here growing up, and Jordan still lives and works in the valley. He built his own house. He's going to be best man."

"He built a house? So he's a builder?"

"No. But good with his hands. Practical. He's an arborist. Tree surgeon."

"Well, there are plenty of trees around here so that makes sense." Maggie brightened. It would be interesting to talk to someone with knowledge of trees. "I wonder if he'd know what to do about our old apple tree?"

"Ask him. Jordan knows everything. He's obsessed with nature and conservation." Rosie kissed her father. "Hi, Dad. Sleep well? Isn't that bed the most comfortable thing you've ever slept on in your life?"

Nick's expression didn't flicker. "Like sleeping on a cloud."

"How's your head, Mum?" Rosie grinned as she dropped

the bag she was carrying onto the sofa. The sofa where Nick had slept a few hours earlier.

"My head is fine," Maggie lied. "Does Dan still want to marry you or has meeting your family put him off?"

"Dan was amused to see you both behaving like honeymooners. Better than having parents who fight, right? Catherine always says that having divorced parents at a wedding can be the most awkward thing ever."

"I can imagine." Maggie's laugh was pitched higher than she'd intended. "I feel terrible that we missed dinner with Dan's family. I was looking forward to it."

"You're spending the morning with Catherine, so you'll get to know her then." Rosie opened the bag. "I have a few things here that might fit you. Dan's aunt left them at Thanksgiving because she knew she'd be back for the wedding. Try them on. They're probably not totally your style, but they'll do until you can find something." She pulled out a sweater in bright pink with a jeweled neck that caught the sunlight.

Maggie felt a stab of pain in her head.

Was Dan's aunt a showgirl in Vegas?

"Thank you."

"And jeans." Rosie thrust them toward her. "Your feet are the same size as mine, so I'm lending you my spare snow boots."

Maggie hadn't worn jeans in at least two decades.

She tried not to think about the carefully chosen outfits packed in her suitcase.

"I'll put these on while you talk to your father." She vanished to the bathroom with the spare change of underwear she'd had the forethought to pack in her hand luggage, and tugged on the clothes.

The jeans were too tight, but by sucking everything in she managed to do them up.

She emerged to find Rosie and Nick talking about the wedding.

"Katie is arriving on the afternoon flight, but Dan has to be somewhere, and I have a final dress fitting. Do you think she'll mind if Jordan picks her up? He offered to drive to the airport."

"She'll be grateful, I'm sure." Maggie wasn't sure of much these days where Katie was concerned. She was looking forward to seeing her face-to-face. "That's kind of him. Is he married?"

Rosie glanced at her. "Don't go there. You know what Katie is like. And honestly I can't think of two people less suited than Jordan and my sister."

"Why? What's wrong with your sister?"

"Nothing. I love her. But you have to admit she is very work focused."

"She has an important job." Katie didn't have it all, either, Maggie thought sadly. She had the work but very little time for anything else.

"She's also a city girl. After two hours in the city, Jordan can't breathe." Rosie stepped back. "You look cute in those jeans."

"They're acting like a tourniquet. There is no blood flowing through the lower part of my body. And I'm two decades too old to be wearing them."

"I think you look great." Rosie handed her gloves and a hat. "Are you ready for your shopping trip? I'll drop you at Snowfall Lodge on my way into town."

Knowing that she couldn't make excuses after her less than impressive performance the night before, Maggie pulled on her coat.

No matter what happened, she was going to try not to embarrass her daughter.

Rosie turned to her father. "Dan and Jordan will pick you up here in half an hour and we'll all meet up later. They're going to bring outerwear to keep you warm and dry."

Mindful that although she'd overacted the night before, she was still part of the same play, Maggie walked over to Nick and kissed him goodbye. To her surprise he took her face in his hands and kissed her back. His mouth was warm and gentle and she felt something unfurl inside her.

Maybe I'm still a little drunk, she thought as she eased away.

She wondered what he'd been about to say before Rosie had turned up.

Rosie rolled her eyes. "You guys! The rest of us have a lot to live up to."

Maggie headed for the door without looking at Nick.

Was she giving Rosie a false impression of marriage by not being honest?

No. She was doing the right thing. This was about Rosie and Dan, not her.

Maggie stepped out of the tree house after her daughter. Last night she'd viewed the forest and the night sky through an alcohol-induced haze, but today her vision was as clear as the perfect blue sky. Fresh snow dusted the trees and she felt the cold air freeze her cheeks. The first thing she noticed was how calm and peaceful it was. She stood still for a moment, enclosed by the forest, listening to the crack of branches and the soft thud of snow. She saw a pond, frozen over and framed by conifers on one side and tall aspen trees on the other.

Catherine was waiting outside Snowfall Lodge, slim

and elegant in jeans, a coat with a fur trim and a pair of oversize shades.

Maggie hadn't expected her to be so casually dressed and instantly felt a little better, even though Catherine looked as if she'd spent half her life in the gym and made jeans look like a high fashion choice.

Still, at least she wasn't carrying a planner.

Rosie made the introductions quickly and Maggie climbed into the car next to her daughter's soon-to-be mother-in-law. The jeans almost cut her in two at the waist. Maybe she should ask if she could lie across the back seat.

"I apologize for not joining you for dinner last night."

"Not a problem! That flight is a killer. I'm probably supposed to commiserate that the airline lost your baggage, but honestly it's a great excuse to shop." Catherine simmered with energy and made Maggie even more aware of her throbbing head and the fuzzy feeling that Nick had told her was jet lag.

"I'm not a very happy flier."

"Me neither. My best friend on a flight is alcohol."

Maggie laughed. Maybe she and Catherine had more in common than she thought. "Do you travel much?"

"I used to. When I was building the business I used to go to all the big wedding shows, but now we have so many word-of-mouth recommendations we can barely keep up, so my work is fairly local. Most of my suppliers are right here in the valley. I use a photographer who has a gallery in town, a local florist, and there's a bridal shop run by a designer who decided she preferred our mountains to the glitter of Manhattan. She has the most exquisite dress for Rosie, I can't wait for you to see it."

"It's generous of you to have given Rosie so much support."

"I adore Rosie. She's so warm and genuine. The moment Dan introduced her I was thinking *let her be The One*. The whole family is thrilled by everything that's happened. Aren't you?"

Was she thrilled? "Dan seems delightful," she said diplomatically. She still wasn't entirely sure what she'd said to him the night before. "But it has all happened rather fast."

"I know. When Dan proposed at Thanksgiving, I almost cried."

Maggie had almost cried, too, although she suspected it would have been a different sort of crying. "So it was a shock to you?"

"You have no idea. It was always going to be a special gathering because Rosie was with us, but I never imagined how special. So romantic and meaningful, because my Dan is not impulsive. Is Rosie?"

Yes, Maggie thought. *Changes her mind with the wind.* "They do seem very much in love."

Did they? She couldn't remember much about that either, but it felt like the right thing to say.

How had Rosie seemed this morning? Pretty normal, although again Maggie had been focusing more on behaving like one half of a couple who were in love. And who was she to judge? She hadn't been able to keep her own marriage going. Even if she was being generous to herself, she had to be at least fifty percent responsible.

Maybe Nick was right. Maybe it was ridiculous hiding the truth.

It wasn't too late to change her mind. Katie was arriving tonight. She and Nick could sit the girls down and explain things. They were bound to be upset, but they were going to be upset whenever it happened and there was still almost a week until the wedding. The wedding could even be a distraction.

Catherine drove toward town. "I can't tell you how refreshing it is to have the bride's parents still married and in love. When we have more time I'll tell you about the last two weddings I helped plan. Nightmare! The bride's parents were in the process of divorcing and let's just say it was *not* harmonious. I know you told Dan this is like a second honeymoon for you."

Had she said that?

Maggie wanted to get out of the car and run fast in the opposite direction, but the jeans made that impossible.

Apart from making a vow never to drink again as long as she lived, what could she do?

There was no way she could tell Catherine, or the girls, the truth.

The timing was all wrong. Nick was right. They should have done it months ago, instead of waiting. This was all her fault.

"We're very definitely married," she said finally. At least that was the truth. "I'm not sure I'd go as far as saying this is a second honeymoon."

"Now you're embarrassed, but don't be." Catherine glanced briefly at Maggie. "Honestly? I envy you."

Maggie stared at her, this sleek, confident, successful superwoman whose jeans definitely weren't cutting her in half. "*You* envy *me*?"

"Yes. You still have your soul mate. Rosie tells me that the two of you met in college. Jonny and I were the same."

"I—I'm sorry for your loss."

"Me too." Catherine gripped the wheel. "But life goes on, right? You keep walking, even when your feet are bleeding and you can hardly stand upright. But it makes me happy to know you two still appreciate your couple time. Some people don't know what they've got until they lose it, but you do. I wish Jonny and I had spent more time together, just enjoying each other, but we were always busy and focusing on the next step, you know?"

Maggie was a fraud, and these jeans were her punishment. "Most people forget to make the most of those small moments."

"But you don't." Catherine reached across and touched Maggie's arm. "We barely know each other, but I'm going to say this anyway and hope you don't think I'm odd—I find you inspirational."

"Me?"

"Yes, you! Why so surprised? You have a wonderful daughter who is open, friendly, intelligent and warm. I know how important Christmas is to you because Rosie told me all about your traditions, and how much you all love this time of year. Most women would have felt resentful and unhappy being dragged away from their home at such a special time, but instead you decide to treat it like a second honeymoon. I want to help in any way I can, so don't hesitate to tell me how I can make the trip extra special. Candlelight dinners? Too cliché perhaps. You can do that at home." Catherine frowned. "Snowshoeing can be romantic. Let me think about it, but I promise you, Maggie, this is going to be a Christmas you'll remember forever."

Maggie wasn't about to argue with that part.

She had no idea how to unravel the tangled mess she'd made.

Couple time. *Oh Maggie, Maggie...*

"You're very kind." Because she had no idea where to take the conversation next, she focused on the scenery.

Mountains rose all around them, and fresh snow gleamed under a perfect blue sky.

"I love that Rosie comes from this warm, stable family. As I say, about half the weddings I arrange, at least one set of parents aren't speaking. It plays havoc with seating, I can tell you. And the photographs look terrible if people are glaring. I had a couple from Texas last month who refused to stand next to each other—the parents, mind you, not the bride and groom. I wouldn't want to be spending Thanksgiving and Christmas with *that* family."

Would that happen to her and Nick?

Would they gradually start to hate each other?

Maybe it would be easier if they *did* hate each other. Maybe then it would at least make sense.

As it was she often lay in the dark, staring up at the ceiling, and tried to work out where and why it had gone wrong. It was a puzzle she couldn't solve and that, somehow, made it harder to accept.

"Do you hold the weddings in the lodge itself?"

"Sometimes. In the winter it's magical because we have the room at the back and with the lights and the glass it makes an intimate venue. In summer, people often prefer to be outdoors. We can cater for an elegant wedding, but if someone wants a more rustic theme I'll sometimes use one of the local ranches."

"Rustic?"

"Yes, but then they often want animals—not that I don't love animals, because I do, but generally I prefer people to do what I say on the day so that things run smoothly, and animals tend to follow their own agenda."

Maggie laughed. She hadn't expected Catherine to be so much fun.

And she hadn't expected to be able to laugh at wedding stories, when her marriage was on its last legs.

"People want animals at their wedding? What type of animals?"

"Sometimes a much-loved family pet. A couple last summer wanted their dog to carry their rings. Unfortunately, the dog was overexcited by all the people and carried the rings off down the valley. We had to improvise."

They were on the edge of the town now, and Maggie had never seen anywhere prettier. Tiny lights edged roofs and windows, so that every building seemed to sparkle. Even the lampposts, rising up from soft mounds of snow, were wrapped in fairy lights and adorned with large red bows.

"It's pretty. Festive."

"This is nothing. I can't wait to show you more of the place. We're going to park here, and then walk. You'll love it. It may not be home, but we do Christmas well, I think. Hard not to feel festive when you have piles of fresh snow to play in. But the town puts on plenty of activities. You can do everything from decorating a gingerbread house, to listening to live jazz. People think it's a glitzy place, but there's also a bit of a country vibe. We're mountain folk."

Rich mountain folk, Maggie thought as she climbed out of the car and noticed the number of designer stores. Did they even sell clothes for people on normal budgets? "How do you improvise a wedding ring?"

"I carry spares," Catherine said. "And I've had to use them on more occasions than you'd imagine. But that's the business. There are always challenges. One bride had her own horse and wanted it in the photographs. That worked out better than you might think. And the horse matched the color scheme perfectly. And then there are the llama weddings, of course."

"Llama weddings?"

"It's a growing trend. On the one hand llamas are quite calming which can be useful, particularly if there are young children involved, on the other hand they also have a nasty habit of eating everything in sight, including the wedding cake on one occasion."

"What happens in the photographs?"

"You have a bride, a groom and a couple of llamas."

"Are the llamas married, too?"

Catherine laughed and locked the car. "No, but they're definitely in a relationship. I'm the first to admit that the whole thing is more country than classy, but it works for some."

Maggie thought about Rosie's asthma. "Please tell me Rosie and Dan aren't having a llama wedding."

"No. Rosie wanted something simple."

That didn't sound like Rosie at all. She was wildly romantic. Maggie would have expected something over the top. Not llamas, of course, but something dreamy. But perhaps the time frame didn't make that practical.

"It's kind of you to organize this at such short notice." She felt stupid for ever feeling jealous. Rosie was lucky to be marrying into such a charming family.

"It's my pleasure, and I mean that literally. There is *nothing* I love more than arranging a wedding, and when my son is marrying the girl of his dreams, then it becomes my dream, too." She slid her arm through Maggie's. "What sort of wedding did you and Nick have?"

The ache was back in her chest. "A simple one. It was the two of us, in a small church in Oxford, with my best friend as a bridesmaid and Nick's closest friend as best man. We were married in winter and the church was freezing, so we exchanged vows as quickly as possible before one of us developed frostbite." And laughed the whole time and kissed. Nick had tried to thaw her frozen hands by tucking them under his jacket, then made indecent suggestions of how they could both warm up. "Afterwards we went to the pub with the whole of his department."

"Your family didn't attend?"

"Nick's mother was there, although I don't remember her smiling much. He never knew his father. My parents didn't approve, so they refused to come. At the time I was miserable about it, but looking back on it I can see it was probably the best thing. A few more people might have warmed the church a little, but I can't imagine they would have added much to the proceedings."

"Why didn't they approve?"

"They thought we were too young. And they didn't understand Nick's career. They thought he was too cavalier and adventurous, and that he needed to get a proper job. He's an Egyptologist."

"I know. Rosie says he's super smart. She showed us a video of him lecturing on YouTube. She's very proud of her dad. Your parents weren't proud?"

"They died soon after we married so they only knew him at the beginning, before he'd made a name for himself, but they didn't understand an academic career. They thought it was a frivolous thing to do. Not a proper job. They were worried he wouldn't be able to support me."

"You didn't work?"

They strolled together through snow and even with a pounding head and a mountain of anxiety, Maggie was charmed.

The whole trip was turning out much better than expected, if you ignored the discomfort she felt from not telling Catherine the truth.

"I worked in academic publishing. Still do."

"What a smart pair you are. No wonder he married you."

Maggie didn't feel smart, particularly when she was with Nick. She tended to listen rather than talk, conscious that anything she said would be boring compared to his tales of the desert. He was a natural storyteller with an ability to embellish each anecdote and hold the attention of an audience. It was the reason his lectures were always standing room only.

"We understood each other. We both wanted to create the sort of family neither of us had growing up."

"Rosie tells me you have the most darling cottage."

"Yes." Maggie thought about the cottage, standing dark and empty over Christmas. She felt something close to guilt, and decided that was ridiculous. A house couldn't feel lonely. What she was feeling was nostalgia for all those wonderful Christmases they'd spent in the cottage. "It's a special place. I hope you'll visit." She said it to be polite, not because she genuinely thought it would happen. How could it? She wasn't going to be living there next year.

"What did you wear?"

"For my wedding? We didn't have much money, and my parents refused to pay for what they saw as a mistake, so I found something in a nearly new shop and told myself it was vintage. Talking of which, you must tell me how much you've spent on Rosie so that I can pay you back."

"Not at all. This wedding is my gift to them. So, tell me, did you lose your baggage on purpose?"

"Excuse me?"

"On purpose. Lost baggage is a fabulous excuse for shopping, isn't it?"

How was she supposed to answer that? Maggie decided that she might be lying about her marriage, but she wasn't going to lie about anything else. "I don't completely love shopping. I never find things I like, and I often find the process intimidating."

"Then you're going to be so happy you met me. Shopping is my superpower, and we have arrived at my favorite boutique."

Maggie took one look at the outside and knew she wouldn't be able to afford more than a pair of gloves. "I think this might be outside my budget."

"Don't worry. I send so many people here, they let me have the clothes at cost."

She propelled Maggie into the welcoming warmth and greeted the woman who was hovering. "This is my dear friend Maggie. She's Rosie's mother—can you see the resemblance? Same eyes and the same beautiful skin. She needs a whole new wardrobe because the airline lost her baggage."

The woman's face lit up even as Maggie's heart sank. She was going to have to sell Honeysuckle Cottage to pay for this.

"My case might arrive. I only need a few things."

"Let's see what leaps out at us, shall we?" Catherine trawled the clothes like someone on a mission, picking up a dress here and a sweater there. Black pants, a couple of shirts, a cashmere poncho, a coat with a fake fur strip on the hood. She was a force to be reckoned with. *Trust me, you will look great in this.*

With considerable difficulty Maggie removed the jeans and wriggled into the black pants and a fitted roll-neck sweater in a completely impractical shade of cream. Neither were things she would have chosen herself. She tended to wear tunics that covered all the bits of herself that she didn't like. She tried to reject a soft wool dress with a hint of sparkle, but Catherine insisted it would be perfect for Christmas Day. Her powers of persuasion eclipsed Maggie's reluctance.

Was this what she'd been like with Rosie choosing a wedding dress?

Maggie took a breath and forced herself to look in the mirror.

"Oh."

"What?" Catherine opened the door to the changing room. "Well, hello, gorgeous. That sweater is perfect."

"I don't usually wear skinny sweaters. I'm too fat."

"Fat? Don't be ridiculous. You look fabulous. Although you could lose a couple of inches from your hair. Or maybe we scoop it up into a messy bun—" She slid her fingers into Maggie's hair, twisted it and secured it with bobby pins extracted from her purse. "I like it. Put some makeup on."

"I don't have any."

"Oh, that's too bad. It's in your missing suitcase?"

"No, I don't usually wear much. Lipstick occasionally."

"You don't—?" Catherine looked stunned. "We need to fix that. Do you know what we're going to do together while you're here? A spa day. Hair. Nails. Makeup. Girly chat. Maybe a glass or two of champagne while we get to know one another better."

Maggie's brain was still throbbing from the last glass of champagne. "I've never had a spa day."

"Really?" Catherine went from stunned to faint, but she recovered swiftly. "How do you pamper yourself?"

"Er—I read in the bath?"

"That doesn't count. I can't believe you've never indulged in a spa day. We're going to change that." Catherine flashed her a smile and handed over the coat. "Try this. Your face will look so cute peeping out from the fur."

Maggie, who was sure she'd never looked cute in her life, put the coat on. "What do you think?"

"Perfect. And it will keep you warm while you're here. When you go out on the snowmobiles, or for a husky ride, we'll lend you something more substantial." She took the coat back. "You don't need much makeup at all, you have excellent skin. You obviously use sunscreen."

"I work indoors in a windowless building half the time, so that's its own kind of sunscreen."

"I'm starting to understand why you don't love your job. Now let's try on a few more things."

Each outfit Maggie tried, Catherine was there to pass opinion, but to be fair she had a good eye.

Before she could overthink it, Maggie handed over her credit card.

Shopping had never been fun, but this was fun.

Or maybe it was Catherine who was fun.

"What about nightwear? If this is a second honeymoon, then you should dress accordingly." Catherine studied Maggie for a moment and then grabbed a selection from the rack. "Black would drain you. Try ivory." She handed over a sliver of silk with straps that crossed at the back.

Maggie had never worn slinky nightwear. The only way to survive Honeysuckle Cottage was by favoring sturdy brushed cotton over silk.

"This isn't practical."

"What you wear in the bedroom should never be practical."

Maggie closed the door and stripped off again.

If she bought this, Nick was going to think she'd gone mad.

She was *definitely* going to say no.

She eased it over her head and it slid down to midthigh. Maggie stared at herself.

With her hair tousled and her lips red, she looked—she looked—

"Oh boy, oh boy, you look super sexy in that." Catherine gave a slow smile as she peeped around the door. "Nick will not be able to resist you."

Maggie was fairly sure Nick had no problems resisting her. If he did, he wouldn't have moved out. They hadn't been intimate for—how long? The fact that she couldn't remember said a lot.

What if he saw the nightdress and thought she was trying to seduce him?

It would be unspeakably awkward.

She did not need a slinky nightdress, and she was going to hand it back to Catherine right this minute.

Keeping it would be nothing short of ridiculous.

Katie

KATIE PLOWED HER way through the crowds at the airport. Elbows dug into her ribs and Christmas gifts with sharp corners bruised her legs. A baby howled in misery and she turned instinctively before remembering that his welfare wasn't her responsibility. She was off duty. Today she wasn't a doctor. She was just another person going home for the holidays. Except that in her case, this wasn't her home. And technically she was on sick leave, not vacation.

The throng of people made her feel uneasy and anxious. Maybe she should have taken those antidepressants instead of shoving the prescription into her purse.

A woman in front of her shrieked and sprinted toward a man with scruffy hair and an eager expression who swung her into his arms.

What must it be like to be greeted like that?

She was probably never going to find out. Unless she got a cat.

Should she get a cat?

No. She was already responsible for the lives of too many living creatures. Did she really want to add another to the list?

And what would it do when she worked long hours?

It probably wouldn't even be pleased to see her when she walked through the door. It would be like Vicky, disapproving of her lifestyle choices.

She tightened her grip on the case and walked past the couple, trying not to listen.

I love you.

I love you, too.

In that moment, their lives seemed perfect. Katie hoped there was nothing grim waiting for them around the corner. That single, dark thought annoyed her.

What was the matter with her? Was she really so warped by her job that she'd forgotten good things happened to people, too? People fell in love, babies were born, friends were made. Some people went through their lives without ever needing the services of the emergency department.

She had enough insight to know that her vision of the world was distorted.

Being a doctor in emergency medicine was like peeping through a window at a crisis. You saw a glimpse of someone's life, but never the whole picture. She rarely saw this reality. There was a businessman striding through the crowd, talking on the phone as if the people around him didn't exist; a couple hugging; a little girl balanced precariously on a suitcase.

And she saw smiles. People who were pleased to see each other. People who didn't live their lives waiting for a disaster to happen.

She felt another twinge of envy as she saw a family of three generations embrace. Envy and a hollow feeling of loneliness. She felt as if everyone in the world was connected apart from her.

Maybe if Rosie had been here to meet her, she would have felt differently. Instead Rosie had sent the best man, who no doubt was as excited about the plan as she was. Four hours in a car making conversation with a stranger.

Oh joy.

Why wasn't Rosie here? Did she really have a dress fitting or was she mad at Katie for expressing doubts about Dan?

But if she'd kept quiet and then Dan made Rosie miserable, how would she have felt?

Maybe this journey was a reprieve. A few hours of rest before she had to try to pull it together in front of her family. Given that Mr. Best Man didn't know her and was simply doing his duty, he wouldn't be able to identify that she was more stressed than usual. And who better to question about the groom than the best man? Maybe she could tempt him to spill all the gory details he was thinking of including in his speech.

But before that, she had to actually find the man.

How was she supposed to recognize him? Rosie, presumably distracted by wedding arrangements, hadn't sent a description. All she'd said was that he would be waiting at arrivals.

There seemed to be a million people waiting at arrivals.

She glanced around to see if anyone was holding a card with her name on it.

Maybe she'd end up spending Christmas in the Denver airport. At least it was more cheerful than the emergency department.

"Katie?" A deep voice came from behind her, and she turned and found herself staring at a broad chest and a pair of powerful shoulders.

Happy Christmas, Katie.

She lifted her gaze past the dark shadow of his jaw to a pair of ice-blue eyes. "Hi." Her voice emerged as a croak and she cleared her throat and tried again. "I mean, *hi*. Dry throat. I'm probably dehydrated from the flight."

"That happens. I'm Jordan. Friend of Dan's, and best man." He stuck his hand out and she shook it, her fingers enveloped by strength and warmth.

"Katie. Big sister and, apparently, maid of honor." The words sounded ridiculous to her. He was probably trying to picture her at a wedding. "How did you know who I was?"

"I had a description. Lone female, dark hair, stressed expression."

"Excuse me?"

"Your sister warned me you'd probably look tired and stressed, so I looked for someone pale who didn't look pleased to be home for the holidays."

"I'm not home for the holidays. I'm in Colorado." Being met by a stranger, who had blue eyes and the shoulders of a fighter. Best man. He was certainly the best-looking man she'd seen in a while. She could hear Vicky's voice in her head, urging her not to ignore an opportunity like this one.

She ignored imaginary Vicky in the same way she ignored real-life Vicky.

"You don't seem too pleased about it. Is this all your baggage?" He reached out to take her case and she tightened her grip.

"Thanks, but I can handle my own suitcase."

He raised an eyebrow. "Sure, but it's a walk to my car, and—"

"It has a handle and wheels, and I have biceps. I've got this." Was he one of those men who thought a woman needed a man to help her through the average day? If so, they were in for a rough week. If he was going to patronize her, she might have to inject him with something.

He studied her and for an unsettling moment she had

a feeling he could see right through her. "Are you always this prickly?"

"I'm not prickly." *Cactus Katie.* "I don't need you to carry my case, that's all. And if that threatens your manhood in some way—"

"My manhood is doing fine, but I appreciate you thinking of it."

"I wasn't thinking of it. Did I say I was thinking about it?"

Their eyes held for a moment and then he gave a glimmer of a smile and gestured toward the exit. "Let's go, before you say something that's going to keep you awake tonight."

"Why would something I say keep me awake?"

"Because you're the type who would lie there simmering, wishing you'd said something different."

"You are so wrong." *He is so right.* Why did she feel as if she'd lost a fight, when there hadn't been a fight? "We should go."

"Is it all right if I show you the way? Or would you rather I gave you the address of where I'm parked so that you can find it yourself? I can meet you there if you prefer?"

She was about to snap a retort, but then she saw the gleam in his eye.

At least the guy had a sense of humor. "From what Rosie told me, we have at least a four-hour drive ahead of us."

"Could be longer because it snowed today."

"I'm sorry. That must be inconvenient." As was the news that she might be trapped with him for more than four hours. Still, at least he wasn't puny. He looked capable of shoveling snow if the need arose.

"Around here we like the snow, so we're willing to take a little inconvenience. Snow means a good ski season, and that's good for the local economy."

She thought about what she'd read. "I thought your economy was kept afloat by up-market retailers and eye-wateringly rich people who spend their billions in your town."

"That, too, but most of those eye-wateringly rich people love the outdoors and sports, which gives everyone something in common. Also, those same rich people keep me in business and give me a life I love, so I'm not complaining."

He loved his life? Right now she was willing to kill anyone who loved their life.

He gestured toward a door on the far side of the terminal building. "We're going that way."

She walked briskly, not because she was in a particular hurry but because she didn't know another way to walk. Time was a precious commodity and she couldn't afford to waste it.

They walked through the airport and out into an open-air plaza. "Is that—?" she narrowed her eyes and stopped walking "—an ice rink?"

"Yes."

"There's an ice rink in the airport?"

"Not technically inside the airport, but yes." He shrugged. "Welcome to Colorado. Do you skate?"

"Not intentionally. I'm the one who sticks people back together after they've skated. We have a couple of rinks in London that open for Christmas, so that pushes up our workload a bit. I've never understood why people think it's a good idea to have a Christmas drink and then show off their prowess, or lack of it, on the ice." She watched as a girl in a red coat executed a flashy jump and landed perfectly. A group of people were singing carols. "I've never seen an ice rink in an airport. It's Christmassy."

"You're a Christmas lover? Somehow that surprises me."

"I get to sleep in, eat too much, drink too much, and

not have to tell yet another family that their child has been stabbed and we weren't able to save him. What's not to like?" Damn. Had she really said that? She didn't even *know* this guy.

He was going to think she was pale, tired, stressed and also very possibly insane.

"Rosie mentioned that you work in the ER." His tone was gentler than it had been a moment earlier. "That must be stressful."

"The—? Oh, yes. We call it the emergency department. And it's not too bad. You get used to it. After a while it becomes a job. Something you deal with."

"Right."

"I mean, to some extent you're a well-trained machine." She felt herself tense as a little girl wearing a red scarf and a pair of furry antlers skated across the ice to her daddy. Any moment now she was going to fall and bang her head. Technically Katie was off duty, but she knew she wouldn't be able to walk past an injured person.

Jordan cleared his throat. "We should probably get going."

"In a minute—" The girl in the red scarf was halfway across the ice now, right in the middle of the rink with people swirling round her. She looked so small and vulnerable.

"Katie—"

"Why isn't her dad holding her hand? She could fall and bang her head."

"A machine." He folded his arms and glanced from her to the girl. "Yeah, that's what I'm seeing. You don't give a damn, do you? No emotion there at all."

She gave him the look she usually reserved for Vicky at her most annoying. "There's nothing emotional about being an advocate for accident prevention."

"Nothing at all. But that kid probably grew up skating. She'll be fine. Let's go." Jordan stepped past her just as the girl reached the other side and was swept into the arms of her proud father.

Katie relaxed. "Right." *Breathe, breathe.*

"If you're a machine, then it figures that you can switch off the doctor mode. Program yourself to shut down."

"I admit that particular switch might be broken. My systems might have crashed."

"You'll be better after a few days in the mountains. Fresh air, sunshine and snow is the best cure for that."

"Let's hope so." She had a feeling that it was going to take more than a few days in the mountains to make her feel better.

His car was warm and comfortable, and Katie relaxed into her seat, relieved to have to think about nothing but being a passenger. She closed her eyes, but unwanted images immediately returned so she opened them again. Part of her had been hoping she'd left it behind, but it had obviously come with her.

"You said you love your life. What do you do?"

"I'm an arborist." He eased into the flow of traffic. "A tree surgeon. You're a human doctor and I'm a tree doctor, so we have that in common at least."

She turned her head. "Trust me, we have nothing in common." Instantly she felt guilty. What was wrong with her? The guy had met her at the airport for goodness' sake, and she was behaving as if he'd kidnapped her against her will. It was as if life had drained all her usual self, leaving only a shell. Maybe she was a machine. "You've known Dan a long time?"

"We met in ski school. I was ten and he was eight."

"And how old are you now?"

He raised an eyebrow. "Am I allowed to ask your age, too?"

"I'm one hundred and three."

He laughed. "And I'm thirty. Dan is twenty-eight."

Six years older than Rosie.

"And you're still friends. So I guess that means he's loyal, at least." She felt a twinge of anxiety for her sister, who was so gentle and always saw the best in people. "Tell me about him."

"What do you want to know? Dan has always loved sports. He's a great skier, he rowed in college, and now—"

"Not that. Give me the bad stuff. Drugs? Drinking? Narcissistic tendencies? Arrests? Tell me all the embarrassing moments from your friendship."

"The term 'friendship' doesn't usually include badmouthing your friend." There was an edge to his voice and he shifted his grip on the wheel. "Do you ask these questions of all the men you date?"

"No. But I ask them of the men my sister dates, because she never sees a dark side to anyone."

"That fits with what I know of her. She's very open. Trusting. Good for Dan."

What Katie wanted to know was whether Dan was good for Rosie. "So what are you going to say in your speech?"

"Speech?"

"You're best man. You give a speech, where no doubt you wheel out stories about wild weekends with prostitutes. A gambling habit? Cocaine? The day you left him chained naked to the Empire State Building?"

Jordan's gaze slid briefly to hers. "If that's an example of a best man's speech, you must have been to some interesting weddings." He slowed as they hit traffic. "When you go on a date, do you send them a questionnaire first?"

"I don't date."

"If those are the questions you ask, I'm not surprised."

"I don't date because I don't have time, not because I don't get offers."

"Ah, so the machine has feelings." A smile played around his mouth and she glared at him.

"We're not talking about me. We're talking about Dan."

"No, you were interrogating me about Dan. Why haven't you asked your sister these things?"

"My sister thinks she's in love. She's incapable of thinking objectively."

"You don't think she can make her own decisions?"

Katie stared ahead of her. How much should she say? "She's my sister. I love her. I'm protective."

"I'm sure."

"What's that supposed to mean?"

"You have a touch of the Rottweiler about you, that's all. Does your sister need protecting?"

"Sometimes." Katie frowned. "A Rottweiler? You're not only saying I'm a dog, you're saying I'm a savage dog."

"I'm comparing personality traits. It's something I do when I meet someone. Helps me figure out who they are. And Rottweilers aren't savage. They're intelligent working dogs."

An intelligent working dog. Maybe that wasn't such a bad description. "So if I'm a Rottweiler, what's my sister?"

He thought for a moment. "Possibly a cocker spaniel."

Katie typed it into her phone and scrolled through the results. "Loyal, gentle and affectionate." She pulled a face. "Not bad, in fact. Seems as if you know my sister."

"Or she could be a Labrador. Kind. Makes a good assistance dog."

Katie thought about the times Rosie had visited the elderly lady who lived next to them when they were growing up. Whatever her mother had been cooking, Rosie had taken one of whatever was cooling on the kitchen table to Enid. Cupcakes. A slice of warm apple pie. It had been Rosie who had insisted Enid join them for Christmas lunch because no one should be on their own on Christmas Day. Rosie, who couldn't bear to see anyone hurt and never wanted to do the hurting, which was one of the reasons she was slow to ditch bad boyfriends. And she'd had a few.

"She could be a Labrador."

"You have a dog?"

"My lifestyle isn't conducive to pet ownership."

"Nothing removes stress lines better than a dog. Maybe you should rethink your lifestyle."

Lately, she'd done nothing else. "I've been a doctor for a decade. Longer if you count medical school."

"And?"

"And you don't rethink something you've been doing for that long." She stared out of the window, wondering if she'd even be able to care for a dog. A dog would need regular meals, and pizza probably didn't count. And what if her sister visited? "The mountains are pretty. And the forest. Is that where you work?"

"I work wherever I'm needed."

"But half the trees are covered in snow. Are you quiet this time of year?"

He smiled. "Busy. People want Christmas trees. And they want lights strung around their houses."

"You do that? I get delivering a Christmas tree, but lights?"

"I'm used to heights and climbing up things with awkward angles."

"I would never have thought of employing someone to put up Christmas lights."

"You don't decorate? You don't like Christmas?"

"I don't *not* like it, but I don't go over the top. There's something about Christmas that makes people a little silly—wearing festive sweaters you wouldn't be seen dead in the rest of the year, kisses under the mistletoe you always live to regret."

"You regret the kisses you've had under the mistletoe?"

She'd fallen right into that one. "I don't think decisions as important as who you're going to have sex with should be decided by a plant, that's all. And a poisonous plant at that."

"Next you'll be telling me you don't believe in Santa. I'm going to have to ask you to keep that thought to yourself. I can't handle it."

"Did you know that people can actually catch infections from Santa outfits?"

"You are full of snippets of information I never wanted to know."

"You're welcome." She had a feeling he was laughing, and she was so tired she smiled, too. "Look, I don't mean to interrogate you, but I love Rosie. I've never met Dan. I want her to be happy, that's all."

"And that's your responsibility?"

She stretched out her legs. She could tell him about Rosie's unsuitable boyfriends, and maybe he'd understand. But then she'd feel disloyal to her sister. And Jordan was on team Dan, not team Rosie. "She has always been my responsibility."

"Younger sister? Big age difference?"

"I was joking when I said I was a hundred and three."

He laughed. "I'm rethinking Rottweiler. You're more of a terrier. Spirited and loves an argument."

"What makes you think I love an argument?"

"Maybe because you keep starting one."

"Which is possibly because you're annoying. What breed would you be, then?"

He thought about it. "I'm an energetic, outdoor type. Reliable, protective of those I love same as you are, easygoing, unless someone crosses a line."

She wondered where that line was.

Everyone had limits, didn't they? She'd recently discovered hers. "So you're a Labrador, too."

He pulled a face. "I'm not that easygoing. Maybe more German shepherd."

The road curved through a narrow valley. Huge walls of granite and limestone rose steeply, silver gray and stark, mostly too steep to hold the snow. Patches of white clung to the less vertiginous sections, and coated the trees.

"This is an impressive place."

"Welcome to Glenwood Canyon."

"I can't imagine how they built this road through the mountains."

"It was a compromise between the engineers and the environmentalists. It's one of the main routes through the Rocky Mountains. That's the Colorado River right there."

It was spectacular.

She gazed out of the window at the soaring walls of the canyon. There was something soothing about being in a warm car, looking out at the snowy mountains outside. Her life felt distant, too far away to be more than a niggle of anxiety. For once she had no responsibility, no one relying on her judgment. Jordan was a good driver, confident, not flashy. Not that she had any intention of telling him that. She had a feeling he was a man who already had the true measure of his worth.

"Does this road ever get blocked in winter?"

"It can have its tricky moments. There's a rest area up ahead at Grizzly Creek. We'll stop there for a short time. Are you hungry?"

She discovered that she was.

After a hastily eaten snack she headed down to the water with him, her hands wrapped around the drink he'd bought her. The air was fresh and cold, the mountains rising straight up from the river. Snow clung to boulders and the water bubbled past patches of ice.

"I bet that water is cold."

"Icy." He stood, legs spread, hands thrust into his pockets. "Dan and I used to spend our summers rafting on this river. Further downriver you have the Shoshone rapids—Tombstone, The Wall and Maneater."

"Funny, none of those names are tempting me to ask you to take me white-water rafting. I can't think why."

"Come back in the summer and I'll take you. I think you'd enjoy it."

"What makes you think that? Do I look sporty?"

"No, you look tense. And clinging to the side of a raft while you're being thrown around in wild water surrounded by breathtaking scenery is a good way of making you forget everything except the moment."

"I'm going to have to take your word for it."

"You're missing out on a real adrenaline rush. It's pretty thrilling."

She took a sip of coffee, feeling the warmth spread from the cup to her fingers. London, with its gray skies and rain, seemed like a long way away. For the first time in a while she felt half-human. "Thanks but I think I'd prefer to get my thrills elsewhere."

He finished his coffee. "You shouldn't be afraid of adventure."

"Who says I'm afraid?"

"You've been grilling me about Dan, which means you're the type who researches everything in detail before you commit to something. You don't trust your instincts."

"I don't have instincts where Dan is concerned. I've never met him."

"Precisely." He dropped his cup in the trash can. "But you're assuming he has a past he needs to hide. And you're not even the one who is marrying him. Are you always this cautious?"

"I'm not cautious."

"No? When did you last do something that scared you?"

Seeing Dr. Braithwaite had scared her, and lately she'd been scared every time she'd arrived at work. "We should probably get going. My family will be expecting me."

He studied her for a moment. "Sure. If that's what you want."

They headed back to the car, and negotiated the next section of road in silence.

They reached a town called Glenwood Springs, and he followed the signs for Aspen.

Katie must have fallen asleep because when she woke they were driving down a snow-covered drive toward a brightly lit building.

"That's pretty."

"Welcome to Snowfall Lodge."

"This is it?" She gazed at the sloping roof outlined by tiny lights. There was a deck and what appeared to be a Christmas tree in every window. Her spirits lifted for the first time in weeks. Even she should be able to heal in a place like this. "It's charming."

"It's a cool place. But you're not staying here. You're staying in one of the tree houses in the forest."

It was like being shown paradise and then being told your ticket wasn't valid for that stop.

Lately her emotions had been all over the place, but even she was taken aback by the depths of her disappointment.

She didn't want to stay in a tree house in the forest. She wanted to stay in this luxurious place, with its twinkling lights and fairy-tale aura. Snowfall Lodge was so far from her everyday life it seemed like nirvana. She wanted to be wrapped by its welcoming warmth and cocooned by the flickering fire she could see through the glass doors. But apparently that wasn't on the agenda.

Goodbye spa. Goodbye massage and thermal pool. Goodbye any hope of recovery.

"A tree house." It was a struggle to keep her tone light. "With the spiders. Yay. Very Hitchcock."

"It's not so bad once you're up there, although I admit pulling yourself up on the rope can be a challenge. How are your muscles, Doctor?"

She didn't have muscles. "You pull yourself up on a rope?"

"How else would you get into the tree? And don't worry about spiders. They're big, but they're not poisonous. Most people find the worst thing is the motion sickness, but you're a doctor so I'm sure you have all the medication you need for that."

"Motion sickness?"

"The place is built in a tree. When it's windy, the branches sway and the house sways with it." He focused on the road, his lights picking up the mounds of snow piled along the edge. "Some people strap themselves to the bed so they don't fall out in the night. Same principle as turbulence on an airplane."

Katie had been sick on the plane when they'd encountered turbulence. She hadn't been able to use the swing in the park when she was a child. She wanted to tell him to turn around. She didn't want to do this. She couldn't do this.

"Are you sure there aren't any vacant rooms in Snowfall Lodge?"

"They reserved this place specially for you."

Karma. They must have sensed that she was here to disrupt the wedding rather than celebrate it.

And Jordan wasn't showing her a morsel of sympathy.

"Look, I really don't think I can—"

"We're here." He pulled up and flashed his headlights. "There. Look up."

She lifted her gaze slowly, reluctantly, braced for the worst. Thanks to him she'd pictured a rickety structure, lashed together by cobwebs and possibly with a haggard old crone in the doorway to greet her.

The reality was so far from the picture he'd painted that it was a moment before she could speak.

The tree house wasn't built into branches, although the design was such that at first glance it appeared to be. It was perched on a slope, surrounded by tall trees, their branches bowing under the weight of snow. A two-story hideaway nestled into the trees as if it had grown there along with the forest.

A beautiful wooden staircase wound up to the front door. "No rope." She saw his faint smile and felt stupid. "I hate you."

"I didn't think you'd take me seriously."

"But I did, so why didn't you tell me the truth?"

"Because you were wound so tight I thought you could do with a laugh."

"Do you see me laughing?"

He gave her a long look. "No, which is a shame, because I'm willing to bet you look cute when you laugh."

Something shifted inside her. Something that made her feel more uncomfortable than she already was. "Just so you know, I really am thinking of killing you."

"But then you'd spend Christmas behind bars, and this place is more comfortable," he said easily. "More hedonism than horror, don't you think? The tree houses are some of the most sought-after places to stay around here. Most of us normal mortals couldn't ever afford to stay in one."

"I'm definitely going to have to kill you." She hesitated. "Do the tree houses sway when it's windy?"

"They're rock solid. I can guarantee that, because I helped build them."

"You?" She dragged her gaze from Snowfall Lodge to his profile. "I thought you were a tree surgeon?"

"I also work with wood."

"So I am sleeping twenty feet above the ground, in something you built. If I fall, I'm going to sue you." But the sense of relief was overwhelming. The place was idyllic. Like her own private corner of the forest. Lights shone from the tree house, lending a warm glow to the wood. A large Christmas tree was visible through one of the windows and snow had settled on the railing around the deck.

Her tension levels, permanently stuck in the red zone for months, finally eased. That tiny adjustment to her equilibrium gave her hope. If she couldn't relax and unwind here in this enchanting, almost otherworldly place, she wouldn't be able to unwind anywhere. It felt a million miles from the crowded streets of London and her small cramped house. A million miles from her real life.

Jordan gestured to a winding path, illuminated by lights strung through the trees. "We have to walk from here. There's a bridge over the creek and it can be icy. You'll need to be careful."

Deep snow smothered the contours of the surroundings. Katie decided that the world seemed a better place when it was covered in snow. Softer. Fewer hard edges.

"I'll be fine." She saw her sister appear in the window and waved.

Was Rosie mad with her because she'd asked if they could share for the first few nights? She'd used Christmas as the excuse—*Christmas is our time together*—but the truth was that she wanted time alone with her sister so she could try to understand what had triggered this wildly impulsive decision. And if Rosie and Dan really *were* getting married (heaven help all of them), a few nights apart wouldn't kill them, would it?

Having reasoned her guilt back into submission, she stepped out of the car and felt the cold seep through her clothing. She'd always hated winter, but now she realized that what she hated was winter in London and those long dreary days that cloaked everyone in gloom. Rain that soaked through shoes and turned a girl from dressed up to drowned rat. This was different. Here, the air was dry and crisp, and above her a million stars studded the clear night sky. This was winter as she'd always imagined it should be. Not dark, damp and dispiriting, but light and bright and crisp.

She breathed in, savoring the delicious smells. A hint of wood smoke. Fir trees. It made her think of those Christmases when she was young, when she and her mother had taken Rosie to choose a tree. They'd argued about the size and then trudged home with it and dressed its lush, spiky branches with decorations stored from year to year in a special box. Her mother had treasured each one. There was a star Katie had made in school the year Rosie was born. A wonky angel Rosie had made in the hospital the Christmas she'd had a bad asthma attack. Then there were the weird and wonderful decorations her father brought home from his travels. A jeweled camel that sparkled under the lights, handblown glass ornaments picked up from a bazaar in Cairo.

There would be no star this year. No tree dressed with memories.

Katie blinked. It wasn't like her to get emotional. Any minute now she'd be crying on his shoulder. She could imagine what he'd make of that. "Thanks for the ride, Jordan."

"Are you going to forgive me for teasing you?"

"Maybe next century."

"Good to know you have a sense of humor." He retrieved her suitcase. "I'll carry this up for you."

"I've already proved I can carry my own suitcase, and given that I don't have to climb a rope with it," she sent him a look designed to wither, "I can manage." Truthfully she wasn't looking forward to carrying the case because she was still nurturing her bad shoulder, but she had another perfectly good free hand and she'd rather dislocate both shoulders than ask for help from him.

"The bridge might be icy. They clear it every day, but sometimes it's—"

"Don't tell me. There's a troll in the water that might leap out and eat me. I'll handle it." A flood of light illuminated her surroundings and she glanced up and saw Rosie framed by the doorway. Her sister was wearing a warm cable-knit sweater, a pair of skinny jeans and thick socks. Katie felt a rush of love so powerful it took her breath away. Whenever she saw Rosie after a stretch of time, she remembered her as a toddler. Affectionate. Trusting. "Thanks, Jordan. See you at the wedding."

She wasn't sorry to leave him behind. She'd felt a wider range of emotion trapped in a car with him for five hours than she had in the past five months. She hoped they wouldn't be spending much time together.

"I'll help you over the bridge."

Katie felt her temper snap. "Because I'm a woman? Because you think my DNA makes me less capable of walking than you? I'll have you know I graduated top of my class from the best medical school in London. I average twenty thousand steps a day, on a quiet day, and I've managed to stay upright for all of them."

"I believe you, but that doesn't mean you have the right—"

"The right what? I can assure you I have everything I need." She hauled her suitcase over the snow and realized right away that this wasn't as easy as she'd thought it would be. For a start, the surface wasn't smooth. The path had obviously been cleared earlier but another layer of snow had fallen since then and it was slick and icy. Still, at least the creek was frozen so if she fell in she wasn't going to drown.

As she hauled her case, she started to sweat. And she still had to carry it up those charming, but frighteningly twisty stairs to the front door. To make it worse Jordan was watching, which meant that if she fell her pride would be broken along with her bones.

Why didn't the man leave?

When she reached the bridge she felt her feet start to

slither and grabbed for the handrail, but it was buried under a pile of snow. Her legs went from under her and she was wondering if Jordan was the type to say *I told you so*, when strong arms grabbed her and held her firmly.

"I was trying to tell you that you didn't have the right footwear. You're mad at me, I get it, but take my help now and be mad at me later." Jordan's voice was in her ear, deep and steady. It should have made her feel safe, but somehow it didn't. She'd never needed anyone before and she didn't want to need anyone now, not even to help negotiate an icy slope. She needed some evidence that she was still the same person she'd always been. Competent. Independent.

"I slipped on purpose, to give you a chance to rescue me and then feel good about yourself." It was because she was locked against hard muscle that she felt him laugh.

"I knew there was a sense of humor buried in there somewhere. And you're right, of course. I can't sleep at night unless I've rescued at least ten trees and five maidens in distress during the course of my working day."

There was something about his solid strength that was annoyingly comforting. "Do I seem in distress to you?"

"Yes, although I doubt that had much to do with the ice and I know you won't thank me for noticing." His voice softened. "Let go of the suitcase and put your arms around my neck, Katie." The way he said her name sent tingles up and down her spine.

"I will not be putting my arms round your neck now, or at any other time, unless it's to strangle you."

"In that case—" He let her go. Immediately her feet slithered. She grabbed at the front of his coat.

"Damn."

His eyes gleamed. "You know, it's all right to accept a little help from someone once in a while."

The occupational health doctor had said the same thing. "I do not need help."

"You have romantic intentions?"

"Excuse me?"

"There has to be a reason you're locked on to the front of my coat. If it's not because you need help, then it must be because you're about to kiss me. Or maybe you're waiting for me to kiss you."

"I'm not the waiting type, Mr. Tree-Doctor. If I wanted to kiss you, I'd have already kissed you." What would he do if she did? And why was she having thoughts like that? Desperation, maybe. It had been almost six months since she'd kissed a man, and the attraction had been nowhere near as powerful as it was between herself and Jordan. "I need a solid object to grab on to, that's all." She gasped as he swept her up and slung her over his shoulder in a fireman's lift. "What are you *doing*?"

"Giving you the help you won't ask for. My duty as best man is to look after the groom. If the bride's sister breaks both her legs, that's going to hold up the wedding. Also, I don't want my best friend threatened with a lawsuit."

"I hate you."

"I know." But still he didn't put her down.

As she thumped his back with her fists, she could hear her sister laughing.

To heap on the humiliation, he carried her case in his free hand with no visible effort.

"This is uncomfortable. You're going to rupture my spleen."

He ignored her and carried on walking, his boots crunching through the surface of the snow.

"There you go." He lowered her gently to the ground.

"Bones in one piece, spleen intact, temper and smart mouth also thriving."

They were at the bottom of the curving staircase that led up to the deck.

"There is nothing wrong with my mouth, thank you."

He looked at her for a long moment and the corners of his mouth flickered into a smile. "Finally, something we agree on."

She was so taken aback she was mute.

His smile widened and he picked up her case and vanished up the stairs as if it weighed nothing.

She heard him laugh and murmur a few words to Rosie, and then he was standing in front of her again.

Before she could move, he leaned forward and brushed his lips across her cheek. "Admit it, Doctor. I rock your world."

"My world hasn't moved an inch. Not a tremor."

His gaze dropped to her mouth and lingered with such intensity that she stopped breathing. If a patient had showed any of the signs she was showing, she would have called the resuscitation team. She would have been hitting the red button and yelling *can I have some help in here?*

She said nothing.

He said nothing.

And then his eyes lifted back to hers and the sizzle of electricity almost knocked her off her feet. Her world wasn't so much rocked, as jolted and shaken. It made no sense. She was an expert at freezing men out. He should be stepping back. He should be giving her a similarly frosty look while he decided she definitely wasn't his type. He shouldn't be looking at her the way he was looking at her. As if he wanted to—as if—

In a delicious trancelike state, she tilted her head. Her

mouth drifted toward his, as if she were being pulled by an invisible force. Her eyes started to close.

And then, when she thought her heart might pound its way through her chest, he spoke.

"Enjoy your time with your sister. And you should ask Dan to take a look at that shoulder while you're here. I don't know how you injured it, but he's good at sports physio."

The words yanked her back to reality. Her eyes opened, but he was no longer in front of her.

What? Where?

Dazed, she turned and watched as he walked back to the car. What had just happened? Was she ill? She pressed her palm to her forehead. She wanted to take her temperature, and maybe run some blood tests. A scan. She *had* to be ill, surely? There was no other reason for her strange symptoms.

Had he noticed?

Get a grip, Katie.

She stared after him, frustrated by every confident stride. And how had he known about her shoulder? *Slip on the ice, damn you.*

"Not even a ripple on the Richter scale," she called after him. "And I could have walked across that bridge without you. I would have been fine."

The last thing she heard before he slid behind the wheel was laughter.

Damn the man.

If she never saw him again, it would be too soon.

She walked up the steps carefully, not because she was afraid they might be slippery, but because her legs seemed to have forgotten their purpose.

And now she had another problem looming. What to do about her sister. Her matchmaking, romance-loving, dreamy sister. Katie was sure that if she examined Rosie's blood under a microscope, her red blood cells would be shaped like little hearts.

"Hurry up, I'm letting out all the heat," Rosie yelled down to her from the door of the tree house. "What's taking you so long?"

Katie wasn't sure there was a clinical term that covered her current symptoms. She realized Rosie hadn't been able to see what had happened. The wraparound deck had provided shelter from prying eyes.

"I'm coming!" She hauled herself up the last few steps. "Where's my baby sister?" She emerged onto the deck and was enveloped in a hug. Rosie held on to her so tightly she thought her ribs might crack. She opened her mouth to protest and ended up with a mouthful of her sister's hair. "Hey. Good to see you, too. Ouch. That's quite a welcome." She brushed hair out of her mouth and tried to ease out of her sister's embrace. "Have you been using the gym? You almost crushed me."

"I'm pleased to see you, that's all. And of course I've been using the gym. My fiancé is a sports fanatic. Slouches not allowed. Come inside and see your new home, and tell me what you thought of Jordan. I can't believe you let him carry you!"

"I wasn't given much choice."

"Isn't he cute?" Rosie opened the curved door of the tree house and Katie hauled her case over the threshold.

"I would have gone with *annoying*." Trying not to think about Jordan, she glanced around the room. An enormous tree stretched upward toward the cathedral ceiling. Tiny lights shimmered in the branches and decorations glinted and gleamed. In keeping with the forest theme, the decorations were delicate leaves, small birds and butterflies, the colors changing from iridescent pearl to lustrous silver in the shifting light. Katie stared at it in awe. "Well, this puts the artificial tree I bought online to shame."

"You bought an artificial tree? Why would you do that?"

"Because I'd kill a real one." And she hadn't wanted another death on her conscience. "This looks as if it's been decorated by an interior designer."

"It's all Catherine's work. She designs a tree for each tree house, and six for the communal guest spaces in Snowfall Lodge."

"She has a talent for it." The tree was perfect, but still Katie felt a pang as she thought of the decorations that usually adorned their tree at home. Maybe they weren't perfect, but they all told a story. "She's the one who has taken over your wedding plans?"

"Yes, but in a good way. I wouldn't be able to do it all myself."

Katie glanced out of the window and wondered if Catherine was putting pressure on her sister. Rosie was so kind, she'd never tell anyone to back off.

Snow fell steadily, each flake following another on its downward journey, swirling in lazy pirouettes. "It's like living in a snow globe."

"Isn't it fabulous? I'd live here forever if I could. I envy Jordan."

Katie didn't want to think about Jordan. She especially didn't want to think about that embarrassing moment where she'd kissed thin air.

She bent to tug off her boots. "How are you feeling?"

"About what?"

"The wedding. Have you changed your mind? Because you can always—"

"No!" Rosie glared at her. "Stop it. I'm happy, Katie. I love Dan. I hope you'll love him, too."

"I'm sure I will, but let's not speculate a moment longer. Where is he?"

"You'll meet him in time."

Katie wanted to meet him now. The wedding was less than a week away and the clock was ticking. The closer they got to the big day, the harder it would be to sort this mess out. She knew there was no way Rosie would break it off at the last minute. She was the type who would go ahead and get married because she didn't want to hurt someone's feelings. But she knew better than to push too hard. *Softly, softly, Katie.* "How is everything else? Did Mum survive the flight?"

"She had a little help."

"You mean Dad?"

"No, I mean alcohol. She was actually drunk when she got off that plane, can you believe that?" Rosie flopped onto the comfortable sofa and stretched out her legs. "She was so embarrassing I almost opened the car door and pushed her onto the side of the road."

"Why was it embarrassing? Dan was disapproving? Upset?"

"Dan wasn't upset. *I* was upset. You don't exactly want your mother to be drunk the first time you introduce her to your fiancé."

"Why? Were you afraid he might dump you if you thought your mother had an alcohol problem?"

Maybe her mother hadn't been drunk at all. Maybe it had been an act on her part to test the mettle of her new son-in-law to be.

No, her mother didn't think that way. And Rosie had inherited her kindness of spirit.

"I wasn't afraid Dan would dump me. What is *wrong* with you?" Rosie's cheeks darkened with color and her jaw lifted. "Has it occurred to you that this relationship might be the best thing that ever happened to me?"

"No, but I don't think like that. You're the romantic in this family. I'm the practical one, remember?" Katie walked toward the fire and warmed her hands. She felt frozen, inside and out.

"You mean you're the pessimist. Why do you always assume everything will go wrong? There's a light side to life, too, Katie."

Katie felt a stab of guilt. The last thing she wanted was to fall out with her sister. "I'm sorry." Contrite, she turned to look at Rosie. "I'm tired, cranky, and it's been a tough few weeks."

"Oh no!" Rosie swung her legs down and stood up, instantly concerned. "Because of me?"

"No, not because of you. Believe it or not, kiddo, I do have a life that doesn't involve you."

"So why have you had a tough few weeks? Tell me."

Realizing she'd fallen into a trap of her own making, Katie prevaricated. "Busy time at work. Don't worry about it."

"Are you sure? Because you can talk to me, you know."

As sisters they'd always been close, although Katie was aware the relationship was different from the one she shared with Vicky or other friends. There was an element of the maternal in her feelings for Rosie. In her relationship with her sister she was the leaned on, not the leaner. She'd never shared her own problems, and she wasn't about to start now. She was the strong one. "Nothing to talk about," she said. "I'm fine."

"Well, you're on holiday now, so you can stop being a doctor for a few weeks."

She'd stopped being a doctor for at least a month, although her sister didn't know that. "Once a doctor, always a doctor. Are you using your inhalers?"

"Yes. I'm not stupid. I haven't had an attack in ages so you can stop worrying about me."

That, Katie thought, *is never going to happen.*

She gazed up at the soaring roof of the tree house. "So where is Dan? When do I get to meet the guy who swept my little sister off her feet?" She wanted to examine him under her metaphorical microscope. She wouldn't have minded examining a few of his cells under a real microscope, too. Maybe she could yank out a hair, or take a small slice of him to send off to the lab for testing.

"Tomorrow."

"What's wrong with right now?"

"He's over at the lodge catching up on paperwork. You've been traveling fourteen hours. You said you wanted us to have sister time."

"I do, but there will be time for that later. Call him. Get him over here. By the time he arrives I'll be showered and human again."

Rosie was looking at her as if she'd grown horns. "I thought you'd want to go to bed. I was going to suggest cheese, wine and an early night."

"I'll take the cheese and wine. Sleep can wait. I want to meet Dan." The clock was ticking. "What about Mum and Dad? Where are they now?"

"Mum spent most of the day shopping with Catherine, which must have been interesting with a hangover. They had lunch in town, so she and Dad are having a quiet evening. They assumed you'd have an early night, so we're all meeting up tomorrow at Snowfall Lodge for a big family breakfast to discuss wedding plans."

Katie's only plan was to stop the wedding.

"Shopping? That doesn't sound like Mum." First her sister announced she was getting married, and now her mother was shopping? What had happened to her world?

"The airline lost her luggage. If you're sure you want to meet Dan, then I'll tell him to come over." Rosie brightened and then paused, her phone in her hand. "You're not going to interrogate him, are you?"

"Me?" Katie assumed an innocent expression. "Why would you think that?"

"Past experience. Remember the time you frightened Anton away?"

"Anton?" Katie cast her mind back. "Skinny guy, studied geography? All I did was ask a few searching questions."

"Searching enough that he decided to dump me."

Katie felt a flash of guilt. "That was my fault?"

"Yes, and by the way at the time he was very anxious about his parents' divorce, which was why we got together in the first place. I found him crying in the library and took him back to my room and made him a cup of tea."

"And then he developed a fixation on you, and you didn't want to hurt his feelings by telling him you weren't interested. But you weren't interested, were you?"

Rosie turned pink. "Not massively."

"Right. So you were actually with him because you felt sorry for him."

"I wouldn't exactly put it like that, but it's true he wasn't my soul mate. I was eighteen. I've learned a lot since then."

About the dangers of whirlwind relationships? Apparently not. "You don't always make the best decisions about men. I was helping you."

"Did it ever occur to you that perhaps all the wrong choices I've made have helped me make the right one this time? I love Dan, Katie. Be kind to him. I don't want you to do your Rottweiler act on him."

That was twice in one day she'd been called a Rottweiler. If it happened again she might bite someone.

"I'm always kind. Unless a man ditches my sister in a seedy club in the middle of a night. That, I admit, brings out my vicious side."

While Rosie picked up her phone and called Dan, Katie prowled around the living room and paused by the bookshelf.

She didn't want to listen in on the conversation, but it was impossible not to.

She heard Rosie's voice soften as she talked. *Yes, she's here. Yes, why not bring some pizzas. Good idea. No, she's not too tired.*

Katie selected a book about mountain climbing.

I love you.

There it was. Those words she'd never said to anyone and probably never would.

She put the book back and turned as her sister ended the call. "Where's the shower?"

She followed Rosie into a luxurious bathroom with a freestanding tub overlooking the forest. "What if someone walks past?"

"They won't. This is private property. If you're lucky you might see an elk."

"Mm." Katie nudged her sister out of the room, stripped off her clothes and stepped into the shower. She'd expected the bathroom in a tree house to be rudimentary at best. A thin trickle of water, probably cold. Instead she was deluged by powerful jets of hot water. She stood for a moment, letting the warmth pour over her and seep into her skin. Then she washed her hair and reluctantly emerged from the steam she'd created.

She grabbed two of the fluffy towels warming on the rail, and wrapped her hair in one and her body in the other.

She rubbed the steam from the mirror and turned so that she could see her shoulder. The scars were visible. Walking out of this room wearing a towel would invite questions she didn't want to answer, so she grabbed one of the robes that were hanging on the back of the door.

Suitably covered, she stepped out of the room. "Rosie?"

"I'm in your bedroom." Rosie appeared from a room next to the bathroom. "Here. This is the bedroom I chose for you. It overlooks the forest. The other is on the shelf and it's gorgeous, but this one is more private."

It was sumptuous, with soft green throws pooling onto the wooden floor. The room became part of the forest. Katie eyed the bed, wishing she could fall into it.

Why had she insisted on meeting Dan tonight?

"This place is gorgeous."

Rosie stepped forward and hugged her again. "I'm glad you're here. I'm sorry I messed up Christmas."

Her whole life was a mess, not only at Christmas. "The whole family is together. What more do we need?"

Rosie eased back. "All those years we sat in the window of Honeysuckle Cottage and hoped for snow so that we could build a snowman. And now, finally, we have a white Christmas and all the snow we could want or need."

"If you're suggesting what I think you're suggesting then the answer is no. I'm too old to build a snowman."

"How about a snowball fight?"

"Definitely too old for that."

"Husky ride? Snowshoeing?"

"Maybe snowshoeing. Is there a hair dryer?"

Rosie produced one, along with a pair of thick socks in cream and gray. "These are an early Christmas gift. They're perfect for keeping your feet warm indoors. I'll be in the living room when you're done. Dan and Jordan will be here in about ten minutes."

"Wait—did you say Dan *and* Jordan? Why is Jordan coming?"

"Because he and Dan were spending the evening together going over a few things when I rang. And anyway, he's best man. You need to get to know him."

"I spent five hours in the car with the guy. I know everything I need to know. I thought it would be the three of us. I want to get to know Dan."

"You can tell a lot about a person by the friends they keep. Dan and Jordan have been friends since they were children. Hurry up and put clothes on or you'll be naked when they arrive."

Katie waited for Rosie to leave the room and then opened her case. She pulled out underwear, clean jeans and a soft white sweater. Despite the snow falling past the window, the tree house was cozy, warmth spreading upward from the underfloor heating.

She pulled on her clothes and dried her hair.

Jordan.

That was an inconvenience.

Slipping her feet into the thick socks Rosie had given her, she walked back into the living room and stared at the elegant Christmas tree. "I would never in a million years be able to make a tree look as perfect as that. The decorations match."

"I know. Not like ours at home. Mum still uses the angel

I made at school when I was six. And there's that weird sequin thing you made."

"It's a star." She touched the branches and breathed in the scent. The smell alone was enough to conjure Christmas. It made her think of laughter and cozy days opening presents in front of the fire. Family. She felt a sudden pang for the past. Had everything been simpler then, or was it wishful thinking?

Rosie poured red wine into two glasses. "Mum and Dad have been acting a little weird."

Katie took the glass from her and took a sip. She knew that if she drank much she'd fall asleep on the sofa. "Weird how? You know Mum hates flying. It was probably the drink. Never underestimate how it can change someone's personality. We see it all the time at work."

"How were they when you last saw them?"

Katie took a sip of wine. "I haven't been home in a while." Something else to add to her list of failures.

"But Mum comes up to London to have lunch with you."

"Not since our big family farewell to you in the summer."

Rosie put her glass down. "You haven't seen our parents since the summer?"

"I've been working hard. We had a date in the diary for October, but then—"

"Then what?"

Katie's heart pounded harder. She remembered his hands on her throat, squeezing. The agony in his voice, and in her shoulder. "Things got busy. I canceled." She hadn't been able to talk to anyone about what had happened. And now she felt guilty. She should have found time for her parents. She was a lousy doctor and not such a great daughter, either.

"Did you know Mum hates her job?"

"What? Who told you that?"

"Mum told Dan. She said it in a matter-of-fact voice, as if it was something we all probably should have known. I always thought she loved her job, didn't you?"

"I—I never thought about it." When Katie had been young her mother had always been there when she came home from school, willing to offer whatever was needed. A home-cooked meal, help with homework or just someone to listen. Her memories of her father were of him coming and going, but her mother had been the one constant. "Are you sure that wasn't the alcohol talking?"

"It might have been the drink that made her say it, but that doesn't mean it's not true."

"I wouldn't worry. Flying probably made her feel wobbly about life."

"I hate to think Mum might be miserable in her job."

"If she was that miserable, she'd leave." Or would she? Katie was pretty miserable, and she hadn't left, had she? It wasn't that easy in practice, to walk out on something you'd done for all your adult life.

Rosie strolled to the window. "They're here. With two large pizza boxes. Always a good sign." She waved madly, her smile lighting up her whole face. "It's only a few hours since I saw him but it feels like forever. Is that seriously cheesy?"

"I'm guessing you're not asking me about the pizza. And no, it's not cheesy." It was scary. "I can't wait to meet him."

She heard male laughter, the sound of heavy boots and then Rosie pulled open the door and there was a flurry of cold air and her sister was flinging her arms round a tall, dark-haired man whose shoulders were dusted with snow.

Katie stood awkwardly while they kissed.

Her eyes met Jordan's.

He held her gaze for a moment and then handed her the pizza boxes, tugged off his boots and hung up his coat. A hint of a smile touched his mouth. "Hello, Dr. Frost."

"Nice." She smiled sweetly and walked past him to the man who was embracing her sister. "Hi there." She held out the hand that wasn't balancing pizza. "I'm the scary big sister. Katie."

Dan untangled himself from Rosie's enthusiastic embrace and shook her hand. "Good to finally meet you."

He might not think so after she'd asked the questions she intended to ask. "Shall we get to know each other over food? This smells good and I'm starving."

"We'll get plates." Rosie grabbed Dan's hand and together they walked to the kitchen area. There was clattering and laughter and Katie stood awkwardly with Jordan.

He leaned toward her. "Cute together, aren't they?"

She gritted her teeth. "Adorable."

"Look at you two, already talking in whispers as if you've known each other forever." Rosie put plates and napkins on the counter, and opened the pizza boxes. "Let's eat while it's hot. They have a pizza oven in the kitchens over at Snowfall Lodge." She pushed the box toward Katie. "This is the best pizza you'll ever eat. And before you nag me about my diet, this is a rare treat."

Katie slid onto a stool. "So, Dan," she said, helping herself to a slice of pizza, "tell me everything. I want to hear all about you, and how you met Rosie."

Jordan sent her a sharp look and she smiled and sank her teeth into the pizza slice. *Rottweiler.*

Dan poured iced water into glasses for everyone. "Do you want the censored version or the uncensored version?"

Rosie groaned. "*Don't* say things like that to my sister."

"Censored editions are for parents." Katie chewed. The

cheese was smooth and melting. She tasted the richness of tomato laced generously with oregano. Rosie was right. The pizza was delicious. "All I know is that you work as a personal trainer."

"That's right. I'd finished working with a client and there was Rosie."

Katie raised her eyebrows. "My sister? In a gym?"

Rosie blushed. "I'd just arrived in Boston, and I decided I was going to try to develop healthy habits."

Dan helped himself to pizza. "I could see her form wasn't good so I went across to help. We got talking. She wanted a fitness program, but she wasn't sure if it was worth spending money when she could go for a run in the park instead. Then she told me about how tough it had been growing up, keeping her asthma under control and how important it was that she was fit and kept exercising." He grabbed a napkin. "And she told me how hard she found it to be motivated to exercise. I loved how open and trusting she was, right from the start."

Alarm bells went off in Katie's head. "That's my sister. She's like that with everyone, from the mailman to the person behind her in the supermarket."

"I'm not like that with everyone." Rosie shot her a look and reached for her wine.

"You think the whole world is good and that everyone can be trusted."

"I do *not* think the whole world is good, but neither do I think it's all bad. And people *can* usually be trusted."

"Not in my experience." She wanted to add *not in yours, either*, but decided a comment like that might get her forcibly removed. Not by Dan, who seemed remarkably relaxed, but by Jordan who was watching her intently, his mouth set in a grim line. She had a feeling that if she said the wrong thing, he'd sling her over his shoulder again. Next time, she'd thump him in the kidneys.

Dan's gaze was friendly. "Rosie tells me you work in the ER. That can't be easy."

Hands around her throat. The sound of glass shattering. *Call yourself a fucking doctor? I'm going to kill you, bitch.* Appetite gone, she put her pizza slice down. "It isn't easy."

"Rosie is so proud of you, aren't you, honey?" Dan reached across and took Rosie's hand.

Katie watched, mesmerized, as his thumb gently stroked her sister's palm.

The two of them gazed at each other, sharing a look so personal, so intimate, that Katie felt as if she should leave the room.

"Here." Jordan topped up her glass. "Drink."

She wondered if he felt as uncomfortable as she did. "I already had a glass."

"Well, have another glass. It might mellow you out some."

"I'm mellow."

He raised an eyebrow. "What are you like when you're tense?"

"Scary." She picked up her pizza again and cleared her throat. Rosie and Dan broke apart. "So Rosie told you she was a couch potato, and you saw her as a great way of building your client base."

Jordan's eyes narrowed, but Rosie laughed and gazed at Dan with adoration.

"He doesn't need more clients. He already has a waiting list."

"And yet here you are with muscles, so presumably you somehow jumped to the front of the queue." *Flaw number one*, she thought. It wasn't very professional to bump her sister up the list.

"I always make clients with medical issues a priority." Dan poured more water. "I knew I could help her. It's all about finding what motivates people. That's the best part of the job."

"And he was so great to work with," Rosie said. "You know how much I hate exercising. I'd so much rather lie on the sofa eating doughnuts and watching movies, but Dan made it fun. He made me want to get fitter. Those sessions turned into the best part of my day. We talked about everything." She reached for his hand. "Do you remember that night we did a late-night session and we talked for so long that the entire gym had emptied and the place was dark?"

Dan smiled. "I remember."

Katie licked her fingers. The pair of them couldn't stop touching. How did they ever get anything done? "And how did you get home after your late-night session?"

Rosie looked puzzled. "Dan took me home."

"Oh. Okay." So at least he'd seen her sister home safely. She couldn't find fault with that. "And what first attracted you to Rosie, Dan?"

Rosie choked on her food. "What sort of a question is that?"

"An intrusive one," Jordan said.

For a guy who supposedly lived a chill, outdoor life, he seemed extraordinarily tense.

He'd seemed pretty relaxed in the car. Maybe it was her. Maybe she brought out the worst in him. It wouldn't be the first time she'd had that effect on a man.

Dan ignored him. "First time I saw Rosie she was doing battle with a treadmill."

"It was a complicated machine," Rosie said. "All I wanted to do was run."

Dan leaned forward. "Running is good, of course, but fitness is about more than cardio. I knew that if I could get Rosie working with weights, it would help her. Remember that first day?" He smiled at Rosie. "You had your hair pulled back in a ponytail, and half of it had escaped. I spent my whole time surrounded by these super groomed, super confident women who are all CEOs or lawyers, and then you showed up—and you were so different. So gentle, and kind."

Oh yeah, Katie thought. That was Rosie.

Rosie wasn't looking at her. She was looking at Dan. "And you had muscles like I'd never seen before. I felt intimidated."

Katie frowned. "Intimidated?"

"Intimidated by his fitness levels."

"Okay, so you fell for his luscious body and his promises to turn you into a fitness goddess."

"Not only that. He was so easy to talk to."

Dan leaned forward and kissed her. "It took me about ten minutes to figure out that Rosie was as smart as she is beautiful."

Katie took another slice of pizza. Had anyone ever looked at her the way Dan was looking at her sister? No, they hadn't, and if they had she would have sent them for testing. "So looks are important to you?"

"Not particularly, but if you're asking if I find your sister beautiful, then yes, I do."

Katie chewed. "You've worked in the same place for a long time?"

"Five years. Before that I coached rowing, before that I rowed myself, when I was in college."

"Do you own your own place?"

"I have a small apartment in the same quiet neighborhood where I grew up."

"How long have you lived in your apartment?"

Jordan swore under his breath.

"Four years. Would you like references?" Dan sounded amused but Rosie was glaring at her.

"Stop it! What is *wrong* with you, Katie?"

"She's checking whether I'm on Santa's naughty or nice list." Dan winked at Katie and she found herself smiling. At least he seemed even-tempered.

"I'm getting to know Dan, that's all. In less than a week we will be related by marriage. I like to know a little about the people I call family."

"Well, it's coming across as interrogation." Seemingly mortified, Rosie took a slug of wine and Dan covered her hand with his.

"It's fine. Relax. Our relationship moved pretty fast. It's natural that your family would have questions."

"Mum and Dad asked you virtually no questions."

Katie sipped her drink. Why not? Still, at least he seemed kind to her sister, she'd say that for him.

"Sorry if it came across as interrogation. That wasn't my intention."

Jordan made a noise that sounded like a growl, but when she looked at him his expression was blank.

She smiled sweetly at him.

She still hadn't made up her mind about Dan, but Jordan was definitely on the naughty list.

Rosie

ROSIE WAS AWAKE early after a sleepless night.

She rolled over in bed, hoping for a cuddle and then remembered she wasn't in bed with Dan. She was in the tree house with her sister. It was supposed to have been a cozy night catching up on gossip like the old days, but it hadn't turned into that.

Instead of hot chocolate and pajamas, there had been a tense atmosphere and Rosie had felt utterly miserable.

"You don't like Dan," she'd said as Katie had cleared the kitchen and made her way to bed.

"I never said I don't like him. I don't know him, that's all."

"Why can't you get to know him over time, the way normal people do?"

"Because there is no time. You're marrying him in a few days."

"Exactly. *I'm* marrying him. *I'm* the one who is going to be spending the rest of my life with him, so why does it matter to you?"

"Because I love you, and I want you to be happy. I'm scared you're making a mistake. You can't know someone in three months."

"It's exactly the same amount of time Mum and Dad knew each other before they were married." And she was using that fact to support her belief that her relationship could work and wasn't doomed from the start. "They've been together more than thirty years, Katie. You know how happy they are. They were virtually ripping each other's clothes off in the back of the car on the way from the airport, which isn't something I particularly want to relive if I'm honest, but it's proof that they're still blissfully happy after all these years. If they can do it, why can't we?"

"I'm sure you can." Katie had looked exhausted. "I'm sorry. Ignore me, Ro. I love you, that's all. You're my little sister, and the thought of you being unhappy terrifies me. It's possible I overreact a little occasionally."

Rosie had felt a rush of love. "A lot. You overreact a lot."

"I'm tired. Long journey. Forgive me?"

"Of course." Rosie had hugged her then, relieved. The last thing that she wanted was to fall out with her sister. "Get some sleep. Tomorrow we're joining everyone for a big family breakfast at Snowfall Lodge, and then we're going for a snowmobile ride into the forest."

In the end Rosie had managed very little sleep. That tiny flame of doubt was still flickering in her brain, lit by her sister.

She woke feeling as tired as she had when she'd gone to bed. She wished she was waking up with Dan. That was a good sign, surely? If she missed him, then that had to mean she loved him. Those feelings she'd been battling with at the airport seemed to have vanished.

She grabbed her phone to message him, and saw that he'd already sent a message to her.

Miss you, babe.

Her eyes stung as she texted him back.

Miss you, too.

His reply came back instantly.

Hope you're having fun with your sister.

Not so far, but hopefully today would be different.

Anxious to mend fences, she showered and dressed, made coffee and took one to her sister.

She opened the door and Katie, who had been in the process of removing her pajamas, gasped and grabbed a robe.

"Don't you ever knock?"

Since when had they knocked? And why was Katie clutching her robe around herself as if she had something to hide? It wasn't as if sharing a bedroom was unusual for them.

"I'm sorry." The bond between them bruised again, she put the coffee on the nightstand. "I thought you'd want coffee. I'll meet you in the living room when you're dressed."

What was wrong with Katie? Was this because Rosie was marrying a man she hadn't known for long, or was there more to it than that?

She walked back to the living room, gathered together her outdoor clothes and was tugging on gloves when Katie appeared.

"I didn't mean to snap. You surprised me, that's all." She joined Rosie by the door and pulled on her coat and boots. "Remember when you were little? You'd crawl into bed with me on Christmas Eve and tug open my eyelids to see if I was awake."

Rosie was relieved her sister seemed back to normal.

"Because Mum told us I couldn't get up and open my stocking until you were awake."

"So you thought you'd help me." Katie wrapped Rosie's scarf around her mouth and nose. "I don't want you breathing in cold air and triggering an attack."

Rosie's love for her sister was threaded with frustration. She hadn't seen her sister since early in the summer and was surprised Katie couldn't see how much she'd changed in that time. But maybe it was going to take time. Before she'd met Dan, Katie had always been her first phone call in an emergency. Rosie hadn't called for anything other than a chat since she'd arrived in the US. She felt stronger. More confident, and she knew that was Dan's influence.

When they'd spent a few days together, hopefully Katie would see how she'd changed.

"Let's go. I know Mum and Dad are dying to see you, and I want you to meet Dan's family. And you're going to love being out in the forest." And she couldn't wait to be alone with Dan. Admittedly it would be on the back of a snowmobile, but it was better than nothing. And maybe he'd pull in somewhere so that they could sneak a few moments alone in the snowy forest. The thought cheered her. "It's a ten-minute walk along the forest path to Snowfall Lodge, or someone can pick us up if you prefer."

"Let's walk." Katie pulled on her boots and they closed up the tree house, clomped their way down the steps and found the path that led through the trees. "I've never been in love, but I might be in love with this place."

"I fell in love with this place the first time Dan brought me here. The leaves were starting to change color and it was spectacular. I thought it was my favorite season, but now it's winter." Rosie stooped to pick up a fir cone. She handed it to her sister. "Snow on the ground. Fir trees. This is how Christmas is supposed to be, don't you think?"

"Maybe." Katie turned the fir cone in her hands. "Where are you and Dan going to live when you're married? Have you talked about it?"

Rosie pushed her hands into the pockets of her coat. They hadn't talked about it. They hadn't talked about anything, but to admit that would simply feed her sister's anxiety. "We'll stay at his apartment, as we do now." She hesitated. "I'll still be coming home to visit. And you can come and stay with me."

"Sounds good." Katie pocketed the fir cone. "We'd better see what Mum and Dad are up to."

They walked through the foyer of Snowfall Lodge, past the enormous Christmas tree and the fire and up the stairs to the top floor.

The dining room seemed to be full of people, and the table groaned under the weight of food.

There was no sign of their parents.

"Here she is! The beautiful bride." Catherine crossed the room in three strides and hugged her tightly. "We were about to send out a search party, honey. And this must be your sister, Katie. Or do I call you Dr. White?" She embraced Katie warmly.

"Definitely Katie." Katie returned the hug awkwardly. "I'm off duty. At least I hope I am."

"Rosie has told us so much about you. And Maggie and I had a good chat yesterday, too. I already feel like I know you. She told me all about that spelling contest at school where you made one mistake and you were so mad with yourself you locked yourself in your room for twenty-four hours. How if you made one mistake in your writing you'd throw out the whole page. I'm the same. I want everything perfect. It used to drive Dan's father crazy, but I'm a detail person, and every detail has to be exactly right. Now come and meet everyone. On my side it's my mother—Dan's grandmother—Granny Sophie. And her sister, Great-Aunt Eunice. On Dan's father's side—" she pulled Katie around the room, introducing her to everyone.

Katie looked a little shell-shocked. Rosie didn't blame her for that. Catherine was the kindest person she'd ever met, but sometimes being with her was like standing in front of a snow plow. If you didn't move out of the way fast, you were flattened.

Still, at least so far Katie wasn't bombarding Catherine with questions about Dan.

She was charming to everyone, and after a few minutes she glanced around the room.

"Catherine, have you seen my parents?"

"Maggie called and said they were running late. It was probably that exquisite French lingerie I persuaded her to buy yesterday." Catherine gave a saucy wink. "Jordan is on his way, so he's going to give them a ride over, to save them walking."

Rosie was trying to delete the image of her mother parading around the tree house wearing sexy lingerie.

"Jordan?" Katie's friendly smile froze in place.

"Believe me, your parents will be safe with him. Everyone is safe with Jordan. He's like a son to me. And what that boy doesn't know about trees isn't worth knowing. I told your mama, with her love of the garden she should be grilling him for information. Katie, help yourself to food, honey. Don't hold back. The pancakes are excellent, the bacon is cured right here in the kitchens and the maple syrup comes from Great-Aunt Eunice's trees so you don't want to miss that."

"Sounds good. So tell me, Catherine, what was Dan like as a child?"

Oh for— "This is *not* the time to get out the baby photos." Rosie grabbed her sister before Catherine could answer, and headed toward the food. "Eat. Fill your mouth. Anything to stop you talking."

She'd piled their plates with pancakes when her parents appeared in the doorway, hand in hand.

They were both rosy-cheeked and out of breath, as if they'd been rushing. Her mother was tugging at her clothing with her free hand, as if she'd dressed in a hurry.

"Sorry we're late. We lost track of the time."

Rosie felt a rush of embarrassment. *Enough already!* But hopefully this display of marital harmony would be enough to silence her sister. She added syrup to her pancakes and leaned closer to Katie. "You see? Lovebirds, after thirty-five years."

Katie swallowed a mouthful of pancake. "They're not usually so demonstrative. Especially not in public."

Rosie added blueberries to Katie's plate. "Have some vitamin C. You're looking pale. Mum told Catherine they're treating this like a second honeymoon. I can't decide if it's romantic or embarrassing. Why are you frowning?"

"Because it's out of character for them to be romantic. Last year Dad gave Mum a dishwasher for Christmas."

"That's romantic if you hate washing dishes."

"I'd kill a man who bought me a dishwasher. Hold this for a moment." She handed Rosie her plate, and crossed the room to greet their parents.

Rosie put both plates down and followed her.

She saw their father put his arm around Katie's shoulder and squeeze. Her sister winced and eased away.

Rosie frowned. Had she hurt her shoulder?

She realized that Katie had said next to nothing about herself since she'd arrived, only that work had been stressful and busy.

"My girls! I've missed you so much." Their mother wrapped them both in a hug before turning to kiss Katie. "It's been so long since we saw you both."

And it was playing on Rosie's mind. She'd been in the US of course, but what was Katie's excuse? Why hadn't she seen their parents since the summer?

"Hey." Dan appeared, fresh from the shower, his hair still damp. He headed straight for Rosie and kissed her on the mouth. "Have you eaten all the pancakes?"

She felt the tension leave her, as it so often did when she was with Dan.

"I'm sure we left a few." She grabbed his hand, walked back to the table and loaded up a plate. "While we have a moment alone, I wanted to say that I'm so sorry about last night. I know Katie went over the top, but she only did it because she loves me."

"I know that." He added blueberries to the plate she was holding. "You don't have anything to apologize for."

"You're not mad with her? Tell me you don't hate my sister."

He took the plate from her and set it down on the table. Then he pulled her into his arms. "I definitely don't hate your sister. I love that she cares about you. You're lucky to have her."

And she was lucky to have him. Why couldn't Katie see that?

They didn't have a chance to talk further because his mother joined them to talk wedding details.

Dan ate while they talked, and after breakfast they made

their way to the back of the hotel where the snowmobile tours were arranged.

Catherine had arranged down suits and helmets for everyone. "You may think these are unflattering, but you'll be thanking me when you're out in the cold and wind."

Katie pulled hers on. "Where are we going?"

"To the Maroon Bells." Dan helped her with her helmet. "Mountains. You'll want to bring your camera."

"Am I driving my own snowmobile? Don't I need a license or something?"

"No license. We thought you might prefer to be a passenger this time around." Dan tightened the strap. "That way you can have all the fun of the ride and the views, without any of the responsibility."

"Sounds good. Who is the best driver?"

Catherine laughed. "My Dan. Jordan is good, of course, but he drives too fast for me. Leaves my stomach somewhere behind on the mountain every time I partner up with him."

"I'll go with Dan," Katie said and Rosie opened her mouth to say that she was going with Dan, but her sister was already sliding her leg over the back of the snowmobile and resting her hands on Dan's waist.

Was Katie choosing him because she thought he was the safest driver, or was this another of her "getting to know you" activities?

On the other hand, maybe it would be good for them to spend time together. At least then Katie would see what a great person Dan was and ease up on the questioning. They were going to be related. She loved them both. She wanted them to get along.

She saw her parents climb awkwardly onto a snowmobile, her mother driving, and turned away, intending to ride by herself.

Jordan gestured to her. "Come with me. You look tired. Bad night?"

"Didn't sleep well." She strolled across to him, her feet crunching on the snow. "This should wake me up."

"Maybe you should stay with Dan tonight. We can't have the bride showing up with dark circles under her eyes."

"I can't. I haven't seen my sister since the summer. I really want to catch up, but last night she was—"

"—like a dog with a bone?"

"I was going to say protective. She wants to know I'm doing the right thing. We need to talk, that's all."

"This is your relationship, Rosie, not hers." He spoke gently. "Your opinion is the only one that matters here. As long as you're sure you're doing the right thing, that's the important thing."

She was sure. Wasn't she? Was she sure? She wished people would stop asking her that. The more she thought about it, the less sure she became.

"I'm sure." Had he sensed her hesitation? What if he said something to Dan? She should be discussing this whole thing with Dan, but she had no idea how to broach it. Plans for the wedding were almost done. In a few days the florists would arrive to transform the dining room of Snowfall Lodge into a magical winter wonderland, fit for a fairy-tale wedding.

Nowhere in that scenario was there room for the bride to have a panic attack.

"Why is your sister riding with Dan?"

"I expect she wants to spend time with him."

He swung his leg over the snowmobile. "I'll bring your

sister home with me. That way you and Dan can have some time together."

"Thank you. Did you and she get along okay on the ride from the airport?"

Jordan's expression didn't change. "We got along fine, don't you worry. Now let's get going before we're too far behind to catch up."

She wrapped her arms around his waist as they sped along the snow, following the groomed trail that led through the valley into the mountains, through aspen groves and vast glittering snowfields that in the summer would be meadows splashed with the color of wildflowers.

Today the landscape was a million different shades of white.

The mountains rose up out of forests of spruce and fir, the reflection of the craggy, snow-covered peaks shimmering on the surface of the partially frozen lake.

The cold stung her cheeks and bit through her thick layers of clothing.

They arrived at the lake to find Katie and Dan already sipping mugs of hot chocolate.

"That was incredible." Katie's cheeks were flushed, her hands curved around the mug. She looked happy and relaxed for the first time since she'd arrived. "What a perfect place. Dan was telling me he used to come up here before dawn so he could take photos of the sunrise."

"In summer this place is so crowded it's hard to find a place to stand on the lakeshore," Jordan said. "Even at sunrise."

Catherine was taking photographs, tall and slim in a white winter jacket and black ski pants.

"She already has a thousand," Dan said. "But still she takes more."

"I'm doing a wedding here in the spring," his mother called over her shoulder, bracing her legs as she took a succession of shots.

Rosie glanced around and saw her parents standing a little distance away, facing each other. "What are they doing?"

Katie grinned. "Having a fight. Apparently Mum is a scary driver. Dad told her he'd ridden camels in the desert that were smoother. That didn't go down well."

Rosie didn't want to hear that they were fighting.

She wanted evidence that they were still blissfully happy.

As if on cue, her mother stood on tiptoe to kiss her father. And then pushed a snowball down his neck.

There was a brief moment when her father stood frozen in shock and then he retaliated, scooping up snow where he stood and chasing after Maggie.

She ran, arms windmilling as she struggled through the ankle-deep snow, shrieking like a teenager, trying to protect her head and neck.

"I never knew she could run that fast," Katie said mildly.

"Me neither. Ouch." Rosie winced as she saw her father catch up. He swung her mother around and held a huge ball of snow aloft.

Their voices carried across the snow.

"Remember, Mags, you started this." He pushed it down her neck and she gasped with the cold and scooped up more snow, pummeling him as he ducked and laughed. They continued to spar, ducking and diving as they grabbed soft scoops of snow and hurled it until they were both covered.

Rosie couldn't remember ever seeing her parents as relaxed as this. Normally her mother fussed over her, checking she was feeling okay, that she'd used her inhalers, that she didn't feel a cold or flu coming on. Since arriving in Aspen, Maggie seemed different. Rosie couldn't quite identify what had changed, but something had. If anything her parents seemed closer than they had when Rosie had been living at home. Presumably relationships changed as people did.

Rosie snuggled inside her coat and smiled. It was good to see them so happy, and not only because it made her feel better personally.

Katie walked over to say something to Dan and Rosie turned to Jordan.

"Do your parents behave like this?"

"Did they fight? Yeah, all the time. Only they threw plates and other heavy objects instead of snow. Eventually they divorced, so I guess they grew tired of throwing things."

It was the first time he'd revealed anything personal about himself. All she really knew about him was that he loved the outdoors, was a skilled carpenter, and had been a loyal friend to Dan for most of his life.

Her parents' shrieks faded into the background.

She touched his arm. "I didn't know. I'm sorry."

"Don't be." He thrust his hands deep into his pockets. "It was a relief for everyone who knew them. You didn't need to be an expert on relationships to know they should never have been together."

"Why?"

"Because they didn't like each other. Everything she did annoyed him, and everything he did annoyed her. Not a good basis for a marriage. If you wanted me to find one word that encapsulated my parents' relationship, it would be *contempt*."

"Ouch. Is that why you never married?"

There was a pause. "I've been married. Once. A long time ago."

"What? But—Jordan! I had no idea." She turned to look at him but couldn't read anything from his profile. "Dan never mentioned it." And why hadn't he? How many other important facts had he failed to mention?

"He knows it's something I prefer to forget. And our relationship was nothing like yours and Dan's, in case you're worrying."

"Am I that obvious?"

"I happen to think that being easy to read is a quality, not a flaw. Generally I'm not big on advice, but I'm going to give you some anyway because Dan's like a brother to me and I don't want to see him hurt. I don't want to see either of you hurt." Jordan stared straight ahead of him. "Don't compare your relationship to anyone else's. The only people who know what goes on inside a marriage are the two people involved."

Her heart was pumping against her ribs. "You think I'd hurt Dan?"

"Not intentionally. But I think, perhaps, you listen to too many voices that aren't your own."

He was right of course. "I—I'll remember that."

"And here's another piece of advice—if you're worrying about something, your wedding for example, talk to Dan, not your sister."

That was good advice. It was what she needed to do.

"You don't like my sister?"

There was a pause.

"She's the first woman I've wanted to kill within five minutes of meeting her."

"Oh!" Rosie didn't know what to say to that. "It was so generous of you to meet her at the airport. I'm sorry if she was—if she seemed—prickly?"

"Don't be. She loves you. But she is so busy protecting

you, she doesn't think about whether you actually want, or need, her protection."

"She's actually the warmest, kindest person I know."

"I believe you, but don't let her wreck what you have, Rosie." He turned to look at her then, his eyes filled with warmth. "Not that you should be at all interested in my opinion, because the only opinion that matters is your own, but I happen to know you're the best thing that ever happened to Dan."

Rosie felt her chest ache. "What makes you say that?"

The corner of his mouth flickered. "I met his other girl-friends."

Maggie

"I AM SOAKED through and freezing and it's all your fault. Did you have to push that last snowball right down my front?" Maggie shivered as she stripped off her outer layers. She was cold but buzzing. She felt more alive than she had in years. For a moment back there by the lake with the sun beaming down on them, she'd thought about nothing but the fun of the moment. The impulse. The delicious rush of semifear as Nick had chased her across the snow, and the laughter. Her ribs still ached from the laughter. "I can't believe we did that." She was too old to have snow melting down the inside of her jacket.

"Had a snowball fight?"

"We've never done anything like that before."

"We've never had snow like this before." Nick pulled off his boots. "Blue skies and sparkling snow bring out my inner child."

She knew it was more than that.

When had they last had fun like that together? When had they last laughed hard at something?

Life had become a series of tasks to be completed, to-do lists to make, places to be.

"Did we embarrass our girls?"

"Probably, but isn't that what parents are for?" He hung up his coat. "And it was no more embarrassing than you kissing me and talking second honeymoons."

"That's different. That was done for a purpose." She handed him her jacket and pulled off her boots. The snow had seeped through every layer of clothing, and now her sweater and her thermal top stuck uncomfortably to her body. She tugged them away from her skin. "This was spontaneous. We behaved like children."

"Maybe. Or maybe we behaved like adults without responsibilities. Which makes a nice change. I haven't heard you laugh like that in a long time. Let me help you with that—" He reached out and pulled off her damp sweater, resisting its attempts to cling to her soaked arms.

And suddenly she was standing in front of him wearing nothing but her borrowed pair of ski pants and her bra.

The change in his expression reminded her that the bra was the one Catherine had chosen, the one she'd initially rejected for its decadent lace embellishments and general unsuitability for this stage of her life. She'd purchased it because it felt luxurious against her skin, and because she wasn't a match for Catherine's persuasive powers.

She hadn't thought anyone but her would see it. Or perhaps, on some level she hadn't examined her reasons too closely. It had been an act of defiance, a way of proving to herself that although her marriage might be dead, she wasn't. That she should look at the miles ahead of her, not the mileage behind.

But she hadn't intended to be standing in front of him wearing nothing but lace.

"I lost my suitcase—" It seemed imperative that she remind him of that fact, in case he was thinking she'd bought it to seduce him. Even as the thought went through her head, she dismissed it as ridiculous. You couldn't seduce a man you'd been with for more than thirty years.

"Yes." His voice was husky, his hands still on her arms. She felt the gentle drag of his thumbs as he warmed her chilled skin.

It had been so long since he'd touched her, since they'd stood like this connected by anything other than the shared life that lay behind them.

She stood still, hardly daring to breathe, hoping that he wouldn't take his hands away and yet at the same time wanting him to because his touch confused her. The soft stroke of his fingers against her skin stirred feelings she'd thought were dead forever. As those feelings grew and spread and deepened, she felt a flutter of panic. She didn't want this. She didn't want to know those feelings were still there, because where would that leave them?

Their separation had been mutual. They'd agreed that whatever they'd shared had burned itself out in the fires of life.

She'd believed it, and yet here she was remembering what it had been like to kiss him and curl her body into his in the dark of the night. She remembered everything that lay behind them, all the shared experiences and life events. Their marriage was like a library full of stories they'd written themselves. And they were about to tear that down.

She felt a moment of panic. Were they doing the right thing?

She had to believe they were. She couldn't have doubts now. That would be unfair on him, and also on her. The decision was made. They needed to plow through it, and she needed to make what lay ahead as easy as possible to bear. Feelings would mean pain, and somehow she'd managed to keep herself numb.

Numb was good. Numb was easy.

His fingers had stopped moving but still he held her, his grip firm as if he was afraid to let go of what he was holding.

A strand of hair had fallen over his forehead. He looked rakish, and younger than his years. For a moment she saw the man she'd fallen in love with. The student who had been so wrapped up in his subject he'd barely known whether it was day or night. In those first few years he'd lived in college and she'd occasionally arrived at his rooms to find him unshaven with bloodshot eyes because he'd been reading all night.

She was the one who had forced him into the shower and then dragged him to breakfast in their favorite café, tucked away in one of the narrow cobbled side streets that were a feature of the ancient university city. He'd devoured bacon and eggs while telling her about his plans to join a dig that summer. He'd talked about pyramids and burial chambers, about gods and burial rituals. Right from the first moment they'd set eyes on each other in the Bodleian Library, she'd been captivated. She'd been taking refuge from a hot, sweaty summer. He'd been absorbed in research. She'd loved his passion, and she'd envied it.

She'd chosen to read English literature, because her parents had pushed her in that direction and she'd found no reason to argue. She enjoyed it, but not in a million years would she have described it as a passion.

Once they were married, her life had fallen into a pattern. She'd tended the girls, she'd tended Honeysuckle Cottage, she'd tended her garden. Somewhere along the way she'd forgotten to tend her marriage. She wasn't a martyr. She didn't take all the blame. Nick was at least half as responsible, but somehow that didn't make her feel better.

Their marriage hadn't exploded or died a dramatic death; it had simply withered and died of neglect.

She felt a spasm of regret, but under the ache was an emotion far, far more dangerous.

She fought against the rebellious swirl of feelings that rose up inside her.

The only way seemed to be to remove herself, so she stepped back and scooped up her wet clothes. "I'll take that shower before hypothermia sets in."

He didn't answer and when she glanced at him there was a tiny furrow between his brows as if he was trying to figure out what had just happened.

If he'd asked, she wouldn't have been able to tell him.

Her heart had been as frozen as her skin, but his touch had thawed it and now all she felt was pain and more than a little confusion.

She locked the bathroom door, stripped off the last of her clothes and stepped under the hot water.

By the time she'd dried her hair and dressed, he'd made hot drinks and that brief moment of intimacy had passed.

"We had a delivery while you were in the shower." His voice sounded so normal it made her wonder if the awkward moment earlier had all been in her imagination.

"What type of delivery? Please tell me it's not a crate of champagne."

"An envelope. It's addressed to you—from Catherine."

She took the envelope from him and opened it, smoothing the page. Would he notice that her hand wasn't steady? "It's an itinerary."

"For what?"

Maggie sat down hard on the sofa. "This is awkward. Catherine has arranged some special activities for us."

"Why is that awkward? It's thoughtful. What sort of activities?"

She fiddled with the envelope. "Couples activities." She didn't look at him. "Romantic activities." And then she was thinking of that moment again, the moment when his touch and breathing had altered.

Nick joined her on the sofa. "Why would she do that?"

"Apparently I told Dan this was a second honeymoon for us, and he passed that information on to her." She looked at him. "Sorry."

His eyes gleamed. "That's what happens when you drink too much champagne."

"That's what happens when someone forces me onto a plane." She flopped her head back against the sofa. "How can one small modification of the truth create such a ripple effect? And I don't want you to answer that. If you say 'I told you so' I'll push more snow down your pants."

"I would never say I told you so. That would make me smug. I have many faults, but I'm never smug. I have sympathy with human frailties."

She lifted her head. "You're saying I have frailties?"

"No, you're perfect, apart from the occasional small modification of the truth. If the price we have to pay for that is a few shared activities, I can live with that."

But could she? Acting a part in public was one thing, but actual togetherness was something different. After what had happened earlier she needed a little distance, not closeness. "What do we do?"

"We can't offend her when she has been so generous with her hospitality. There's only one thing we can do. We say thank you and go along with whatever she has arranged."

"Even if it includes a naked mud bath?"

"Does it?"

"I don't know. I saw the words *second honeymoon* and *special activities* and then my mind blanked with panic." She glanced down at the paper. "What a tangled mess. I'm starting to realize there is no easy way to tell people you're breaking up. No right time. You just have to do it. Perhaps we should—"

"No. We shouldn't. We made a decision and we're sticking with it. You can't get cold feet now. We're in this all the way. For better or worse." He removed his glasses and rubbed the bridge of his nose. "Sorry. That wasn't tactful." He reached across and tugged the paper out of her hand. "I'd like to read what it takes to keep a marriage alive."

"What if she's arranged for us to exchange vows under the stars?"

"You could vow never to be economical with the truth again." He smoothed the sheets of paper on his lap. "Whatever it is, we have to do it."

Her mind was a jumble of thoughts and feelings. She needed space to think, not more of his company. "We could tell her we'd rather chill and enjoy each other's company here."

He ignored her, his attention on the paper he was reading.

"Well?" She started to feel nervous.

"This afternoon we're going dogsledding. We're being picked up from here, given the right clothes to wear and taken into the forest to a mystery place where it seems that being close to nature will rekindle my romantic tendencies." He adjusted his glasses. "Did I ever have those? I'm not sure there is anything to rekindle."

"I suppose it depends on how you define romance."

He gave a faint smile. "That sounds damning. Maybe I

shouldn't have asked." He glanced down at the paper again. "It might be fun."

"What does it involve? We ride in the back of a sled?"

"No, I think we're the ones driving." His gaze flickered to hers. "Clearly they've never seen you drive. After that snowmobile, I'm not sure I trust you with dogs."

"You're not funny. How do you drive dogs?"

"Presumably we'll be taught. Can't be more unmanageable than camels."

If they were driving, she thought, there wouldn't be much opportunity for awkward conversation. As long as she wasn't freezing cold, maybe it wouldn't be so bad. "Is that it?"

"No, that's only the beginning. Then we come back here, have an hour to shower, warm up and change before being driven to an intimate dinner in a restaurant."

She swallowed. "What's intimate about it?"

"It's the two of us, for a start. Also, it's halfway up a mountain. No easy access and no easy escape. Once we get there, you're my captive."

"Maybe you're *my* captive." She felt a flutter of panic. "I want to spend time with the girls. I've barely seen them."

"Unless you want to change your story, seems like you're stuck with me." He lowered the paper to his lap. "Is that so bad?"

"I'm not sure." It didn't feel bad, and that in itself was strange and unsettling. Couples getting a divorce were supposed to argue and talk through lawyers, not enjoy candlelit dinners together. "This whole thing feels—weird."

"Why? We used to go on trips and enjoy intimate dinners. Remember?"

"I don't remember candles, except for the time we lost power in the cottage that winter. I remember picnics in fields, and days spent clambering through the ruins of ancient castles. We didn't have the money for fancy restaurants."

He fiddled with the paper. "You chose the wrong guy. You should have married an economics student. He would have gone into banking. Probably would have ended up running the bank. By now you would have had a house in Mayfair and a country pile in Surrey."

"That sounds like a lot of work."

"At least five cars."

"There's only one of me. What would I do with five cars?"

"You definitely would have had staff."

"Staff would have been welcome." Or would they? She'd happily hand over dust removal duties but creating a home was so much more than a compilation of domestic tasks. And she wouldn't have relished having other people around the house.

"Your parents would have approved of your choice."

"If my parents would have approved, then I know I would have hated him."

"I hate him, too, and I never even met the guy." He reached across and took her hand. "I'm sorry, Mags."

"For what? For not running a bank, owning two houses and five cars? That's not the stuff that makes people happy, although perhaps it fills a hole if someone isn't happy."

"You're wise. Have I ever told you you're wise?"

"You're the professor."

"You're the professor of life." He glanced back at the paper. "Want to hear the rest?"

"There's more? Please tell me we're not white-water rafting. The power shower was enough for me."

"Tomorrow morning you're up at dawn, joining Catherine for a spa morning. Hair, nails, massage and pampering."

"Dawn? I'm not sure I like the sound of that. What are you doing while I'm putting my back into relaxation?"

"I can choose between a massage and a few hours at leisure. I think I'll choose the leisure. There's a book on the shelves I'd like to dip into."

"I hate you."

"After that we're going up on a gondola to the top of the mountain for lunch."

"A gondola? Is this Venice?"

"A gondola is a ski lift."

"What happens after lunch? Or is that the end of our second honeymoon?" She saw Nick's expression change. "Nick?"

"The suggestion is quiet time back in the tree house."

"Quiet—?" Maggie gasped. "You mean sex?"

"I'm guessing that's what she has in mind."

"Is there a hidden camera somewhere? Is someone going to watch us? Tick it off the list?" She closed her eyes. "I am never telling a lie again. From now on it's the truth all the way, no matter who it upsets."

"We can talk about that later, but in the meantime we have to get ready for sledding. According to the brochure, it's something we're never going to forget."

Maggie didn't have any trouble believing that.

Spending time getting up close and personal with Nick hadn't been on her agenda.

It wasn't real, she reminded herself. All this was still part of the pretense.

Katie

KATIE STOOD SELF-CONSCIOUSLY while the woman fussed over the dress she was trying on.

"It's a little loose. Your measurements have changed since you sent them to Rosie."

Katie smoothed the fabric over her hips. "I may have lost weight. Sometimes I forget to eat when I'm working."

Rosie shook her head in disbelief. "I hear people say that and I don't get it. I have never forgotten to eat in my life. How does that even happen?"

"Sometimes I'm too busy, and sometimes the stuff I see puts me off my food."

"Katie is a trauma doctor," Catherine explained to the seamstress. "This woman is a heroine."

"Not a heroine." Katie wriggled, as uncomfortable about the conversation as she was about the dress. "It's a job."

"It's so much more than that. Your mother told me all about how you wanted to be a doctor from the moment Rosie had her first asthma attack. She's proud of you. Thank goodness there are people like you in the world." Catherine leaned forward to pinch some fabric over her hip. "I think we could take it in here."

Katie had never felt less like a heroine.

I'm a fake, she thought. *A total fake.*

"Honestly, the dress is fine. It looks great. Better than anything else I own, I promise you that." It was a struggle to stand still. "There's no time to adjust it. The wedding is in four days. Unless you feel like postponing?"

Rosie's eyes widened. "Are you joking?"

"Ha! Of course I'm joking." She wasn't joking. "I'm surprised you managed to pull all this together in such a short time, that's all. That's put a lot of pressure on Catherine."

"It was Catherine's idea," Rosie said and Katie stopped wriggling.

Was that why her sister was doing this? Why hadn't that thought occurred to her before? Maybe she'd been pressured by Catherine. Well-meaning pressure, but still—

"I love a winter wedding," Catherine said, "and I have never seen two people more in love than Rosie and Dan, so it seemed right."

It didn't seem right to Katie. Why was she the only one questioning the speed of this?

She wanted to hold up her hand and yell *stop, stop!*

Was this really what Rosie wanted?

Admittedly Katie hadn't so far discovered anything about Dan that provided her with an excuse to step in and halt proceedings, but that didn't mean there wasn't something there.

Maybe there were incidents in his childhood that might offer up clues as to his character.

"Parents always talk about what makes them proud of their children," she said. "They rarely talk about the things that embarrassed them. Did my mother mention the time she was called into school because Rosie had freed the school rabbit from its life of incarceration?"

Catherine laughed. "That is so like Rosie."

"It wasn't only me." Rosie gathered up her hair and studied herself in the mirror. "There was that time Mum had to go to school because you'd been accused of cheating in an exam. You denied it, and there was this huge bust-up. You yelled at the teacher for calling you a liar. They said you needed to learn respect, as well as not to cheat."

"I remember that. I've never been good at dealing with injustice."

"Mum was called in," Rosie told Catherine. "They wanted Dad, too, but he was on a dig in Egypt."

Katie shrugged. "Dad never dealt with that kind of thing anyway. He left it to our mother."

"Yes, and she asked to see the paper, and then she said *did it not occur to you that my daughter might have known the answers?* The teacher told her it wasn't possible to get a perfect mark, so Mum asked her to give you another exam and you got a perfect mark in that, too." Rosie beamed at her. "She always knew you were super smart, and she made sure everyone else knew it, too. You'd told her you wanted to be a doctor, and she wanted to do everything she could to support that and make sure you reached your full potential."

And now Katie was considering throwing it all away. All the work. All the training. The thing she'd spent a third of her life doing.

She was going to be a disappointment to her whole family, especially her mother.

She really ought to talk to them, but she had no idea where to start. *Hi, Mum, you know how proud you feel when you tell people your daughter is a doctor? Well, you're going to have to start telling them your daughter gave up being a doctor. Sorry.*

No, that wasn't going to work. And if this wedding was

going ahead, she didn't want to be the one to kill the atmosphere by talking about her own issues.

"How about Dan?" Katie turned slowly as the seamstress checked the hem. Her nerves were so frazzled she half expected them to be poking out through the dress. "Did he ever embarrass you?"

"No, but he gave me a few white hairs. I guess that's what little boys do to their mamas." Catherine stood back and narrowed her eyes. "I wonder—maybe a flower in your hair?"

"He was naughty?"

"More adventurous than naughty. As a toddler there wasn't a surface too high for him to climb onto, and as a teenager there wasn't a slope too steep for him to ski. And he was stubborn. When there was something he wanted, nothing was going to stand in his way. That boy could wear down rock."

Was that it? Had Dan's determination to get what he wanted put pressure on Rosie? Rosie hated confrontation. She might find it hard to speak up in that situation.

Rosie was focused on the dress Katie was wearing. "Is the color okay? Is it what you imagined? I've been scared you might not like it."

"I love it." The dress was a pale, silvery gray that shimmered in the light. It was understated and elegant, and something that Katie would have chosen herself if she'd ever had the need for such a thing. It wasn't the dress that worried her. What worried her was the fact that the wedding was now only four days away and she still wasn't convinced Rosie wasn't making a huge mistake.

Was her judgment off? It wouldn't be the first time, but the fact that her sister kept using their parents as evidence that a whirlwind relationship could sustain in the long term, concerned her. You only needed evidence if you were trying to prove something. You only needed to prove something if you doubted it.

She shouldn't need evidence, should she? She should *know*. And if Rosie was so excited about getting married, why did she seem so tense? It couldn't be workload, because Catherine seemed to be doing all the work. And that was another thing that bothered Katie. Rosie was a romantic. She'd played weddings with her dolls. She'd made bouquets with daisies from the garden. Surely she should want more say on the detail of her own special day?

"The sparkle lifts it, I think." Catherine was focused on the dress again, making notes on her phone and adding a few recommendations of her own. "Instead of the silk wrap, try it with the faux fur. It will be warmer."

Without thinking, Katie shrugged off the silk and heard Rosie gasp.

"What happened to your shoulder?"

She'd been so preoccupied with weddings, she'd forgotten about her shoulder. "Nothing."

"Nothing? Katie, you have a huge scar. You've hurt yourself."

"I fell, that's all and it's healing well." Katie grabbed the fur wrap from Catherine with a quick smile of thanks. "No need for drama."

But of course Rosie wasn't going to let it go that easily. "Fell how? Where?"

"Through a glass door. Silly me. Forget it, it's embarrassing. I love this fur." She turned sideways and looked at her reflection in the mirrored walls of the store. "It's warm and it has a certain glamour, don't you think?"

Rosie wasn't looking at the fur. "Why would you fall through a glass door?"

"I lost my balance. I was wearing heels. You know what I'm like in heels. Lethal."

"No, I don't know." Rosie was frowning. "I've never known you struggle in heels. And I've never known you lose your balance. It doesn't seem like you."

"I was tired after a long shift."

"So why were you wearing heels? Were you on a date?"

Katie bit back a hysterical laugh. "Not exactly. Can we stop talking about this? It wasn't my finest moment." It was probably the first truthful statement she'd made about that night. "This fur is great, I think, don't you, Catherine?"

"I like it." Catherine gave her a long, steady look and then smiled. "We need to decide what to do with your hair. Your cut is—unusual."

Katie fiddled with the ends, grateful that Catherine was supporting the change of subject. "That's because I used the kitchen scissors." She saw Dan's mother physically flinch. "I know. It's a crime, but there you go. It was getting on my nerves and I didn't have time to get to the salon. The scissors were clean, I promise."

To her credit, Catherine recovered quickly. "I suppose we should be grateful it wasn't a scalpel, and it's nothing that our stylist at the lodge can't sort out. I'll call her right now and she can fit you in this afternoon. I thought maybe a loose updo for the wedding." She gathered up Katie's kitchen-scissored hair and twisted it gently. "Something subtle and pretty. Rosie, show your sister your dress."

Katie wondered if Rosie found it strange to be trying on dresses without their mother there. And how did their mother feel about it?

Apparently her parents had an alternate engagement doing something romantic.

Rosie vanished and reappeared with a flourish, wearing her wedding dress.

Katie felt a thickening in her throat, a surge of emotion that blocked speech. Love. It had filled her heart from the first moment her mother had carefully put her newborn sister into her arms. *Be careful. Support her head. Don't drop her.* She'd grown up understanding that love brought with it anxiety. She'd seen it in her mother's face during her sister's first asthma attack, and again every time her sister started to wheeze. She'd seen a lot of things in her time working in emergency medicine, but there wasn't much that was more frightening than not being able to pull air into your lungs. She'd watched her mother closely, noticing how she stayed calm even when she didn't feel calm. Katie had copied that, not knowing then that it was a skill she would use time and time again in the future with frightened patients and scared relatives. She'd sat quietly by Rosie's bed, forgotten and ignored, not understanding the medical terms but having no trouble understanding the grave expressions of the medical team. There had been times when her body hadn't felt big enough to contain all the love she felt for her sister. She hadn't only felt the weight of that fragile bundle in her hands, she'd felt it in her heart.

Was this why she found it so hard to have a lasting relationship with someone?

Subconsciously had she held back from experiencing that intense, terrifying depth of feeling?

She moved through life with such purpose, she rarely stopped to reflect.

Had she, somewhere along the way, rejected love?

Maybe not love, but vulnerability. She'd rejected vulnerability. She witnessed it constantly in her work. The fear in the face of a relative, the panic in the face of a patient who felt life sliding out of control.

Her experiences in her job had reinforced those same feelings of helplessness she'd experienced as a young child and she'd unconsciously wrapped her heart in layers of protection so that she felt the blows less.

She didn't like feeling vulnerable, but she felt it now as she looked at her sister.

"Wow, you look—" she swallowed "—you look gorgeous. The dress is gorgeous."

"I love it, too." Rosie did a twirl, ivory silk catching the light, her hair sliding over her shoulders in shiny waves.

Catherine narrowed her eyes. "When I see you with your hair loose like that it makes me wonder if you should wear it that way. It's more you than a structured updo, isn't it? What do you think, Katie?"

"She prefers to wear it down." She thought of all the times she'd done her sister's hair before school. Braids. Ponytails. She'd learned them all.

Catherine twisted a strand of Rosie's hair around her fingers, visualizing the options. "We're keeping the flowers simple. Locally foraged foliage, white orchids. Maybe it *would* work with flowers in your hair."

"I like the sound of that. I forgot to tell you, Katie." Rosie turned to her sister. "We're going to have a hot chocolate bar, for guests who need to warm up."

She had to pull herself together.

"That's where you'll find me. There, or next to the champagne. Catherine, would you take a photo of both of us so that I can send it to our mother?"

Catherine took the photo and Katie stood still as the woman made a final adjustment to the hem of her dress.

Finally they were done, and she and Rosie picked their

way through fresh snow to the car while Catherine lingered to discuss final details. Rosie slipped her arm through Katie's.

"Does it hurt?"

"Does what hurt?"

Rosie gave a growl of frustration and unlocked the car. "There are times when I could strangle you."

Katie stared at her. "What?"

Rosie climbed into the car and Katie followed.

The car provided sanctuary from the cold, but not from her sister.

Rosie pulled off her gloves and blew on her hands. "It hurts my feelings, Katie. I tell you pretty much everything, and it hurts me that you don't feel able to confide in me. Don't," she said quickly as Katie opened her mouth, "don't tell me there's nothing to talk about or I really will have to strangle you. The truth is you don't see me as an equal, do you?"

Katie was shocked into silence. Rosie hated confrontation. She'd do virtually anything to avoid it.

"I have no idea what you mean."

"You don't treat me like a sister or a friend, you mother me. You've always mothered me."

Be careful. Support her head. Don't drop her.

"I'm protective, that's true."

"I feel protective of you, too, but there's a big difference between being protective and being motherly. It's natural to hide things from our parents, everyone does that, it's part of growing up and obviously we don't want to freak them out with tales of real life, but it's *not* natural to hide from a sister. We should be sharing things, but you don't let me in. Why not? Don't you trust me?"

Katie had never had to answer to her sister before. "Of course I trust you."

"Really? Because the basis of almost all our conversations is you checking up on me—am I using my inhaler, have I been in hospital, am I sure I want to marry this man. When do you ever lean on me?"

"I—" She swallowed. "I don't really lean on anyone."

"Exactly. And why not? We're family, Katie. I'm not some random stranger you can't trust."

"We talk all the time."

Rosie shrugged. "Whenever we talk, it's mostly you sorting out my problems and most of the time I don't even want you to sort them out. I don't need you to interfere."

She was being caring, not interfering. Wasn't she?

She forced herself to examine whether that might be the truth. It was a deeply uncomfortable experience. She could see how it might be possible to interpret her intervention as interference rather than loving concern.

"I suppose the reason I don't share my own problems is the same reason I do everything else. I'm protecting you."

Rosie didn't smile. "You don't have to protect me from life, Katie. I'm living it, right alongside you. When did we last do something fun together?"

Catherine arrived before Katie had a chance to formulate a reply. She wasn't sure if she was frustrated by the reprieve, or relieved. Mostly she was worried. It was unlike Rosie to be confrontational.

And there was no sign of her apologizing or softening in any way. She didn't reach for Katie's hand or mouth *sorry* or any of the things Katie would have expected.

And when *had* they last had fun together?

As they drove back to the lodge, Rosie sat silent next to her.

"I hope your parents are having fun," Catherine said. "Dogsledding is usually a highlight for our guests."

Katie couldn't begin to imagine her parents sledding, but what did she know? Right now she wasn't thinking about her parents, she was thinking about her sister. According to Rosie, she was no fun.

She answered Catherine politely and then looked out of the windows at the mountains, feeling as if she'd somehow let her sister down.

Despite the discomfort, she forced herself to analyze their relationship. It wasn't that she didn't see her sister as an equal, it was more that there was an imbalance in their relationship. Katie had been ten years old when Rosie was born. When Katie had been sixteen, Rosie had been six. They'd moved through each phase of life at different times.

"I'm going to drop you girls back at Snowfall Lodge because I have the floral designer coming at three," Catherine said. "Katie, Becca can't do your hair until five, but I thought you and Rosie might like a swim, or a massage, in the meantime. Have a little sister time."

Sister time.

What was that supposed to look like?

Katie shifted in her seat. It was up to her to make the change, and she needed to do it now. "A swim sounds good, but I didn't bring a swimsuit." Would swimming count as fun? She didn't even know.

"We sell swimsuits. Snowfall Lodge places great emphasis on aquatic recreation." Catherine turned toward the lodge. "Your parents are having their romantic dinner in town tonight, and I have my book group which I can't miss because it's our last one of the year and I'm responsible for the food, so will you two be all right?"

Rosie nodded. "I'm having a quiet dinner with Dan. Is

that all right with you, Katie? You could order room service to the tree house and chill with a movie."

No, it wasn't all right. Suddenly it seemed urgent that she and Rosie have fun together.

"As we're having our hair done and getting all glammed up, maybe we should have one last fling as single sisters and go dancing. There has to be somewhere to dance in Aspen?"

"Dancing?" Rosie was looking at her as if she'd suggested looting an art gallery.

"I feel like celebrating. And it would be good to have fun together."

Her sister held her gaze. "All right."

"I think it's a wonderful idea," Catherine said. "It's been all wedding, wedding, wedding lately and this will give you the chance to relax with your sister. Dan won't mind. You two have the rest of your lives to be together."

Katie focused on her breathing. That surge of panic that enveloped her at the thought of Rosie spending the rest of her life with a man she barely knew? She was ignoring it. Mindfulness. Meditation. Medication. Whatever it took. She wasn't saying anything else about it. Rosie was an adult, capable of making her own decisions.

Maybe her sister was right. Maybe she was too protective. And what did she know about love anyway? Nothing. She wasn't sure she knew much about having fun, either, but she was determined to address that.

They spent the afternoon swimming in the heated rooftop pool that was the crowning glory of Snowfall Lodge. Covered by a glass dome, it was like being outdoors in the mountains.

She and Rosie had the place to themselves. As Katie slid into the pool, the water warmed her skin and relieved some of the tension in her muscles.

Keeping her body and shoulders beneath the surface of the water, she admired the jagged mountains and the tips of the snowy trees. It was as if the world had been painted in white.

If it weren't for the circumstances, she could almost have relaxed.

Rosie floated next to her, eyes closed.

"Are you mad with me?"

Rosie opened her eyes. "No. But sometimes it's a little frustrating that you still treat me like a child."

"Not true." Katie wiped the water out of her eyes. "Maybe it is true, but I think that's because you're my baby sister."

"I'm twenty-two."

"You'll always be my baby sister, no matter how old you are, in the same way we'll always be Mum's children even when we're fifty."

How would Rosie react if Katie confided in her? Not only about the attack, but her doubts about her career choice?

She noticed Rosie looking at her shoulder again and took off across the pool, swimming laps until the sun dipped in the sky and someone came to tell her the salon was ready for her.

She showered and changed quickly, then sat placidly allowing the hairdresser free rein.

"Can I add a few highlights around the front?"

"Anything," Katie said. "Whatever you think would look best."

"I'll be doing your hair the morning of the wedding," Becca said, "so it's good to have a chance to work with your hair before then. Is there anything you love? Anything you hate?"

"She's conservative." Rosie unscrewed the cap from her water bottle. "Don't do anything radical."

"Maybe radical would be good." Katie stared at herself in the mirror. Did she really look that pale? She needed to wear more makeup. Or find a way of getting more sleep.

Rosie took a sip of water. "Do you have anything to wear dancing?"

"No. I'm going to raid your wardrobe and pretend I'm a teenager again."

Three hours later all evidence of the use of kitchen scissors had been erased and Katie's hair fell in soft layers around her face.

"You look amazing." Rosie stroked Katie's hair back. "All you need to do now is stop frowning."

"Am I frowning?"

"Always. You're always serious." Rosie hugged her. "This is my wedding. You're not allowed to frown at my wedding."

"Where are we going tonight? I don't want to bump into our parents and invade their second honeymoon."

"That isn't going to happen. We're going to a place that has the best DJ around. It's very cool. And I have the perfect dress for you. I bought it to wear to a party in the summer."

"A frostbite dress. Yay. Do I need to point out that there are several feet of snow on the ground?"

"I've messaged Dan. He is going to drive us there, and pick us up after so we won't be outdoors for long. And you can wear your coat."

Back in the tree house, Rosie delved into the suitcase she'd quickly packed at the lodge. "Here." She pulled out a dress. "Try it. I fell in love with it the moment I saw it."

"Like you did with Dan?"

Her sister laughed. "I guess so. Only he's a whole lot warmer than that dress."

Katie pulled the dress over her head. "I am too old to wear this."

"No, you think you're too old and you act too old, but tonight you're going to leave your overdeveloped sense of responsibility behind and throw your young and sexy self onto that dance floor."

"They probably won't let me in."

"It's exclusive, that's true, but everyone knows the Reynolds family around here."

"We're not members of the Reynolds family."

"We soon will be." Rosie wriggled into a scarlet jumpsuit. "Rosie Reynolds sounds cool, don't you think?"

"You're marrying him for his name? Only kidding!" Katie intercepted Rosie's warning look. "You look incredible. Like something that fell off the Christmas tree."

"I'm pretending that's a compliment."

"It is a compliment. You're very stylish. I've always said so."

"Wait until the wedding. It's going to be perfect."

"Catherine seems to have done most of it, and she's not even your mother." And she'd wondered about that. Was their own mother upset that she wasn't more involved in the detail of her daughter's wedding? Was she watching the plans drift past her, just beyond her reach and feeling sad that she was an observer and not a participant? While Catherine chose silk, and flowers, and pondered over menus, did their own mother feel grateful or replaced? She was such a hands-on, involved and caring parent, she had to be upset, surely? Thinking about it, Katie had a renewed respect for her mother, who never put pressure on either of her girls. Not once had she been anything but supportive of Rosie. "Talking of our mother, I need to forward that photo. She'll love it."

And tomorrow morning first thing Katie was going to check on her. Give her a chance to talk about how she felt about the wedding.

"Catherine is amazing. What woman wouldn't want to have the whole thing arranged for her by a professional?" It didn't seem to have occurred to Rosie that their mother might have feelings on the topic.

"You. You used to daydream about weddings." Katie dug in her bag for her mascara. "Normally you'd be saying, *I really want eucalyptus—oh wait, I've changed my mind—maybe ivy*—but when it comes to this wedding, you don't seem to say much. You're happy with everything? I'm worried she's railroading you." Even without looking at her sister's face she knew she'd done it again. "Forget I said that. She loves you. I can see that."

"You can't help yourself, can you?" Rosie's cheeks were flushed. "Why are you so convinced that this marriage is a mistake? You're as bad as Grandma."

"We never met our grandmother."

"I know, but Mum has told us how she disapproved of them getting married so fast. And look how it turned out."

Katie thought about her parents rolling together in the snow like children, and off on a romantic date. "You're right. I'm being ridiculous." She had to stop this. She had to stop always looking at the evidence that supported the bad, instead of the good. Why was she such a mess? Whatever the reason, it was up to her to sort it out.

She had to stop protecting her sister, and instead support her.

She crossed the room and hugged Rosie. "Tell me you're happy. That's all I want to hear."

"I'm happy."

"That is the only thing I care about. Apart from dancing, of course. I care about dancing. Is that Dan outside?" She grabbed her coat and her bag. "Let's do this. Let's have fun."

From now on she was forcing herself to focus on the positive, not the negative.

Every time a dark thought entered her mind about the risk of whirlwind relationships, she was going to think of her parents rolling in the snow. Her parents kissing like teenagers.

It had worked out for them. There was no reason why it couldn't work out for Rosie.

Maggie

"WHEN CATHERINE SAID the restaurant was in the mountains, I didn't realize it was literally in the mountains and that we had to ride in a snowcat to get here." Maggie walked the few steps to the cabin and into the welcome warmth. She sniffed the air. "Herbs and garlic. Smells good."

"And we're going back on the horse-drawn sleigh. I'm not sure if that will be better or worse." Nick handed his coat and scarf to the restaurant staff, scattering snow across the floor. "Are you cold?"

"No. Those blankets they gave us were warm." And she'd had to slide close to him on the seat to make room for others. Her thigh had pressed against the length of his thigh, her arm against his arm, two halves pressed together as if they were a whole. She'd had to remind herself that they weren't a whole. That their two well-fitting pieces had been split apart. But her mind had refused to cooperate and had dragged her back to that moment earlier in the tree house. Heated from the inside, she'd barely noticed the cold.

Even now, as he helped her with her coat, she noticed the light brush of his fingers against her neck. It was as if her body was suddenly supersensitive to his touch.

He handed her coat to the staff. "Apparently it's possible to snowshoe up here, too."

"I'm glad we took the snowcat option. There are limits to my need for adventure and I don't want to have to work that hard for my dinner. Are we seriously going back down in a horse-drawn sleigh? Will the horse be friendly?"

"As long as it gets us safely back down the mountain I don't much care about its personality."

"I suppose you're going to tell me that camels are worse."

"Camels are definitely worse."

They were shown to their table, and Maggie slid into her chair by the window. Even though she felt unsettled and more than a little confused by her own feelings, it was impossible not to be charmed by the atmosphere. As they'd crawled up the slope in the snowcat, she'd wondered if the journey would be worth it, but her first glimpse of the place had convinced her that it was. The Alpine-style restaurant nestled in the trees, halfway up the mountain. It was a cozy retreat from the frozen world outside, its wooden walls lit by tiny lights, and the air scented by wood smoke and wholesome cooking.

It was dark outside so the view was limited, but the lights from the cabin lit up the surrounding forest and trails.

"It's pretty." Snow floated and swirled past the window, gentle but relentless. "Do you think we'll be snowed in?"

He slid on his glasses and opened his menu. "I don't know, but being trapped in a restaurant wouldn't be the worst thing in the world. The wine list looks good, and at least we won't go hungry."

She glanced around her. All the tables were occupied. "It's obviously *the* place to spend a romantic evening."

"Presumably that's why Catherine chose it."

Maggie felt like a fraud. They were surrounded by couples enjoying their relationship. She and Nick were faking theirs.

"Champagne, courtesy of Mrs. Reynolds."

Two glasses were placed in front of them along with a small plate of canapés and Maggie waited until they were alone again before she caught Nick's eye. "Don't say it."

"What?"

"You were going to make a reference to what happened last time I drank champagne."

"I was not. This is one glass, Mags. You emptied the drinks cabinet on the flight. In fact France might now have a champagne shortage."

"Thank you for your tact and delicacy, and for respecting my wish to forget it."

"Why would you want to forget it?"

"Because I was an embarrassment to my entire family. Well, not Katie because she didn't witness it, but no doubt Rosie will have shared the horrors of it by now." She'd always been pleased that the two girls had each other. She would have loved a sibling.

She studied the menu and then put it down and caught Nick smiling at her. "What?"

"I happen to think you were adorable."

"Adorable?"

"When you consumed the champagne. You lost your inhibitions."

"You mean I all but molested you in front of my daughter and her soon-to-be husband. And told them this was a second honeymoon. If it weren't for that champagne, we wouldn't be sitting here now."

"I can't think of anywhere I'd rather be." He raised his glass, "To us."

Her heart gave a little kick. "There is no 'us,' Nick. We're divorcing, remember?"

"Not tonight. Tonight we're on our second honeymoon, although I feel compelled to point out that we had no money on our first honeymoon so the food and drink were nowhere near as impressive. This version is vastly superior."

Everything about him was light, whereas she felt weighed down and heavy.

Pretending in front of the people she loved was one thing, but this was different. This felt real.

"No one is watching."

"We don't know that. You want it to get back to Catherine that we repaid her hospitality by fighting?"

"We don't fight." She felt exhausted. It could have been the physical activity but she thought it was probably something else. Something she didn't want to think about.

"You're right. We don't." He studied her. "Why don't we?"

"I suppose after all the years we've been together, we've learned what works and what doesn't." Marriage was like a dance, trying to move to the rhythm of life, searching for a pace and a path that suited both people. Some floundered, but they hadn't. They'd simply spun away from each other.

She lifted her glass. She didn't want to toast "us." She didn't want to toast the future, because right now she wasn't sure she liked the way it looked. Toasting the past was likely to make her feel sad. The only thing left to toast was the present. "To now. This evening. May the horse not run away with us down the mountain."

"That sounds like a metaphor for life." He tapped his glass against hers. "To an evening of fun."

"Fake fun."

"The fun doesn't have to be fake." He closed the menu.

"There was nothing fake about our snowball fight. I enjoyed it. Probably because I won."

Maggie choked on her champagne. "*I* won!"

"That's not how I remember it."

"Then you have a selective memory."

"That last shot that went right down your front? That was a winner."

"Next time I'm not going to spare you. Prepare to be defeated, Professor."

"Your aim isn't good enough to defeat me." He pushed his glasses up his nose and the familiarity of the gesture made her heart ache.

She missed this. She missed their little exchanges across the meal table. She missed those small gestures that were part of him, and that she knew so well.

He pushed the plate of canapés closer to her. "Why are you looking at me like that?"

"I was planning my strategy for the next snowball fight." She put her menu down and selected a small creation of smoked salmon and fresh chive.

"It doesn't matter what your strategy is, I'm ready for you. You're going to lose. Have you chosen?"

"I'm having the goat's cheese."

"You can't. I'm having the goat's cheese."

"We're allowed to eat the same thing."

He frowned. "We never eat the same thing in a restaurant. We always split. That way we try more than one dish."

Splitting dishes was something they'd done when they were young and didn't have the money to eat out often. It was a way of trying as many different things as possible on the menu. *Try this. Taste this.* "Not always. Remember the lobster?"

"Of course. That dinner is scarred into my soul. You refused to share. It was the one and only time."

"It was good lobster."

"You're telling me that now? Have you no heart?"

She definitely had a heart. Hers was bruised and sore, as if someone had reached inside her chest and punched it. Far from being a respite, this trip was making it worse.

"If you want to share, why don't you have the smoked fish?"

"Good plan."

They ordered the food and she took a sip of her champagne. "It tastes like celebration, which is somewhat ironic in the circumstances. What are we celebrating?"

"Our skills at performing arts, maybe. Certainly not your aim with a snowball."

She was grateful for the humor. "There's nothing wrong with my aim. I was being gentle with you. I didn't want you to be soaking wet for the ride home."

"I believe you. You don't have a ruthless bone in your body. The woman in charge of the place told me you're the first client who has ever asked if she is too heavy for the sled dogs."

"It seemed like a perfectly reasonable question to me. Dogs aren't that big. I worried about them, that's all." She fiddled with the stem of her glass. "I had a good time."

"Me too. I am never going to forget your face when those dogs took off. They didn't seem to have much trouble pulling you." He was laughing and suddenly she was laughing, too.

"They didn't take off. I was in control at all times." She saw a woman sitting at the next table glance at them. "We're being too loud."

"I don't care. It's good to hear you laugh." He paused. "We had fun this afternoon."

"We did. It was relaxing. Being out in the forest, with nothing but the sound of the dogs and the cold air on your face—" and being with Nick. The man she'd once loved and still loved as much as ever. Despite the broken pieces, she still loved him.

The realization came as a shock.

His gaze held hers. "When did we stop having fun, Mags? When did we stop doing things together?"

Their appetizers arrived before she could answer, and she picked up her fork.

He leaned forward. "Let me ask a different question— *why* did we stop doing things together?"

"I don't know. Life, I suppose. You were busy. Working. Traveling. I was focusing on the girls. It happens."

"Fun should have happened, too. We should have made the time. Been creative. Let's be honest, would we have thought to do any of these things if Catherine hadn't arranged them for us?"

"No. Because these are couples activities, and we're not a couple. We haven't been for a while. We're together because our daughter is getting married."

"That's my point—we wouldn't have done them even when we were a couple."

Maggie's phone buzzed and she reached for her bag, grateful for the distraction. Did she really want to dissect the past? How was that going to help?

Nick sighed. "Do you have to check that? This is supposed to be a romantic dinner."

"Fake romantic dinner. And Catherine isn't likely to be watching over our shoulders, is she? One of the girls might need me." She glanced at her phone.

"They're adults, Mags. They can handle life for five minutes without your intervention. If it was an asthma attack they'd be calling you, not messaging."

Maggie ignored him. Katie had sent her a photo of the two of them wearing their dresses, arms looped round each other, smiles on their faces. *Her girls*. "They had a dress fitting this afternoon." While she'd been on a sled ride with Nick. She felt a pang, as if she'd lost something she'd never get back. "Catherine must have taken the photo. Look." She turned her phone so that he could see the screen and he gave a brief smile.

"They look great. Happy."

"Yes. And they're going dancing tonight. That's good. I've been worried about Katie. Something isn't right."

"She's probably tired. Jet lag. And she does a tough job."

"I know, but she's been doing a tough job for a decade and—" She broke off, unable to explain a mother's instinct. "I feel something is wrong."

"You worry too much. It's probably nothing."

She hoped he was right and that nothing was bothering Katie.

Her mind shifted to her younger daughter. "I like Dan very much. He's kind and attentive, he has a good sense of humor and he seems to know Rosie. But do you think it's a mistake for them to get married so young?"

"I've been married once in my life and I made a mess of that, so I don't think I'm qualified to answer."

She put her phone back in her bag. "You didn't make a mess of it, Nick. Marriages end. It's a fact of life."

"It's also a fact that there has to be a reason for them to end." He drained his glass. "I've been wondering lately if things would have turned out differently if I'd done a different job."

"Nick, that's crazy. What else would you do?"

He shrugged. "Maybe a museum job, with better hours."

"Museum jobs frequently come with hideous hours, and worse pay. And you love what you do."

"But I was away so much I ended up living on the fringes of the family."

She frowned. "What are you talking about?"

"Even now, we're at dinner, but you take calls from the girls. You're like this inseparable trio and occasionally I join in."

Their food arrived, but neither of them touched it.

He was looking at her and she was looking at him.

"Are you saying you felt shut out?" She felt a rush of frustration and something close to guilt. "I never complained about your job, Nick. I never complained when you were gone for weeks at a time, when you returned with half the dust of the desert in your bag. I understood it was what you needed to do. It was the life you wanted. But you can't blame me for building a life that worked for me. A life that I wanted. You know what my upbringing was like. Sterile. Lonely. My parents were detached. I used to think they loved me, but didn't know how to show it. Now I'm not even sure that's true. I think maybe I prefer to think that because it's easier to handle than the alternative. There was nothing cozy about our home. Nothing warm or welcoming. I wanted to build something different for our family. And I'm proud of what we created, and what we had for such a long time."

"*You* created." He picked up his fork. "You made our family what it was."

His use of the past tense felt like a physical blow. "That's not true. You were part of that family, too."

"All I did was show up occasionally."

"I don't resent your work, Nick. I never did. You were following your passion, and I was following mine."

"But yours was making our family work."

"You make it sound self-sacrificing, but it wasn't like that. I wanted to create the family environment I'd dreamed of having when I was growing up. I wanted warmth and love, good food, laughter. I did it for me."

"I was selfish. I see that now." He put his fork down. "I keep thinking of that time I was packing for that trip and Rosie had an asthma attack. Do you remember?"

She remembered. She could smile about it now, but at the time she hadn't felt like laughing. "You asked me where your boots were."

"And you told me where you'd put those boots if you knew where I'd left them."

She blinked innocently. "I'm sure I would never have been so vulgar."

"I deserved it. I deserved a lot worse than that. Our daughter couldn't breathe and I was packing for my trip." He ran his hand over his face. "It wasn't that I didn't care, or wasn't worried."

"I know that." Had she known that? Had she occasionally felt exasperated and angry that his priorities seemed to be in the wrong place?

He let his hand drop. "You handled it with more skill and grace and calm than I ever could. You didn't only calm Rosie when she couldn't breathe, you calmed us all. You never panicked."

"I panicked constantly. Inside I was a wreck."

"I never saw that."

"I didn't dare let anyone see."

"It made me feel inadequate."

"I felt inadequate, too."

"When?" he demanded. "When were you ever inadequate? Give me an example because I don't remember a single time."

"Most of my life I suppose." She finished her champagne. "I was never quite what my parents wanted me to be and then, for a little while when we were first together it felt so right nothing else mattered. But then as you climbed the career ladder, things changed. People judge you by what you do. All those dinner parties where I was introduced as *Professor White's wife.* As if without you I wouldn't exist as a person. Even though I knew that raising the girls was probably the most important thing I would ever do in my life, I still felt—" she struggled to find the right word "—less. I felt less."

He frowned. "I never once felt you were less. I never made you feel that way."

"Your colleagues did. Once they discovered I wasn't one of them, I wasn't worth their attention except as a way of getting to you."

"Academics can be a strange bunch."

"People can be a strange bunch." Her toes were warm, her whole body relaxed. "When people asked me what I did, I talked about academic publishing as if that gave me the credentials I needed to be accepted into the group, but my job was something I did to bring in extra money. You were the success."

"As I said the other day, I may have succeeded at some things, but I didn't succeed at our marriage."

"There is no blame, Nick. And there's no pass or fail with a marriage." She spoke softly. "Maybe we got the balance wrong. I don't know. I didn't want the girls to feel your absence, so I worked doubly hard to make sure we had fun when you were gone. I didn't want to spend the time counting the days waiting for you to come home."

Was that why they'd drifted apart? Was it her fault?

In the beginning his absences hadn't mattered so much. If anything they'd added an exciting edge to their relationship and his homecomings had been accompanied by passion and a greater appreciation of each other.

She picked up her fork. "I suppose life got tougher. The demands were greater. My focus was always on keeping the family stable and happy. We were a three, and sometimes a four, but hardly ever a two. The truth is it took effort to be a two, and I didn't have much energy left."

"I was the same. Work and family came first, and that didn't leave anything much for the two of us. Maybe if we'd done more things like we've done today we'd still be a couple."

She didn't want to think about that. She *couldn't* think about that. If it was true, then it was heartbreaking. "It's not easy to have a snowball fight in Oxford. And dog-sledding through the Bodleian Library would definitely be frowned on."

His gaze softened. "We had fun today, Mags."

"I know."

"We had fun *together*. We were a couple."

"We were pretending."

"We might have been pretending to be a couple, but the fun part was real enough." His tone was rough. "Rosie left home four years ago. The last four years was our chance to reconnect. To make time for us. We should have grown closer, not farther apart."

She ate half the goat's cheese without tasting any of it and then they swapped plates.

"I'm sure we're not the first couple who has grown apart."

He put his fork down. "Do you hate me, Mags?"

"What? Do I—?" She was astonished by the question. "No! How could you even ask that?"

"Because all the divorced couples I know hate each other. John and Pamela don't communicate at all. Ryan and Tracy aren't even in the same country."

"She moved?"

"He moved. Took a job in Frankfurt."

"Oh." She pondered that new piece of information. "I suppose some people might find that easier." But not her. She liked the life she'd built, and the comfortable nest of memories that cocooned her when times were hard. Was this a good time to mention that she didn't want to sell Honeysuckle Cottage? No. That conversation would be better had another time. Probably when she'd worked out a way to afford it by herself. Maybe she could rent a room to a student. There was demand for it.

"I feel responsible."

"For the fact that Ryan took a job in Frankfurt?"

There was a gleam in his eyes. "For the demise of our marriage."

She nibbled at her half of the fish. "It's a shared blame, Nick. It takes two."

"Does it? Because I see a lot of things I did wrong— things I regret—but I don't see anything you did."

"You implied that I shut you out."

"No. I was telling you that I felt on the edge. Not the same thing. There are things I'd change if we had our time again."

"Mm?" She tried to sound casual. Did she want to hear the alternate scenario? The one which might not have ended

in divorce? No, not really. The time to have had this conversation was long past.

"For a start I'd notice that you didn't love your job.
Thinking about it now, it's pretty obvious. You love being
outdoors. You always have. You love nature. I should have
seen that any job that kept you trapped indoors would be
the wrong one."

"I made my own choices. And I'm not like you. I didn't
have a burning passion. I applied for lots of different jobs,
and took one that made me an offer. I'm sure millions of
people do the same thing. We land in a place as much by
accident as design."

They finished eating, although she barely tasted the
food.

"Instead of having dessert and coffee here, why don't we
go back to the tree house? We can sit in front of the fire and
finish our conversation without half the world listening in."

She thought about it. "I suppose the horse pulling the
sleigh might be less tired if we go early."

They bundled up and made their way out into the cold.

They had the sleigh to themselves for the short ride down
to the village. From there, they'd take a car back to Snowfall Lodge.

Maggie snuggled under the thick blanket and Nick put
his arm around her and pulled her closer. Maybe she should
have pulled away, but she didn't want to.

It was for warmth, she told herself. For warmth, that
was all.

She realized how rare it was to travel like this, with no
car fumes, impatient drivers, or stop-and-start traffic. The
horse and the sleigh left no human footprint, and there was
something magical about it.

They could have been alone in the world, the only sounds

the muffled sound of the horse's hooves on the snow and the occasional soft swish of its tail as they made their way down the trail that led to the village. They snuggled together under the blanket, watching the stealthy swirl of snow that fell silently around them.

Maggie was glad of the layers she'd put on, and also glad for Nick's strength and warmth.

She leaned her head against his shoulder, enjoying the clean, freezing air and the steady presence of the trees that guarded the edges of the trail.

The end came too soon, and when they climbed into the waiting car she felt a pang of disappointment.

Back in the tree house, Nick headed straight for the kitchen and she stripped off her outer layers and stood in front of the flickering fire.

"Here." Nick handed her a mug full of scalding hot coffee. "This will warm you up. It's snowing again—can you believe that? And there's a blizzard forecast for tomorrow."

"All those years I dreamed of having a white Christmas, and suddenly there is so much snow there's a chance we'll be snowed in."

"Do you hate it? Are you missing Honeysuckle Cottage and our usual Christmas traditions?"

Maggie walked to the window and stared out at the trees. Trees always made her feel calmer. "No. I love it. It's the most perfect place I've ever stayed."

"You're enjoying yourself?"

"Yes. Real life seems a long way away."

"But in a week we're going back to that life. And you're returning to a job you don't like. Resign, Mags. Make that the first thing you do when you get home."

"Without another job to go to?" He'd always been more

impulsive and adventurous than her. "It's a good thing one of us is sensible."

"I'm not sure I agree. Not if being sensible traps you in a life you don't like. Give yourself the gift of a fresh start."

She blew on her coffee to cool it. "I've already had about fifty rejections. It's pretty obvious that I don't have the qualifications or professional training to do the job I want to do. If I resign, all I'll give myself are money worries. What's good about that?"

"The job you'd like to do is garden design?"

"Some of my happiest moments have been spent in our garden, and I'm proud of what I've created. I think losing the garden will be one of the worst things about selling the house. A garden isn't something that happens instantly. It matures and changes over time." She looked at him. "Like a marriage, I suppose."

He held her gaze. "Do the training. Get the qualification."

"I'm too old."

He raised an eyebrow. "If you can learn to drive a sled pulled by huskies, I'm sure you can learn garden design. That lead dog was a character."

"He was adorable."

Nick sat down on the sofa and put his mug on the low table. "You don't have to factor in the kids anymore, Maggie. They have their own lives. Katie's career is going well and Rosie has only just started her postgrad and is about to be married. Time to think about yourself."

"What about the cost? I wouldn't only lose my income, I'd be out of pocket. That sort of course would cost a fortune."

"We have the money, Mags. We can afford it."

Should she point out that they were no longer a "we"?

"A divorce is expensive. Lawyers. Two properties. Two sets of bills."

His eyes darkened. "We'll find the money for this. It's about priorities."

Her heart softened. Another man might have fought hard to keep as many of his assets as possible. Nick wanted her to do a course that would be of no benefit to him whatsoever.

"And what if I do the course, get the qualification, and then can't get a job? What a waste of money that would be."

"Maybe you'd enjoy the process, in which case the money wouldn't be wasted. And maybe you would get a job. There are no guarantees, unless you don't do it in which case it's pretty much guaranteed that you won't be a garden designer. Promise me you'll think about it."

"I'll think about it." She finished her coffee. "I suppose we should get some sleep if we're to be up and about for tomorrow's romantic challenge."

He finished his coffee and stood up. "I enjoyed tonight, Mags."

"Me too."

"I'll make up the sofa. Unless you think the girls might pay us an impromptu visit before we go to sleep. Do you think we should share the bed, to be safe?" There was a tense, awkward pause and for a moment his gaze met hers. Her skin tingled, and she thought back to the moment after the snowball fight.

Only a few days before, the future and her feelings had been clear, but now suddenly everything was tangled and murky. If they shared a bed it would become more complicated. And it didn't feel safe.

She was the one who had started this. She'd insisted that they keep up this pretense, and at first it hadn't seemed a hardship. But she'd been thinking only of the girls, and now suddenly, she could think only of herself.

Something had changed in her. Shifted.

"I don't think that's necessary. We already agreed to meet over at the lodge for breakfast at ten tomorrow. They have no reason to come here. I'll fetch the bedding," she said. "I put it away in the basket upstairs so that the girls didn't see it."

She busied herself making up the couch, plumping pillows and tucking in blankets. This part she was good at. The practical stuff was easy. It soothed her and calmed her.

"Good night, Nick." She smiled and walked to the bedroom, hoping she looked more composed than she felt.

By the time she'd finished in the bathroom, he'd turned the lights out in the living room.

From her vantage point on the shelf she could see his bulk curled up on the sofa.

She felt a shimmer of emotion that she didn't fully understand. They'd had more honest exchanges in the past couple of days than they'd had in the past couple of years. Would it have made a difference if they'd had those conversations sooner?

Telling herself that it didn't matter, she slid into bed and propped an extra pillow under her head so that she could watch the snow falling. There was something calming and hypnotic about that silent swirl of flakes, blurring the edges of the world outside.

At some point her eyes drifted shut and she dreamed of walking through the snow hand in hand with Nick.

When she woke the fire had gone out, and the snow had stopped. Sunlight poked its way through the trees. The delicious aroma of fresh coffee told her that Nick was already up and around.

Pulling on a robe, Maggie went down to the kitchen and poured two mugs of coffee.

When Nick emerged from the bathroom, she handed him one.

"Did you sleep?"

"Not as well as I would have expected to after all that exercise. Thanks." He took the coffee from her. "You?"

"Not bad. What kept you awake?"

"Our conversation. This situation." He walked over to the sofa, put his coffee down and lit the fire. "It feels wrong somehow."

Was he talking about their separation?

Her heart skipped. Was he about to suggest that they tried again?

The chemistry was still there. The last few days had made her aware of that. Their love was still there, too. But could they really start again?

He'd picked the sofa that faced the bookshelves rather than the window. Because this conversation seemed too important to have from a distance, she sat down next to him with her back to the door.

If he suggested they try again, what would her answer be?

She nursed her coffee, giving herself time. "What exactly are you suggesting?"

"I don't know." He looked as confused as she felt. "But I think we should talk about the divorce, don't you?"

Maggie heard a faint sound behind her seconds before she heard her daughter's voice.

"Divorce? You're getting a divorce?"

Drenched in horror, Maggie turned and saw Katie standing a few feet away. She was holding a box of pastries and staring at them as if they were strangers.

No need to ask how long she'd been standing there or how much she'd heard. The answer was visible in the agony on her face. She'd obviously heard everything and neither Maggie nor Nick had even heard the door open.

Maggie forced herself to stand up. Her legs shook. Her hands shook. Her coffee sloshed on her leg, but she ignored the burn. She had bigger things to worry about. She'd spent months planning the best way to tell the girls. She'd ached over how and when. Never once had this scenario crossed her mind.

She wanted to blame Nick, but she knew it wasn't his fault. If she'd listened to him, they'd have done it a long time ago, and they would have done it together.

A tiny part of her wondered what, exactly, Nick had wanted to talk about before Katie had interrupted them but she ignored that, too. Right now, the priority was her daughter.

Katie looked as if she was in shock. As if she'd witnessed something she hadn't yet managed to process.

Maggie knew she'd never forget the look on her daughter's face. "You should have told us you were coming over."

"Why?" Katie glanced at the tumble of bedding on the couch. "So you could both climb into the bed and pretend to be together?"

"We need to talk. Sit down, Katie."

"I don't want to sit down." Her steady, reliable, calm and unflappable daughter looked distraught. "I want to know what's going on. You've told everyone this is a second honeymoon. You two have been glued together since you arrived here and frankly it's been a little embarrassing. But suddenly here you are getting a divorce? I don't understand." She looked so hurt and confused that Maggie rushed across to her and tried to wrap her in her arms.

"Katie—"

"No!" Katie pushed her away. "I don't want hugs, I want answers. It was all an act, wasn't it? The *we're so in love* thing you and Dad have going on. An act."

Maggie knew her face was probably the color of a Santa suit. "We probably should have told you before now, but it hasn't been easy and I was trying to find the right time, and that time wasn't immediately before your sister's wedding."

"How could I have been so stupid? I thought it was odd that the two of you were so demonstrative all of a sudden, but I assumed it was because you were making the most of taking a holiday together."

"We—" Maggie glanced at Nick. "I thought it was best to wait and tell you after the wedding."

"Does Rosie know? No, of course she doesn't." Katie paced to the kitchen area and put the box of pastries down on the counter. "She keeps using you as her inspiration. Holding you up as an example of a perfect marriage. So what's the plan? Is Dad going to move out? Or have you split Honeysuckle Cottage in half or something?"

Maggie swallowed. "Dad's already moved out. He has a room in college. We've been living apart for a while."

"How long is a while?"

"Since the summer."

Katie stared at her. "The summer? Oh my—" She choked on the words. "I can't—"

"Katie—" Maggie stepped forward but Katie headed for the door.

"Don't touch me. I need some air. Space. Time to think." She was stammering. Stumbling.

Maggie felt as if her heart had been ripped in two. "Please, Katie—" But her daughter was already at the bottom of the steps and flying down the snowy track that led to the tree house as if she was being hunted.

Maggie whirled to Nick who was standing silently by the sofa, staring after his daughter. "Why didn't you say something? Why didn't you *do* something?"

"You heard her. She wants space. Best to let her have that space and then we can talk properly later."

She wanted to blame him, but she knew that all the blame rested with her. She was the one who had insisted on waiting.

"This is all my fault. You wanted to tell them months ago."

"And you wanted to wait."

"And that was the wrong decision."

"I don't believe it was." He shook his head. "The last few days have been the most fun we've had in years. We've talked more than we have in years. I feel as if I know you better than I have in years. I'm sorry Katie walked in when she did, but I'm not sorry for any of the rest of it."

Everything he said was true. But what did that mean? What did it change?

"What are you saying?"

"I don't know." He ran his fingers through his hair. "I don't know what I'm saying."

She understood his confusion because she felt it, too. "It doesn't even matter. All that matters is Katie."

Frustration crossed his face. "Do you really think Katie is what matters here? What about us? We have to talk about *us*, Mags—"

"—and we will, but first we have to check on our daughter. I'm worried about her." She grabbed her phone and called Katie's number but predictably it went straight to voice mail. "I can't focus on anything else until I know she's okay, don't you understand that?"

He was silent for a moment. "Yes," he said. "I understand that." His tone said that he understood it but didn't like it, and his body language said the same thing as he clomped to the door and reached for his coat. His shoulders were slumped. He looked defeated, and she felt as if she was being tugged in two directions.

She felt a moment of loss, followed by panic. "Where are you going?"

"To find our daughter. That's what you want, isn't it?" He shrugged on his coat and reached for his scarf. While he wrestled with layers and wool, she wrestled with guilt and questioned her priorities.

"She's probably gone back to the tree house to tell Rosie." They all protected Rosie. And now Katie, her strong, determined, reliable Katie was hurting and alone. Of course they should put her needs first.

"Katie isn't the sort to sob out her problems on someone's shoulder. She never has been. And she'd want to protect Rosie. It's what she does. It's what she's always done. My guess is that she's gone for a walk to let off steam."

They were talking about the girls, but she was thinking about him. About *them*. About their evening together. And now the closeness had gone, and she was the one who'd killed it. She badly wanted it back but it was like trying to grab handfuls of that steam he'd mentioned.

She felt numb. If Katie hadn't walked in when she had, what would she and Nick be talking about now? Would the closeness, the intimacy, have continued?

Had there ever been an example of worse timing?

And what was he going to say to Katie when he found her?

They were getting a divorce. That was a fact and it was a fact that stayed the same no matter who had the conversation. "Nick—"

"I know, you're worried and want me to hurry up." He tugged open the door and she felt a rush of desperation. She could stop him. She could call him back now and maybe, somehow, they could find their way back to that place they'd been when Katie had walked in.

But then what about Katie?

She opened her mouth but before she could decide what to say the door slammed and Nick stomped off into the snowy forest to look for their daughter.

Katie

SHE WAS LOST.

Katie turned to look behind her, and then to the sides. She'd been on the trail, but then she'd seen a couple of people snowshoeing up ahead, and because she'd been crying and her cheeks were wet and her eyes were red and the last thing she wanted was to engage with another human being, she'd turned onto an unmarked trail that led into the forest. She hadn't meant to go far, but she'd walked and taken another couple of turns and now she was definitely lost.

The trail climbed steeply uphill, guarded by towering trees, the forest thick in parts and coated with fresh snow.

It had been easy to walk on the main trail in her snowshoes, but harder here where the snow was deeper and the surface untouched. Sunlight poked through the trees, making the surface of the snow glisten.

Katie closed her eyes and breathed in the air and the peace. She was lost, but so what? Being lost worked for her. It felt like a metaphor for life. She was lost physically and emotionally. Her parents, two people she thought would be together forever, were getting a divorce.

The world no longer made sense. If they couldn't make it, what chance was there for anyone else?

She wanted to pretend it wasn't happening, but she knew denial wasn't a good thing so she kept forcing herself to think the word.

Divorce.

Of all the things she'd expected to happen this Christmas, that hadn't been on the list.

It felt as if her entire life was falling apart. First her job, and now this.

The irony was that she'd gone to her parents' cabin unannounced because she'd wanted to check on her mother. She'd been worried she might be upset that Catherine seemed to be organizing Rosie's wedding. Through the windows of the tree house she'd seen them seated on the sofa together, deep in conversation, and had thought how cute they were together. She'd envied them the closeness and felt a little guilty at disturbing them on their second honeymoon.

They hadn't heard her knock on the door.

It wasn't until she'd stepped inside the tree house that she'd realized the conversation absorbing both of them was focused on the details of their divorce.

She knew things hadn't always been rosy at home— she'd witnessed the strain Rosie's illness had put on their relationship, but that had been years ago and she'd assumed they'd somehow weathered it. The fact that they hadn't put another dent in her view of relationships.

She'd thought her family was unbreakable and yet here it was, apparently broken.

Why now? It didn't make sense.

And why was she so upset about it? That didn't make sense, either.

She was an adult, not a little girl. The way her parents chose to live their lives shouldn't impact her, but suddenly all she could think of was the fun times the four of them had spent together. All those idyllic years spent in Honeysuckle Cottage. Her parents taking turns reading her stories, lying on the bed next to her and letting her turn the pages. Her dad taking them all to see Egyptian mummies at the museum.

Christmas.

Christmas had always been her favorite time of year. From the moment she arrived at Honeysuckle Cottage and saw the candles flickering in the window and the trees decorated with tiny fairy lights, the stresses of the year somehow slid from her.

But she knew that what really made Christmas so special wasn't the fairy lights or the candles, nor even her mother's fabulous cooking—it was being home with her family.

She gasped in air as she struggled up the steep slope. Her parents added a level of security to her life, even though she didn't see them that often.

Her life was so crazy she dashed from one moment to the next with little control over her time. Most days she felt like a leaf blowing in the wind. She'd shared a house with Vicky for a decade, but it still felt like somewhere she slept and ate. It didn't feel like home. Honeysuckle Cottage was home. Would they sell it?

Katie stopped walking because she could no longer breathe properly or see where she was going.

She brushed away the tears, angry with herself.

Her parents were both alive and healthy. She of all people should know that was what was important. And of course they'd sell the cottage. They couldn't hold on to a house that was too big for one person, simply to accommodate the family a couple of times a year. Why did that make her sad?

Maybe it was because the rest of her life seemed unstable. She'd had relationships over the past decade, but none of them had lasted more than a couple of months and she'd barely shed a tear when they ended. She had friends she was often too tired to see because she was always working, and a job she wasn't even sure she liked anymore.

Her whole life had shifted precariously. She'd been so sure about being a doctor, but now she was questioning that.

She thrust her hand into her pocket and dug out her phone.

She shouldn't be thinking about herself. She should be thinking about her parents. Her mother must have been miserably unhappy, and presumably she was unhappy now. Why hadn't she said something?

Katie waved her phone in frustration, looking for a signal.

Guilt crawled over her flesh as she remembered all the times she'd avoided calling home. Maybe if she'd been better at staying in touch, her mother would have found it easier to confide in her.

And what about Rosie? Rosie, who kept using their parents' solid marriage as evidence that a whirlwind romance could work. Impetuous and impulsive Rosie, who still believed in happy endings. Katie had used that evidence, too, to reassure herself that her sister's relationship would sustain.

Katie was going to have to tell her the truth. But not now, because her phone wasn't working.

She put it back in her pocket and stood still, staring into the trees. It was only now, when she stopped trudging through the snow, that she realized how cold it was. Her breath left smoky clouds in the air ahead of her.

She started walking again, planting her feet firmly in the deep snow. The surface was scattered with pine cones and whispers of fir and the only sounds were the soft thud as snow fell from a tree, the call of a bird, the snap of a branch as the weight of its burden grew too much.

She came to a fork in the trail and stopped. A decision had to be made. Left, right, or turn back? Better to keep going forward in the hope that she'd see a sign.

She was surrounded by peaceful, scented forest. Snowy peaks rose above the tops of the trees and she could hear the rush of water from the river somewhere far down below. It was beautiful. So beautiful it was almost humbling.

She thought about London, with its streets choked with cars. When she'd first moved there she'd found the city exciting and energizing. Lately, she found it energy-sapping. Everyone was in a rush, in a crowd, in a temper.

Here, it felt as if she was the only creature on the planet.

She wasn't sure what made her glance up, but she did it and immediately clashed with a pair of yellow-gold eyes.

For the second time in a month she knew real, gut-wrenching fear.

She was not the only creature on the planet.

What *was* that thing? It was *huge*. And it was looking right at her, and not in a friendly way.

Could she run in these stupid, cumbersome snowshoes?

Given that walking had been a challenge, the answer had to be no.

A moment ago she'd been freezing cold, but now she was shivering for a different reason.

Maybe she could sidle into the trees and hope he didn't think she looked like something worth following.

She took a single step and the animal sprang down from the tree in a series of fluid, athletic leaps and landed on the trail in front of her.

This is it, Katie thought. *This is how I die.*

And they'd never find her body because no one knew where she was.

A familiar male voice came from behind her. "Don't move."

Relief weakened her knees. Never in her life had she thought she'd be pleased to see Jordan, but as he stepped beside her, she was. It took all her willpower not to fling herself at him. "What is that thing?"

"Mountain lion."

Lion?

Katie wished she was back in London. She was never, ever, complaining about the city again. "We should run."

"Do not run." His hand closed over her shoulder. "Are you going to accuse me of going all macho on you if I step in here?"

"Please—" Her mouth was so dry she could hardly speak. "Step anywhere, preferably in front of me." She could have sworn she heard him laugh, and then he did step in front of her.

His bulk blocked her view, but she saw him spread his arms and heard him shout at the lion. For a moment it stood, all coiled muscle and strength, and then it vanished into the forest.

Katie thought her legs might give way.

Jordan turned and closed his hands over her arms, as if he realized she needed holding up. "We were lucky."

"Yes." She tried to smile, but it didn't happen. "I'm relieved you arrived when you did."

"I meant we were lucky to see the lion. They generally try to avoid humans."

"I wonder why this one decided to make an exception?"

"You're a lone hiker, which makes you more interesting.

He was probably fascinated by the difficulties you were having walking through the snow."

"You mean he was waiting for me to fall down so that he could eat me?"

"I doubt he would have eaten you." He let go of her but only to zip her jacket up to the neck. "Keep this closed. It's no wonder you're shivering. What are you doing all the way out here?"

"Taking a walk."

"This isn't a marked trail. You were lost."

"Not exactly *lost*. More freely walking wherever the impulse took me."

"The impulse took you into the path of a mountain lion. And if you'd carried on walking to the left you would have fallen off the mountain. It's steep, and the trail ends at a big drop-off."

"Good to know." She licked her lips. "Should we get away from here, in case that lion has friends? And shouldn't he be hibernating or something?"

"Mountain lions don't hibernate, but it's rare to see one in the middle of the day. They tend to be more active at dusk and dawn. The heavy snowfall we've had the last couple of weeks has probably driven him down from the mountains. Or maybe he followed his prey, a deer or an elk, and then came across you."

"Great." Katie shivered. She'd been prey before, and it wasn't an experience she was in a hurry to repeat.

"They're not usually interested in humans. It's food they're after, but it's good to be alert. You didn't answer my question. What were you doing all the way out here?"

She hadn't even realized she'd come this far. She'd been so upset she'd walked without thinking. "I needed time to myself. I didn't realize it was dangerous."

"There's other things more dangerous than that mountain lion." He shifted his backpack. "You could find yourself up to your neck in snow, or you could slip on the ice and bang your head. Take someone with you when you hike. And if you meet a mountain lion, make yourself look large. Look it in the eye so that it knows you're not afraid."

"I wasn't afraid. What makes you think I was afraid?" She saw a gleam in his eyes.

"Great. In that case I'll say goodbye." He turned and started to walk up the path away from her and she stared after him in disbelief.

Was he really going to leave her here? No, he was trying to annoy her. Making a point. Any moment now he'd turn round and walk back to her.

But he didn't. He kept walking, his long powerful legs making it look easy.

"Jordan!" She wasn't proud that her voice shook.

He turned. "What?"

It almost choked her to say it. "Don't leave me."

There was a pause and then he strode back toward her at a considerably slower pace than he'd walked away. "Let's be clear about this so there's no mistake. You're asking for my help?"

She gritted her teeth. "Yes, I'm asking for your help."

"You're admitting that you're lost and that you can't do this by yourself?"

The man was maddening. "Yes, I'm admitting that."

"Wow." He folded his arms. "I bet this is a first for you."

There was humor in his voice and normally she would have made a smart retort, but she didn't have one available. She felt lost and sad and totally unlike herself. She didn't want to go back to Snowfall Lodge, but she couldn't keep wandering in the forest. "Point me in the right direction and I'll walk home by myself."

"What if you meet another mountain lion?"

"I'll handle it."

He reached out and gently removed her sunglasses. "You've been crying."

"I have not. The cold makes my eyes water."

All traces of humor vanished. He slipped her glasses into his pocket, pulled off his glove and stroked her cheek with his fingers. "You'd rather die than show vulnerability, so it must be something bad. Did something happen? What's wrong?" He studied her face and then glanced back down the trail. "What are you doing all the way out here?"

"I told you. I was walking."

"Because you're upset. You wanted to get away, and you didn't even care where you were walking."

It started to snow again, huge fat flakes that settled on her hood and her jacket.

The world obviously hated her.

He frowned. "Did you know a storm was forecast?"

"I wasn't thinking about the weather. The sky was clear when I left."

"It's not clear now. It's snowing and it's going to get heavier. We should move." Instead of walking back down the path he continued upward.

"This isn't the way to Snowfall Lodge."

"We're not going back to Snowfall Lodge."

"Where are we going?" She stumbled in the deep snow and he paused and held out his hand.

"My home is closer."

She hesitated and then took his hand. It was that or face plant in the deep snow. "You live here? On the trail? There are houses here?"

"Not houses, no. My cabin is a ten-minute walk from here. We can shelter and wait for the storm to clear."

His cabin.

She stopped walking.

She was in the middle of nowhere, with a man she didn't really know. Was this a wise move? Events of the last two months had made her jumpy. Once, she'd moved through life with confidence, but she no longer trusted her judgment. The doubts snaked in from nowhere, making her second-guess every decision. Was this safe? Was she making a mistake? Was she going to look back on this moment and feel like kicking herself for doing something stupid?

She breathed deeply. Sometimes life required you to make a choice between two less than perfect options. A storm was coming in, so trying to find her way back on her own wasn't going to end well. This man knew where they were, and he knew how to find shelter. And he wasn't a stranger. She knew him. He and Dan had been friends forever.

He waited, surprisingly patient. "You're anxious, but you don't need to be."

This was embarrassing. "You think I'm stupid."

"I don't think that."

Still, she felt compelled to explain. "I don't always—" She brushed snow away from her face. "I made a bad judgment a little while ago, and it didn't turn out well."

"And now you don't trust yourself because you're worried you'll misjudge a situation." He let go of her hand and pulled the hood of her jacket farther over her head to keep out the cold and the snow. "This isn't one of those situations, Katie. Everything is going to turn out fine. Providing we move now, before we both get frostbite."

She'd expected sarcasm, or one of their usual barbed

exchanges. She hadn't expected gentleness. He had kind eyes. Why hadn't she seen that before?

"Let's go." This time she took his hand, and she held tightly as the snow deepened and the trail narrowed. The trees were barely visible and the world became nothing but swirling snow. The visibility was reducing by the minute and she shivered, partly from the icy wind, and partly at the thought of what might have happened to her if she hadn't met him on the trail. She would have been caught in this alone and unprotected.

She was grateful for his strong grip and solid presence, but she didn't understand how he could know where he was. The world was a blur. "Are we lost?"

"No. Be careful here—" He held a branch back for her and she stumbled past, conscious of the weight of snow pressing down on the branches above her.

"It's like Narnia." She glanced at him. "From *The Lion, the Witch and the Wardrobe*."

The corners of his mouth flickered. "Just because I live in the mountains doesn't mean I didn't get an education."

"I didn't mean to sound rude. Not everyone reads the same thing, that's all."

"Careful. That sounded almost like an apology."

"It was an apology." She trudged next to him, the deep snow tugging at her boots. Walking was exhausting work, even with snowshoes, and she was relieved when he paused at the edge of the trail and she saw the flicker of lights through the trees.

"We're here." The snow smothered all sound, but the lights kept flickering through the trees and then suddenly the forest opened up and she saw the cabin.

"Oh—" She stopped and stared through the swirl of snowflakes.

"What? It's not fancy like Snowfall Lodge, but it's home." He gave her hand a tug and they walked the last few steps to the cabin.

"It's incredible. Like something out of a fairy tale."

He pushed open the door. "Those are the stories where someone always dies, right? You think there's an evil witch inside who is going to feed you cookies?"

"I hope so. Right now I would wrestle a witch for a cookie." She was surprised by the warmth of his smile. It was impossible not to smile back. She followed him inside, grateful to be out of the snow. "Isn't it lonely living all the way out here in the middle of nowhere?"

"I happen to think this place is somewhere, not nowhere. And I'm happy in my own company." He reached out and helped her unzip her coat. "You're shivering. Sit by the fire and I'll make a hot drink."

She slid off her boots, rubbed her hands with her arms and stepped through an arch into the living area of the cabin. She fell in love instantly. With the thick, soft rug that covered the wooden floor. With the crowded bookshelves that lined three of the walls. A pair of antique skis hung on the wall above the stone fireplace. The place wasn't carefully put together; it was lived in. The books were thumbed, the skis scratched and well used.

"They were my great-grandfather's." Jordan glanced at her as he walked through to the small kitchen. "He'd laugh if he could see what we use now. Your clothes are wet. Do you want to take a shower and change?"

Into what?

"I'm fine, but thanks." She didn't plan on staying long.

"Are you hungry?"

She'd taken pastries to her parents, intending to eat

breakfast with them and it had never happened. "Yes, but I feel guilty suddenly landing on you like this."

"A day ago you would have taken delight in inconveniencing me, so I'm declaring myself officially worried. I'm going to change, then make us something to eat."

He left the room and was back a moment later holding a towel. "Here—at least dry your hair."

She took the towel with a nod of thanks and watched as he left the room. Being with him made her a little uncomfortable. If she hadn't been in a slightly weakened state she might have been more sparky.

She heard the sound of a door opening and closing, and then the sound of the shower running. She tried not to think about how good it would feel to be standing under a jet of hot water.

Absently drying the ends of her hair, she sat down on the sofa.

When he came back into the room he was carrying a tray loaded with food. His hair curled damply over the neck of his thick, cable-knit sweater. "Help yourself."

"Thanks." She tried not to notice the way his jeans fit snugly around his thighs. Her trousers clung, too, but because they were damp and uncomfortable. But what was the point of taking them off when she'd have to put them back on to walk back to the lodge? And then there was the fact that she didn't want to run around his cabin in her underwear.

He put the tray down and took the towel from her. "Sure you don't want a hot shower?"

"I'm fine, thanks. This looks delicious."

There was a fresh loaf and a slab of creamy butter. Plump tomatoes, mountain ham and chunks of cheese.

Trying to ignore her damp clothes, she picked up a plate.

"The bread looks delicious. Did you go to the store this morning?"

"I baked it myself." He smiled at her surprised look. "What? You think all I'm good for is rescuing women from ice and snow?"

"I didn't need rescuing."

"That's more like it. I was missing the argumentative side of your nature." He cut a couple of thick slices of bread, speared one and put it on her plate.

She knew she was being ungracious. Her shoulders sagged. "You're right. I needed help. And I'm grateful. Thank you. Not only for the food, but for rescuing me."

He piled ham and cheese on her plate. "Are you going to tell me what's wrong?"

She buttered the bread, took a bite and moaned with pleasure. "This is *good*. I haven't had freshly baked bread since the last time I was home, which is months." She helped herself to cheese, caught his eye and put the plate down. She wasn't being fair, was she? "I suppose I do owe you an explanation."

He stretched out his legs. "On second thought, it can wait. Eat. Stop worrying for five minutes."

That was easier said than done, but she ate hungrily, knowing she was going to need fuel for the trek back to Snowfall Lodge. "What time does it get dark?"

"In a couple of hours."

She glanced at her watch and realized five hours had passed since she'd left her parents' cabin. "I had no idea it was so late." She scrambled to her feet. "I have to get going."

Jordan sliced off another chunk of cheese and added it to his plate. "Where exactly are you planning on going?"

"Back to Snowfall Lodge. Where else? My family will

be wondering where I am. My parents, particularly my mother, will be worried." And for once she was the cause. She, who tried hard never to worry her parents, had stormed out of their tree house without even allowing them to explain. She'd told no one where she was going because she hadn't known where she was going.

What were they thinking right now? Maybe they'd already called search and rescue.

"They won't be worried. They know you're with me."

"How could they possibly know that?"

He cut more bread. "I texted Dan earlier, when I saw you on the trail. More cheese?"

"No, thanks. You texted him?" She frowned. "I couldn't get a signal."

"It comes and goes. You can relax. No one will be worrying."

"I'd still like to talk to them myself." What exactly had she said to her parents? The whole conversation was a blur. Had she hurt her mother? That was the last thing she wanted, but she'd been so *shocked*. "Can I use your phone?"

"There's no signal in the cabin. You have to walk up the trail a little way, and you can't do that in this weather. Settle down, Katie. We're going to be here awhile, so you might as well calm down."

"You do know that telling someone to 'calm down' is a sure way of making them super stressed and mad, don't you?"

"Yes." He spread butter on the bread. "I like you better when you're mad. All this amenable vulnerability is starting to rattle me."

She had no idea what to say to that. "I have to get back. Even if my parents aren't worried, I still need to talk to my sister. And I need to do it urgently. There are reasons."

"Are those reasons connected with why you were wandering aimlessly through the forest when I found you?"

She moved closer to the fire. "I found out this morning that my parents are getting a divorce."

If he felt any surprise, it didn't show. "And that was a shock?"

"Yes! You've seen the way they are together. They act like teenagers. We all thought they were on a second honeymoon." She saw a faint change in his expression. "You didn't think that?"

He cut another slice of cheese. "I thought they looked like a couple who were trying too hard. Putting on a public display."

She stared at him and then sat back down again. "Damn, you're right. Why didn't I see that?" She put her face in her hands and then let them drop. "Once again I completely misjudged a situation."

"Once again?"

"Never mind." She bit her lip and stared into the fire. "They *were* trying too hard, you're right. It was so unlike them." The fact that she hadn't asked more questions bothered her. She was trained to be observant, and yet she hadn't noticed. "I'm so mad with them. And sad. And—" She glanced at him. "Sorry. You don't need to hear this."

"Talk, Katie." He pushed his plate away. "It sounds as if you need to."

Would talking even help? She wasn't sure. All she knew was that she felt thoroughly miserable. "I can't believe they didn't tell us. And it's a mess. It changes everything. The reason I was lost in the forest was because I overheard them talking and was upset. I went there for breakfast because I wanted to check on my mother, and that's when I heard them discussing their divorce. I walked out. Which probably wasn't my most adult moment, but I wasn't thinking clearly."

"You didn't turn to your sister?"

"I needed time to process the information, and decide how best I could support her."

"What about someone supporting you? Do you ever lean on anyone?"

She frowned. "No. I don't need to."

He watched her for a moment. "So you walked, without really knowing where you were going."

"I was on the main trail, but I was trying to avoid people and took one of the smaller paths. Before I knew it, I was lost. And met a mountain lion—" She curled her legs under her, trying not to think about how badly her walk of distress could have ended. "You probably think I'm unbelievably stupid and irresponsible."

"I think you were upset. Finding out that your parents are breaking up is always a shock."

"It's not as if I'm a toddler or a teenager. It shouldn't matter."

"They're still your parents. It's natural to feel upset. I did when my parents divorced, which made no sense given the way they were together."

His parents were divorced. She wasn't the only person on the planet to have gone through this.

Tears closed in on her again. Crying in front of Jordan? Really? She blinked. "I'm angry with myself for letting my emotions cloud my decision making." The last time had come with serious consequences.

"If you feel like crying, cry. Don't hold back on my account."

"I never cry."

"Are you a robot?"

"Excuse me?"

"Ever since I met you at the airport you've been acting as if someone programmed you. You're angry that emotions affected your decision making, but that makes you human. Frankly I'm relieved to see your emotions are still alive. I was afraid you might have strangled the life out of them, you hold on to them so tightly."

"My job requires me to be in control of my emotions. I can't break down every time I see something sad or stressful."

"You don't need to defend yourself against me. I'm not attacking you."

"It feels that way."

"Because you don't like to admit that you're human like the rest of us. You get angry with yourself when you fall short of what you see as perfect. I bet you grade yourself at the end of every day."

She did exactly that. "You are the most annoying man who ever lived."

"My ex-wife would agree with you."

Her mouth fell open. "You were married?"

"Hard to imagine, I know." He looked tired. "Let's start this again. I was trying to be sympathetic, but I guess I'm better with trees than words. I'm sure you're an excellent doctor, but you're allowed to be off duty once in a while. Give yourself a break, Katie."

She leaned her head against the sofa and stared up at the roof of the cabin. "I'm not an excellent doctor. After this morning, I'm pretty sure I'm not a great daughter either. So that only leaves sister. That, I'm not sure about. I try hard, but I don't think I'm what Rosie wants or needs. Did you know that I went to a nightclub last night? Rosie told me we never have fun, so I went to have fun. I danced."

"That's rare?"

"About as rare as a mountain lion sighting in the middle of Oxford. You should have seen me. I was the life and soul of the place. I'm not saying I didn't have a little help from a couple of margaritas." She eased herself to her feet again. All the muscles in her body ached. "I need to get back. I need to be there for Rosie. Our parents will have told her by now, and she'll be in a state."

"Because of the divorce?"

"Not only that. Rosie has been using my parents' whirlwind courtship and long marriage to convince herself that her marriage to Dan will work. When she discovers they're splitting up, it will change things." She caught his eye. "You think I'm meddling, but you don't know Rosie the way I do. She's impulsive. Spontaneous. I'm not at all sure that she hasn't been swept away with the romance of all this, and that deep down it's not what she wants." On the other hand, could it be that her judgment was as flawed about that as it had been about other things?

"You don't think she should be the one to decide that?"

"I do. But the news about our parents might influence her decision making."

"A marriage is as unique as the two people involved. Your parents' relationship has no relevance to your sister. If she has doubts, she should be discussing them with Dan, not you."

"I've known her for her whole life. He's known her for a couple of months. Never mind—" She held up her hand. "We can agree to disagree. She's my sister. I won't see her hurt."

"Either way, your conversation with your sister is going to have to wait."

And this, of course, was their biggest area of disagreement.

"I know you think you're protecting your friend, but Dan doesn't want to marry a woman who is having doubts. I'm saying that I need to talk to her."

"And I'm saying that your talk will have to wait until tomorrow. You can't leave."

"Of course I'm leaving. What are you suggesting? That I stay the night?"

"I'm not suggesting. I'm telling you that's what's going to happen."

"Are you trying to provoke me? Is this you being all macho again?" She folded her arms. Tapped her foot. Tried to ignore those blue, blue eyes watching her every move. "I'm in your man cave and that's where I'm staying, is that it? Why don't you throw me over your shoulder like you did before and carry me straight to the bedroom? Or maybe you're planning on locking the door and tying me to the sofa?"

They stared at each other for a long moment. Each second blended into the next until she lost track of time. Her heart started to punch hard at her ribs.

They were enveloped by the warm wood of the cabin, the falling snow, the force of the chemistry.

He was the one who eventually broke the tense silence. "When did you last look out of the window?" His voice was gentle. "It's called a blizzard."

"It's snowing, I know, but if you point me in the right direction I'll be fine."

She paced over to the window, sure he was exaggerating. It took one glance for her to realize that he wasn't. At some point during their conversation the storm had worsened. The trees that surrounded the cabin were no longer visible. The world around them had lost all definition. All she could see was a swirling mass of white. She felt a flash of panic. She was trapped. "You must have a snowmobile or something that I could borrow. Something with headlights. Some way of getting back down that trail."

"You'd be dead before you even found the edge of the trail, and you'd put the lives of the search and rescue team at risk. I can't let you do that."

No, of course he couldn't, because as well as having the bluest eyes she'd ever seen, he was also a decent human being.

She felt a rush of desperation. "How long will the storm last?"

"As long as nature intends."

It maddened her that he was so relaxed. "You're enjoying this, aren't you?"

"Don't flatter yourself. So far you've not been great company, although I'm sure that could change if you'd settle down some."

She felt a stab of guilt. Without him, she would have been attacked by a mountain lion, or lost in that snowstorm. "I'm a bit stressed."

"I'm getting that."

"I have to check on Rosie. You must have some way of being able to contact someone. This is an emergency."

"We have different views on what constitutes an emergency."

"We have different views on most things. It's all about perspective. Being snowed in without any form of communication is an emergency in my book."

"Today you're reading from my book, not yours. I keep the cabin well stocked. I have a generator in case the power goes out. I have pretty much everything I need to survive in a situation like this one. You won't starve and you won't freeze."

"How often does this happen?"

"A couple of times every winter. Sometimes more. We're in the mountains."

She rubbed her arms and paced back toward the fire. This whole situation was unreal. What had possessed her to walk into the forest? Why hadn't she gone to the bar at Snowfall Lodge and ordered a large vodka and processed her issues in warmth? "There must be a phone signal somewhere."

He dug his hand into his pocket and pulled out his phone. "Check for yourself. And while you're at it, take a look at the message from Dan."

She took the phone, saw that he had no signal at all, and read his last message to Dan.

Found Katie. Will keep her here with me overnight.

Dan had replied: Thanks. Will let family know.

She was dismayed, but also relieved. At least her mother wouldn't be imagining her dead somewhere in the forest. She handed the phone back. "So what happens now?"

"Well, I don't intend to throw you over my shoulder and carry you to the bedroom, so I guess we need to find another way to pass the time."

She felt awkward. "So—you want to swap life stories?"

"I'm going to throw another couple of logs on the fire. You should sit down and relax."

"You should know by now that I don't know how to relax."

"Try." He walked out of the room and closed the door.

She pulled a face at the door, and then felt childish. If

he hadn't found her when he had, she'd still be on that trail and the blizzard would have wiped out any chance of her finding her way home.

Fretting about her sister, she paced over to his bookshelves. Jordan was obviously a big reader. There was more nonfiction than fiction, a concentration of books about Arctic exploration and climbing. Several shelves were devoted to biographies.

When he walked back into the room a few minutes later, she was curled up on the sofa, her nose deep in a book on Ernest Shackleton's ill-fated trip to Antarctica.

He dropped the logs he was carrying into the basket next to the fire. "That book won't warm you up."

She closed the book. "Judging from your bookshelves, you love the outdoors."

"I do." He carefully added a log to the fire. "I'm guessing you're an indoor, city type."

"I work in the city, and my job is indoors so I don't have much choice about that. Most people don't choose their career based on the environment. But I bet you did."

"I wouldn't want to live anywhere but the mountains."

"You disapprove of me. You think I'm controlling and interfering."

He stood up. "I think you love your sister."

"Are you an only child?"

"Yes."

"And your parents?"

"My mother lives in the next valley. My father's whereabouts are unknown since the divorce."

"He didn't stay in touch with you?" She couldn't imagine not having her dad in her life. "I'm sorry to hear that."

"It's life. Things happen. Are you warm enough?"

"Yes. Thank you. I'm sorry you have an impromptu

house guest." Maybe one day she'd be able to talk about her parents' divorce in the same calm tone he used. To steady herself, she stood up and walked around the room, taking in the small details. The custom-built bookshelves. The beautifully carved wooden staircase that led up to the loft. "This place is amazing. How did they manage to build something like this, right in the middle of the forest?"

He sat down on the sofa. "There were challenges, that's for sure."

She ran her fingers over the handrail. "This is beautiful work."

"Thanks. At the time the work half killed me."

"*You* built this?"

"Why so surprised?"

"Well, because—" she studied the staircase again "—because this is incredible. You have real talent and skill. To be honest I've never even thought about people making staircases."

He smiled. "You're the type of person who lives in a house without wondering who made it."

"I don't have any admiration for the person who built my current place. In fact if I ever met him, I might have to kill him. The boiler gives up every winter, there's damp in my bedroom. The one good thing about my work is that it keeps me from seeing too much of the inside of my house."

"You don't like your work?"

"Yes, but it's tough sometimes." She shut him down, the way she always shut people down when there was something she didn't want to talk about. She'd always handled her problems herself. She was Dr. Kathryn Elizabeth White, and she had life sorted.

At least, she used to. Now she was Dr. Kathryn White,

total mess. She was used to being the calm one, the person who took control. Others looked to her to lead.

Right now she wanted to hide, but Jordan looked at her as if he could see everything.

"You don't strike me as a woman who has a problem dealing with 'tough.'"

"I guess everyone has their limits." She wrapped her arms around herself and walked to the window, turning her back on him. She could hold herself together. It was what she did.

She breathed slowly, her breath forming a cloud on the glass. She resisted the temptation to draw a heart. That would be frivolous, and she wasn't frivolous.

Beyond the window, the snow was falling steadily. There was something about all the pristine white that made the outside world seem distant and unreal. She lived most of her life in a sterile environment. Long corridors. Beeping machines. The pace was always urgent. If there was a word that never appeared in her vocabulary it was *slow*.

"I love this place. And does that surprise me? Yes, it does a little." She leaned her head against the window. The glass was cold. "Maybe I'm learning something new about myself." Lately it was happening a lot. It was like inhabiting the body of a stranger.

"So where do you usually vacation? You strike me as the sort who would choose a city break. Culture. Galleries."

"I don't take vacations."

He frowned. "Never?"

"Hardly ever. I work. If I have the energy to string a sentence together, I see friends or family. If I have a day off I generally spend it sleeping off the previous seven I spent at work. Honestly? I'm not sure I do love my work." The words left her lips without her permission, as if they'd been trapped inside her for too long. "I can't believe I said that aloud."

"Why?"

She turned. "Because saying it makes it real, and the whole idea that I might not like my job terrifies me. I've wanted to be a doctor since I was a little girl. I saw my sister sick, and that was it. Right from that first moment in the hospital I knew that was what I was going to do. I wanted to develop the skills to fix her. To take that scared look off my mother's face. So I worked. I worked so hard. Every exam I took as a child, every book I read. It was a ladder, and I climbed every rung of it and when I got my place at medical school my parents were so proud, and so was I. I was the first doctor in the family."

"Which makes it harder for you to confess that you're not sure you want to carry on with the job. Not easy to walk away from something you've given so much to. Have you talked to them?"

"No. I don't want to worry them."

"Seems to me you spend a lot of time protecting your family, Dr. White." He stood up, walked to the kitchen and returned with a bottle of wine and two glasses. "Drink?"

"I don't usually drink during the day."

"Make an exception. It might do you good to let go of those strict rules you set for yourself. And anyway, it's almost dark." He poured wine into two glasses and held one out to her. "Come and sit down."

She took the glass from him and sat down on the sofa. Leather. Ridiculously comfortable. She sank into it and wondered if a sofa like this would encourage her to relax more.

"It's crazy to even think of giving up something I've trained for my whole life, isn't it?"

"Is it? Are you still enjoying it?"

"It's not as simple as that."

"Life rarely is." He sat down next to her.

"Once you start down a track like medicine, it isn't easy to change to something else. And the longer you stay on that track, the harder it gets. I always wanted to be a doctor. I thought this was it. This is who I am."

"People change. And that's allowed. There's no rule book that says you have to do the same thing your whole life."

"I can't give up."

He looked at her. "Why? Do you have dependents? A couple of kids you've failed to mention?"

"No."

"Loans then. A big mortgage?"

"I'm still renting with a friend. I've been saving for a deposit on my own place, but I'm always too tired to look. And I like complaining about our broken boiler. It's part of my routine."

"So you have a financial buffer."

"I suppose I do." She'd never seen it that way. "But what would I do?" She took a mouthful of wine, and then another. "This is good. I should have had a glass of this to calm myself down this morning instead of going for a walk and getting lost."

"Then you would have said, and done, things you later regretted. Wine for breakfast tends to have that effect on people." There was a smile in his eyes as he toyed with the stem of his glass. "The reason you want to give up—does it have anything to do with the bad judgment you think you made?"

Apart from that appointment with the occupational health doctor, she hadn't talked about it. It surprised her to discover that she wanted to. Maybe it was because Jordan was virtually a stranger. He wasn't Vicky, who was well-meaning but clumsy. Or her parents, whom she needed to protect. She didn't need to think about his feelings. He was as close to an impartial observer as she was going to get.

She took another sip of wine. "Yes, although if I'm honest I think I was starting to have doubts a long time ago but it was easy to talk myself out of those doubts. Medicine is a track you stay on for life. I never considered I might change direction. But when something big like that happens—" she paused "—you start to wonder if you're even good at it. If, maybe, you'd be doing the world a favor by switching to a different job."

"Is this another one of those instances when you're being hard on yourself? Not that I know much about practicing medicine, but I can imagine the answer isn't always clear."

"But every decision you make has consequences." She stared into the fire. "A girl died. Her name was Emma. She was fourteen years old, on a night out with her friends to celebrate her birthday. There were four of them, walking arm in arm, laughing. They were probably talking about clothes, and the boys they liked. The car came from nowhere. He mounted the pavement—sidewalk—"

"I know what a pavement is."

"Yes. Of course you do." Her breathing was fast. "He smashed into Emma, tossed her in the air like a rag doll, drove off without stopping. Can you believe that? He hit a girl, a human being, and didn't stop." Even after everything she'd seen in her life, she couldn't accept what one person would do to another. She glanced at Jordan and saw the shock in his face. The fact that he found it shocking was comforting. He wasn't judging her for not treating it as routine. "She was brought in to us—we had the trauma team ready, surgeons, everyone, but it was—" Why did she find it so hard to talk about it? "Her dad arrived at the hospital. Single dad. Looked after Emma since his wife died. She was his life. His baby. He begged us to save her. Begged us. *Don't let her die, don't let her die.*"

Jordan reached out and removed her wineglass. Then he covered her hand with his. She didn't even feel it. She was back there, with Emma's blood all over her surgical gloves and a father's desperate hope in her hands.

"We couldn't. Her injuries were—catastrophic."

"I'm sorry." His hand tightened and this time she felt the firm pressure of his fingers locked protectively over hers.

"Her father was distraught. I had to tell him. That was my job. And he was on his own. She was all he had in the world. His little girl." His love, and his heartbreak, had been so palpable that she'd lived the agony with him. She'd hated her job then. Hated its limitations. *Her* limitations.

"I can't even imagine how hard that conversation must have been."

"It's part of the job. The worst part." She clung to his hand. "He couldn't make sense of it, and there was nothing much I could say because how can you make sense of something that makes no sense?"

"I'm guessing that was a particularly difficult conversation."

"We were talking, he was asking me for details. The police came. They'd found the car. One of the girls gave a description and—" she closed her eyes "—there was— they were able to identify the car because—DNA—traces of blood—it doesn't matter. You don't want to know." She opened her eyes and looked at him. "You're probably thinking that a good doctor should be able to detach from it."

"I'm not thinking that."

"He was drunk. The man who killed her. They picked

him up and arrested him. I think that tipped the father over the edge. His baby, killed by a guy who should never have got behind the wheel. Senseless. Avoidable." She felt the sympathy coming off Jordan in waves. "The police went to talk to the other girls, I was left alone with her father. I don't know what happened. Everything changed in a moment. He was—deranged with grief. He picked me up by my throat and slammed me against the glass window of the relatives' room. Kept saying, *Why couldn't you save her? Why?*" She'd seen stars, then darkness, then his voice—*call yourself a fucking doctor?* "A nurse came into the room. Tried to pull him off, but he was too strong so she left the room to get help."

"He let you go?"

"The glass behind me shattered. I think it shocked him. He let me go, people arrived to help—that was it."

Jordan swore and ran his hand over his face. If he'd looked shocked before, now he looked shaken. "You were badly hurt?"

"Cut my shoulder. It was nothing. He lost a child. He lost his baby. I wanted them to show that drunken loser her broken body. I wanted him to see what he'd done, but of course that isn't how it works." She picked up her wine again and took a mouthful. Her hand shook. She'd told him. She'd told someone. "When you're a doctor, you try to let things slide off you. If I allow myself to feel, I can't do my job. That doesn't make me callous, it makes me efficient."

"But you're human."

It was a quiet statement of fact and it made her feel better. For the first time in weeks she wondered if, perhaps, she wasn't such a failure. Perhaps she was human.

She drained her glass. "That incident—that death— didn't slide off me. It buried itself in me like a shard of that glass. On the outside, I've healed." They'd removed pieces of glass, stitched her, told her she'd have a scar. She hadn't even cared. Part of her even thought that maybe she deserved it. "I wanted to save his little girl. That's why I became a doctor. I kept wondering if there was more we could have done to save that child, even though I knew there wasn't. My brain keeps thinking of scenarios where she'd been brought in sooner, where the ambulance had taken five minutes instead of ten—I don't even know that would have made a difference, but I haven't been able to let it go."

"Flashbacks?"

"All the time. *If only. What if.* Did we do everything? Did we try everything?"

"Of course the real question is why he had a drink and then got behind the wheel."

"I know you're right. But logic doesn't make me feel better." But Jordan did. He made her feel better, as if his thoughtful, carefully chosen words were stitching together those parts of her that had been torn apart.

"Technically he assaulted you." He let go of her hand and reached for the bottle of wine. "Knowing you, I'm guessing you didn't press charges."

"No. The man was beside himself. He—" Her eyes filled. "It wasn't the first sad, difficult case I've handled. I don't know why that one got to me, but it did. I feel—I've lost confidence."

"Because you couldn't save his daughter?"

"Not only that. I should have seen how upset he was. I should have seen the risk. I misjudged it totally. It could have been one of my staff he attacked, and not me. It could have been worse. And then he would have been dealing with assault charges on top of grief."

He was silent for a moment. "You ask a lot of yourself,

don't you? You're human, Katie. You feel. You have compassion."

"I was so busy feeling, I abandoned judgment. He was distraught, understandably. Angry, too. I probably should have anticipated the possibility of violence."

"You're a mind reader? You're supposed to be able to predict human behavior?"

"To an extent, yes. I'm wondering if I was tired, if I wasn't engaged enough in the job. Or maybe I'm not good enough. And now I can't untangle any of it."

He topped up her glass. "You expect perfect. I bet you were a Grade A student all the way."

She managed a smile. "You're a psychologist?"

"No, but even I can see that you can't apply that kind of grading system to a real life situation. You're struggling to be detached and do your work. And you think, for some reason I'm not understanding, that makes you a bad doctor."

"I think I was doubting myself anyway and this has made me doubt myself even more. I've been on the edge for weeks. I'm on sick leave, did I tell you that? My family don't know. They don't know about any of this. I try never to cause them worry. It's hell for a parent to worry over a child. I saw that anxiety in my mother's face every time Rosie was taken into hospital. I saw it in my father's face."

"So you force yourself to handle your feelings alone. It's okay to lean on people, Katie. Everyone needs support."

She wondered who gave him support. Dan presumably. And other friends. His mother. "I'm going to be fine. Well, apart from the headache I'm going to have tomorrow from all this wine." She breathed and put her glass down. "Who would have thought it would be you who made me feel better?"

A ghost of a smile touched his mouth. "I thought I was the most annoying man who ever lived?"

"Turns out you're not so bad."

His smile vanished and he took her hand again. "It's not your fault, Katie. None of it."

She knew she should probably pull away, but she liked the way his hand felt on hers.

"You don't know that. You can't know."

"I know for sure that if I was ever injured I'd be lucky to have someone like you in charge of my care. You're shivering." Giving her hand a squeeze, he stood up and put another log on the fire. "I'm sure you're a fine doctor, but that doesn't mean you have to carry on doing a job that no longer works for you."

"To give up something I've worked this long and this hard for—" she bit her lip "—that would make me stupid, don't you think?"

He waited until the flames started to lick around the log and then sat back down next to her. "I would have gone with brave."

"Brave?"

"The easy route would be to carry on doing what you're doing and not question it."

"Yes, that's the low risk option."

"To me the risk is that you look back in twenty or thirty years and regret that you spent your life doing something you didn't love. But you could always take a break. Instead of making an immediate decision, take time to think it through."

It was an option she hadn't considered. Her brain had been dealing with all-or-nothing scenarios. Why hadn't she thought of a compromise? Why hadn't she thought of taking a break?

"I can't believe I'm saying this, but you occasionally talk sense, Jordan."

They were sitting close together. The only sound was the crackle of the fire and the howl of the wind beating against the walls of the cabin. What had felt cozy before, now felt intimate. Her leg was pressed against his and she felt a rush of desire that almost knocked her flat.

She glanced at him and then looked away quickly, but not before she'd seen a response in his eyes. "How about you? Do you love what you do?"

"Most days. And then sometimes I'm freezing off my fingers and toes in a blizzard—"

"—and you think you'd like a nice, warm office job?" There was a shift in the atmosphere. She sensed he was aware of it, too.

He gave a soft laugh. "That has never been the dream. I wanted to live and work in the mountains. That was the most important thing for me."

She envied the fact that he was so sure about what he wanted. "I can't believe you built this place." She stood up, drained from her own emotional outpouring and more than a little embarrassed.

"Shaped every log and board myself. Lost most of the skin on my fingers in the process."

She tipped her head back and glanced up at the roof. "You have no TV and no Wi-Fi."

"That's right."

"So how do you occupy yourself?" She turned her head and met his gaze.

Humor glimmered there. "Are you propositioning me, Dr. White?"

Her mouth felt dry. "I might be. Of course it could be the wine." She'd probably read him wrong, in which case her embarrassment was about to triple. "As it doesn't seem that I'll be going anywhere tonight, can I change my mind and use your shower?"

He stood up, too. "I'll fetch you towels and leave some dry clothes on the bed." The bed. One bed. The reality of it struck home. She was snowed in with Jordan.

"Do you have blankets for the sofa?"

"Yes, but I'll take the sofa." He disappeared, and reappeared moments later with towels. "Shower is straightforward."

She stripped off her clothes, put her underwear on the heated towel rail to dry off and stepped under the jets of water. It turned out to be a rainhead shower and she lathered her hair, soaped her body and realized at some point that she felt better than she had in a long time. Maybe it was the wine. Or maybe it was because she'd finally talked about it. Jordan, it turned out, was a good listener.

Wrapped in a towel, she rescued her underwear and stepped across the hall into the bedroom. He'd laid out fleece-lined sweatpants, T-shirts and a sweater.

She tied the waist of the sweatpants and turned up the bottoms so she didn't fall over them. Her own sweater had somehow stayed miraculously dry so she pulled that back on.

She wasn't going to win any fashion contests but at least she was warm and dry.

The bedroom was dominated by the large bed and the fireplace. Like the rest of the cabin, the focus was on the quality of the wood and the workmanship. The floor was heated, the bed draped in soft layers to keep the chill out on cold nights. There were books stacked on both nightstands, and the soft glow of a lamp sent a shaft of light across the bed. It was more rustic than elegant, but there was something about the place that made her want to crawl into that bed, sink against the pile of pillows and read until her eyes drifted shut.

Instead she dried her hair and joined Jordan in the living room. He was seated on the sofa, his legs stretched out as he stared into the fire.

She sat down next to him and picked up her glass. "Now I understand why you've been so protective of Dan. He's like a brother to you. You think of him the same way I think about Rosie."

"Not exactly, but yes—" he shrugged "—there's a similarity."

"Do you think the marriage will work? Are they rushing things?"

"Unlike you, Dr. White, I don't do a risk assessment on every situation, or try to predict every outcome. I tend to let life happen."

"I envy you. But what's your best guess?"

"My marriage lasted six months, so I don't consider myself qualified to comment or advise on anyone else's relationship, but I know what rushing looks like and I don't think I'm seeing it here."

"But your own experience hasn't made you cynical about relationships. If it had, you'd be warning Dan off marriage."

"It was a long time ago. We were eighteen. Dan is nothing like me. And, as I said before, I don't believe one person's relationship experience has relevance to someone else's. We're all different. How about you? Engaged? Seriously involved?"

"Neither. I never get in that deep with people. That time when you threw me over your shoulder? That's the most action I've had in a looooong while."

"Any particular reason for that?"

She sat up and put her glass down on the table. "Yes. I'm a coward. There. I said it. I'm a coward. Every time you love someone you risk getting your heart beaten to a pulp."

"Cheerful thought."

"I'm risk averse. I'm not brave. You were wrong about that. I can't handle that bone-deep anxiety that comes from loving someone. I only understood that recently. So apparently I'm now a psychiatrist as well as a specialist in emergency medicine. The one thing I'm not good at is relationships, but hey we can't all be good at everything."

"But you must date."

"Usually I see a man once. No one calls me a second time."

He raised an eyebrow. "Why?"

"It could be because I always hand out a fake phone number."

His eyes narrowed with amusement. "Dr. White, you shock me."

"I also give them a fake name. And I have no idea why I just told you that."

He started to laugh. "Tell me the name. No. Let me guess—you go by the name of Tiara. Or maybe Aurora. Geranium?"

"Karen."

"No. I don't believe you. No way are you a Karen."

"Karen. Is there any more wine? If this is confession time, I'm going to need it."

"Yes, Karen." He topped up their glasses. "Sorry, but you are not a Karen. Guys in London must be stupid."

"How about you?"

"I don't have a fake name. Never seen the need."

"I mean, do you date? You must have been involved since your wife."

"I guess I'm pretty wary, too."

They were side by side on the sofa, elbows touching, thighs touching. She was acutely conscious of him.

"Jordan?"

"What?"

"The other day, I lied."

"About what?"

"When I told you the earth didn't move." She turned her head and found he was already looking at her. Her stomach curled.

"It moved?"

"It might have moved. A little."

His gaze slid to her mouth. "You're not sure?"

"The wine has made things a little hazy." She inched a little closer. "If I kissed you now, would you be shocked?"

"Try it and I'll let you know."

The last of the daylight was fading and the only light came from the flickering fire. It was as if nothing existed beyond the wooden walls. The cabin had become a cocoon.

She sat up and put her glass down on the table. Then she did the same with his.

"I can see you're focused," he murmured. "A woman on a mission, seeking an answer to the question of whether the earth is going to move."

"This is a controlled, clinical trial. Nothing more." She lowered her mouth toward his and then stopped, her breath mingling with his. "To clarify, if the earth should happen to move, you're not going to ask for my number, are you?"

He slid his hands into her hair, holding her head close to his. "Not much point, since I already know it will be fake. Karen."

Their mouths hadn't touched, but she was excruciatingly

aware of him. Those blue eyes, veiled, watching her. His fingers, strong as steel, gently cupping her face.

The teasing atmosphere had vanished, leaving only delicious tension.

Was this a mistake? She didn't know. All she knew was that she was sick and tired of feeling bad and being with Jordan felt good. Rosie said she'd forgotten how to have fun. She needed to know that part of her was still alive and well.

She moved her mouth even closer to his. "You can still stop me."

"Why would I stop you?"

They moved at the same time, mouths colliding, hands seeking. She'd intended it to be a kiss, that was all. One kiss. But the moment his hand stroked down her back she knew one kiss was never going to be enough.

Without breaking the contact he shifted himself so that he was lying full length on the sofa and she straddled him.

She fumbled with the buttons of his shirt then gave up and tore at it, sending a couple of buttons flying. Later she'd wonder what it was about him that brought out a wildness in her, but right now she wasn't thinking. When she felt him pull at her sweater she raised her arms and he removed it so the only barrier left was silk and lace. His mouth closed over her breast and then he decided to get rid of the silk and lace and her bra went the way of his buttons.

He took her face in his hands and broke the kiss long enough to look at her, and there was a white heat in his eyes that thrilled her.

"What?" She touched her lips to his forehead, his cheek and the roughness of his jaw. "Something wrong?"

"Yes."

She stilled and drew back a little, question in her eyes. He gave a slow smile. "You're still wearing too much."

She smiled back and then shivered as he drew his hands down her bare arms.

"I can fix that." She sat up, still straddling him and felt his hands move to her waist. Her heart thudded harder as he slid his fingers into the waistband of the track pants and pushed them down her thighs. Her underwear followed and she shifted position and let it fall to the floor. She felt his eyes on her but did nothing to cover herself. Instead she reached for the snap of his jeans and eased his zipper down.

"Now I'm intimidated." She saw him frown and gave a soft laugh. "Your abs. You look like you've spent a lifetime in training."

"It's called the hefting-great-tree-trunks workout." He slid his hand behind her head and drew her mouth down to his. "Don't be intimidated. I've been admiring your sexy self since you stalked off that plane looking ready to kill someone."

"The only workout I do is the overworked doctor routine." She teased his lips with her mouth, felt him touch the tip of her tongue with his and then he was kissing her hard and she felt as if she was falling, *falling*...

She felt his hands slide down her back, cup her bottom and then move down her thighs. And all the time he kissed her, and she kissed him back until her whole body ached and she was consumed by the delicious rush of desire. She touched her lips to his jaw, moved lower to his neck and then his chest. And as her mouth seduced, her fingers moved lower, teasing, exploring until his breathing fractured and he closed his hands on her hips and shifted her so that she was underneath him and he was the one on top. It wasn't the easiest of maneuvers on a sofa and she clutched at his shoulders, caught between a moan and a laugh.

"Smooth, huh?" His fingers were in her hair, his mouth

on hers, kisses punctuated by his own muffled laughter. "I might be feeling a little impatient."

"Impatient works for me—" She wriggled under him and curved one of her legs over his. "Whatever you do, don't stop." It was obvious he had no intention of stopping and he moved only to give himself better access to her trembling body. He kissed as if he already knew everything there was to know about her, as if he already knew her secrets and quivering need turned to aching pleasure as he teased her intimately, his fingers slow and sure. She reveled in the warmth of him, the weight of him, pressing her down and then he moved down her body and she let her eyes drift closed, lost in the relentless skill of his mouth and tongue.

The concept of time slid away from her and there was only this moment. This man. And then he moved again and this time reached for something from the pocket of his jeans, now abandoned on the floor.

The interruption frustrated her and she slid her hands over the slope of his shoulders, feeling hard muscle ripple under her fingers. He murmured her name into her hair, whispered what he intended to do to her, and then she felt the heated hot slide of him, the thickened pressure as he surged into her, taking her gasps into his mouth. He slid his hand under her bottom, lifting her into him, each slow, measured thrust taking him deeper. She was overwhelmed by an excitement so intense that she found it hard to draw breath. She tried to say something, to tell him how she felt, but the words wouldn't come and then she stopped thinking and sank into a world of pumping heat and sensation.

She came apart in a rush of delicious spasms and felt him thrust deep as he reached the same peak. They rode it out together, mouths fused, bodies locked, each slick spasm deepening the intimacy.

When her body finally calmed she opened her eyes and stared at the ceiling in stunned disbelief.

Jordan collapsed half on top of her, fighting for breath. "That was—"

"It was."

There was a pause while he tried to recover. Then he lifted his head. "You may not know your own phone number, Karen, but you sure know how to rock a guy's world. For what it's worth, I'd give you a solid grade A."

Grinning, she turned on her side so that she could look at him. How could she feel this comfortable with him? It didn't make sense, but right now she wasn't in the mood to analyze it. "Only an A?"

His eyes drifted shut. "It's the top mark, honey."

"What about an A with a star? Or an A plus?" She slid her hand down his body and heard him groan.

"Seriously?" He opened his eyes and turned his head to look at her. "You expect a lot. I'm beginning to understand why men never call you after that one night. You think it's the fake number that keeps them away, but it's probably that they're lying spent in the gutter somewhere trying to recover enough energy to move."

"What can I say? I've always been an overachiever. Want me to prove it?"

He pulled her closer. "If that's what it takes to boost your confidence, I'm all in, Karen."

Rosie

ROSIE LAY WITH her head on Dan's chest. "That was—" she pressed her mouth to his heated skin "—amazing."

"You're amazing." Dan pulled her closer.

They were in his bedroom at Snowfall Lodge. Catherine was out at a charity carol concert and they'd had the apartment to themselves all evening. Dan had grilled chicken, Rosie had made a salad. They'd shared a bottle of wine and then decided on an early night. Lying in his big king-sized bed, watching the snow falling beyond the window, made her feel more relaxed than she had in days. This was all she'd needed. Time together, away from everyone.

She smiled to herself. "I missed you."

"I missed you, too." He turned on his side and ran his hand slowly down her body. "I was reaching the point where I was going to grab you and ravage you behind the nearest tree house. A quickie."

"Sounds like a quick route to frostbite." She leaned in and kissed him. "I feel a little guilty for being secretly pleased that Katie got herself snowed in with Jordan."

"Why would you feel guilty?"

"Because they don't get on well. She'll be hating every minute. I suppose he will be, too. They irritate each other."

"Not your problem, honey." Dan pulled her closer and she curled her body into his.

"It is my problem. She's my sister. I love her. And I feel bad. I'm the reason she's here, and now she's snowed in with a man she doesn't like. I bet they're going crazy trapped together. What do you think they're doing?"

"Knowing your sister, she's probably grilling Jordan for information on me."

"That's a possibility. She hasn't exactly been relaxed since she arrived. I assure you she's not normally this bad. Has she upset you?"

"No." He stroked her hair gently. "But it hasn't been easy to steal time together, has it? She's done her best to keep us apart."

"Not on purpose." Or was it on purpose? "Katie and I haven't seen each other for a while. Christmas is always a time when we catch up properly. We have a bedroom each at home, but at Christmas we always share and talk until about three in the morning."

"I understand."

"It matters to me that you don't think badly of her. I never really thought about it before, but of course a marriage is more than the joining of two people. It's the blending of friends and family. I want you to love her, too."

"Relax. I like your sister very much."

She was conscious that he'd only spent a few days with Katie and she'd been in her full-on protective sister mode the whole time. And now Rosie was the one feeling protective. Had she been too hard on Katie? She knew how much her sister loved her. Had she been unfair? "Something happened to her, Dan. She has this scar on her shoulder."

"Did you ask her about it?"

"Yes, and she dismissed it. Said it was nothing, but it

didn't look like nothing to me. I wish she'd talk to me. It's annoying. Or maybe *frustrating* is a better word."

"Not everyone likes to talk about their problems."

"But she's my sister. I talk to her all the time. I always have. She's been there for me through thick and thin. Our relationship feels—I don't know." She frowned. "Unbalanced. I'd like to be there for her once in a while."

"I guess in a family we pick our roles, and it isn't easy to change that. She's the big sister. The strong one. She supports you. She's not the one looking for support. Confiding in you would fundamentally change the relationship."

She lifted herself up on her elbow and looked at him. "You're right. That's exactly it."

"And you two have quite an age gap. Seems to me she sees herself almost as a parent."

"She does. And I've probably made it worse by turning to her instead of our parents whenever I had a problem." She thought for a moment. "So is it fixed, this whole 'role' thing? Or can I get her to change?"

"I guess only your sister can decide that."

"I have to persuade her to let me be the big sister for a while?"

He pulled a face. "Can't see that working. The best you can hope for is equals."

"Like twins?"

"That would work." He pulled her down and kissed her. She melted into him and then pulled away.

"What if she and Jordan kill each other in that cabin?"

"They'll be fine."

"If she grills him, is he going to give her anything she can use against you?"

"I guess we'll find out. If she comes roaring in here telling you to run for your life, we'll know Jordan divulged my biggest, darkest secret." He stroked a strand of hair away from her face. "I love you, Rosie White. I love your little anxious frown. I love the way your hair swings when you bounce across a room. I love the way you care so much."

"I have an anxious frown?"

"You do, and it's cute."

"I love you, too." She really did. How could she have doubted it? "It's good to be together like this. It's good to be able to talk." Her doubts had gone, chased away by a quiet evening spent together with the man she loved.

Everything was going to be okay.

He curved his hand around the back of her head and brought her mouth to his. His kiss was gentle, skilled and turned her brain and body to mush. When he lifted his head, she gave a murmur of protest and wriggled closer.

"Dan—"

"You've been a little quiet this week. Not quite yourself."

Her heart pumped a little harder. If she was going to talk to him about her doubts, now was the time. But what was the point? She knew for sure now that this was what she wanted. *He* was what she wanted.

"It's nothing—a combination of my parents being here, my sister overreacting, and the wedding plans."

"It's crazy, isn't it? The dress, the guests, *are these the right flowers*." He cupped her face in his hands and held her gaze. "I get it, baby, I really do. My mother is a little overwhelming, and you have been so patient and kind letting her take over and plan the whole thing."

"It's been so much work for her. I feel guilty about that."

"Don't feel guilty. She loves to be busy. Ever since we lost my father, she's been the same. It's as if she's afraid to slow down. Doing this for us is making her so happy, and you're kind to let her do it. Your kindness is another of the many things I love about you."

What about her indecisiveness? Her tendency to flit from one thing to another? Did he love those things, too?

He did, she told herself. He absolutely did. He'd *seen* that side of her. He'd seen her making up a million excuses to not get out of bed to exercise, he'd seen her dither over a dress choice, and fret over whether she'd picked exactly the right subject to study.

"I find your mum inspirational. She keeps going. Keeps moving forward, even when her heart is broken and her feet must hurt."

"Yeah, that's my mother. But still, it can be exhausting being around her. And I'm going to make you a promise, Mrs. Reynolds."

"I'm not Mrs. Reynolds."

"A couple more days, and you will be." He rolled onto his back, taking her with him. "We're going to keep smiling and get through this wedding, and then next summer I'm taking you to Hawaii. White sand beaches, palm trees, lazy evenings sipping cocktails. It's going to be incredible."

A warm feeling of contentment spread through her.

This, she thought, was true happiness. It was one of those moments you wanted to bottle so that you could bring it out when times were hard.

"I'm still worried there are things we don't know about each other. For example did I ever tell you that when I was eight years old I wanted to be a journalist?"

He pulled her close. "I thought you wanted to be a fairy when you were eight years old."

"I did, but then I found out that being a fairy has lousy career prospects."

"Was that the day before you decided you wanted to be a ballerina?"

She felt a rush of warmth. He *did* know her. "Are you suggesting that I flit from one thing to another?"

"You do, and it's another thing I love about you. Your brain is bursting with possibilities and options."

"That doesn't annoy you?"

"It's fun. And being with you comes with a guarantee that we will never, ever be bored."

"You don't mind that I change my mind?"

"As long as you don't change your mind about me, no."

She felt a flash of guilt and was relieved she hadn't said anything. Yes, she'd had doubts, but they were normal doubts. Marriage was a big step. She was allowed to ponder on it and worry a little. It wasn't something he needed to know.

"I'm glad we're on our own tonight."

"So am I." He trailed slow kisses across her jaw and down her neck.

She closed her eyes.

She'd had relationships before, but nothing that had felt like this. Nothing to anchor her or cause her to question her choices or her plan for the future. But the moment she'd met Dan it had felt different, and not only because he'd managed to get her to actually like exercise. They'd connected in a way that felt fresh and special. Her other relationships had all felt right at the time, but it wasn't until Dan that she'd realized she'd never known intimacy. Being with him had made her more confident and stronger in every way.

Feeling warm, loved, and utterly content with life, she drifted off to sleep and woke only when Dan walked into the room with breakfast on a tray.

"What time is it?" She yawned and sat up in bed.

"Nine o'clock. You were tired."

"And whose fault is that?"

He winked at her and put the tray on her lap. There was a basket of warm, buttery croissants, freshly squeezed juice and coffee.

"You're spoiling me." She patted the bed next to her. "This doesn't look like the usual health food you force down my throat."

"I think we used up enough calories last night for it not to matter." He kissed her, and stole half a croissant. "The good news is that it has stopped snowing and the sun is shining. I had a text from Jordan. He's bringing Katie back now, and they're coming here. Apparently, she wants to talk to you."

Rosie paused with the glass halfway to her mouth. "What about?"

"No idea. Maybe she's decided she can't be maid of honor, if Jordan is best man."

"She'd grit her teeth and get through it. Maybe she wants to explain why she sprinted into the forest by herself, because I can tell you that is definitely out of character." She watched him chew. "Are you going to let me eat any of this breakfast you made for me, or did you make it to torture me?"

"Sharing is caring." Dan tore off another piece of croissant, but this time he fed it to her. "I know there's a lot to do today, but let's try to snatch an hour together this afternoon."

"Sounds good to me." She ate the rest of the croissant, finished her juice and slid out of bed. "If Katie is on her way, I'd better take a shower. I'll drink the coffee in a minute."

Dan followed her to the bathroom. "Need help?"

"No!" She pushed at his chest. "I do not want to be naked when my sister arrives."

Ten minutes later, after the fastest shower on record, she was dressed and in the kitchen.

The moment she saw Katie's face, she knew this wasn't about the wedding.

"You look serious. Were the roads terrible? You're here, so I assume you managed to dig yourselves out?"

"Yes. Jordan handled it." Katie took her hand. "I've been worried about you."

"Me? I'm not the one who was lost in a blizzard. Thank goodness Jordan found you. It all sounded very scary. Why did you go off like that without telling anyone where you were going?"

"I—" Katie held tightly to her hand. "I thought you'd be upset. I was expecting you to have had a sleepless night."

Rosie caught Dan's eye and blushed. "Well, I didn't get that much sleep, but—to be fair we haven't had any time alone lately—"

"I meant because of Mum and Dad."

"What about Mum and Dad?"

Katie stared at her. "You didn't talk to our parents yesterday?"

"We had breakfast. They were worried about you, until the text arrived from Jordan." She smiled at him. "That was thoughtful of you."

"No problem." Jordan was tense. Watchful. His eyes on Katie as she paced over to the window.

"So—how do you feel about what they told you?"

Rosie glanced at Dan, wondering what she'd missed. "What did they tell me? Er—" She thought hard. "They told me they'd had a great time on the sled safari. Apparently Mum fell in love with the lead dog. And they loved the restaurant." She smiled at Dan. "It sounded romantic. We need to do that—"

"Wait," Katie interrupted her. "That's it? You didn't talk about anything else?"

"What else were we supposed to talk about?"

Katie let go of her hand and took a deep breath. "You don't know, do you?"

"Er—if you tell me what it is I'm supposed to know, I can tell you if I know it." She watched as her sister walked to the window and stared out. "Katie? What's wrong?"

Her sister didn't answer.

The silence stretched from seconds to a full minute. Rosie glanced at Dan but he shrugged, clearly as mystified as she was.

Was this to do with Katie's shoulder? The secret she was obviously hiding?

Rosie walked over to her sister and put her hand on her arm. Outside the sky was a clear blue, and the snow sparkled fresh and untouched.

"I love you. You can tell me anything, you know that don't you?"

Her sister swallowed. "I—I thought they would have told you. I didn't realize I was going to have to do it."

"Do what? Told me what?"

"They're getting a divorce, Rosie." Katie's voice was so soft the words were barely audible.

"What?"

"A divorce." Katie rubbed her fingers over her forehead and only now did Rosie see how tired she looked. "I thought they would have told you yesterday."

Rosie thought back to the interactions she'd had with her parents. They'd been concerned about Katie. She'd seen her father take her mother's hand and squeeze it. He'd been reassuring and loving.

"You're wrong. They love each other. They're happily married. This last few days they've been behaving like honeymooners."

"It was all a lie. An act. They've been living apart for months." Katie sounded exhausted. "They're not happily married."

"I don't know why you would think that. It's insane." Rosie felt Dan slide his arm around her shoulders, offering comfort. Why did he think she needed comfort? "It's some sort of misunderstanding."

"I know this is upsetting and the timing sucks, which is presumably why they hid it from you yesterday. They're planning on carrying this charade through to the end."

"They *told* you they're getting a divorce?"

"I overheard them talking about it yesterday. Learned a lesson never to drop in on someone unannounced. They were so deep in a divorce discussion they didn't even hear me arrive."

"Maybe they were talking about someone else's divorce."

"Think, Rosie." There was a note of exasperation in Katie's voice. "Even you admit they've been behaving oddly since they got here."

"They're demonstrative, but it's nice."

"It's fake. It's an act especially for us."

Rosie felt wobbly. "I don't believe you."

"I honestly wish it wasn't true, but it is and as you don't believe me there's only one way to deal with this." Katie took her hand and pulled her toward the door.

"Where are we going?"

"To see our parents. If we show up unannounced they won't have time to prepare for us. It's time they told you the truth."

Katie

DRIVEN BY FRUSTRATION, Katie strode along the snowy path that led to the tree house. If she'd been walking in heels on a marble floor her footsteps would have been loud and purposeful. Heads would have turned, and people would have speculated. As it was, the snow muffled the emotion that flowed into each stride. The few birds searching vainly for food paid little attention.

"Katie!" Rosie's voice came from behind her. "Slow down. Better still, stop."

The sun was shining and the only reminder of the blizzard was the fresh layer of snow coating the trees and catching the light with blinding beauty.

For once, Katie didn't notice the beauty. How could her parents not have told Rosie the truth? Why was she the one who'd had to deliver the news and hurt her sister? They'd had all day to do it and yet, apparently, they'd kept up their "second honeymoon" act, and even gone out to dinner again the night before. It seemed that they were determined to continue their deception. Not only that, but they now expected Katie to join in and play her part. And that wasn't going to happen. No way. It was wrong. Why couldn't they be open and honest?

She ignored the tiny voice in her head that reminded her she hadn't been open and honest with her family, either. That was different. Totally different.

Avoiding that thought, she stomped up the steps to the tree house, holding tight to the wooden rail so she didn't slip. That rail made her think of Jordan, and the night they'd shared.

He'd been quiet on the drive over to the lodge. She'd been equally quiet. She'd had no idea what to say after a night like the one they'd shared. They were intimate strangers.

Ignoring her own inner turmoil, she opened the door of her parents' tree house.

It was ten in the morning, but there were no signs of life.

Had they already gone out somewhere? Another bonding activity?

She stepped inside and tugged off her boots. Moments later, Rosie appeared, breathless and pink-cheeked. Dan and Jordan were with her.

Katie hadn't expected them to come, too, but maybe it was better that everyone found out the truth at the same time. It would save repeated explanations.

The living room looked faintly abandoned. A stray cushion lay on the floor forgotten. There were no blankets on the sofa. No sign that this had provided a bed for her father.

The lights on the Christmas tree twinkled, and she wondered how it could still look so festive and cheerful. Surely some of the gloom and sadness should have dimmed those lights?

On the table stood an empty bottle of wine and two glasses.

She turned away and something on the floor caught her eye. A wisp of fabric. A bra. A lacy, silky confection that looked as if it had been torn off and abandoned in the heat of the moment. Katie stared at it, and then at the trail of clothes that marked a path to the bedroom. The door was open a crack, as if the last person to walk through it had been too distracted to close it.

And then she heard sounds. A low moan.

Her brain froze and all the words she'd gathered up ready to speak froze right along with it.

Rosie put a hand on her arm. "We need to get out of here." She whispered the words and glanced toward the bedroom door.

Katie shook her off. Had their parents heard them arrive? Was this another of their fake togetherness scenes?

"We're talking to them now."

"What? No!" Rosie's face flamed. "I absolutely do not want to walk in on our parents having sex!"

"They're not having sex. They're pretending to have sex." Katie walked across the room, pushed open the door and heard her mother's horrified gasp.

"Nick! Oh God—" She grabbed at the covers, pulling them high.

Katie heard her father swear for possibly the first time in her life.

"We're so sorry," Rosie blurted out, yanking at Katie's sleeve. "We'll come back later."

"No." Katie had never been more confused in her life. "I don't understand. You're getting a divorce."

"Katie—" Still clutching the sheets with one hand, her mother held out her other hand. "I know how upset you were yesterday. We tried calling you."

"There was no signal." And she'd been with Jordan, and—

She wasn't going to think about that now.

Her father sat up, keeping the sheets carefully across his chest. "We were worried."

"We're so sorry." Rosie tugged at Katie again. *"Please—"*

Katie didn't budge. She was so frustrated by the situation she felt as if she might explode. "You can't do this! You have to be honest. We're adults."

"Katie—" Her mother frantically smoothed her hair. "Your father and I need to talk to you. Perhaps that's best done alone."

"Of course." Rosie turned away, relieved, but Katie grabbed her.

"No." She focused on her parents. "You have to be honest. Rosie keeps using the two of you as reassurance that her own relationship will work."

Rosie gave a horrified squeak, but Katie plowed on.

"She's been having doubts and she's handling those doubts by telling herself that because you met and married in a whirlwind, as she plans to do, and are still happily married after thirty-five years, that means her relationship is going to be okay, too. So you need to tell her the truth. You need to tell her you're getting a divorce, so she can figure out what that means for her own feelings and her own relationship."

There was a taut, agonizing silence. She realized that her parents weren't looking at her, they were looking at Rosie.

So was Dan.

He was staring at Rosie as if he'd never seen her before. "You've been having doubts?"

"No!" Rosie sounded horrified. "I mean maybe a few, but that's natural, and—it was nothing."

"Oh sweetheart." Their mother's face was a picture of concern. "You should have said something. Why didn't you?"

"Good question." Dan's voice was thickened by emotion. "Why didn't you?"

Rosie whirled on her sister. "What have you *done*?"

What had she done?

Katie started to shake. "I didn't—I thought you should know the truth about our parents, that's all."

Her mother had the sheet clutched tightly across her breasts. "We're not getting a divorce, Katie."

"But—"

"Katie—" This time it was her father who spoke. "Your mother is telling the truth. We're not getting a divorce."

"But yesterday—I overheard—"

"Your mother and I were working through some issues, that's true, but after you walked out yesterday we spent the day talking and figuring out some things we probably should have figured out a long time ago."

Katie shook her head in confusion. "You've been living apart since the summer."

"And that's given us the space we needed to see our relationship through fresh eyes."

Rosie gasped. "Since the summer? And you never said anything to us?"

Katie had no idea what to say, either. This was why she was no good at relationships. It was all too confusing. "When you arrived here, you were pretending. This whole second honeymoon thing was an act."

Her parents exchanged looks.

"That's true," Maggie said, "but somehow in the middle of all that pretending, we found each other again. We rediscovered all the things we love about each other. We've had fun. We've enjoyed spending time together. We won't be getting a divorce. We intended to talk to you both about it this morning."

"But we barged in on you, because Katie was so sure she had the evidence she needed to stop my wedding." Rosie's cheeks were scarlet as she turned to her sister. "From the moment you arrived here, that's what you've been trying to do."

"No. I mean, yes, perhaps, a little—" Katie sank down onto a chair. "I wanted to make sure you knew what you were doing, that's all."

"All?" Tears slid down Rosie's cheeks. "You interrogated Dan, and you interrogated me, and not only that but you kept us apart on purpose. It's been hard for us to find time to be together. That's probably why Jordan kept you in his cabin last night!"

Jordan frowned. "Rosie—"

"There was a blizzard," Katie said. "We were snowed in."

"Yes, there was a blizzard, but Jordan has all the gear up there. He works in the forest. It's his job. His life. Do you honestly think he couldn't have got you out if he'd wanted to?"

Was that true? No, it couldn't be true. He wouldn't have done that. Their night together had been the one authentic thing that had happened to her lately. She looked at Jordan, expecting him to deny it and saw instantly that there was nothing to deny. "It's true? You could have got us out?"

He hesitated. "Technically, yes, but that wasn't what—"

"It doesn't matter." This had to be one of the most humiliating moments of her life. Fortunately she'd had plenty of experience of stifling uncomfortable emotions. She turned back to Rosie. "I was worried about you. You were using our parents' marriage as inspiration. You needed to know about the divorce."

"So they hit a rough patch," Rosie said. "It happens. They've worked through it. If anything, I'm more inspired than ever." She turned to Dan. "I'm sorry about my sister, but you have to believe I love you. I really do."

"I'm not worried about your sister. I'm worried that you've been having doubts and didn't talk to me. Why not?"

"I did try to mention it a few times but I couldn't find the right words. And honestly, I wasn't even sure they were real doubts. I'm a doubty sort of person, and you *know* this. I change my mind about what I want for breakfast, what I want to wear—"

"And who you want to marry." Dan was white-faced and when Rosie took a step toward him, he took a step back.

Jordan spoke for the first time. "I think we should leave Maggie and Nick to get dressed, and meet up in Snowfall Lodge at lunchtime. Dan and Rosie, go and talk this through on your own. You don't need an audience."

Rosie's eyes were glistening. "Dan, please—"

"Hello? Anyone around?" Catherine's voice sang out from the living room. "The sun is shining, the mountains look like something from a Christmas card, I have freshly baked pastries and a plan for a perfect romantic day for the two of you. Oh—" She stopped as she saw the crowd gathered in the doorway of the bedroom. "I'm sorry. I didn't know you had company."

"Come in," Nick said dryly. "It's a free-for-all."

Catherine looked bemused. "What's going on?" She saw the tears on Rosie's face and immediately went to her. "Oh honey, what's wrong?"

She was kind, Katie thought, her brain and body numb. And she seemed to genuinely care about Rosie.

"Is it something to do with the wedding? Because all you have to do is tell me, and we'll fix it right away."

"There's nothing to fix." Dan pushed past his mother, snatching his coat on the way. "There isn't going to be a wedding."

Maggie

Maggie lay on the bed, stunned, the covers pulled up to her chin. "I can't believe that happened."

"Neither can I." Nick plumped the pillows and made himself more comfortable. "Ironic, really. The girls live at home with us for a couple of decades and never walk in on us having sex, and here we are thousands of miles from home and suddenly we have the entire family, plus a bunch of almost strangers, in our bedroom. It's the only time I've been grateful you always insist on having sex under the covers."

"That's what you're dwelling on? The fact that the girls walked in on us having sex?" She sat up, still clutching those covers. "Nick, this is serious. Rosie looked devastated."

"Katie looked worse."

Maggie had been so horrified at being caught naked in bed by her children, that she hadn't paid too much attention to the finer nuances of body language. "After what she heard yesterday, it must seem very confusing for her. I can see why she was reluctant to believe us, but did she really think we'd go as far as faking sex?"

"Well, to be fair we've been faking everything else, Mags, so we can't really blame her for not trusting us."

"I know." She covered her face with her hands and then let them drop. "I have messed this up. I was so busy thinking about us, and keeping up a convincing act, that I didn't focus on the girls. Rosie was having doubts. Our baby was having doubts and I didn't even notice? And I've been worried about Katie for a while. I should have pushed harder. Spent more time with her. Parenting is *so hard*, and it never gets easier. I wanted so badly to be a better mother than my own."

"Oh believe me, sweetheart, you aced that one." He leaned closer and kissed her. "You can't force someone to talk to you, Mags. And as you say, we were rather focused on our own relationship. Which made a change if I'm honest."

She felt a stab of guilt.

"You're right, and we do need to focus on ourselves, but how do we do that when our girls are both going through such a bad time?" She flopped back down on the bed, trying to relax the tight knot in her stomach. "How are we going to fix this? The wedding is in two days."

"From what Dan said, there isn't going to be a wedding."

"You think he meant that?" A few weeks ago that might have come as a relief to Maggie, but not now.

She felt responsible. Admittedly it had been a somewhat tortuous chain of events, but still she knew the blame lay with her. "Why would Katie tell us that Rosie was having doubts about Dan, while Dan was standing there?" Maggie tried to shake off her own embarrassment and examine the facts. "What was she thinking? Unless Rosie and Dan had already discussed it."

"He looked as shocked as we were. And I'm not sure

Katie was thinking. Which isn't like her. Katie always thinks everything through."

"She gets that from me. You and Rosie are the impulsive ones." She glanced at him. "Sorry. That sounded like a criticism and I didn't mean it to. I'm—panicking, I suppose. This whole situation has turned into a nightmare." Grabbing her robe she contorted herself to put it on under the covers and then slid out of bed.

"Not the whole situation." Nick grabbed her hand and tugged her down next to him. "Last night was—"

"It *was*." She leaned in and kissed him, her heart full, but her mind somewhere else. "And I know we still have so much to talk about and work through, but our priority right now has to be our girls. And I don't even know which one of them to go to first."

"Maybe they don't need us wading in. They need space. You heard Katie. They're adults. They want to be treated as adults, and that means leaving them to sort out their own problems."

"Leave them? You mean not go to them?"

"Our role is to support, Mags, not fix."

"But they're both hurting." And she'd never grown used to the fact that when her children hurt, she hurt, too. It was as if there was a physical connection. How could she not go to them at a time like this? "And what did Rosie mean about Jordan intentionally keeping Katie away for the night so that she and Dan could be together?"

"I don't know. There have obviously been things going on between the girls that we don't know about."

"Now I think about it, you're right. Katie looked upset. Do you think something happened between her and Jordan?"

"Jordan? What would happen between her and Jordan?"

"Oh Nick." Maggie shook her head. "You must have picked up the tension between them."

"Exactly. Tension. So nothing is likely to have happened, is it? Except that if he did keep her there on purpose then the guy will probably live to regret it."

"How can someone so smart be so clueless?"

"Jordan?"

"You! I don't mean angry tension, I mean sexual tension. Are you seriously telling me you haven't picked up the chemistry between them?"

"Chemistry?"

"Let's just say they're not indifferent to each other, and I can't believe you haven't noticed that."

"What can I say? My brain has been full of my own romantic issues, and intrigue is definitely not my area of expertise. I need coffee. Maybe then I'll be able to process this. Go to the girls." He sounded tired. "I know you want to, and it's fine." He walked to the kitchen and she watched him go, torn in two. How many times had she put the girls first? The answer was every time. She hadn't nurtured her marriage, assuming with a flagrant carelessness that it didn't need tending and would be fine. Neglected, it had withered, but apparently it hadn't died. New shoots were visible, and there was definitely life in their relationship. But not if they were simply going to carry on as they had before.

She wanted to go to the girls. She wanted to dress their wounds, hug them tightly and help them heal. She could tell herself that this was a crisis moment, that they needed her now, and that next time she'd take a step back. But there would always be a crisis, wouldn't there? That was life. There were always explosions, whichever path you walked.

And Nick was right. They were adults now. They needed

to find a way to deal with their own problems. If they wanted to come to her, they'd come to her.

She slid out of bed, ignoring the almost physical pull to go to her children.

And it wasn't only the girls of course. What about Catherine? She'd put so much effort into making this the perfect wedding and right now it didn't look as if it would happen.

She reached for her phone and then put it down again. Catherine probably needed time to process what had happened, too. It would be fine to call later.

She slipped on a robe and walked to the living room.

"You're right, this time I'm putting us first. If the girls want us, they can call."

He paused, a mug in one hand and the jug of coffee in the other. "I understand if you want to go to them, Mags."

"I don't." She was sure of it now. "They're important, but we're equally important. I don't want to lose this, Nick. I'm not even sure what 'this' is, but I want to give it the attention it deserves." She needed to know she'd done everything she could to hold on to this marriage that was so precious to her. How could she have let something so special go without a fight? How *could* she?

He held her gaze and she saw something in his eyes she hadn't seen in a long time. Something that was hers alone. Something that no one else could share. After so many months unable to reconnect with the man she'd married, she'd finally found him. And she wasn't letting him go.

"I'll take a shower while you're making coffee." She turned and walked into the bathroom, wondering how it was possible to feel light and heavy at the same time. She was worried about the girls, but that didn't take away the memory of the night before and the hope for the future that was wrapping itself around her like a hug.

Her feet were bare and she pressed them into the heated floor. Maybe they needed to refit the bathroom in Honeysuckle Cottage.

She realized that she and Nick hadn't even mentioned the house in their discussions. There were so many things they hadn't talked about. But it would happen, she knew it would. This wasn't an ending, it was a new beginning.

Katie walking in when they'd been talking about divorce had shaken them both.

There had been a moment of panic. A moment when both of them had focused on their eldest daughter and her feelings. After they'd realized she wasn't going to pick up her phone and talk to them, they'd been forced to talk to each other. Not a fake interchange, like the ones they'd been having since they'd stepped off the plane in Denver, but an honest discussion. They'd talked about the day he'd made the decision to move out, a decision she hadn't challenged, and they'd traced the loose thread of their relationship back until they could identify when the first holes had appeared in the fabric of their marriage. They saw that a series of wrong choices had brought them here, choices that at the time had seemed so trivial they hadn't even registered. The late-night tea she'd refused when he'd returned from one of his trips, because she was tired. His decision to sleep in the spare room when she was up and down in the night with Rosie. The dinners out she'd refused because she was afraid to leave Rosie with a babysitter. The time they'd synchronized calendars to make sure all home and family obligations were covered, but hadn't put in time for themselves. Each seemingly insignificant choice had eroded their time together. At some point he'd taken her hand, and still they'd talked. She acknowledged that her life had become consumed by the girls, that Rosie's frequent trips to the hospital had caused her more anxiety than she'd admitted. He'd confessed to guilt that she'd handled that anxiety alone, and he'd acknowledged that he'd let work overwhelm family life. The touching, the physical contact, had been gradual. A lacing of fingers, a hand on a thigh, an arm around a shoulder and then finally the connection had become more intimate. Lips, hands, bodies. The past had retreated as they'd focused on the moment and gradually stitched together all the threads that had been untangled. Under the sparkle of Christmas tree lights, he'd led her to the bedroom, undressing her on the way. The way he'd touched her had felt familiar and yet new.

Would that even have happened if Katie hadn't walked in when she did and overheard them talking?

Maggie turned on the shower and stepped under the jets of water.

She was anxious and a little sad, so how could she also be feeling happy?

She was thinking about Nick's hands on her body when she heard a sound and then felt his actual hands on her body.

She gasped, opened her eyes and almost drowned. "What? You're supposed to be making coffee."

He flashed her a smile and wiped the water from her face. "Coffee is brewing. No sense in taking two showers. This is the eco version."

"It's daylight."

"Why do you think I'm here? You look cute when you're wet, have I told you that?"

"Cute is for twenty-year-olds." She felt ridiculously self-conscious.

"I can promise you it isn't." He lowered his head and kissed her neck and then her shoulder.

Her heart kicked up a few paces, but this time reality

kept her feet on solid ground. "Nick, we can't—the girls—seriously—after what just happened?"

"There was no lock on the bedroom door, but luckily for me—and you—there is a great lock on the bathroom door. And I used it. Relax." His mouth slid to her shoulder and she felt her legs go weak.

"If I relax, I drown. I'm too old to have sex in a shower."

"Where is this 'I'm too old' coming from?"

"Maybe from the fact that I *am* too old? And so are you."

"Now you've bruised my ego." He kissed her slowly, deliberately, taking his time. "I'm going to have to prove you wrong."

"We've never had sex in a shower."

"Because the bathroom in Honeysuckle Cottage has a sloping roof and sex in the shower would most likely result in a serious head injury, but *this* shower—" He lifted her easily and she gasped and wrapped her legs around him.

"What are you doing?"

"I'm sweeping you off your feet. Enjoying my second honeymoon. And I have to say, Mrs. White, so far it's been as much fun as the first."

"You can't do this!" She squirmed self-consciously. "I'm too heavy."

"Are you saying I'm feeble? You're denigrating my manhood?"

"No, I'm saying I weigh too much for you to pick up! And I don't want to have to call for help because you've slipped a disc and are lying naked in a shower. Our daughters would never speak to us again, that's if they still are, and as for Catherine—goodness knows what Catherine thinks of us. This is crazy, Nick. Put me down."

"Haven't you heard?" He kissed the corner of her mouth. "The couple who half kill themselves in the shower together, stay together. It's a bonding activity recommended by therapists the world over."

"That's not the version I know. Nick, I'm serious. We can't—"

He kissed her.

His mouth was gentle on hers, coaxing her lips apart. She felt the erotic slide of his tongue and the knowing stroke of his fingers over her bare skin.

She melted into him, shocked by the intensity of her own response.

Married couples didn't feel this way, did they? That frantic, heart pumping, heat-in-the-belly type of excitement came with youth and unfamiliarity. It didn't come after two children and more than thirty years of shared history.

Or maybe it did. He *knew* her. He knew exactly how to touch her, *where* to touch her. There was no fumbling, or clumsy exploration. Just an urgency she didn't recognize, a desperation neither of them had felt in a long time. They'd been apart for months, and before that they'd been sleeping in separate rooms. In some ways this *was* new.

She kissed him back and slid her hands over his shoulders. She'd always loved his shoulders. She'd loved to sleep with her cheek pressed against his chest, she'd loved watching him sweep the girls off their feet and gallop around the garden with them riding those shoulders. Years had passed, but those shoulders were still broad, and still strong. There was a physical aspect to his job, and he kept himself fit.

She felt his muscles flex as he lowered her, not because he couldn't hold her, but because he wanted full access to her body. As he closed his mouth over her breast she gasped and almost inhaled the water still raining down on them.

He shifted her slightly so that the water was away from her face, and then slowly worked his way down her body.

Those hands had lost none of their skill. Neither had his mouth. And she knew, deep in her heart, that he wasn't only showing her that he knew how to give her pleasure, he was showing her that he loved her. Every stroke, every intimate touch, sent pleasure surging through her body and when he finally entered her she cried out his name and held on to him. He set the rhythm, but she followed, matching him, taking him until the sensation built to almost unbearable levels and they both tipped over the edge together.

Afterward neither of them moved. They stayed locked together in the steamy warmth of the shower.

Her breathing and her heart were in a race. She leaned her head against his chest, and felt the answering thump of his heart. She felt his hand curve around the back of her head, cradling her there.

"I can't believe I almost lost you." His tone was raw. "I can't believe I almost let you go. I love you, Maggie. God, I love you so much."

She squeezed her eyes tightly shut, afraid to open them in case the moment disappeared.

She wanted to speak, but she couldn't, and still his arms stayed locked around her.

"I know we still have things to talk about." He eased her away from him and smoothed her wet hair back from her face. "Many things. But I need to know we're going to find a way. I need to know that you *want* to find a way. Will you look for a way with me?"

"Yes." She placed her palm on his jaw, feeling the scrape of stubble. "We'll find a way. I want that, too."

She wasn't going to let them drift apart again.

She wasn't going to let that happen.

"We should probably get dressed." He pressed a kiss

against her hair. "In case we have more visitors. It seems to happen a lot."

"Good plan. Pass me a towel."

"First, let me look at you. Do you know how long it is since I've seen you naked?"

She was conscious of the beam of sunlight. "Nick—"

"No more undressing in the bathroom and sex in the dark. Promise me."

"I'm not comfortable walking round naked. I have stretch marks. This body has given birth to two children."

"Our children." He murmured the words against her mouth, and then her neck as he inhaled the scent of her. "We made those children together. And I love your body. I think I already proved that given that I had the staying power of an adolescent."

She leaned her forehead against his chest. "This feels strange. Different. How can it feel different? How can I feel shy with you when we've known each other for so long?"

"I don't know." He cradled her close. "Maybe it's because we're starting again. Maybe it *should* feel different. We want it to be different."

"I feel guilty that we lied to the children, but part of me is wondering whether this would have happened if we hadn't come here and spent this time together."

"I like to think it would, but you're right that it brought us together. That and your alcohol moment."

"You're never going to let me forget that, are you?"

"Never. In fact if we were to renew our vows I'd make you promise to consume a bottle of champagne a night for as long as we both shall live."

"We probably wouldn't live that long if we drank a bottle of champagne a night." It scared her to think that they might not have reached this point without Rosie's wedding.

And now it seemed the wedding might be canceled. Why was life always so complicated? "We need to get dressed."

"Yes." He kissed her and stepped out of the shower. He knotted a towel around his waist and passed one to her. "I'll pour coffee."

"I would kill for coffee, but get dressed first. We've subjected our kids to enough trauma."

He flexed his biceps. "You don't think it would do them good to see their father in such great physical shape?"

"Get dressed, Professor." She sent him a look and he gave her that same cheeky lopsided grin that she'd fallen in love with all those years before.

He left the bathroom and Maggie wrapped the towel around herself and gazed out the window into the snowy forest.

She wasn't getting a divorce. She and Nick were staying married.

Thank you, thank you, thank you.

She hadn't even realized this was the outcome she'd wanted, but now she realized she'd wanted it the whole time. She'd missed him. Not the dry, sterile, polite relationship they'd had for the past couple of years, but the warmth, friendship and passion they'd shared before that.

She brushed at her tears impatiently. Why was she crying? She didn't even know. Relief, perhaps. Or maybe it was the release of so much emotional and physical tension. Or maybe it was anxiety about her children.

Weak with gratitude, she dried her hair, dressed quickly and joined Nick in the kitchen.

"So what do we do?" She took the coffee from him and curled her hands around the mug.

"We're going to start by talking about your work, and what you want to do when we get home."

"I've already told you, I'm too old. And I don't have the right training."

"We can fix the training part. And I don't think age plays a part."

"I think it does. I can't give up secure employment, spend all that money and time on training, and then find no one will give me a job."

"They might give you a job once you have the training."

"But we don't know."

"There are no certainties in life, but one thing I know for sure is that we need to make some changes. And you should do something you want to do for a change, no compromises. No making a choice that fits with the family."

"You're telling me to be selfish."

"Doing something for yourself doesn't make you selfish. My students tell me it's called *self-care*. Are you hungry? I could fry bacon."

"You won't keep that hot body if you keep eating bacon, Professor."

"I need to keep my strength up, to keep you satisfied." He topped up her coffee. "Talking of which, we should probably pick your underwear up from the floor."

"My—" She turned her head and gasped. "They must have seen it when they walked in."

"You'd think it might have given them a clue. Good job Katie is a doctor and not a detective. Criminals would be able to act without fear of reprisals."

"This is not funny." She scurried across the room and scooped up their discarded clothes. "It is a little strange that she didn't realize what was going on."

"She thought we were faking it. She probably thought those sounds of utter bliss that came from your mouth were exaggerated for effect, whereas in fact it was a response to my sexual prowess."

She flung her bra at him and he caught it one-handed.

She felt strange—a combination of giddy teenager and anxious mother. She knew life did that—it dished out good and bad on the same plate and you were expected to eat it all up. She knew from experience that it was possible to smile and cry at the same time. To grieve and rejoice in the same breath.

Her phone pinged and she whirled around, searching for it.

"That will be one of the girls. Where did I leave it?"

"Try looking down the back of the sofa."

She rummaged and found it. "It's not the girls. It's Catherine. She's inviting me to join her for breakfast in town. You're invited."

"I don't know. I can excavate ancient remains, but digging my way out of emotional situations is different. That's your territory."

"It's obviously a crisis meeting—she wants to talk about the wedding. Perhaps it would be easier if I went on my own. But I wanted to talk to the girls."

"Rosie will be talking to Dan. At least, I hope she will."

"But Katie—what about Katie?"

"I'll go and find her. Talk to her."

"You? But you never—" She bit her lip. "Sorry. That's probably on the list of things you're not supposed to say to your partner, isn't it? *You never*, along with *you always*. I didn't mean it that way, it's just that I'm the one that usually talks to the girls when there's a problem."

"I know, and I think it's time that changed, don't you? I may not have had as much practice as you, and no doubt

I'll say totally the wrong thing, but at least they'll know I care. I want them to know that."

"Oh Nick, they know you care—"

"I've always taken the easy parts of parenting and left you with the hard parts. I'm having that conversation with Katie. And if she yells, at least she'll be yelling at me."

Maybe Maggie was partly responsible for the fact that the girls turned to her. She'd always assumed she'd be better at it. She'd taken that role without considering whether it was a role that should be shared.

"You're right, you should do it. Let her talk, Nick. Don't try to fix it."

"Should I punch Jordan?"

"You've never punched anyone in your life. Why on earth would you punch poor Jordan?"

"For hurting my daughter." There was a fierce look in his eyes that she couldn't remember seeing before.

"We don't know he hurt her." She softened. "You're in good shape, Nick, but I think he might get the better of you. And then there's the fact that I think Katie likes him. If it turns out that we've wrecked Rosie's relationship, I'd rather we didn't also wreck Katie's. No, a conversation with your daughter is all that's needed. One where she does most of the talking, and you do the listening."

"I can do that. Good luck with Catherine."

"I don't know which part I'm dreading most. Admitting our relationship was fake, or explaining why Dan stormed out and canceled the wedding."

"Our relationship isn't fake anymore. Maybe you don't have to mention it."

"If I don't tell her that we were pretending, none of the rest of it makes sense." She rubbed her fingers over her forehead. "No, I have to tell the truth. It's the only way we're going to stand a chance of unraveling this." She sighed. "I was dreading meeting her, I felt so intimidated, but the truth is I like Catherine. I like her a lot."

"I like her, too. Go and talk to her. I'll clear up here and then find Katie."

Maggie bundled up and trudged through the snow to the trail that led to Snowfall Lodge.

When she saw Catherine waiting in the car, she felt a flicker of nerves.

She knew how much work Catherine had put into planning this wedding, and how badly she wanted it to go ahead. She was probably furious with Maggie.

Oh well—

Bracing herself for a difficult conversation, she opened the car door and slid inside.

Catherine looked immaculate as ever, her eyes shielded by oversize sunglasses.

"I'm so happy you've come." She waited for Maggie to fasten her seat belt and then headed toward town. "We have to talk."

"I know." Maggie leaned her head back against the seat. "Catherine—"

"Let's wait until we get to the coffee shop. I didn't want to risk being disturbed in the lodge. Dan took a snowmobile out somewhere, but I suppose he'll be back at some point and I didn't want to risk being interrupted."

"He took a snowmobile?" Maggie slumped in the seat. "I was hoping he and Rosie would be talking about their issues."

"He'll be back. When Dan is hurt or has something to work out, he often takes himself off. His father was the same. There are so many things I want to say, but I need to focus and the roads are terrible after yesterday's blizzard. And I'm dying for a soy latte."

Maggie had a feeling they were going to need something a lot stronger than a soy latte to make them both feel better, but who was she to argue? And, as Nick had pointed out, alcohol was at least partially responsible for the position they now found themselves in.

She felt awkward. She wanted to tell the truth. She wanted to apologize, but Catherine had made it clear she wanted to postpone the conversation. And underneath it all was a simmering anxiety for both her daughters. Hopefully Nick would speak to Katie and not put his foot in it by saying something tactless, but what about Rosie? Was she on her own and upset somewhere?

"How was your day with Nick yesterday?" Catherine drove confidently. "Was the sledding fun? Was dinner romantic?"

Every word Catherine spoke reminded Maggie how much this woman had done for her. And how much she had to explain. "It was all great, thank you."

"That's good to know."

"The sleigh ride back from the restaurant was magical."

"It's a wonderful thing. I once had a man propose to the love of his life on that sleigh ride." Catherine glanced at her and Maggie noticed how pale she was. As if she'd been crying.

Guilt stabbed her.

"Catherine—"

"Well, look at that—parking, right outside my favorite coffee shop. It's meant to be." Catherine eased carefully into a space and the two of them picked their way across the snow and into the warmth.

Catherine picked a small table by the window, close to the fire. "What can I get you?"

"A cappuccino please." Maggie reached for her bag to pay, but Catherine waved her away.

While Catherine went up to the counter to order, Maggie tried to rehearse what she might say, and then decided that there was no best way to confess that you'd been lying. She needed to come straight out with it.

When Catherine settled in the seat opposite, she took a deep breath.

"I'm glad we have this chance to talk privately. There are a few important things I have to say."

"Me too, but can I start by saying thank you to you for at least agreeing to listen. I thought you'd be furious. You probably *are* furious, and I don't blame you for that at all. I'm furious with myself. Thank you for at least giving me a hearing."

Maggie was thrown. "A hearing? I don't understand."

"I'm sure you don't. There are so many things I need to explain, but I thought it was best if we did it somewhere private so we're not interrupted. I've been dreading this all morning. And talking about this morning, I apologize for walking in like that. I was going to slide my envelope with my suggestions for your romantic day under the door and leave the pastries outside, but then the door was open and I saw everyone else inside and assumed you were up and around."

"That's the least of our worries." Maggie wanted to forget about the fact that half of Colorado had seen her in bed with Nick.

Catherine picked up her spoon and poked at her coffee. "This is my fault. I don't even know where to start."

"Start by telling me how you can possibly think any of this is your fault. If anyone is to blame, it's Nick and I."

Catherine frowned. "Why?"

Maggie didn't understand why Catherine wasn't angry, then realized it was because she didn't have the facts. "You go first. Then I'll go."

"All right." Catherine sat back in her chair. "When my husband died, I—well, let's say it was a tough time. There were mornings when I didn't get out of bed. I couldn't. I lay there, wallowing in misery and self-pity. Why him? Why me? All the usual thoughts that you don't want to admit to because you're not proud of them. Dan was away at college, and I knew he was worried about me. I pretended I was fine. I spoke to him in a bright, cheery voice, told him I was keeping busy."

"But you weren't."

"No, and I guess he sensed that. He insisted on coming home, so I knew I had to pull myself together. I'd told him all these lies about how I was keeping busy, so I had to find something to be busy with. I was telling a friend about it and she suggested I help organize her wedding. It was her second marriage, she was working full-time and hating every minute of arranging details. I took everything off her hands. I did it so that Dan wouldn't worry about me, but within weeks I was feeling better. I had a reason to get up in the morning. Something to work for. I told myself I was doing it so that my friend could carry on working and not have a stress attack, but really I was doing it for myself. I had never imagined work could be therapy, but that's how it turned out. Also turned out that I was good at it. It was a big wedding. Word spread. I was invited to do more. What began as a hobby turned into a business. Soon I needed an assistant. And I loved what I was doing.

I'd never had a career. I met Jonny in college, and Dan arrived almost right away. Jonny was so busy building his business, I wanted to support him. And many would think that was an old-fashioned approach, I know."

"It was your choice," Maggie said, thinking of her own life up until this point. "It was what you wanted."

"Yes. There was nothing I wanted more than to be Dan's mother, but equally once Jonny died there was nothing I wanted more than to show my son I was okay. He's very protective. I didn't want him worrying about me, and doing something stupid like give it all up to come home. You raise a child to be independent. I understood that. You raise them to leave, even though the leaving breaks your heart into pieces." Catherine rummaged in her bag for a tissue and blew her nose. "Sorry."

"Don't apologize. I cried for weeks when Rosie left home, but don't tell her." Maggie reached across the table and took her hand. "I think you're inspiring. And brave."

"I don't know about that. Anyway, when Dan first brought Rosie home I could see right away how much he loved her. He was devastated when he lost his father and seeing him so happy was a huge relief to me. I felt excited, as if we were entering a whole new phase of life." She pulled her hand from Maggie's and picked up her coffee. "I'm telling you this because it may have contributed to the way I behaved."

"I don't understand."

Catherine put the cup down. "From the moment Dan proposed, I took over. I was the one who suggested they get married at Christmas. And I did it at a big noisy family dinner, without thinking that it would mean sweet Rosie wouldn't be able to express her views on it."

"If she'd had doubts, she would have said so."

"We both know she probably wouldn't. She's a kind, generous girl. And I do believe she loves Dan, otherwise I never would have pushed so hard. I don't really know why I did, except that getting married at Christmas seemed romantic and I wanted the two of them to start their new happy life immediately." Her eyes filled again. "I all but hauled her down to that dress shop. Looking back on it, I could see she was a little panicky, but did I hold back? No, I told myself bridal nerves were normal. I didn't want to think that maybe this was all moving along too quickly. And I didn't think about you. She's your girl. Your baby. And I was doing all the things a mother should do."

"Catherine, *please*!" Maggie leaned forward. "Stop torturing yourself. I wasn't here to do those things, so I was grateful to you for doing them. And grateful to you for your kindness to our daughter."

"I love her. That part isn't in question. But my affection probably contributed to the fact I railroaded her."

It wasn't easy having children, Maggie thought. It wasn't easy getting the balance right. She saw that so much more clearly now. Love and caring could so easily turn into smothering, and it wasn't easy to know where to draw the line.

She sat up a little straighter. "I think you're being too hard on yourself. If she'd had doubts, about the relationship or the speed of the wedding, she should have talked to Dan."

Catherine sniffed. "You think so?"

"Yes." Maggie said it firmly, to convince both of them. "If they're adult enough to get married, they're adult enough to sort out any problems they encounter."

"You're so rational and mature."

Maggie burst out laughing. "I wish. Let's just say I had an epiphany recently."

"Dan is as focused and stubborn as I am. When he wants something, he goes for it. It's a strength, but it's also a flaw. Maybe Rosie tried to talk, and he didn't listen. And now he's in shock."

Maggie finished her coffee. "I like Dan, a lot. I'm sure he and Rosie will work this out."

"And if they don't?"

Maggie tried to ignore the sick lurch in her stomach. Would she ever lose that impulse to reach for her phone and check on her daughter? "Then they both will have learned something from it. And we will pick up the pieces and support."

"I don't understand why everyone was in your bedroom this morning. And why so much tension? No one told me anything."

Maggie fiddled with her coffee cup. "This is the part of the conversation where you're going to be mad with me."

"I can't imagine that ever happening."

They were about to find out. "About our second honeymoon—"

"I think it's so romantic."

"It's not romantic. It's fake. Or it was fake. Nick and I have been living separately for months." She told Catherine everything, from the slow demise of her marriage, to their decision to fake their relationship for a little longer so that they didn't spoil the wedding.

Catherine listened without saying anything and when Maggie had finally finished, she stirred.

"So I brought you back together?"

"Yes. It's been years since Nick and I spent time as a couple. Enjoyed ourselves. Our relationship had turned into something close to an administrative arrangement. Because we were faking this second honeymoon, we were forced to do all the things you'd so kindly arranged. The sledding. The romantic dinner. We haven't done anything like that in long time."

"And it turned into something real. You fell in love again." Catherine pressed her hand to her heart. "You have no idea how happy that makes me. But what does this have to do with this morning?"

"Yesterday, Katie overheard us talking about divorce. Naturally, she was upset. She walked off, and that's how she ended up spending the night in Jordan's cabin. But she obviously assumed we would have told Rosie. When she discovered we hadn't—well, she's very protective of her sister."

"Of course she is," Catherine murmured. "Isn't that what sisters are for?"

"She seemed to think Rosie was having doubts, and was using our marriage as evidence that a whirlwind relationship could work. Katie felt it was her responsibility to tell her the truth. I assume Rosie didn't believe her, so Katie dragged her over to our tree house for an honest conversation."

"But you were in bed, enjoying your new relationship." Catherine started to laugh and Maggie felt herself blush.

"I can assure you having your grown kids walking in when you're having sex is not funny."

"I know, I know." Catherine wiped her eyes. "But honestly, you couldn't make this up. But Katie must be thrilled to know you're getting back together?"

"I don't know. We haven't spoken to her. Dan heard her trying to convince Rosie not to use our marriage as reassurance, and he was understandably upset. That's when you arrived."

"So do the girls know that you and Nick are together again?"

"They should do. We tried telling them. But it was rather chaotic, and then there's the fact that Katie doesn't trust us much right now. She'll probably never believe a single thing I say ever again. You think this is your fault but I think it's mine. If I'd told the girls the truth from the beginning, Katie wouldn't have come charging in this morning, Rosie wouldn't have followed and Dan wouldn't have found out she'd been having doubts."

"But then you and Nick might not be together. I think it's good that Dan found out. They need to find a way of communicating. If you can't be honest with the person you're choosing to spend the rest of your life with, then how is that ever going to work? Dan can be very stubborn, and sure of himself, but maybe he needs to learn to listen more." Catherine finished her coffee. "I need to apologize to Rosie for taking over. For pushing. I made it hard for her to speak up. This whole episode has made me realize a few things about myself, too. I need to give people space to breathe and move, and make their own decisions." She straightened and glanced at the time. "We should be getting back. I might have a wedding to cancel. Unless you and Nick would like to renew your vows?"

Maggie gave a wan smile. "I don't think that would be tactful in the circumstances."

"Or maybe it would be exactly what everyone needs. And it would certainly persuade Katie that this time you're telling the truth." She stood up. "Are we really going to give up on this wedding?"

"It's up to the two of them. I'm not going to interfere even though it half kills me not to."

"I'm trying not to reach for my phone and call Dan."

"We need to find something else to do with our hands."

She saw Catherine grin suggestively and felt her cheeks burn. "Catherine Reynolds, you have no shame."

"You're right, I don't. In fact, I'm feeling quite proud. I feel responsible for bringing you and Nick back together. Fate's a funny thing, isn't it? Maybe I pushed too hard to have this wedding quickly, but if we'd done it next year you and Nick would have been divorced."

Maggie felt her heart tumble. She liked to think they would have found the way back together somehow, but maybe they wouldn't. She reached out and hugged Catherine. "Whatever happens with our children, I hope we can stay in touch."

"Of course!" Catherine eased away. "I was so nervous about meeting you."

"*You* were nervous about meeting *me*?" Maggie started to laugh. "I was terrified of meeting you. You're so successful, and you run your own business."

"I run my own business because I'm far too picky to ever work for anyone else. No one would ever hire me. Why are you staring at me?"

"Because—I never thought of that option. Working for myself." Why hadn't she thought about it? Why let others decide whether she'd be a success at something or not?

"You should think about it. There's nothing like being the boss. You can give yourself a raise, and take tea breaks whenever you like." Catherine picked up her bag and coat. "We should get back."

They walked to the door and Maggie paused. "For what it's worth, I'm sure they're in love."

"I'm sure of it, too."

"She's changed. She's more confident. Being with him has made her more confident." Maggie held the door open.

"They're good together. We have to hope they'll realize that themselves."

"And if they don't?"

"Then it won't be a very merry Christmas."

Rosie

"ROSIE, WAIT! *WAIT*."

Rosie heard her sister's voice and carried on walking. It was Dan she needed to talk to, not Katie. Katie had already said more than enough.

"Please—" Breathless, Katie caught up with her and put her hand on Rosie's shoulder. "We need to talk."

Rosie shrugged her off. "You've already said what you wanted to say, and I heard you." She was desperate to talk to Dan. Where had he gone? The fact that he'd disappeared so quickly worried her more than anything. He didn't want to be found. She wasn't even going to be given a chance to fix this.

"Rosie—I need to explain—"

"No, you don't." Rosie whirled round to face her sister. "What is *wrong* with you? I don't believe for a moment you'd try to intentionally hurt me, so what is this? Are you jealous? Is that what's going on? Are you envious that I've finally found someone I love and who loves me back?"

Katie recoiled. "Of course not. It isn't that at all."

"Then what? Because I don't believe this is all about protecting me. You haven't protected me from hurt, you've given me the hurt. You've taken away the one thing I wanted more than anything in the world. I love him, Katie."

"But you were having doubts—"

"I haven't once told you I was having doubts. It was you who said that."

Her sister looked stricken. "But you were using our parents as evidence. I thought—"

"You thought you knew better than I did, even though this is actually my relationship, my feelings." She stepped closer to her sister. "And do you know what? If I'd had doubts, those would have been my responsibility and handling them would have been my responsibility, too. This is my life, and I'm allowed to feel the way I want to feel. And if I make a mistake and mess up, then that's on me, too. And what qualifies you to think you know better than I do? When did you last fall in love?" She felt a flash of guilt as she saw the agony in her sister's eyes.

"You're right." Katie's words were barely audible. "I don't know anything about love, but I know you."

"You know one side of me, the side you think is vulnerable and needs protecting. You've asked a ton of questions, trying to find a reason why this is the biggest mistake ever, but you haven't once asked me why I love him. I'm an adult, Katie, and yes, I have a tendency to change my mind about things, but that's part of who I am. And by the way, I change my mind a lot less since I've been with Dan because he doesn't make me doubt myself the whole time. Being with him is the best thing that has happened to me. I love him, and I won't be changing my mind about that, but even if I do that has nothing to do with you. I don't need you to make my decisions for me. And I don't need you to question the ones I make."

"You're right. And I'm sorry. But our parents—"

"It doesn't matter to me what's happening with our parents. Their relationship is their business. I'll love them and respect them whatever they decide. And my relationship is my business, and I expect you all to love me and respect me whatever I decide. You want to know why I let Catherine arrange the wedding? Because arranging the wedding is making her happy, and I like seeing her happy. Turns out that all the little details don't matter to me. All that really matters to me is marrying Dan. I don't care how or where. You're worried that Dan and Catherine have been bulldozing me, but you're the biggest bulldozer of them all. And before you say you're mothering me, remember that there's a single letter separating *mother* from *smother*. From now on if you want to interfere with a relationship, get one of your own." She turned sharply and walked away, her legs shaking so badly from the encounter that it was challenging to put one foot in front of the other.

She was close to tears. She'd never confronted Katie before. This was her sister, her *sister*, whom she loved with her whole heart. And she'd hurt her, but she was hurting, too. Usually she avoided confrontation, but being with Dan had given her the confidence to believe in her opinions and stand up for herself. And although part of her wanted to run back to Katie and beg her forgiveness, she wasn't going to do that. Katie had to respect her decisions, and right now her priority was Dan. Her relationship with Dan. She was willing to fight to protect that, even if doing so felt horrible.

She started to cry, but crying made it harder to walk fast and breathe, so she forced herself to calm down. There was no way she was going to have an asthma attack now, in this crucial moment of her life.

She had to talk to Dan, or even the fight with Katie would have been for nothing.

She arrived back at the lodge, only to find that he'd taken a snowmobile out on one of the trails.

She'd been hoping for a private conversation in a cozy, private place like the kitchen at Snowfall Lodge, but it seemed there was no chance of that.

Could he have made it more obvious that it was over between them?

Tears stung her eyes. How could he not want to talk to her?

They were supposed to be getting married in forty-eight hours. Surely he at least owed her a conversation?

She ignored the little voice in her head reminding her that her inability to talk to him was the reason they were in this mess.

She had to talk to him. She had to explain, and it couldn't wait. She didn't want him to think it through without at least hearing her side of the story. But if she wanted to talk to him, she was going to have to go to him.

She sweet-talked Rob, who looked after the snowmobiles for the lodge and sometimes took guests out.

"You want to take a snowmobile?" He scratched his head. "You shouldn't ride alone."

"I won't be riding alone. I'll be with Dan. We were supposed to go together, but I was held up." She delivered her most charming smile, pulled on a snowmobile suit and climbed onto the snowmobile with as much confidence as she could muster.

She tried to remember what Dan had taught her. She was pointing in the right direction, the key was on and the emergency kill switch was up.

Trying to look confident, she jerked her way along the track that led away from the hotel.

Chances were that Dan would have taken the same route

they'd taken the other day. She knew he loved the area around Maroon Bells. Her guess was confirmed when she saw what had to be his tracks.

She opened the throttle and went a little faster. The fresh snowfall created a powdery dust as she traveled, reducing visibility. Nerves flickered through her. She was going to put the damn thing in a ditch, or maybe she'd break through ice and drown. Did this trail cross water? She tried not to think about the fact that she'd failed her driving test five times.

There was no sign of Dan, but that didn't surprise her. He always drove too fast. If she wanted to catch up with him, she was going to have to do the same. She had to do this. She had to talk to him.

She went faster, the snowmobile cutting through the snow. The sky was blue, the trail was empty. Had it been a different day she might have thought this was bliss.

Finally, she reached the frozen lake and there, standing on the shoreline, was Dan.

He must have heard her approach, but he didn't turn until she'd walked up behind him.

"Dan?"

"I came here for some space. I needed to think."

"I know, and I'm sorry. But—" She reached out and touched his arm, and felt something close to physical pain when he shrugged her off. "We have to talk. Please. You owe me that." She felt cold. So, so cold and she knew it had nothing to do with the outdoor temperature.

"You're urging me to talk? Do you see the irony of that?" He turned to look at her and there was a hardness in his face she'd never seen before.

"Of course I do." Her chest felt tight. Was it misery and distress, or the beginnings of an asthma attack? One sometimes led to the other. She wished she'd remembered to put her inhaler in her pocket. She pulled her scarf over her mouth. "I understand why you're angry, but I need you to know I love you. I really love you, Dan."

His eyes didn't soften. "You wouldn't tell me if you didn't."

She thought of all the things she'd said to her sister. "I'd tell you."

"Then why didn't you tell me you were having doubts?"

"I tried a few times but you—you misunderstood me, and—"

"So it's my fault?" He didn't yield. He didn't give an inch, but neither did she.

Even though she hated confrontation, she was prepared to do whatever it took to make him at least understand her feelings. "I'm not saying it's anyone's fault. Only that I didn't find it easy to say, and every time I tried you thought I was saying something else, so in the end I didn't say anything at all and honestly I wasn't even sure my doubts were real. I was doubting my doubts." She tried to laugh, but her body refused to cooperate. She felt as if she was fighting for her life. She was certainly fighting for her love. For *their* love.

He turned away again, as if looking at her hurt too much. "It doesn't matter now."

"So—what?" Her throat felt thick. "This is it? You don't love me anymore."

He gave a humorless laugh. "You think I can switch it on and off? I wish I could. I still love you."

"Then—" She spread her hands. "I don't get it. Why can't we talk about this and move on?"

"Because what happens next time, Rosie?" His voice was raw. "Next time you have an issue you want to talk about, something that is worrying you, something that maybe threatens our marriage, are you going to talk about it? Or are you going to hold it inside until it gradually infects what we have. I can't marry someone who doesn't feel they can talk to me. It's fundamental for making a relationship work."

She couldn't breathe.

Tears made it hard for her to see him. She felt strange. If he'd told her he didn't love her anymore, maybe she could have accepted it but to tell her he loved her but was still breaking it off—it was like being kicked hard in the chest. She felt broken. "I can't believe you're being so stubborn."

"I'm doing what I feel is best."

She made a last desperate attempt to understand. "Is this about your dad? Are you scared?"

"This is about us, not my dad."

She didn't believe him. There had to be more going on, surely? But if he wouldn't talk to her, what could she do?

Underneath the thick blanket of misery, she felt the stirrings of anger. Anger that he wasn't prepared to talk it through with an open mind. Anger that he was so easily throwing away what they had.

"Don't do this, Dan. Seriously, don't do this. You said you knew me. If you truly know me then you'll know I struggle with confrontation and difficult conversations. I'm working on it. I've probably made more progress in the last day than I have in the last ten years, but you have to be patient." She swallowed. "I'm asking you to be patient."

He turned away. "It's over, Rosie."

In that single moment anger eclipsed misery. "Yeah? Well, it's good to know that what we had was worth fighting for. You say you can't marry someone who won't talk to you, well, I can't marry someone who won't listen and is so inflexible." She stomped away and somehow made it back to the snowmobile. Scrubbing the tears from her eyes, she jammed the helmet back on her head and sped back down the trail. She wanted to find somewhere warm to sob in comfort. Frozen tears were no one's idea of fun. And she could feel herself wheezing. If she went to the main lodge she ran the risk of bumping into Catherine. She couldn't handle her parents right now. Which left the tree house she'd been sharing with her sister.

With luck, Katie wouldn't be there.

She delivered the snowmobile safely back and made it to the tree house.

The first thing she saw was the Christmas tree glistening, and the second thing was her sister. She was wearing her coat and scarf, and pacing across the living room.

So luck wasn't on her side.

With a sigh, Rosie tugged open the door and was instantly enveloped by her sister.

"I've been so worried. You didn't answer your phone."

She hadn't even heard her phone. "I was busy. Why are you wearing your coat indoors?" And then she noticed the suitcase. "You're leaving?"

"I—I've ruined everything." Katie stopped hugging her and took a step back. "You're mad at me, and I don't blame you. And Mum and Dad are probably mad, too, because of my performance earlier. And I'm not even going to think about what Dan and Catherine probably think. It's best if I leave, but I couldn't leave before checking on you first. How are you doing?"

"Your wish came true. The wedding isn't going ahead."

Katie's skin color matched the snow beyond the windows. "That wasn't my wish. I didn't want that. I wanted you to be sure, that's all. I didn't mean this to happen. I'm so, so sorry. You didn't find him?"

"I found him, but the conversation didn't go the way I wanted it to." Rosie peeled off her coat and hung it up. "Maybe I should fly home with you. We could all fly home and have Christmas in Honeysuckle Cottage." Once, that would have sounded so appealing, but for some reason it no longer did. She felt sick and a little panicky. She'd lost something she knew she'd never get back. She was frustrated, miserable and a little angry, but mostly she was sad.

"We're not flying home." Katie looked horrified. "We're going to fix this. You're getting married. Do you want to get married?"

"Of course! But it's too late."

"It can't be too late. He'll change his mind."

Rosie thought about Dan. "He's not going to change his mind. And you don't think I should be marrying him anyway."

"I do. All I ever wanted was to make sure this was what you wanted. That night on the phone when I was working, and you told me he was perfect—it freaked me out a little. I'd come from dealing with a woman in an abusive relationship. At the beginning she thought the guy was perfect. He made damn sure of it until he'd reeled her in. I suppose I don't believe in perfect people, and then you used that word and it worried me."

"I never said Dan was perfect. No one is perfect. I said—" Rosie frowned. What had she said? "I think I said he was perfect for *me*. That's not the same thing."

Katie looked stricken. "You're right. It's not the same thing at all. Which proves I should never take personal phone calls when I'm at work because yet again my judgment was flawed."

"It's done so now let's drop the subject. I'm cold, and I need to warm up."

"You're mad, and upset and—" Katie placed her palm on Rosie's cheek "—and you're cold. Freezing. Where have you been?"

"To talk to Dan. On a snowmobile."

"A snowmobile?" Katie removed her own scarf and wrapped it around her sister's neck. "Who can have a conversation on a snowmobile?"

"Not us." She tugged off her boots. "But I'm starting to think we can't have a conversation anywhere."

"This is all my fault."

"It's not your fault." Rosie flopped facedown on the sofa. "It's my fault for not having confidence in my own decision making. I'm sorry I yelled at you."

"I deserved every decibel. And I feel terrible. What can I do?"

"Nothing." Rosie's voice was muffled by the sofa cushions. "I tried talking to him but he's made up his mind."

"Well, that's ridiculous." Katie stroked her back gently.

It made her remember being little, being poorly, when she'd snuggle on her sister's lap and listen to her read a story.

"If I ask you to grab my inhaler from my bag, are you going to freak out?"

"Your—of course—" Katie scrambled to her feet and dug her hand into the back pocket of her jeans. "Here. Sit up. Breathe. Good technique, remember? Why didn't you have this with you? Never mind, use it, that's all that matters. I'm not freaking out, I promise."

"You carry an inhaler in your pocket?" Rosie sat up and took it from her. "Since when have you suffered from asthma?"

"I don't, but you do so I like to be prepared. Stop talking. I can't believe you went out in the freezing cold like that. But I'm not going to worry and be overprotective. You're an adult."

"I had a scarf but it was colder than I thought." And she hadn't been thinking about her breathing, she'd been thinking about Dan.

She closed her eyes and used the inhaler twice.

Katie took it from her and knelt down in front of her. "Sit for a minute, don't try to talk. I'll do the talking. I'm really sorry for everything. I haven't been in a good place the last few weeks."

"Stop." Her chest felt so tight. She should have used her inhaler sooner. "Everything you said was true. I do change my mind about things. I'm like a grasshopper, leaping from one thing to the next. And Dan is right. I should have been able to talk to him. But sometimes he plows right over me, and he doesn't even know he's doing it."

"And when he calms down, you can tell him that." Katie stroked her hair. "A conversation requires two things, someone to talk and someone to listen. Maybe he's upset that you didn't talk, but you're upset that he didn't listen. Fifty, fifty, Rosie. No, don't talk. If your breathing doesn't improve in a few minutes, we're going to the hospital. You should be so mad with me."

"I'm not mad."

"Stop talking. I've been a bad sister. I've been overprotective, I know that, but from the moment you were born I wanted to make sure nothing hurt you. I fell in love with your funny little face the moment I saw you."

"I don't have a funny face."

"Check out your baby photos." She took Rosie's hand. "I'm going to stop being overprotective. I can't promise to get it right overnight, but I can promise to work on it. Moving forward if you ever want to talk to me as a friend, I'll be here, but no more advice from me. Turns out I'm not great at it anyway. Apart from the inhaler thing. I'm totally great at that, so still no talking."

"You're a great sister. And a great doctor."

"I am not either."

Rosie pressed her hand to her chest. She felt a flutter of fear. There was nothing, nothing, more frightening than not being able to breathe. "This is—there's a good hospital here, right?"

"You're not going to need a hospital." Her sister was calm. Rock solid. "I'm here, and you're fine."

"Distract me."

"Distract you? Okay—well, you wanted me to open up to you, so this is me opening up. I always wanted to be a doctor, you know that. Right through school. Right through medical school, I thought I was doing the only thing I could do. This was me. It was a vocation." Katie had her eyes fixed on Rosie's chest, watching the rise and fall. "Until it wasn't. I don't even know what happened. Slowly, without me even noticing, my love for the job started to drain away. Nothing dramatic. A drop at a time. A slow hemorrhage of enthusiasm. I didn't even notice. I told myself I was tired. Stressed. So what? Show me a doctor who isn't tired and stressed. I didn't give it a second thought." She paused. "How's your chest? Are you doing okay?"

Rosie nodded. She couldn't remember ever hearing Katie talk to her like this before. She waved a hand to urge her to carry on.

"Two months ago, there was an incident at work. It was—upsetting. Usually we try to detach, it's a requirement of the job, but none of us did so well that night. I don't need to give you the details—"

"Give me the details." If her sister had dealt with it first-hand, the least she could do was hear about it secondhand. She needed to understand. And she didn't want to think about her breathing.

Katie hesitated and then started talking and every word she spoke increased Rosie's respect for her sister. How did you handle something like that and not be affected? Did Katie really think it was possible to stay detached?

"He attacked you."

"It was understandable."

"And frightening."

Katie rubbed her fingers over her forehead. "Yes, and frightening."

"Did you get support?"

"Not until last week, when I finally saw a doctor. Who signed me off sick. Yes," she said, and gave a wry smile, "I'm actually on sick leave. I'm officially sick, which would be a useful explanation for the way I've been behaving. And now you're going to ask me why I didn't tell you before. I'm not sure why, except that you're proud that I'm a doc-tor. I thought you might think less of me."

"I'm your sister. I love you. How could I think less of you?" Rosie leaned forward and wrapped her arms around her sister.

"Oh—that's nice. Does this mean I'm forgiven? Don't give me sympathy. I'm better if I just—"

"It's okay, Katie. It's okay to feel shitty after something like that."

"I'm fine, really, I don't—"

"It's okay." Rosie hugged tighter and felt her sister sag against her.

"I'm not okay. I'm not okay." Finally Katie cracked. Tears flowed out of her, and she cried, great jerking, broken sobs that tore through Rosie like a knife. Her sister had never, ever, cried on her before. Her own cheeks were wet and she realized she was crying, too. She didn't know what to say—what could she possibly say?—so she simply held her sister and murmured meaningless words of comfort.

Eventually the crying stopped and Katie slumped against her. "And now I have a headache. And I didn't even drink to get it."

Rosie gave a choked laugh. "We could fix that."

Katie sniffed and pulled away. "Bet you preferred me in my role as smother mother."

Smother mother.

Despite everything, Rosie laughed. "Not true. I feel as if I finally know you a little. And it explains a lot about how you've been the last few weeks."

Katie blew her nose and flopped down next to Rosie on the sofa. "I have some big decisions to make. And I have no idea what to do. Here's the learning point from this sorry tale. You think there's some magic decision fairy that makes every choice a clear one, but there isn't. We're all muddling our way through, doing the best we can. We make decisions based on many factors, and sometimes that can lead to one hell of a mess. My life is an example." She looked at Rosie. "Yours might be, too, but that's my fault. I have managed to screw up your life as well as mine."

It was something of a shock to discover that her sure, confident sister was wrestling with doubts, too. A shock and a comfort.

"You're an amazing doctor."

"I don't know. I try to be—but that doesn't mean I don't wish I'd chosen another profession."

"You really feel that way?"

"I think I do. And it's taken me a while to admit it, because the thought makes me panic. I've devoted my whole adult life to this. It's hard to walk away from that without wondering if it was all a waste."

"Whatever you do in the future, the past is never a waste." Rosie leaned her head against her sister's shoulder.

"Jordan said something similar."

"You discussed it with Jordan?"

"He's a good listener. And it helped that he wasn't emotionally invested. Sometimes when a decision feels huge, you want someone to tell you you're doing the right thing."

"I know. One of the things I love about Dan is that he's so confident about everything. And his confidence rubbed off on me a little. He's not scared of life. Being with him made me braver. He doesn't talk himself out of doing things that are difficult. He looks at the obstacle and either goes over it or around it. He makes me think about the things I can do, not the things I can't."

Katie pulled her closer. "Tell me what else you love about him."

"I don't know. It's a thousand small things, isn't it? Like the way he makes me tea because he knows I love it even though he never drinks it himself, and the way he watches romantic movies because that's what I want to do."

"He watches romantic movies? Does he pull a face?"

"No face."

"He looks at his phone during the sloppy parts?"

"Never."

"Wow, that's—definitely love. And he does better than I do, by the way. If Vicky chooses a romantic movie I moan all the way through it. What else?"

"He's so calm and patient. The first time I met him, in

the gym that day, I had an asthma attack." She felt her sister tense.

"You never told me that."

"Because I knew you'd overreact. I was using the treadmill and—" she waved a hand "—it doesn't matter. But Dan noticed, and he was by my side in an instant and then came with me to the hospital and handled all of it because I hadn't been in the US long. And he was calm. So calm. You already saw that when you were subjecting him to interrogation." She felt her sister wince.

"You're right, he could have punched me and he didn't."

"He would never do that. He would think that if there was something you needed to say, then you should say it." She sighed. "And I didn't."

"And that was my fault. I'm sorry I made you doubt yourself. And for what it's worth, I don't think those doubts came from you. I put them there. I created this problem and I need to fix it."

"It's my problem. I could have shut you down. I could have told Dan how I was feeling." Rosie didn't want to think about that. "You discussed this with Jordan, too?"

"We were snowbound for the best part of fifteen hours. Talking about the weather got old after twenty minutes."

She was dismissing it, but to Rosie it seemed momentous that she'd talked to Jordan.

"What else did the two of you talk about?"

"A lot of things. Including my overdeveloped protective instincts."

"He's seriously hot."

"Rosie White, you're about to be married."

"Doesn't seem that way, but even if I was it doesn't stop me noticing when a man is hot. Just stops me doing something about it. Jordan is smoking hot."

"He is." Something in the way her sister said it made Rosie wonder.

"Did you have trouble staying warm when you were snowbound in that cabin?"

"No. I was toasty. There was a perfectly good fire."

"So no body warmth, then."

"I didn't say that."

"Katie!" Rosie sat up and stared at her sister. "Did you—?"

"Yes, we did. Several times in fact. Probably would have been more but he ran out of condoms. There. That's my first ever kiss and tell. I'd carve his name in my bedpost, except my bed doesn't have a post."

Rosie hadn't thought she was capable of being cheered up, but for some reason this cheered her up. "How long is it since you've been involved with a man?"

"Who said anything about being involved? I'm not involved. We spent a pleasurable physical night together, that's all."

"Apart from the fact you told him things about yourself you've never told anyone else."

"That too."

"And he knows your real name."

"Now you're freaking me out. Fortunately for me, as you pointed out, he kept me there so that you and Dan would have time alone, so I don't think either of us need to worry that this is going to be a lasting relationship."

"And you're not mad with him for that?"

"The only person I'm mad with right now is myself. I am going to call the airline, then a taxi. And I will take advantage of the long flight to rethink my life." Katie heaved herself to her feet. "But first I need coffee, and now that your breathing seems to have settled down you need a hot shower to warm up."

"Please don't leave. If we leave, then we'll leave together. I still need to talk to Catherine. Promise me you won't leave?"

Katie stilled. "I thought you'd had enough of me."

Rosie stood up, too, and wrapped her arms around her sister. "I've had enough of you protecting me, but I haven't had enough of you."

"Okay, well—" Katie hugged her back. "I won't leave until you do. That's a promise."

"What about Mum and Dad? Are they splitting up? I'm confused."

"You and me both. They were definitely thinking of it, but once I calmed down I realized they couldn't possibly have known we were all going to show up this morning, so the whole bed thing couldn't possibly have been for effect."

"Can we not talk about the bed thing?"

"Good plan." Katie gave her a final hug and walked to the kitchen.

"Do you think it was my fault they were having problems?"

"Why would it be your fault?"

"My asthma put strain on the whole family."

"It wasn't your fault." Katie handed her a mug. "Relationships are complicated."

"You don't need to tell me that." Rosie took a sip of coffee. She felt exhausted. Drained of energy. And on the verge of tears. Knowing that crying in front of her sister would make Katie feel worse, she put her coffee down. "You're right. I need to take that shower. What are you going to do?"

"I have a couple of errands. First I have to apologize to Mum and Dad, for flinging accusations and invading their privacy. After that," she said, shrugging, "I don't know. Maybe you're right. Maybe we should fly home. Whatever we do, it's been interesting."

Rosie managed a smile. "You can't beat a White family Christmas."

Katie

KATIE PULLED ON her outdoor gear and paused by the door.

She could hear the shower running, and she knew her sister was crying under that shower.

She clenched her hands, fighting the impulse to break down the bathroom door and hug her.

But what good was comfort?

Rosie didn't need comfort. She needed the man she loved. And seeing as Katie was entirely responsible for what had happened, she was the one who should fix things. And that was in no way interfering. How could fixing a wrong be classed as interfering?

It was the natural order of things.

She'd messed up. And it was no good playing the *what if* game and wondering if she might have reacted differently had Rosie not called in the middle of a difficult shift, if Sally hadn't been on her mind, if her head hadn't been full of her own problems, or if the words *perfect* and *whirlwind* hadn't triggered her protective instincts. That was in the past. All she could do was deal with now.

She closed the door behind her and walked toward Snowfall Lodge. It was freezing. Surely Dan wouldn't still be out on the snowmobile? If he was, then she was sunk.

The walk to the lodge gave her time to think, and by the time she stepped into the elegant foyer, she knew exactly what she wanted to say.

Taking advantage of the fact that the reception staff were deep in conversation with guests, she ducked into the private stairwell and took the stairs up to the apartment.

She didn't intend to give Dan warning of her arrival, and when she tapped on the door and he opened it she saw immediately that had been the right decision.

"I know you want to close the door in my face and I don't blame you," she said. "Give me ten minutes. That's all I ask."

"Rosie sent you."

"Rosie would kill me if she knew I was here now."

"But you're willing to take that risk."

"Yes, I am, because all of this is my fault."

He opened the door and she stepped inside.

She could see from his body language that he was in agony. She took that as a good sign.

"So here's the thing." She paced to the window and stared across the now familiar beauty of the mountains. "I came here to stop your wedding."

"Well, at least you're honest."

She turned. "It seemed too quick to me. A wild, crazy impulse. There were some things going on in my life—I won't bore you with details, but taken together with what I already knew about Rosie, I felt I knew her mind better than she did. I was scared for her." She thrust her hands into her pockets. She'd eaten so much humble pie in one day she felt bloated. "I've always seen her as vulnerable. All those times when she was little and I held her when she couldn't breathe—well, that's an image that's hard to shake off." She saw that his expression had changed.

Because she sensed he was listening, she kept talking.

"I was determined to find out more about you, because I was sure that Rosie couldn't possibly know you properly after such a short time. So I asked questions."

"I noticed."

"I asked a lot of questions, and you were gracious and patient and—" she breathed "—and more polite than I deserved. You answered everything I asked. I thought maybe it was time I told you a bit about me."

He frowned. "Katie—"

"Hear me out. I need you to understand why I behaved the way I did. I need you to understand that it wasn't personal. I'm quick to judge. Too quick. I often start with the worst-case scenario and work backward. I'm fiercely protective of the people I love. I'm a perfectionist, which isn't good and I'm working on it." She sat down on the sofa, staring at her hands. She didn't have a plan for what to say, but she knew she had to keep talking. "The first time Rosie had an asthma attack, I thought I was going to lose my little sister. I felt this huge sense of responsibility." She glanced up. "When she went to college, she didn't want to worry our mother so she used to call me when she was in trouble. And that was fine, I was pleased she turned to me—"

"But it cast you in the role of parent, and meant that you carried the burden by yourself."

Katie nodded. "I'm not even sure that I would have gone into medicine if it hadn't been for her."

"She says you're a great doctor."

Katie wasn't going to argue that fact. Her issues weren't important here. This was about Rosie. "I kept at it, because that's what you do when you've had a long and expensive training and you've made a career choice that society assumes will be forever. You're not sure you're enjoying it, but hey, most of your colleagues are burned out and exhausted, too, so in the end it becomes normal. You justify the way you're feeling. And why not, because no one ditches medicine after a decade of practice, do they?"

He sat down opposite her. The defensive look in his eyes had gone. "They do if they no longer want to do it."

"You think it's okay to change your mind about things? You see that as a strength, not a weakness?"

"Yes. I do."

"Good." She stood up. "So go and find my sister and tell her you made a mistake. Tell her you still love her and finally have the talk that you probably only need because I interfered. And if after that talk, you still believe it's not the right thing, then we'll handle it." Her eyes filled. "I can't be the reason you both break up."

"Because she'd never forgive you?"

"No. Because I can see now that the two of you are perfect together. I think you need to each find a way to improve your communication, but hopefully you'll have plenty of years ahead to practice. I want her to be happy. I want you to be happy. Despite appearances, I really like you, Dan, and I hope eventually you might grow to like me. Or at least, forgive me."

"I do like you, Katie, and I respect how much you love your sister."

But he hadn't changed his mind. "You have to understand her." She knew she sounded desperate. She *was* desperate. "Rosie is so kind. She never wants to hurt anyone."

"I know that. I know her. Why do you think I'm in love with her?"

"I—you're still saying that in the present tense." She felt a burst of hope that was instantly quenched by the expression on his face.

"Turns out you can switch off wedding plans, but you can't switch off love."

"But if you're in love, why wouldn't you get married?"

"Exactly for the reason you said. Rosie hates hurting anyone, so if she can't talk honestly with me, how am I ever going to know whether she really loves me? How are we going to solve problems in the years ahead?"

"Are you sure she wasn't talking? Or could it have been you that wasn't listening?"

"I don't know what you mean."

"Rosie says she tried to tell you. Did you hear her trying to tell you?"

"I—no. But—"

"Maybe your listening skills need work. Maybe she needs to speak louder. Or email you. Use a whiteboard in the kitchen, or sticky notes. I don't know—" she spread her hands in frustration "—I know nothing about serious relationships, but I do know that this seems like such a fixable thing to me. You love her. She loves you. The two of you need to find a better way to communicate, that's all. I don't think you know how truly lucky you are. In this often horrible world, where things go wrong for people every damn day, you have found love and friendship and warmth—all the things that truly matter, all the things that are going to make your life good and sustain you in the times when life isn't good—and you're going to turn your back on that? And by the way, if your answer to that is 'yes,' then I've found out what's wrong with you. I rest my case."

"I thought you were a doctor, not a lawyer."

"It felt like the right thing to say." She sniffed and walked to the door. "And now I'm leaving. Before my sister figures out I'm here, and our relationship is blown forever."

She was halfway to the door when his voice stopped her.

"You wanted to know about me, so let me tell you about me. If it's not related to work, or physical fitness, I tend to put things off. I'm a terrible procrastinator. I've been known to pay my taxes late. I miss my dad every damn day, and his death made me appreciate how important it is to hold on to love when you find it."

She turned and he nodded.

"That's the reason I wanted to marry Rosie quickly. It wasn't an impulse. It wasn't because my mother jumped in and suggested Christmas. It was because I knew. I knew she was the one for me, and I wanted to make the most of every moment."

"Stop." She blinked and sniffed. "You're making me cry, and I am the least sentimental person you are ever going to meet."

"Yeah? I know you were upset about Jordan keeping you away."

She had her medical training to thank for the fact that she could keep her expression neutral. "I'm not upset. He did the right thing." She squared her shoulders. "The two of you needed time together and I was getting in the way of that. I'd say he executed his duties as best man perfectly. He's a good friend. You and Rosie are lucky to have him in your corner." And what was there to be upset or sad about anyway? They'd spent a night together, so what? They were two consenting adults. They'd both made a choice. Yes, she felt completely messed up and emotional about it but that wasn't Jordan's fault. It was because she was generally messed up and emotional. She had a sick note to prove it.

"Right now I'm not sure I'm going to need a best man."

She thought for a moment. "Tell me something, Dan. If you know how important it is to hold on to love, why are you letting it go? Do you think there weren't days when your parents had to find a path through a bumpy part of their relationship? Look at my parents. On second thoughts, you probably don't want to look at my parents because every time we turn in their direction they seem to be doing something excruciatingly embarrassing, but my point is that throwing love away simply because you need to both learn to accommodate the way you both are, is a horrible waste."

He didn't answer, so she tried again.

"You said you had plenty of time to get to know each other, but knowing each other isn't only about discovering that one of you once had a pet rabbit, or failed a physics test. It's about understanding how the other person reacts. I see it in the hospital. People who become aggressive when they're frightened. People who are so numb with grief they can't even speak, let alone cry. It's not because they don't care, but because that's their way of handling the fact that they care almost too much. Those are the things you need to know about someone. You've found out something really important about Rosie—she is probably not going to yell in your face when something is wrong. You're going to have to create the environment where she can tell you what's on her mind." And she'd messed that part up, too. Katie knew she hadn't given Rosie the space to talk. "That isn't a reason to break up. It's something to file away and use when you need that deeper understanding. That's what knowing someone really means. And I think it's called intimacy, although that is something I know next to nothing about." She turned and walked out of the apartment without looking back.

Had her words had an impact?

She had no idea.

She arrived back at the tree house to find her father waiting for her.

"Hi, Katkin."

The use of her childhood nickname almost finished her off. "Dad. Where's Rosie?"

"She's talking to your mother."

"Divide and conquer. And you got me. That really is the short straw."

"That's not how I see it." He looked awkward and out of his depth, which wasn't a surprise. She couldn't remember ever having a personal discussion with her father in her whole life. Their relationship had always been about shared activities and adventure. Never about emotions.

"I'm sorry about this morning."

"We're the ones who should be sorry. For not telling you the truth." He thrust his hands into his pockets. "But to be honest, I'm not sorry. Your mother and I had—well, we'd grown apart. We couldn't see a path forward. And then we pretended to still be in love. We spent time together. We had fun for the first time in a while."

"It sounds like the plot of a romance novel."

He gave a tired smile. "Perhaps that's where I went wrong. I never read a romance novel. Maybe if I had, I might have learned a thing or two. Maybe my marriage wouldn't have crashed."

She felt an ache in her chest. "I truly am glad it worked out for you both."

"That isn't why I'm here. I didn't come here to talk about us, although I did want to tell you that our marriage is still very much on. I came here to talk about you."

"You don't need to say anything. I behaved badly, I know."

"You were upset. Worried about your sister." He ran his hand over his jaw. "You haven't seen much of your mother lately."

"I know, and I'm sorry. It's been crazy at work and I'll try to do better."

"Seeing your family isn't a test you have to ace, Katkin. We love you. If you're busy, that's not a problem. You're talking to the guy who spent half your childhood away digging up relics. I understand busy, and so does your mother. But if it's something else—" He walked across to her and put his hands on her shoulders. "If there's something else making you keep your distance. Something bothering you. I hope you'd say something. We're proud of you, I hope you know that."

She knew how proud they were. That was half the problem. She pulled away from him. "I'm fine, Dad."

"I've never claimed to be much of an expert on body language, but I'm working on it. I know you're not fine. What I don't know is why what I said upset you."

"Honestly, Dad—I can't—do we have to talk?"

"I'm not saying the right things, am I?" His shoulders sagged. "Your mother will kill me. You girls always talk to your mother when something is wrong, and I don't blame you, but it means I haven't had as much practice. Should I go, Katie? I don't want to make things worse." He was such a kind man. Such a smart man. *Her dad.*

Maybe Jordan was right. Maybe it was time she leaned on people herself, instead of protecting them.

"You said you were proud of me," she told him. "Of the fact I'm a doctor."

"We are proud of you."

"But I'm not sure I want to be a doctor anymore." There. She'd said it. "And I'm sorry if you feel I'm letting you both down. If you feel—"

"Stop right there. Why would you feel you were letting

us down? This is about you, not us. Your life. Your decision."

"I've wanted to be a doctor forever. I've spent my whole life working to get where I am now."

"And what? You think that means you have to carry on doing something that no longer fits with what you want?"

She swallowed. "You don't think I'm crazy?"

"Crazy to contemplate a shift in career when you no longer love what you're doing? Of course not. Crazy would be spending the rest of your life doing something because you've always done it."

"It feels like a waste."

"Nothing you do in life is ever wasted. Nothing." He gestured to the sofa. "Let's sit down for a minute."

"You said you were proud of me."

"We are proud of you. But not because you're a doctor. Because you're *you*. A smart, determined, dedicated young woman. It doesn't matter what you decide to do, you're always going to give it your all because that's who you are."

She decided not to tell him about the attack. Not because she wanted to protect her parents, but because she wanted to put it behind her. It was time to look ahead, not back. Still, it was nice to know she could talk to him if she ever felt the need. "I don't even know what I want to do."

"That's because you haven't given yourself time to think about it. Resign. Take some time off. Think about it. Give yourself space. If you decide to go back to medicine, fine. If not, that's fine, too."

Hadn't Jordan suggested the same thing? "I could, I suppose. I have savings."

"And we have savings, too."

"Thanks, but I would never take your savings. I'm a

grown woman, and if I decide to leave then I have to figure this out for myself."

"Only you can do the figuring out, but we can all help with the practical side. If you wanted to come home for a while, you could."

"And hang around while you two are kissing and cuddling?" She smiled and nudged him. "Thanks, but no thanks. And this isn't the reaction I was expecting. I thought you'd be disappointed and disapproving. I thought you'd lecture me on throwing my life away and my training. But you almost sound as if you want me to leave."

"What I want," he said, "is for you to be happy. I found out a lot of things this week, but one of those things is that your mother doesn't love the job she's been doing for so many years."

"Rosie told me about that."

He looked at her. "She's thinking about alternatives."

"She is? Like what?"

"Not sure yet, but possibly something to do with landscape design. Garden design."

"That makes sense. Good for her."

"My point is, that you don't have dependents, you only have yourself to worry about. There is no better time than this to make a change. Try something else. And if you want to go back to medicine in a year or two, you can do that."

"You make it sound simple." But hadn't Jordan made the same point?

"I think the complexity is one of perception. You've worked hard for something. You're struggling with the idea of walking away from it. But picture yourself twenty years from now, still a doctor. How does that look?"

"It's not pretty."

"There you go. You're young, Katie. Take a risk. And get

a hobby. Take up yoga. Join a choir. You used to be great at playing the piano. What happened to that? Travel. Do something wild. Buy a horse. Fall in love."

Love.

She thought about those few precious hours with Jordan, and knew she'd never forget it.

"I think Vicky would complain if I moved a horse into our backyard." She didn't want to talk about love. But the other stuff? It was definitely time she thought about that. If there was one thing this week had taught her, it was that she had no balance in her life. There were no mountains, or fir trees. Not enough blue sky and fresh air. She leaned her head on his shoulder. "Thanks for listening. This is the first time we've talked like this."

"It is." He patted her leg awkwardly. "It went okay, I think. We did pretty well."

She smiled and hugged him. "You were great. Thanks for not judging, and for being supportive. Thank you, Daddy."

"You haven't called me Daddy since you were six years old."

"Right now I feel about six years old."

He was silent for a moment. "I might be crossing a line here, and if I am then tell me, but did something happen between you and Jordan? Your sister said something—"

"It's fine."

"I saw your face. It didn't look fine, Katkin. Did he hurt you?" He shifted so that he could look at her. "Because if he did, I'll talk to him."

"Oh my God, Dad, *no*! I can't think of anything more awkward. Except perhaps walking in on you and Mum having sex. That was pretty bad."

"Sex is a normal, healthy—"

"Stop! I beg you, stop."

"All right, but I'm here for you. I can talk to him. Or knock him down. No one hurts my girls."

It should have made her laugh, the image of her father knocking Jordan down, but instead it made her want to cry.

"I can take care of myself."

"Maybe you're not as tough as you think you are."

She was starting to think she wasn't tough at all. Any moment now she was going to start crying. "I'm okay."

"I know, but sometimes it's nice not to have to fight your way through life alone."

His words struck home. At that moment she felt more alone than she ever had before in her life.

She almost told him about Jordan. Almost. She'd find the conversation awkward, and she knew for a fact he would. "I think I might lie down for a couple of hours."

"Good plan. You were probably awake all night worrying about your sister while you were trapped in that cabin."

She didn't share the fact that her exhaustion had a different cause. This new spirit of openness was all well and good, but there were limits. "Thanks again for listening. And for saying all the right things."

"Parenting." He kissed the top of her head and stood up. "There's nothing to it. Now go and lie down, close your eyes and dream about a future that excites you. And if your mother happens to ask how it went, don't forget to tell her I aced it."

Laughing, she gave him a push and watched him leave.

Why had she dreaded that conversation? She should have had it sooner.

She still didn't know what she was going to do, but she'd given herself permission to at least think about it.

And she was glad her parents were still together. Pleased they were happy.

An image of Jordan flashed into her mind. She'd never felt as comfortable with anyone before. Never talked and shared so openly. The closeness had added a layer of intimacy she hadn't known before.

Was that how her parents felt when they were together? And Rosie and Dan?

She felt an ache deep inside her. For a moment, she imagined a different kind of life. A life that was balanced and varied. Instead of coming home half-dead from exhaustion with nothing left to give, coming home to someone who cared about her.

And what? She saw herself doing that with Jordan?

This whole thing with Jordan hadn't been real.

It had been one night, not a whole life.

Her phone pinged and she saw a message from her sister.

Guess what? I'M GETTING MARRIED

Katie closed her eyes. Relief made her weak. Thank goodness. She didn't know the details, and she didn't care. All that mattered was that it was going to be okay. She hadn't ruined her sister's life. She felt a rush of emotion so powerful it almost knocked her flat.

She blinked back tears as she texted back.

So happy for you both.

The wedding was going ahead. Which meant she needed to pull herself together.

She needed to smile, and focus on being happy for her sister. She could figure the rest of it out later.

It was Christmas. This was her favorite time of year.

So why did she feel so low?

She was going to close her eyes for five minutes and see if that helped.

She was halfway to the bedroom when there was a tap on the door.

"Oh for—" She turned and saw Jordan standing there.

Her heart lurched. She wasn't sure she could handle him right now.

She wanted to tell him to go away, but if she did that he'd think she was brokenhearted or something equally embarrassing, and she'd suffered all the embarrassment she could handle for one day.

She waved him in. "Hi, Jordan. Is something wrong?"

"Dan and Rosie seem to have fixed whatever was bothering them."

"She messaged me."

"I'm guessing you had something to do with the fact it's back on."

"If you're asking if I spoke to Dan, yes, I did, although it was more of an apology really, since it was my interfering that almost broke them up in the first place. But in the end they fixed it themselves. Was there anything else or did you just come to talk about Rosie and Dan?"

"I didn't come to talk about Rosie and Dan." He closed the door behind him. "There are some things I need to say."

She was too tired for this.

"Let me save you the effort. I interfere, I know I do. Am I sorry? A little, maybe, for the way this played out but I am never going to stop looking out for my sister, so it would be disingenuous of me to pretend I'm going to change much. I know I'm not your favorite person, but we have a wedding to get through so I vote we suspend hostilities until the celebrations are over. After that I'll fly home, and you never have to see me again."

Jordan stood there. "Are you done?"

"Yes."

"Good, because now it's my turn. About last night—"

"I'm stopping you right there." She raised her hand in a stop sign. "You played me at my own game."

"I wouldn't say so."

"You wouldn't?"

"No." He strolled into the cabin. "For a start, my name really is Jordan. And when you ask me for my number, I'm going to give it to you. My real number. Every digit correct."

She gave a half smile. It was the best she could manage. "Why would I ask for your number?"

"Because it's going to be hard for you to contact me without it."

"Why would I need to contact you? Oh, I get it—" She nodded. "You're worried I might be pregnant. Relax. That's not going to happen."

"That's not the reason."

Then what was the reason? "It's fine, Jordan. We spent a night together and probably won't see each other again once Christmas is over, it's no big deal. In fact, it's how my relationships always turn out. You don't have to worry. You're not dealing with some dreamy princess who thinks life is a series of happy-ever-afters."

"That's good to know, because dreamy princesses aren't really my type."

"No?" She picked up a few of Rosie's clothes that had been strewn around the living room. If she kept busy and didn't look at him, she could get through this, she knew she could.

"This is the part where you ask me what my type is."

Did he have no tact at all?

"Sorry, I haven't memorized the script." She kept it light. She also kept her back to him. "What is your type?"

"That's the strange thing. If you'd asked me a few weeks ago I would have said I didn't have a type, but it turns out I'm partial to a certain moody doctor with a brain as sharp as the business end of a scalpel and an impressive knowledge of anatomy."

She didn't move.

"Katie?" His voice was rough. "Look at me."

She turned. "I've told you—"

"You're not interested in relationships, I know, but hear me out." He kept his gaze fixed on hers. "I didn't keep you in that cabin because I wanted to give Dan and Rosie time together, although I did think they needed time together. I kept you in the cabin because it wasn't safe to leave."

"Rosie said—"

"I'm telling you Rosie was wrong. Think about it, Katie. When have you and I held back on telling each other what we think? Not once. You've been speaking your mind since I gave you a ride from the airport, and I've been speaking mine. So why would I concoct some elaborate plan to keep you away from your sister? If that was the reason for keeping you in the cabin, I would have said so. I would have told you right out that I wasn't going to let you go home and interfere. I would have locked the door and put the key in my pocket. We would have fought. With luck, you would have wrestled me for it." There was a gleam in his eyes that she hadn't seen before.

"We really were snowed in?"

He shrugged. "Could I have got us out? Maybe, but not without risk to life. I'm not sixteen anymore. Taking risks like that doesn't have a whole lot of appeal."

"I thought you were adventurous."

"There's adventure, and then there's stupidity. Even if I'd been willing to risk my life, and that of the rescue teams who would undoubtedly haul themselves out to search for us, I wouldn't have risked yours." He paused. "In the spirit of honesty, I ought to also admit that I wanted you there. If the snow hadn't cooperated, I would have found another way."

She felt warm for the first time all day. "You—would?"

"Yes. Was that your dad I saw leaving?"

"Yes." What exactly was he saying? She wasn't sure. Wasn't experienced enough at this to interpret his words.

He strolled across to her. "You talked to him? Are your parents okay?"

"They are. Seems they're not getting divorced, and this whole pretend thing is part of the reason. Which means the sex was, in fact, real. And that's something I'm trying not to think about." She rubbed her fingers over her forehead and stiffened as he took her hand.

"Headache? That's lack of sleep. And stress of course. Have you taken something?"

"No."

"You're a doctor. Aren't you supposed to know how to treat yourself?"

"I'm right at the back of the queue."

"I can see that self-care isn't high on your agenda. You might want to think about that, Dr. White."

"I intend to. I intend to think about a lot of things, including my career." She stared at his chest. "Thanks for listening, by the way. It helped to talk about it."

"I'm pleased you felt able to talk to your dad." He slid his fingers under her chin and lifted her face to his. "So have you decided what else you'd like to do?"

"No. I might resign, and take some time to think about it. Sleep in late. Go to yoga. Buy a horse."

"A horse?"

"Never mind." She smiled. "I have no idea what comes next, and in a way that's scary but it's also surprisingly freeing. Turns out I like the idea of a clean slate."

"You'll go back to London?"

"Where else would I go? I could stay with my parents in Oxford, but as they're rekindling their relationship I think that could be uncomfortable for everyone involved."

He has the bluest eyes, she thought. *The bluest eyes.*

"I've never been to London, but it doesn't sound like a peaceful place. Not an easy place to think. Also, you're a Rottweiler, and Rottweilers need exercise and stimulation or they get into trouble."

"Is that right?"

"Mm. You might be better somewhere with more outdoor space. Like a cabin in the mountains, for example. Somewhere cozy. Wooden walls, great views, log fire. When the snow melts it's surrounded by spring flowers. You can walk all day and not meet another person. And the air is fresh and clean, no pollution."

Her heart beat a little harder. "It sounds great. Do you know of a place like that?"

"As it happens, I do." He cupped her face in his hands. "Stay, Katie. If you have thinking to do, then do it here. I can guarantee you won't find a better place."

Her mouth felt dry. She wasn't sure what he was offering and she didn't want to clarify because she was so afraid she'd got it terribly wrong. "Are you offering me use of your cabin? Where will you go?"

His eyes creased with laughter. "Funny."

"Your place didn't seem big enough for houseguests. You only have one bedroom."

"How many bedrooms do we need?"

Her heart was hammering. "We?"

"I'm asking you to stay. With me. And I realize you're at a crossroads of your life, which might mean you're vulnerable and shouldn't be making rash choices, or it could mean it's time to make rash choices."

She felt his heart beating under her palm. "Are you a rash choice, Jordan?"

"Maybe." He lowered his head until his mouth was almost touching hers. "All I know is that I don't want to drive you to the airport."

"Because you'll miss me when I go?"

"A little. Mostly because you're a particularly annoying passenger and another five hours in a car with you just might kill me."

She laughed, and she would have carried on laughing except that he kissed her, crushing her mouth under his and reminding her of all the reasons that night in the cabin had been special.

When he finally lifted his head she wrapped her arms around him. "I thought you hated me."

"You really have no experience with men, do you, Karen?"

She grinned. "You're going to have to guess my phone number. Ten digits."

"I don't need your phone number. I have you in person."

She leaned her head against his chest. She'd never said *I love you* to a man, but if she did ever say those words she imagined it would be to someone like him. "I've had so many options running through my head, but staying here wasn't one of them."

"And?"

"Can I think about it? Not because I don't want to do it, but because I have to think about everything. It's who I am."

"I know."

"A cabin in the forest sounds wonderful. Especially as it comes with room service."

He kissed her again. "That room service is the best you'll get anywhere."

"I believe you." She hugged him. "Can we talk about this later? There are things I need to do now."

"Like break up a wedding?"

She smiled. "I was thinking more of making this wedding the best it can possibly be."

Rosie

ROSIE STOOD IN the pretty anteroom with her family. She felt as if a flock of butterflies were playing volleyball in her stomach.

They could hear the sounds of the string quartet wafting through from the main room, along with the low hum of conversation.

Everyone was waiting for her.

"Do I look okay?" She touched her hair, which had been cleverly styled to allow a few curling strands to fall over the shoulders of her dress. "My hands are shaking. If I confess I'm nervous, will you all assume I'm changing my mind?"

"Us?" Katie pressed her palm to her chest. "Whatever would make you think that? We're all rational people here."

It felt so good to be able to laugh at it. She'd been afraid of a rift, but she knew that she and her sister would always heal any rift. Their relationship was too important not to. "I can't believe this is happening, after everything."

"Me neither. I mean, I scared the crap out of the man and he's still marrying you? It has to be love. But remember, it's not too late to change your mind." Katie ducked as Rosie took a swipe at her with her bouquet.

And then they were both laughing and Rosie pulled

Katie into a hug. "I'm going to miss you when you go back to London."

"Er, about that—"

"What?" Rosie stepped back. "You're thinking of staying here to comfort me if my marriage falls apart by Friday?"

"I'm thinking of staying, yes, but not because of you. I happen to like it here. A lot. It's pretty, the air is fresh, the pace of life is slower and—"

"And Jordan lives here." As the answer came to her, Rosie smiled. "You finally agreed to a second date?"

"I'm not sure *date* is the word I'd use, but yes, I'm planning on staying awhile. I still have a few weeks before I have to be back. I thought I'd spend it here, doing some thinking. Mostly about my career." Katie slipped her arm through Rosie's and reached out to their mother who stepped forward and wrapped them both in a hug.

"That sounds like a good decision to me. And if you need to talk it through with myself or your father, or need space—whatever you need, we're here for you."

Rosie closed her eyes, enjoying the moment of closeness with her mother and sister.

She was lucky to have this. She knew she was lucky.

Katie sniffed and pulled away. "We're going to mess up Rosie's makeup. Also, the groom might have a panic attack." She smoothed her dress and turned to their father. "How do we look?"

Nick studied them and Rosie could have sworn his eyes were shiny. "Not bad for a pair of reprobates."

Maggie tutted. "Ignore him."

Nick cleared his throat. "I'm proud of my girls. You both look beautiful. Of course you have your mother's genes, so that's to be expected." He winked at Maggie. "How am I doing? Admit it, that was smooth."

Maggie rolled her eyes. "If you didn't expect praise after every compliment, it would be smoother."

"You do look beautiful, Mum," Katie said and Maggie turned to look at herself in the mirror.

"Catherine helped me pick it out. Turns out losing your luggage can in fact have a good side. And talking of Catherine, if you three are all ready, I'd like to join her at the front. She's probably thinking about Dan's father, and how much he would have wanted to see this day. I want to give her moral support and make sure she knows we're here for her. We're all family now." She kissed both the girls, and Nick, and then walked out of the room.

Rosie took a steadying breath.

She felt her father take her hand and slide it into his arm. "Ready?"

She nodded, and tightened her grip on her father's arm. Together they walked through the door to the main room with its picture windows and stunning mountain views. The chairs faced those windows, the snowy forest and snow-capped mountains providing the perfect backdrop. The floral designer had worked with Catherine to produce a perfect winter wedding. The flowers in the room mirrored those in her delicate bouquet—silver dollar eucalyptus, dusty miller, and pure white lisianthus.

It was everything she could have wanted, and she was pleased she and Dan had decided to keep their wedding small and intimate, close friends and family only.

As the music changed, heads turned to look at her and she felt a flutter of nerves.

And then she saw Dan, standing at the front with Jordan.

He smiled, and she walked toward that smile, oblivious to everyone but him.

It didn't feel scary. It felt like the start of an exciting adventure.

She spoke her words, and heard him speak his. Later, she'd think about those words, but right now everything she needed to know was right there in his eyes.

She heard Catherine sniff behind her, or maybe it was her mother, and then Dan was kissing her and she was kissing him back.

"Well, Rosie Reynolds," he said against her mouth, his eyes laughing into hers, "it's too late to change your mind now."

She wrapped her arms around his neck. "I'm never going to change my mind."

"Anything you want to say to me? I'm checking in, like we agreed. I'm listening."

She smiled. "I love you."

"I love you, too. I also happen to be starving, so shall we get the party started?"

She'd already peeped into the room where the party was going to be held. The tables were decorated with silver pine cones and bunches of white anemones, and delicate strands of fairy lights were twisted through ivy. There was a dance floor, and plenty of champagne and the chef from Snowfall Lodge had prepared a winter-themed menu.

It was going to be a night to remember, but she knew this was the part that would stay in her head forever.

She saw her mother and Catherine, arms linked, bonded by the events of the past week. Her father, beaming and proud, and Katie, her hand in Jordan's.

Turning to face the smiling faces, she stepped forward, eager to start her new life with Dan.

Maggie

"MERRY CHRISTMAS."

Maggie opened one eye carefully and saw that Nick was already sitting up. "Why are you awake so early?"

"It's Christmas Day. I couldn't wait to see if Santa had been."

Even when she was half-asleep he could still make her smile. "You are such a child."

"Says the woman who was the last person on the dance floor last night. Catherine made me promise to take you dancing more often."

"Does she know how clumsy you are?"

"Well, I danced with her, so I'm guessing yes. I trod on her feet at least three times."

"You never take me dancing."

"Probably why she told me to do it more often. Are you ready for your presents?" He looked ridiculously eager and she laughed.

"Last time you were this excited was the year you bought me a lawn mower."

"That was a top-of-the-range lawn mower. But this is a million times better than a lawn mower. Catherine told me a present is supposed to be a luxury, not a necessity."

"You talked to Catherine about gifts?"

"She's family now. That means I can ask her all my stupid questions. Also, I suspect she is feeling at least partly responsible for our renewed relationship and doesn't trust me not to mess it up if left to my own devices."

"She did an incredible job yesterday. It was a beautiful wedding. I will never forget it."

"I will never understand why women get so emotional about weddings."

"Excuse me? I saw a tear in your eye when Dan and Rosie kissed."

"Probably dust. So—are you ready for your presents now?"

She lifted herself up on her elbow. "How can you be so sickeningly awake and lively?"

"It's Christmas. It's snowing, and I'm in bed with my wife."

She felt warm and happy. "I might need coffee."

"I already made you coffee. If you sit up, I'll pass it to you." He patted the bed next to him and she sat up and adjusted the pillows.

"Do we have time for this? Everyone is coming here for breakfast and present opening, so unless we want to have another embarrassing moment we'd better get dressed."

"We have time. And I locked the door, so this time no one will walk in unannounced. I'll unlock the door when you've opened your presents." He reached under the bed, retrieved a stack of untidily wrapped gifts and laid them on her lap.

The wrapping made her smile. There was a reason she'd always been the one to take charge of wrapping at Christmas. Nick managed to somehow make everything look as if it was trying to fight its way out of the paper. If they'd had a dog, she would have assumed the dog had eaten it for breakfast.

Feeling ridiculously happy, she opened the first gift and burst out laughing. "A planner?"

"You obviously aspire to being a planner type of person. I want you to tuck it under your arm and stride around like the power woman you are about to become." He leaned across and flipped it open. "Also, I may have already written a few things in there to get you started."

She glanced down and gasped. "*Sex with Nick.* Seriously? Now I have to hide this from the girls!"

"We're allowed a private life, Mags. And I don't only mean a sex life." He kissed her again. "You're going to need that to schedule in all the adventures we're going to take together."

"Oh Nick." She put the planner down. "I was dreading this Christmas, but it's turned out to be the best ever."

"It's only just beginning. Open the next one."

She dutifully opened it and found a brochure for an upmarket bathroom company. "Er—I don't get it."

"It's time we added a touch of luxury to the cottage. We're treating ourselves to a bathroom, complete with underfloor heating so that you can walk round naked without getting frostbite."

She clutched the brochure to her chest. "Do you know the best thing about all this?"

"Getting to spend the rest of your life with a hot, sexy professor who is great at wrapping presents and never breaks things?"

She rolled her eyes. "That, but also staying in our home. Honeysuckle Cottage feels like family. Does that sound stupid?"

"It sounds like something only a woman would say.

Ouch." He ducked as she smacked him over the head with the brochure. "I was teasing you. Of course the house is family. The reason I know that is because it drains our bank account and causes us stress, just like our kids."

Deciding that she couldn't argue with that, she flipped through the brochure. "This is a great idea. I love it."

"And there's this." He pulled a small slim box from under his pillow. It was beautifully wrapped, with an elaborately tied silver bow that gleamed in the light.

"No way did you wrap this."

"What gave it away?"

"Where do you want me to start? The edges are straight. There's ribbon."

"You're right, I didn't wrap it."

It looked like jewelry, but Nick had never bought her jewelry apart from her engagement and wedding rings. Their gifts to each other were invariably practical. A new coat. Hiking boots.

She removed the bow, slid her finger under the wrapping and stared at the narrow box. "This can't be a washing machine."

"It's something to do with gardening."

Intrigued, she flipped open the box. Nestled on a bed of midnight-blue velvet was a delicate pendant shaped like a pine cone. "Oh Nick. It's beautiful. I love it! And I love that you thought of it, and chose it—wait—are those—diamonds?"

"Yes. Most expensive pine cone ever to fall off a tree. I thought it would remind us both of this place." He removed it from the box and fastened it around her neck. "I thought you could wear it for gardening."

"You think I should wear diamonds for gardening?" She took his face in her hands and kissed him. "Thank you."

"There's one more gift."

She pushed the empty wrapping aside and picked up the envelope. "Don't tell me—we're going dogsledding again."

"No, but we probably should." He watched as she opened the envelope and scanned the letter inside.

"A resignation letter?"

"A draft resignation letter. You might want to personalize it."

She sucked in a breath. Holding the letter in her hand made it seem scarily real. "I've been thinking about this a lot."

"If you're going to tell me you can't resign without a job to go to, then I'm not listening. You hate what you do, Mags. Consider it good parenting to resign, because our Katie also hates what she does and you will be leading by example."

Maggie felt something tug deep inside her. She hated the fact that Katie had kept secrets from them, protected them, but how could she judge when she'd done the same? It was funny what you were prepared to do for love. "That wasn't what I was going to say."

"Then what?"

"It was something Catherine said, about how no one would employ her so she decided to employ herself. If I did the training, maybe I could work for myself? I know I'm a hard worker. I know I'm good with plants, and have an eye for design. I don't have to sell myself to myself, if that makes sense."

"It makes perfect sense." He leaned back against the pillows, looking smug. "So now I'm married to a power woman. That is such a turn-on. Tell me honestly, was it the planner that did it? Much as I'd like to stay here all day, we probably should get dressed before company arrives."

"The girls' gifts are already under the tree. My gift to

you, too." She'd thought about it, worried about it, and come to the conclusion that it was the perfect gift for their new life. She hoped she wasn't wrong about that.

"Can I open it in front of them? Is it a sex toy?"

Her playful shove turned into a hug and then something more and by the time they'd showered and changed, everyone was at the door.

Nick flung the door wide, letting in freezing air and the noise that was their family.

Amidst the chorus of Christmas greetings, Catherine produced Maggie's missing suitcase. "It was delivered yesterday, but in all the excitement of the wedding the message didn't come through to me from reception."

Maggie took the suitcase. "This means you girls will have two sets of presents, because I already bought a replacement set."

"Life's tough," Rosie said, "but we'll cope."

Maggie laughed. "Will I have to return my new wardrobe?"

"No." Nick took the suitcase from her. "But I'm pleased to see this, because it contains something very important. Something I need."

"What could you possibly need from my suitcase?" She watched, intrigued, as Nick flipped it open, delved deep and brought out a familiar box.

"Oh *Dad*." Rosie rushed forward and pulled off the lid. "You brought our decorations from home. There's my angel. And the jeweled camel! Now it really does feel like Christmas. You're the best."

Katie was laughing. "This is almost as embarrassing as whipping out baby photos. My contribution is a very impressive Christmas star." She slid her arm around Jordan.

"Please bear in mind that I was seven when I made that star. Don't judge."

"Do I look as if I'm judging?"

Maggie looked at Nick, her throat clogged with emotion. "You packed those decorations?"

"No. They jumped into the case because they didn't want to be left out of a White family Christmas." He shrugged. "And I thought, maybe, you'd be feeling a little nostalgic, and that this box might help. It's a little taste of home, that's all."

"I think it's the most wonderful, thoughtful—" She walked toward him and Rosie stepped between them.

"No! Just—no." She spread out her arms to keep them apart. "I think I speak for all of us when I say how thrilled we are that you and Dad will not be getting a divorce, but we don't need to witness every second of the making up. We're convinced, truly."

"I'm in charge of breakfast," Catherine said, carrying several large bags to the kitchen.

Katie followed her. "I'll help."

Maggie watched as she and Catherine emptied the bags, laughing and talking as they worked smoothly together. Already she saw a change in Katie. She was softer, less sharp and jumpy and the glances she exchanged with Jordan told Maggie that whatever this relationship was, it was making her daughter happy.

There was a pop and a whoop as the first champagne bottle was opened, and then the clink of glasses and the murmur of conversation.

Catherine waved a fork. "Help yourselves to food, then we can open the presents."

There was smoked salmon, scrambled eggs, freshly

baked pastries, and plenty of chilled champagne and orange juice.

Maggie took a moment to appreciate her family. She'd dreaded spending Christmas away from home, and yet it was turning out to be better than ever, which proved that change could be good.

Spending Christmas here had been forced upon her, but it had turned out well.

If she resigned from her job, maybe that would turn out well, too.

"I have a toast." She raised her glass. "To being brave and taking risks."

Everyone joined her in the toast and Nick strolled across to top up her glass.

"I love it when you're brave."

"Do not pour Mum any more champagne," Rosie yelled across the room.

Nick ignored her and poured. "I have no idea why you'd say that. There isn't another woman alive who can tolerate alcohol like your mother."

"Here—put the bottle down and open this, Dad. It has your name on it." Rosie crossed the room and put a box in his hands. "I'll take that." She whisked the champagne bottle away, and passed it to Jordan.

Nick opened the gift and Maggie held her breath. Had she done the right thing?

He opened the box. "It's a soft toy. A dog." He pulled it out, puzzled.

"Yes." Maggie felt ridiculously nervous. "It's a representation of course. The real thing is waiting for you at home. There's a photo of him in the box."

Nick put his hand back in the box and pulled out a photo of a litter of puppies. "Black Labs?"

"The Baxters' dog had a litter last month. I've helped her with them occasionally." When she'd been upset and missing Nick badly. "One in particular took a shine to me. I thought—I know you love dogs, and we've never been able to have one because of Rosie's asthma, but now it's the two of us I thought it was time. Walking it will keep us both fit. And I know we'll need to be careful when Rosie and Dan come to stay—" she smiled at her daughter "—but the Baxters have promised to take care of him whenever we need them to, and we will never let him upstairs in the bedrooms, and our downstairs has wood floors so they should be easy to clean." She waited, watching his face.

"A puppy." Nick studied the photo. "He has intelligent eyes."

"He's so intelligent. I'm already in love with him."

"I could take him to work to soothe stressed students. When is he ready to leave his mother?"

"In a few weeks, but the Baxters will hold on to him for as long as we like. What do you think?"

"I think," Nick said slowly, "that this might be the best gift anyone has ever given me."

"If you're getting a puppy," Katie said, "I might have to rethink moving back home."

"I can't wait to come and stay," Catherine said. "Is February a good month to visit Oxford?"

"Wait until May. Spring in Oxford is gorgeous. It's warmer and it's a perfect month to see all the gardens. We'll walk along the river and I'll take you round the colleges. I'm already looking forward to it." Maggie raised her glass. It seemed unbelievable to think that a month ago she'd been dreading this week, and anxious about meeting Catherine. "We drank to the happy couple yesterday, so today we're drinking to Catherine. Thank you for welcoming us into your home and your life, for giving the White family our first genuine white Christmas, for doing such an incredible job arranging a wedding. To new friends, and new family."

Everyone raised their glasses and chorused her toast.

"Thank you." Catherine was blushing. "I was rather hoping Christmas here could become a new White-Reynolds family tradition. What do you think? Spring in Oxford, and Christmas in Colorado?"

Nick put one arm round her, and the other arm around Maggie, the champagne in his glass dangerously close to spilling. "I'm not sure."

Maggie raised her eyebrows. "What?"

"If you're given more opportunity for practice, you might beat me in a snowball fight."

"I already beat you." Maggie thought about her anxieties that this might be her last family Christmas with her daughter. All she'd thought about was repeating the past. In fact, she'd hung on to the past so hard she'd almost made dents with her fingernails. What a waste of time and energy that had turned out to be. Life did change. Nothing stayed the same. But sometimes the life that lay ahead could be even better than the life they were leaving behind. And whatever happened, she was going to be living that life with Nick. With her family.

She raised her glass again. "Christmas in Colorado."

* * * * *

Keep reading for an excerpt from One More for Christmas *by Sarah Morgan.*

Acknowledgments

I've been writing Christmas books since I was first published, and it's become part of my own festive tradition—one that often stretches until March when the book is delivered! Each time I have a new book published I feel the same sense of excitement, and also gratitude. Much of that gratitude is directed toward my superhuman publishing teams—HQN in the US, and HQ in the UK. So many good (and fun!) people are working hard to bring my stories to readers, and I appreciate their efforts more than I can say.

My editor Flo Nicoll is truly a book magician, so generous with her time and talent, and always able to bring the best out of every story. Working with her is a dream come true.

A published book needs to find an audience and I'm thankful to the many wonderful bloggers and readers who tirelessly read and review my books, and to my publicity dream team, particularly Sophie Calder, Lucy Richardson, Lisa Wray and Anna Robinson.

My agent Susan Ginsburg brings insight, energy, support and guidance to my writing career. I'm grateful both to her and to the whole team at Writers House, for the tireless advocacy.

I'm lucky to have a family who have always been supportive and encouraged my love of writing. Thank you for understanding when I pull out a notebook and start scribbling at awkward moments.

As always, my biggest thanks goes to my readers, so many of whom take the time to contact me with kind messages, book recommendations, and to express enthusiasm for my stories. Thank you for picking up another book of mine and I hope this book will add some warmth and festivity to your winter reading.

Love, Sarah
xxxx

Gayle

When Gayle Mitchell agreed to a live interview in her office, she hadn't expected her life to fall apart in such a spectacular fashion in front of an audience of millions. She was used to giving interviews and had no reason to think that this one might end in disaster, so she sat relaxed, even a little bored, as the crew set up the room.

As usual, the lights were blinding and kicked out enough heat to roast a haunch of beef. Despite the frigid air-conditioning, the fabric of Gayle's fitted black dress stuck to her thighs.

Beyond the soaring glass walls of her office lay what she truly believed to be the most exciting city on earth. Also one of the most expensive—but these days Gayle didn't have to worry too much about that.

Once, the place had almost killed her, but that had been a long time ago. That memory contributed to the degree of satisfaction she felt in being up here, on top of the world, gazing down from her domain on the fiftieth floor. Like planting a stiletto on the body of an adversary, it was symbolic of victory. *I won.* She was far removed from those people scurrying along the freezing, canyon-like streets of Manhattan, struggling to survive in a city that devoured the weak and the vulnerable. From her vantage point in her corner office she could see the Empire State Building, the Rockefeller Center and, in the distance, the broad splash of green that was Central Park.

Gayle shifted in her chair as someone touched up her hair and makeup. The director was talking to the cameraman, discussing angles and light, while seated in the chair across from her the most junior female reporter on the morning show studied her notes with feverish attention.

Rochelle Barnard. She was young. Early twenties? A few years older than Gayle had been when she'd hit the lowest point of her life.

Nothing excited Gayle more than raw potential, and she saw plenty of it in Rochelle. You had to know what you were looking for, of course—and Gayle knew. It was there in the eyes, in the body language, in the attitude. And this woman had something else that Gayle always looked for. *Hunger.*

Hunger was the biggest motivator of all, and no one knew that better than her.

She hadn't just been hungry—she'd been starving. Also desperate. But usually she managed to forget that part. She was a different woman now, and able to extend a hand to another woman who might need a boost.

"Ten minutes, Miss Mitchell."

Gayle watched as the lighting guy adjusted the reflector. In a way, didn't she do much the same thing? She shone a light on people who would otherwise have remained in the dark. She changed lives, and she was about to change this woman's life.

"Put the notes down," she said. "You don't need them."

Rochelle glanced up. "These are the questions they want me to ask. They only handed them to me five minutes ago."

Because they want you to stumble and fall, Gayle thought.

"Are they the questions *you* would have chosen to ask?"

The woman rustled through the papers and pulled a face. "Honestly? No. But this is what they want covered in the interview."

Gayle leaned forward. "Do you always do what other people tell you?"

Rochelle shook her head. "Not always."

"Good to know. Because if you did, then you wouldn't be the woman I thought you were when I saw you present that short segment from Central Park last week."

"You saw that?"

"Yes. Your questions were excellent, and you refused to let that weasel of a man wriggle out of answering."

"That interview was the reason you asked for me today? I've been wondering."

"You struck me as a young woman with untapped potential."

"I'm grateful for the opportunity." Rochelle sat straighter and smoothed her skirt. "I can't believe I'm here. Howard usually does all the high-profile interviews."

Why were people so accepting of adverse circumstances? So slow to realize their own power? But power came with risk, of course, and most people were averse to risk.

"Things are always the way they are until we change them," Gayle said. "Be bold. Decide what you want and go after it. If that means upsetting a few people along the way, then do it." She closed her eyes as someone stroked a strand of her hair into place and sprayed it. "This is your chance to ask me the questions Howard Banks wouldn't think to ask."

Which shouldn't be too hard, she thought, *because the man had the imagination and appeal of stale bread.*

Howard had interviewed her a decade earlier and he'd been patronizing and paternalistic. It gave Gayle pleasure to know that by insisting on being interviewed by this junior reporter she'd annoyed him. With any luck he'd burst a blood vessel in the most valuable part of his anatomy—which, for him, was probably his ego.

"If I don't give them what they're expecting, I could lose my job."

Gayle opened one eye. "Not if you give them something *better* than they're expecting. They're not going to fire you if the ratings go up. What's on their list? Let me guess... My work-life balance and how I handle being a woman in a man's world?"

Boring, boring.

The woman laughed. "You're obviously a pro at this."

"Think of the people watching. Ask the questions *they'd* ask if they were in the room with me. If you were a woman eager to make a change in your life, what would *you* want to hear? If you were struggling to get ahead in the workplace—" *which you are* "—constantly blocked by those around you, what would you want to know?"

Rochelle picked up the papers from her lap and folded

them in a deliberate gesture. "I'd want to know your se-crets—how you handle it all. How you handled it at the beginning, before you had everything you have now. You started with nothing. Put yourself through college while working three jobs. And you've become one of the most successful women in business. You've transformed com-panies and individuals. I'd want to know whether any of your experiences might be of use to me. Whether you could transform *me*. I'd want to come away feeling so inspired I'd call the show and thank them."

"And you think they'd fire you for that?"

The woman stared at her. "No, I don't." She slapped the papers down on the desk. "What is *wrong* with me? I've read all your books several times, and yet I was about to ask the questions I'd been handed. One of my favorite sec-tions in your last book was that bit about other people's ex-pectations being like reins, holding you back. You were our role model in college." She pressed her palm to her chest. "Meeting you is the best Christmas gift."

"Christmas?"

"It's only a few weeks away. I love the holidays, don't you?"

Gayle did not love the holidays. She didn't like the way everything closed down. She didn't like the crowds on the streets or the tacky decorations. She didn't like the uncom-fortable memories that stuck to her like bits of parcel tape.

"Aren't you a little old to be excited about Christmas?" she asked.

"Never!" Rochelle laughed. "I love a big family gather-ing. Massive tree. Gifts in front of the fire. You know the type of thing…"

Gayle turned her attention to the makeup artist, who was brandishing lipstick. "Not that horrible brown. Red."

"But—"

"Red. And not an insipid washed-out red. I want a *look at me* red. I have the perfect one in my purse."

There was much scrambling and an appropriate lipstick was produced.

Gayle sat still while the makeup artist finished her work. "This is your opportunity, Rochelle. Take it and ride it all the way home. If you make an impression on the public, your bosses won't be able to hold you back."

There.

Done.

Gayle had the power to give her a boost and she'd used it. She liked to give people the kind of chance she'd never been given. The rest was up to them.

"Five minutes, Ms. Mitchell." The director scanned her shelves. "When we've finished the interview we might take a few stills for promotional purposes."

"Whatever you need." If her story inspired people, then she was happy. She wanted women to understand their own strength and power.

Rochelle leaned forward. "In case I don't have a chance to thank you properly after, I just want to say how grateful I am for your support. Do you have any idea how inspiring it is to know that you live the life you talk about in your books? You're the real deal. You're right at the top of your game, but still you take the time to reach out and give others a helping hand."

Her eyes glistened and Gayle felt a flash of alarm.

The helping hand didn't come with tissues. Emotion had no place in designing a life. It clouded decision-making and influenced those around you. Gayle's staff knew better than to bring emotion to a conversation.

Give me facts, give me solutions—don't give me sobbing.

Rochelle didn't know that. "At college we had a mantra—what would GM do?" She blushed. "I hope you don't mind that we called you that."

Some said that GM stood for Great Mind, others Guru of Management. A few of her own staff thought it stood for Genetically Modified, but no one had the courage to tell her that.

Rochelle's admiration continued to flow across the desk. "You're afraid of nothing and no one. You've been an inspiration to so many of us. The way you've shaped your career, your life. You never apologize for the choices you make."

Why should she apologize? Who would she apologize *to*?

"Use this opportunity, Rochelle. Did my assistant give you a copy of my next book?"

"Yes. Signed." Rochelle appeared to have reined in her inner fangirl. "And I think it's *so* cool that you have a male assistant."

"I employ the best person for the job. In this case it's Cole."

Out of the corner of her eye she checked the desks of her top executives. She and Bill Keen were the only members of the company to have their own offices. The others worked in the bright open space that stretched the width of the building. Occasionally Gayle would survey her domain from the protection of her glass-fronted oasis and think, *I built this myself, with nothing more than guts and a grim determination to survive.*

The shiny globe of Simon Belton's bald head was just visible above the top of his cubicle. He'd arrived before her that morning, which had boosted her mood. He was a hard worker, if a little lacking in truly innovative ideas. Next to him sat Marion Lake. Gayle had hired her the year before as head of marketing, but she was starting to think the appointment might have been a mistake. Just that morning Gayle had noticed her jacket slung casually over the back of her chair, its presence indicating that Marion was somewhere in the building.

Gayle's mouth thinned. When she gave people a chance, she expected them to take it.

Even now, after all these years, people constantly underestimated her. Did they really think she'd see a jacket draped over the back of a chair and assume the owner was somewhere in the office? There had been no coffee on the desk, and Gayle knew that Marion couldn't operate without coffee. And the place had the atmosphere of a cemetery. Marion had a loud voice and an irritating compulsion to use it frequently—a flaw possibly related to the volume of coffee she drank. If she had been anywhere in the vicinity, Gayle would have heard her.

She often thought she would have made an excellent detective.

"Going live in three minutes," one of the film crew told her, and Gayle settled herself more comfortably, composing her features.

She'd done hundreds of interviews, both live and recorded. They held no fear for her. There wouldn't be a single question she hadn't already been asked a hundred times. And if she didn't like a question, she simply answered a different one. Like everything else, it was a matter of choice. They weren't in control—*she* was.

In her head she hummed a few bars of the Puccini opera she'd seen the week before. Glorious. Dramatic and tragic, of course... But that was life, wasn't it?

Rochelle smoothed her hair and cleared her throat.

"Live in five, four, three..."

The man held up two fingers, then one, and Gayle looked

at the young reporter, hoping her questions would be good. She didn't want to have misjudged her.

Rochelle spoke directly to the camera, her voice clear and confident. "Hi, I'm Rochelle Barnard and I'm here at the offices of Mitchell and Associates in downtown Manhattan to interview Gayle Mitchell—more commonly known as GM to her staff and her legions of fans—one of the most powerful and celebrated women in business. Her last book, *Choice Not Chance*, spent twelve months at the top of the bestseller lists and her latest book, *Brave New You*, is out next week. She's one of the leading authorities on organizational change, and is also known for her philanthropic work. Most of all she's celebrated as a supporter of women, and just this week was presented with the coveted Star Award for most inspirational woman in business at a glitzy event right here in Manhattan. Congratulations, Ms. Mitchell. How does it feel to have your contribution recognized?"

Gayle angled her head, offering her best side to the camera. "I'm honored, of course, but the real honor comes from helping other women realize their potential. We're so often told that we can't compete, Rochelle, and as a leader my role is to encourage other women to challenge that view."

She smiled, careful to portray herself as approachable and accessible.

"You're known to be a fierce advocate for women in the workplace. What drives that?"

Gayle answered, the words flowing easily and naturally.

Rochelle threw a few more questions her way, and she handled those with the same ease.

"People either love you or hate you. There seems to be no middle ground. Does it worry you that some people consider you to be ruthless?"

"I'm tough, and I make no apologies for that," Gayle said. "There are people who will always be threatened by the success of another, and people who shy away from change. I embrace change. Change is progress, and we need progress. Change is what keeps us moving forward."

"In your company you run an internship program with one of the most generous packages of any industry. You also offer scholarships. Why have you chosen to invest in this area?"

Because once, a long time ago, when she'd been alone and desperate, she'd vowed that if she was ever in a position to help someone like herself, then she'd do it.

But she didn't share that. Such an admission might easily be seen as weakness. And how could they possibly understand? This girl sitting opposite her had never experienced the hard grip of fear. Gayle knew how deeply those claws could bite. She understood that fear could make you a prisoner, holding you inactive. Breaking free of that wasn't easy. She was willing to hand a key to a few worthy individuals.

"I see it as an investment…" She talked a little more about the role she'd played fighting for the underprivileged and saw Rochelle's eyes mist with admiration.

"Some people think you've been lucky. How would you answer that?"

Not politely.

Luck had played no part in Gayle's life. She'd made careful choices, driven by thought and not emotion. Nothing had happened by chance. She'd *designed* her life, and now it was looking exactly the way she wanted it to look.

"It's easier to dismiss someone as 'lucky' than it is to admit that the power for change lies within the individual. By calling someone 'lucky' you diminish their achievement, and the need to do that often comes from a place of insecurity. Believing in luck absolves you of personal responsibility. Whatever you do in life, whatever your goals, it's important to make active choices."

She looked into the camera.

"If you're feeling dissatisfied with your life, find a piece of paper right now and write down all the things you wish were different. You don't like your life? Do something about it! You envy someone? What do they have that you don't? How do you want your life to look? Deciding that is the first step to redesigning it."

Rochelle was nodding. "Your last book, *Choice Not Chance*, changed my life—and I know I'm not alone in that."

"If you have a personal story we'd all love to hear it…"

Gayle drew in the audience, as she would if she were speaking to them live. She knew that right now, in living rooms and kitchens across the nation, women would be glued to the screen, hoping for a magic bullet that would fix their lives. Phones would go unanswered, babies would go unfed and unchanged, doorbells would be ignored. Hope would bloom, and a brief vision of a different future would blast away fatigue and disillusionment.

Gayle knew that once the interview ended, most would just sink back into their own lives, but right now they were with her. They wanted to be inspired.

"Hearing people's personal experiences can be motivational and uplifting for everyone. My approach to life is relevant whether you run a household or a corporation."

"I ended a relationship." Rochelle gave a nervous laugh, as if surprised that she'd actually admitted that on prime-time TV. "After I read the chapter 'Obstacles to Ambition,' I wrote down everything that might stop me achieving my goals, and the guy I was seeing was top of the list. And that chapter on auditing friendships…? Decluttering your contacts…? Brilliant! Asking yourself, *How does this relationship bring me closer to my goals?* And I wanted to ask *you*, GM, is this something you've done yourself?"

"Of course. My books are basically a blueprint of the way I've lived my life—but it can apply to anyone's life. The main takeaway from *Choice Not Chance* is to challenge yourself. *Brave New You* focuses on confronting our innate fear of change."

There. She'd slotted in a mention of the book, and because it was live it wouldn't be cut. Her publisher would be pleased.

"I want all women—from the barista who serves me my coffee every morning to the woman who manages my investments—to feel in control of their destiny." She gave the camera an intense look. "You have more power than you know."

Rochelle leaned forward. "You're famous for saying that no one can have it all. Have you made sacrifices for your career?"

"I've made choices, not sacrifices. *Choices.* Know what you want. Go for it. No apologies."

"And you've never had any regrets?"

Regrets?

Gayle's world wobbled a little. How well had this woman done her research?

She sat up a little straighter and looked at the camera. "No regrets."

And just like that, the interview was over.

Rochelle unclipped her microphone. "Thank you."

"You're welcome." Gayle stood up. "How did you get your start in TV?"

"I applied for a ton of things after college but had no luck with anything." Rochelle was relaxed and chatty now the interview was over. "Then I was offered an internship at the studio. I shadowed a reporter, and they let me present a little because they thought I looked good on camera. So I suppose you could say I fell into it."

Gayle winced. You fell into snowdrifts—not jobs.

"Today is a crossroads for you. Doors will open. I hope you walk through them."

"Thanks, GM. I'm never going to forget what you've done for me." Rochelle glanced at the crew and then back at Gayle. "We need photos so we can promote the interview on our site and social media."

"Of course." Gayle walked to her bookshelves and posed in what she knew was the most flattering position, careful that both her books were in the shot, face out.

Did they know that today was her birthday? No, why would they? Her digital team had scrubbed all mention of her birth date from the internet, so her age was shrouded in mystery. Birthdays slid past like the seasons—unmarked and frankly unwanted. She preferred to keep the focus on her achievements.

The photographer glanced around him. "Could we have a photograph with the award?"

The award?

Gayle glanced upward. The award had been placed on the top shelf of the bookcase that lined the only solid wall of her office. Had it been attractive she might have displayed it somewhere more prominent, but it was an ugly monstrosity, the brainchild of someone apparently devoid of both inspiration and artistic skill. The golden star itself was inoffensive, but it had been attached to a particularly ugly base. The first thing she'd thought on being presented with it the night before was that it reminded her of a gravestone.

Her opinion of it hadn't mellowed overnight.

She looked at the award again, loathing it as much as she had when she'd received it—although of course at the time she'd smiled and looked delighted. What message would it send for her to be photographed with something so lacking in aesthetic charm? That she was ready for the grave and had the headstone to prove it?

She glanced outside to where Cole, her assistant, was supposed to be sitting during the interviews in case he was needed. Where *was* he? He should have anticipated this and had the statue ready.

She could either wait for his return—which would mean the TV crew lingering in her office—or she could get the damn thing herself.

Irritated, she slid off her shoes and pulled her office chair over to the bookcase.

The photographer cleared his throat. "I should get that for you, Ms. Mitchell. I'm taller than you, and—"

"Chairs were invented so that women could stand on them when necessary."

Still, she was about to curse Cole for putting it on the highest shelf when she remembered she was, in fact, the one who had instructed him to do that.

Stepping onto the chair, she reached out.

Why had he put it so far back? Presumably Cole found it as loathsome as she did.

She rose on tiptoe and felt the chair wobble slightly.

She closed her right hand around the base of the award, remembering too late that it had required two hands to hold it steady when she'd been handed it the night before. As she swung it down from the shelf, the chair wobbled again, sending her body off-balance.

By the time she realized she was going to fall, it was too late to recover.

She groped for the bookcase with her free hand, but instead of providing solid support it tilted toward her. She had time to make a mental note to fire the clueless individual who had forgotten to secure the bookshelves to the wall, and then she was falling, falling, falling… One of the points of the heavy golden star smashed into her head and she crashed onto the hard office floor.

She was conscious for long enough to wish the decorator had given her deep-pile carpet. And then everything went black.

She missed the sound of Rochelle screaming and the sight of the camera rolling.

For a brief period of time she was blissfully oblivious to the chaos erupting around her.

Her return to consciousness was slow and confusing. She heard a low humming sound, a whirring in her head. Was she dead? Surely not. She could hear things.

She could hear people panicking around her, even though panic was an emotion specifically banned from her office.

"Oh my *God*, is she dead? *Is she dead?*"

"Not dead. She's definitely breathing."

Gayle was relieved to have that confirmed by an outside source.

"But she's unconscious. I called 911. They're on their way."

"Is that an actual *hole* in her head? I feel a little faint."

"Pull yourself together." A rough, male voice. "Did you get the shot, Greg?"

"Yeah, the whole thing is on camera. It'll be a happy day for the headline writers. My money is on STARSTRUCK!"

"Could you be just a little sensitive here?" Rochelle's voice, sounding traumatized. "She's badly injured and you're writing headlines!"

Didn't they *know* she could hear them? Why were people so clueless? She had no idea how long she'd been knocked out. A minute? An hour? A day? No, if it had been a day she'd be lying in a hospital bed now, surrounded by a chorus of beeping machines.

Her chest hurt. Why did her chest hurt?

She remembered the bookshelves falling with her.

Someone must have caught them, or lifted them off her. As for the fate of the award—she had no idea. If the pain was anything to go by, there was a possibility it was still embedded in her head.

There was a crashing sound and the doors to her office burst open.

Gayle tried to open her eyes and give someone her scariest stare, but her eyelids felt too heavy.

She heard more voices, this time firm and confident—presumably the EMTs.

"What's her name?"

Why was he asking her name? Didn't he recognize her? *Everyone* knew who she was. She was a legend. She'd just won an award for being inspirational, and if they couldn't see the actual award then surely they could see the award-sized dent in her skull.

She was going to write to the organizers and suggest a brooch for the next winner.

"Gayle, can you hear me? I'm Dan."

Why was he calling her Gayle when they'd never met? She was either Ms. Mitchell or GM. Young people today had no respect. This was why she insisted on formality in the office.

This "Dan" barked out some instructions to his partner and proceeded to assess her injuries.

Gayle felt herself being poked and prodded.

"Has someone contacted her family? Loved ones?"

"Her...what?" That was Cole, sounding stressed and confused.

"Loved ones. Nearest and dearest." The EMT was pressing something to her head.

"I don't think—" Cole cleared his throat. "She doesn't have loved ones."

"She must have *someone*." Dan eased Gayle's eyes open and used a flashlight.

"That's probably the first time anyone has looked into her eyes in a long time."

Funny, Gayle thought. Until that moment she hadn't even realized Cole had a sense of humor. It was a shame it was at her expense.

"Partner?" Dan again, doing something that apparently was meant to support her neck.

"No. Just work. She loves her work."

"Are you telling me she has no one in her life?"

"Well, there's Puccini..."

"Great. So give this Puccini guy a call and tell him what's happened. He can meet us at the hospital."

Gayle wanted to roll her eyes, but her head hurt too badly. She hoped this EMT knew more about head injuries than he did about culture.

"Puccini was a composer. Opera. GM loves opera. People? Not so much. She isn't a family type of person. GM is married to her work."

Dan clipped something to Gayle's finger. "Oh man, that's sad."

Sad? *Sad?*

She ran one of the most successful boutique consulting firms in Manhattan. She was in demand as a speaker. She'd written a bestseller—soon to be two bestsellers if preorders were anything to go by. What was sad about that? Her life was the subject of envy, not pity.

"Makes her a bitch to work for, actually," Cole muttered. "I couldn't go to my grandmother's funeral because she had a ten o'clock and I needed to be here."

Cole thought she was a *bitch*?

No—*no*! She wasn't a bitch. She was an *inspiration*! That journalist had said so. Yes, she worked hard, but there was a perfectly good reason for that. And if she hadn't worked hard and turned the company into the success it was now, her team wouldn't have their nice comfortable secure jobs. Why couldn't they see that? Maybe she should use that award to knock some sense into her staff on a daily basis.

It was time she showed them she was awake—before she discovered more about herself she didn't want to know.

"I don't get it," the EMT said, slapping the back of Gayle's hand to find a vein. "I guess if you don't have family, then you work. It's that simple."

He slid a needle into Gayle's vein, and if she'd been capable of speech or movement, she would have punched him—both for the pain and his words.

It wasn't that simple *at all*. They were implying she worked because she was lonely, but that wasn't the case. Her work wasn't her backup plan—it was her *choice*.

She'd chosen every single thing about her life. She'd *designed* her life. Written a book about it, dammit. Her life was perfect for her. Custom-made. A haute couture life. Everything she'd ever wanted.

"I guess her life must be pretty empty."

Empty? Had they looked around at *all*? Seen the view from her corner office? True, she didn't often look at it herself, because she was too busy to turn around, but she'd been told it was magnificent. Hadn't they seen the photographs of her with industry leaders?

She led a *full life*.

"Yeah, poor thing…"

She wasn't a poor thing. She was a powerhouse.

All they saw was the businesswoman. They knew nothing else about her. They didn't know how hard she'd had to work to arrive at this place in her life. They didn't know *why* she was this way. They didn't know she had a past. A history. They didn't know all the things that had happened to her.

They didn't know her at all. They thought she had an empty life. They thought she was a lonely, sad figure. They were wrong.

They were—

Were they wrong?

She felt a sudden wash of cold air and saw a blinding light.

That question Rochelle had asked her, echoed in her head: *And you've never had any regrets?*

The faint wobble inside her became something bigger. It spread from the inside outward until her whole body was shaking.

She didn't have regrets. She did *not* have regrets.

Regret was a wasted emotion—first cousin to guilt. Gayle had no room for either in her life.

But the shaking wouldn't stop.

"We'll get her to the ER."

As well as the shaking, now there was a terrifying pressure in her chest. Had they forgotten to lift the bookcase from her mangled body? No. No, it wasn't that. The pressure was coming from the inside, not the outside. Heart? No. It wasn't physical. It was emotional.

"Her pulse rate is increasing."

Of *course* it was increasing! Emotion did that to you. It messed you up. It was the reason she tried never to let it into her life. She had no idea who had allowed it in now—because it certainly hadn't been her. It must have crept in through the hole in her head.

"She might be bleeding from somewhere. Let's move. If there's no one at home to care for her, they'll probably admit her."

She was going to be admitted to the hospital because all she had in her life was work and Puccini. Neither of those was going to bring her a glass of water or check she was alive in the night.

She lay there, trapped inside her bruised, broken body, forcing herself to do what she urged others to do. Acknowledge the truth of her life.

She ran a successful company. She had an apartment full of art and antiques on the Upper East Side and enough money that she never had to worry about it. But she had no one who would rush to her side when she was in trouble.

Cole was here because he was paid to be here, so that didn't count.

She wasn't loved. There was no one who cared about her. Not one person who would hear about the accident and think, *Oh no! Poor Gayle!* No one would be calling a florist and ordering flowers. No one would be delivering a casserole to her door or asking if there was anything she needed.

She was alone in this life she'd designed for herself.

Completely, totally and utterly alone.

She realized why most people were reluctant to examine the truth of their lives. It was an uncomfortable experience.

What had she done?

She'd chosen her life, designed her life, and now she didn't like the way it was looking.

In that moment Gayle had an epiphany—and not a good one.

What if she'd chosen the wrong design? What if all the choices she'd made had been wrong? What if all these techniques she'd recommended to people through her books were wrong, too?

She needed to stop publication.

She needed to tell her publisher she wanted to rethink the book. How could she promote *Brave New You* when she was lying on the floor shivering like a wounded animal?

She opened her mouth and tried to croak out some words.

"She's moving. She's conscious! Gayle— Gayle, can you hear me?"

Yes, she could hear him. She was unloved—not deaf.

She forced her eyes open and saw a uniformed EMT and behind him Cole, looking worried. There was the cameraman, and also Rochelle, scribbling frantically. Making the most of an opportunity, Gayle thought. Taking the advice she'd been given and redesigning her life.

And that was when she had her second epiphany. Who said you could only design your life once? People remodeled houses all the time, didn't they? Just because you'd lived with white walls for decades didn't mean you couldn't suddenly paint them green.

If she didn't like the way her life looked, then it was up to her to fix it.

And, although she didn't regret her actions, exactly, she did regret the outcome of those actions.

Maybe she could have done more.

Maybe it wasn't too late to rebuild what had been knocked down.

But she had to be the one to make the first move.

"My daughter." Her lips formed the words. "Call...my daughter."

She saw Cole's face pale. "She's conscious, but she has a serious head injury. She's confused. She has amnesia."

The EMT frowned. "Why would you say that?"

"Because GM doesn't *have* a daughter."

Gayle thought about the baby they'd put into her arms. The way it had felt to be entirely responsible for the well-being of a tiny, helpless infant, knowing what lay ahead. How hard life could be. If it hadn't been for the child, she might have given up, but motherhood had driven her on. How could she give up when she had her daughter to protect? She'd wanted to swaddle her in steel and surround her with an electric fence to keep the bad at bay.

"Gayle, do you know what day it is?"

Yes, she knew what day it was. It was the day she'd started questioning everything she'd believed was right. The day she'd realized that regret could hurt more than a bruised head and crushed ribs. How could she have got everything so wrong?

She tried again. "Call my eldest daughter."

What if she died before she had a chance to fix things?

"Eldest...?" Cole looked nervous. "She doesn't have one daughter, let alone more. Ms. Mitchell—Gayle—how many fingers am I holding up? Can you tell me?"

Right at that moment she wanted to hold up her own finger. Her middle one.

"Call my daughter."

"She isn't confused. Gayle Mitchell has two daughters," Rochelle said. "I did a deep dive into her background before the interview. My research suggests they're estranged."

Estranged? No, that wasn't right. True, they hadn't seen each other for a while. Maybe a few years. All right, perhaps it was nearly five years... Gayle couldn't remember. But she did remember their last encounter. When she thought about it—which she tried not to—she felt affronted and hurt.

None of it had been her fault. She'd been doing her best for them—which was all she'd ever done. She'd worked hard at being the best mother possible. She'd made sure she'd equipped her children to deal with the real world and experienced a mother's frustration when her girls had made bad choices. She'd discovered the anguish of having all of the anxiety but none of the control. She'd done her best. It wasn't her fault that they preferred the fairy tale to the reality. It wasn't her fault that they were unable to appreciate how well she'd prepared them for adulthood.

Yes, relations between them were tense, but they weren't *estranged*. That was a truly horrible word. A word with razor-sharp edges.

Cole appeared to be suffering from shock.

"She has *kids*? But that means that she—I mean she must have had—"

The fact that he was struggling to picture her having sex wasn't flattering. He clearly thought his boss was a robot.

"All right. If you're sure, then we should call the daughters." His voice was strangled. "Is there a phone number, Ms. Mitchell?"

Would Samantha have changed her number?

She hadn't called, so Gayle had no way of knowing.

She'd been waiting for both of them to call her and apologize. Days had melted into weeks and then months. Shame flooded through her. What did it say about a mother when her own children didn't want to make contact?

If she admitted the truth, would her judgmental staff and the medical team decide she wasn't worth saving?

Instead of answering, she moaned.

That caused more consternation among the people gathered around her.

"She's struggling to speak—can we find out her daughter's number?"

"I'm searching…" Rochelle tapped away on her phone. "One of her daughters is called Samantha."

Gayle gasped as the EMT and his assistant transferred her to a gurney.

Cole was searching, too. "There's a Samantha Mitchell in New Jersey. Comedian. No *way*."

Was he implying that she didn't have a sense of humor? That laughter didn't figure in her DNA?

"There's a Samantha Mitchell in Chicago…a Samantha Mitchell, dog walker, in Ohio. Samantha Mitchell CEO of a bespoke travel company in Boston…" He looked up as Gayle made a sound. "That's her? She runs a travel company?"

Boston? Samantha had moved cities? It wasn't enough not to speak to her mother—she clearly didn't want to risk running into her on the street.

Gayle tried to ignore the pain. She was willing to be the bigger person. Kids disappointed you. It was a fact of life. She would forgive and move on. She wanted to do that. She wanted them in her life. Their relationship never should have reached this point.

And CEO!

Through the ashes of her misery, Gayle discovered a glowing ember of pride. *You go, girl.*

Whether Samantha admitted it or not, there was plenty of her mother in her.

As they wheeled her through the office to the elevator, she caught a glimpse of the shocked faces of her staff, who had never once seen GM vulnerable in all the time they'd worked at Mitchell and Associates.

But she felt vulnerable now. Not because of the head injury, and not even because of the photos that the wretched photographer had taken of her unfortunate accident, nor the prospect of headlines as painful as the injury itself.

No, she felt vulnerable because someone was about to contact Samantha.

And there was every possibility that her daughter wouldn't even take the call.

From award-winning *USA TODAY* bestselling author

SARAH MORGAN

comes this heartwarming, emotionally rich new novel, brimming with her trademark Christmas sparkle!

In the snowy Highlands of Scotland, Suzanne McBride is dreaming of the perfect cozy Christmas. Her three adopted daughters are coming home for the holidays, and she can't wait to see them. But tensions are running high...

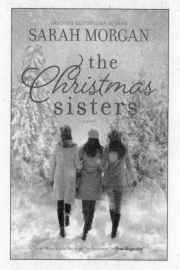

"Sarah Morgan puts the magic in Christmas." —*NOW Magazine*

Order your copy today!

GEOLOGY

by

FRANK H. T. RHODES

Dean of the College
of Literature, Science and
the Arts, University of Michigan

Illustrated by

RAYMOND PERLMAN

Professor of Art, University of Illinois

GOLDEN PRESS • NEW YORK
Western Publishing Company, Inc.
Racine, Wisconsin

FOREWORD

"**THE EARTH**—love it or leave it," is a popular slogan evolving from man's recognition of the perils of an exploding population, a polluted environment, and the limited natural resources of an already plundered planet. Effective solutions to our environmental problems demand an effective knowledge of the earth on which we live.

The object of this book is to introduce the earth: its relation to the rest of the universe, the rocks and minerals of which it is made up, the forces that shape it, and the 5,000,000,000 years of history that have given it its present form. Many topics that are discussed in the book have a very practical and urgent significance for our society, things such as water supply, industrial minerals, ore deposits, and fuels. Others are of importance in longer planning and development, such as earthquake effects, marine erosion, landslides, arid regions, and so on. The earth provides the ultimate basis of our present society: the air we breathe, the water we drink, the food we eat, the materials we use. All are the products of our planet.

The study of the earth opens our eyes to a vast scale of time that provides us with new dimensions, meanings, and perspectives. And it reveals the order of the earth, its dynamic interdependence and its structured beauty.

F. H. T. R.

CONTENTS

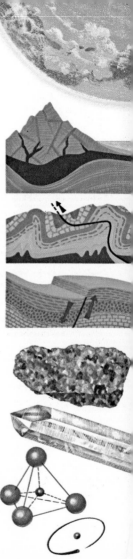

Volcanic eruption in Kapoho, Hawaii. Many islands in the Pacific are volcanic in origin.

GEOLOGY AND OURSELVES

Geology is the study of the earth. As a science, it is a newcomer in comparison with, say, astronomy. Whereas geology is only about 200 years old, astronomy was actively studied by the Egyptians as long as 4,000 years ago. Yet speculation about the earth and its activities must be as old as man himself. Surely, primitive man was familiar with natural disasters such as earthquakes, volcanic eruptions, and droughts.

Gradually, as primitive man's knowledge increased, he became more dependent upon the earth in increasingly complex ways. Today, behind the insulation of our modern living conditions, civilization remains basically dependent upon our knowledge of the earth. All our minerals, fuels, and building and constructional materials come from the earth's crust. Water supply, agriculture, and land use also depend upon sound geologic information.

Geology stimulates the mind. It makes use of almost all other sciences and gives much to them in return.

THE BRANCH OF GEOLOGY emphasized here is physical geology. Other Nature Guides of this series, *Rocks and Minerals* and *Fossils*, deal with the branches of mineralogy, petrology, and paleontology.

PHYSICAL GEOLOGY is the overall study of the earth, embracing most other branches of geology but stressing the dynamic and structural aspects. It includes a study of landscape development, the earth's interior, the nature of mountains, and the composition of rocks and minerals.

HISTORICAL GEOLOGY is the study of the history of the earth and its inhabitants. It traces ancient geographies and the evolution of life.

ECONOMIC GEOLOGY is geology applied to the search for and exploitation of mineral resources such as metallic ores, fuels, and water.

STRUCTURAL GEOLOGY (tectonics) is the study of earth structures and their relationship to the forces which produce the structures.

GEOPHYSICS is the study of the earth's physical properties. It includes the study of earthquakes (seismology) and methods of mineral exploration.

PHYSICAL OCEANOGRAPHY is closely related to geology and is concerned with the seas, major ocean basins, sea floors, and the crust beneath them.

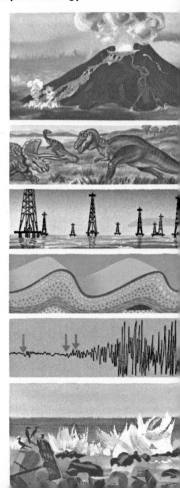

THE SIZE AND SHAPE OF THE EARTH were not always calculated accurately. Most ancient peoples thought the earth was flat, but there are many simple proofs that the earth is a sphere. For instance, as a ship approaches from over the horizon, masts or funnels are visible. As the ship comes closer, more of its lower parts come into view. Final proof, of course, is provided by photographs taken from man-made space craft.

The Greek geographer and astronomer Eratosthenes was probably the first (about 225 B.C.) to measure successfully the circumference of the earth. The basis for his calculations was the measurement of the elevation of the sun from two different points on the globe. Two simultaneous observations were made, one from Alexandria, Egypt, and the other from a site on the Nile near the present Aswan Dam. At the latter point, a good vertical sighting could be made, as the sun was known to shine directly down a well at high noon on the longest day (June 23) of that year.

Eratosthenes reasoned that if the earth were round, the noonday sun could not appear in the same position in the sky as seen by two widely separated observers. He compared the angular displacement of the sun with the distance between the two ground sites, A and B. He assumed that the measured ground distance (x) should represent a portion of the earth's circumference. His measured ground distance was 5,000 stadia, about 575 miles. The angular displacement of the sun (y) was found to be slightly more than 7°; the observer on the Nile saw the sun directly overhead at noon but the observer at Alexandria had to incline his sighting device more than 7° from the vertical to it. Since a reading of 7° 12' corresponds to one-fiftieth of a full circle (360°), the 5,000 stadia ground distance represented one-fiftieth of the earth's circumference. Eratosthenes calculated that that entire circumference was about 28,750 miles.

RECENT DATA from orbiting earth satellites have confirmed that the earth is actually slightly flattened at the poles. It is an oblate spheroid, rather than a sphere. Since the polar circumference is 27 miles less than at the equator, it is also flatter at the poles. The following measurements are currently accepted:

Avg. diameter	7,918 mi.
Avg. radius	3,959 mi.
Avg. circumference	24,900 mi.

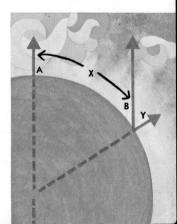

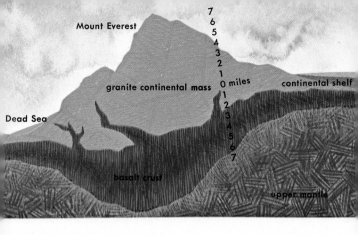

THE EARTH'S SURFACE, for the purpose of measurements, is commonly assumed to be uniform, for mountains, valleys, and ocean deeps, great as some are, are relatively insignificant features in comparison with the diameter of the earth.

But mountains are not insignificant to man. They play a major role in controlling the climate of the continents; they have profoundly influenced the patterns of human migration and settlement. Think, for example, of the influence of mountains on life in the continent of Asia, which contains the highest (Mount Everest, 29,141 feet) and lowest (Dead Sea, 1,294 feet below sea level) points on any of the continents.

Mountain ranges, with very few exceptions, are narrow, arcuate belts, thousands of miles in length, generally developed on the margins of the ancient cores or shields of the continents. They consist of great thicknesses of sedimentary and volcanic rocks, many of them of marine origin. Their intense folding and faulting is evidence of enormous compressive forces.

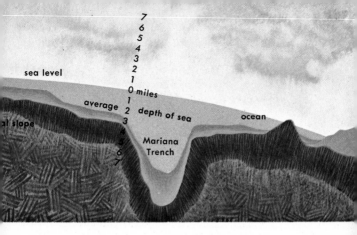

They have distinctive geophysical characteristics, and the fact that they project as such conspicuous topographic features poses profound geological problems.

Mountains are not limited to the land. The ocean floor has even more relief than the continents. Most of the continental margins extend as continental shelves to a depth of about 600 feet below the level of the sea, beyond which the sea floor (continental slope) plunges abruptly down. Both the shelf and the slope vary considerably in width and in slope, and neither has a uniformly flat surface.

The ocean floor adjacent to many island areas has long, deep trenches, the deepest of which, off the Philippines, is about 6 1/2 miles deep (p. 138). A world-wide network of mid-oceanic ridges, of mountainous proportions, encircles the earth. This network, discovered only during the last decade, has geophysical and geologic characteristics that suggest it occupies a unique role in earth dynamics—that along these ridges new sea floor is constantly being created.

9

○ Pluto

THE EARTH

RELATIVE DISTANCES OF PLANETS FROM THE SUN

3,000 million miles

EARTH is one of nine planets revolving in nearly circular orbits around our star the sun. Earth is the third planet out from the sun and the fifth largest planet in our solar

Neptune

PLANETS vary in size and rate of orbit. Mercury, with a diameter of 3,112 miles, is the smallest of the planets and nearest the sun. It orbits the sun in just three earth months. Jupiter, with a diameter about ten times that of Earth (88,800 miles), is the largest planet and fifth in distance from the sun. It takes about 11¾ earth years for Jupiter to make one revolution around the sun. Pluto, the most distant planet, is 40 times farther from the sun than Earth and probably about half the diameter (3,700 miles). It takes about 247¾ earth years for Pluto to make its long, eccentric orbit around the sun.

2,000 million miles

Uranus

THE SUN makes up about 99 percent of the mass of the solar system; the remaining one percent is distributed among all the other bodies in the system. Its immense size may be illustrated by visualizing it as a marble. At this scale, the earth would be the size of a small grain of sand one yard away. Pluto would be a rather smaller grain 40 yards away.

SATELLITES revolve around six planets. Including the earth's moon, there are 32 satellites altogether. Twelve belong to Jupiter, ten to Saturn, five to Uranus, two to Neptune, and two to Mars.

Saturn

1,000 million miles

Jupiter

COMETS are among the oldest members of the solar system. They orbit the sun in extremely long, elliptical orbits. As comets approach the sun, their tails begin to glow from friction with the solar wind.

● Mars

Earth ● ● Venus

Mercury ●

IN SPACE

Mercury •

Mars •

Pluto •

Venus 🌑

Earth 🌑

system, having a diameter of about 7,918 miles. It completes one orbit around the sun in about 365 1/4 days, the length of time that gives us our unit of time called a year.

THE MOON, earth's natural satellite, has about 1/4 the diameter, 1/81 the weight, and 3/5 the density of our planet. The moon completes one orbit around the earth every 27 1/3 days. It takes about the same length of time, 29 1/2 days, to rotate on its own axis; hence, the same side, with an 18% variation, always faces us. The surface is scarred with circular craters that range from a few feet to 160 miles in diameter. Many craters are circled by ramparts reaching up to 15,000 feet in height. A fine, slippery dust composed of beads of glass and irregular fragments of rock covers the moon's surface.

Neptune

Uranus

ASTEROIDS, the so-called minor planets, are rocky, airless, barren, irregularly shaped objects that range from less than a mile to about 480 miles in diameter. Most of the 1,600 asteroids that have been charted travel in elongated orbits between Mars and Jupiter. The great width of this zone suggests that the asteroids may be remnants of a disintegrated planet formerly having occupied this space.

METEORS, loosely called shooting stars, are smaller than asteroids; some being the size of grains of dust. Millions daily race into the earth's atmosphere where friction heats them to incandescence. Most meteors disintegrate to dust but fragments of larger meteors sometimes reach the earth's surface as "metorites." About 30 elements, closely matching those of the earth, have been identified in meteorites.

Saturn

Jupiter

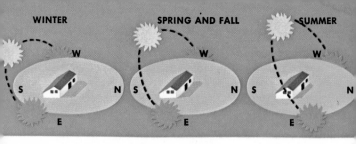

Tilted axis determines different positions of sun at sunrise, noon, and sunset at different seasons in middle north latitude.

THE EARTH'S MOTIONS determine the daily phenomenon of day and night and the yearly phenomenon of seasonal changes. The Earth revolves around the sun in a slightly elliptical orbit and also rotates on its own axis. Since the earth's axis is tilted about 23 1/2° with respect to the plane of the orbit, each hemisphere receives more light and heat from the sun during one half of the year than during the other half. The season in which a hemisphere is most directly tilted toward the sun is summer. Where the tilt is away from the sun, the season is winter.

RELATIVE MOTIONS OF THE EARTH

REVOLUTION is earth's motion about the sun in a 600-million-mile orbit, as it completes one orbit about every 365¼ days travelling at 66,000 mph.

ROTATION is a whirling motion of the earth on its own axis once in about every 24 hours at a speed of about 1,000 mph at the equator.

NUTATION is a daily circular motion at each of the earth's poles about 40 ft. in diameter.

PRECESSION is a motion at the poles describing one complete circle every 26,000 years due to axis tilt, caused by gravitational action of the sun and moon.

OUR SOLAR SYSTEM revolves around the center of our Milky Way Galaxy. Our portion of the Milky Way makes one revolution each 200 million years.

GALAXIES seem to be receding from the earth at speeds proportional to their distances.

THE SUN is the source of almost all energy on earth. Solar heat creates most wind and also causes evaporation from the oceans and other bodies of water, resulting in precipitation. Rain fills rivers and reservoirs, and makes hydroelectric power possible. Coal and petroleum are fossil remains of plants and animals that, when living, required sunlight. In one hour the earth receives solar energy equivalent to the energy contained in more than 20 billion tons of coal, and this is only half of one billionth of the sun's total radiation.

Just a star of average size, the sun is yet so vast that it could contain over a million earths. Its diameter, 864,000 miles, is over 100 times that of the earth. It is a gaseous mass with such high temperatures (11,-000° F at the surface, perhaps 325,000,000° F at the center) that the gases are incandescent. As a huge nuclear furnace, the sun converts hydrogen to helium, simultaneously changing four million tons of matter into energy each second.

Solar prominences compared with the size of the earth

Earth

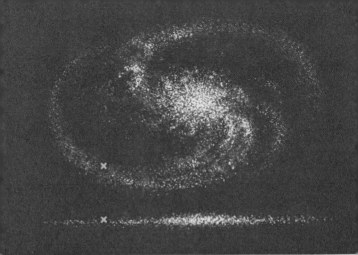

THE MILKY WAY, like many other galaxies, is a whirling spiral with a central lens-shaped disc that stretches into spiral arms. Most of its 100 billion stars are located in the disc. The Milky Way's diameter is about 80,000 light years; its thickness, about 6,500 light years. (A light year is the distance light travels in one year at a velocity of 186,000 mi. per sec., or a total of about 6 trillion miles.)

GALAXIES are huge concentrations of stars. Within the universe, there are innumerable galaxies, many resembling our own Milky Way. Sometimes called extragalactic nebulae or island universes, these star systems are mostly visible only by telescope. Only the great spiral nebula Andromeda and the two irregular nebulae known as the Magellanic Clouds can be seen with the naked eye. Telescopic inspection reveals galaxies at the furthermost limits of the observable universe. All of these gigantic spiral systems seem to be of comparable size and rotating rapidly. Nearly 50 percent appear to be isolated in space, but many galaxies belong to multiple systems containing two or more extragalactic nebulae. Our galaxy is a member of the Local Group which contains about a dozen other galaxies. Some are elliptical in shape, others irregular. Galaxies may contain up to hundreds of billions of stars and have diameters of up to 160,000 light years. Galaxies are separated from one another by great spaces, usually of about 3 million light years.

Many galaxies rotate on their own axes, but all galaxies move bodily through space at speeds of up to a hundred miles a second. In addition to this, the whole universe seems to be expanding, moving away from us at great speeds. Our nearest galaxy, in Andromeda, is 2.2 million light years away.

About a hundred million galaxies are known, each containing many billions of stars. Others undoubtedly lie beyond the reach of our telescopes. It seems very probable that many of the stars the galaxies contain have planetary systems similar to our own. It has been estimated that there may be as many as 10^{19} of these. Chances of life similar to that on earth occurring on other planets would, therefore, seem very high.

WHIRLPOOL NEBULA in Canes Venatici, showing the relatively close packing of stars in the central part.

GREAT SPIRAL NEBULA M31 in Andromeda is similar in form but twice the size of our own galaxy, the Milky Way.

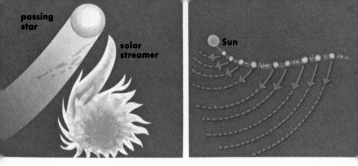

passing star

solar streamer

Sun

Artist's interpretation of the planetesimal theory

THE ORIGIN OF THE SOLAR SYSTEM is obscure, but two more or less distinct methods have been suggested. Both theories assume the sun to be the parent of the rest of the system. Early theories suggested the earth formed from an incandescent nebula, but growing evidence indicates that perhaps the earth accumlated in a relatively cold condition. It seems unlikely that the atmospheric gases of the planets could have survived a molten condition.

THE PLANETESIMAL THEORY suggests that tidal forces set up by the close approach of another star caused the ejection of streamers of swirling gaseous material from the sun, which later condensed to form planets. This theory accounts for the similar sizes of planets at roughly similar distances from the sun and for the rotation of the planets. But it seems probable that, far from condensing into planets, any gases erupted from the sun would disperse, and the emptiness of space makes the postulated near approach of a star an improbable, though not impossible, event.

THE DUST-CLOUD THEORY, the more modern theory, suggests a colder "dust cloud" of helium and hydrogen, with some heavier elements. The contraction of this disc resulted in the formation of "protoplanets," which later became planets, revolving around the residual mass of the sun. This theory accounts reasonably well for the spacing of the planets, and explains the presence of the smaller, denser planets in the inner orbits, and the large, low-density planets in the outer. Segregation of material within the Earth was probably the result of radioactivity.

THE ORIGIN OF THE UNIVERSE is unknown, but all the bodies in the universe seem to be retreating from a common point, their speeds becoming greater as they get farther away. This gave rise to the expanding-universe theory that holds that all matter was once concentrated in a very small area. Only neutrons could exist in such a compact core. According to this theory, at some moment in time—at least 5 billion years ago —expansion began, the chemical elements were formed, and turbulent cells of hot gases probably originated. The latter separated into galaxies, within which other turbulent clouds formed, and these ultimately condensed to give stars. Proponents refer to this as the "big bang" theory, a term descriptive of the initial event, perhaps as long as 10-15 billion years ago.

CONTINUOUS CREATION is an alternative to the whole "big bang" theory. It holds that matter is being created continuously at exactly the same rate that it is "lost over the horizon of the universe . . ." Most astronomers now tend to reject this theory, however. A substitute theory states that the universe may be alternately expanding and contracting.

Artist's interpretation of the dust-cloud theory

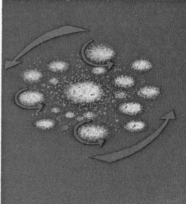

THE EARTH'S ATMOSPHERE is a gaseous envelope surrounding the earth to a height of 500 miles and is held in place by the earth's gravity. Denser gases lie within three miles of the earth's surface. Here the atmosphere provides the gases essential to life: oxygen, carbon dioxide, water vapor, and nitrogen.

Differences in atmospheric moisture, temperature, and pressure combined with the earth's rotation and geographic features produce varying movements of the atmosphere across the face of the planet, and conditions we experience as weather. Climatic conditions (rain, ice, wind, etc.) are important in rock weathering; the atmosphere also influences chemical weathering.

Gases in the atmosphere act not only as a gigantic insulator for the earth by filtering out most of the ultraviolet and cosmic radiation but also burn up millions of meteors before they reach the earth.

The atmosphere insulates the earth against large temperature changes and makes long-distance radio communications possible by reflecting radio waves from the earth. It also probably reflects much interstellar "noise" into space that would otherwise make radio and television, as we know them, impossible.

Composition of air at altitudes up to about 45 miles	Composition of air at altitudes above 500 miles
	helium 50%
nitrogen 78%	
	hydrogen 50%
oxygen 21%	
argon 0.93%	
carbon dioxide 0.03%	
other gases 0.04%	

THE RATIO OF GASES in the atmosphere is shown in the chart at left. Clouds form in the troposphere; the overlying stratosphere, extending 50 miles above the earth, is clear. The ionosphere (50-200 miles) contains layers of charged particles (ions) that reflect radio waves, permitting messages to be transmitted over long distances. Faint traces of atmosphere exist in the exosphere to about 500 miles from the earth's surface.

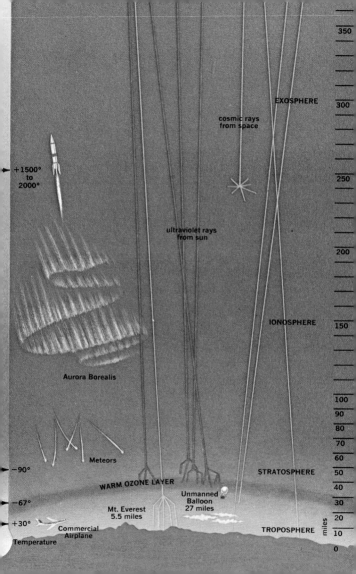

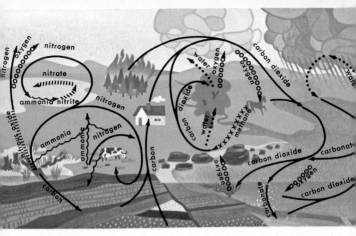

Atmospheric circulation involves the continuous recirculation of various substances.

THE ORIGINAL ATMOSPHERE was probably different from that of the present. If the earth ever was molten, the present atmosphere may be a remnant of the original gaseous material. This would mean that the atmosphere is as old as the earth, although its composition may have changed. The original atmosphere probably consisted of water vapor, hydrogen, ammonia, and methane. Eventual oxidation of methane and decomposition of ammonia would produce carbon dioxide and nitrogen. But the earth more probably accumulated from "cool" material. Then its atmosphere could have evolved from chemical reactions and volcanic action, and consisted of nitrogen, carbon dioxide, and water vapor. In either case, the present oxygen content of the atmosphere could result from oxygen released by water vapor during solar radiation and later from plants during photosynthesis. The origin of water on the earth is associated with the origin of the atmosphere.

THE EARTH'S CRUST: COMPOSITION

Man has so far been able to penetrate to only very shallow depths beneath the surface of the earth. The deepest mine is only about 2 miles deep, and the deepest well about 5 miles deep.

Where man cannot go, he uses geophysical methods to "X-ray" the earth. Careful tracing of earthquake waves shows that the earth has a distinctly layered structure. Studies of rock density and composition, heat flow, and magnetic and gravitational fields also aid in constructing an earth model of three layers: crust, mantle, and core. Estimates of the thickness of these layers, and suggested physical and chemical characteristics form an important part of modern theories of the earth (p. 148).

The crust of the earth is formed of many different kinds of rocks, each of which is an aggregate of minerals (p. 92).

Grand Canyon of Colorado River, Arizona, is 1 mile deep, but exposes only a small part of upper portion of earth's crust.

MINERALS are naturally occurring substances with a characteristic atomic structure, and characteristic chemical and physical properties. Some minerals have a fixed chemical composition; others vary within certain limits. It is their atomic structure that distinguishes minerals from one another.

Some minerals consist of a single element, but most minerals are composed of two or more elements. A diamond, for instance, consists only of carbon atoms, but quartz is a compound of silica and oxygen. Of the 105 elements presently known, nine make up more than 99 percent of the minerals and rocks.

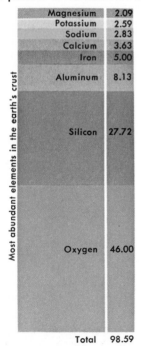

Most abundant elements in the earth's crust	
Magnesium	2.09
Potassium	2.59
Sodium	2.83
Calcium	3.63
Iron	5.00
Aluminum	8.13
Silicon	27.72
Oxygen	46.00
Total	98.59

OXYGEN AND SILICON are the two most abundant elements in the earth's crust. Their presence, in such enormous quantities, indicates that most of the minerals are silicates (compounds of metals with silicon and oxygen) or aluminosilicates. Their presence in rocks is also an indication of the abundance of quartz (SiO_2, silicon dioxide) in sandstones and granites, as well as in quartz veins and geodes.

Smoky Quartz

The most striking feature of minerals is their crystal form, and this is a reflection of their atomic structure. The simplest example of this is rock salt or halite (NaCl, sodium chloride), in which the positive ions (charged atoms) of sodium are linked with negatively charged chlorine ions by their unlike electrical charges. We can imagine these ions as spheres, with the spheres of sodium having about half the radius of the chlorine ions (.98 A as against 1.8 A; A is an Angstrom Unit, which is equivalent to one hundred millionth of a centimeter, written numerically as 0.00000001 cm or 10^{-7}cm).

SODIUM ATOM joins CHLORINE ATOM

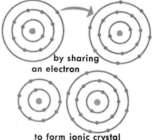

by sharing an electron

to form ionic crystal sodium chloride

X-RAY STUDIES show that the internal arrangement of halite is a definite cubic pattern, in which ions of sodium alternate with those of chlorine. Each sodium ion is thus held in the center of and at equal distance from six symmetrically arranged chlorine ions, and vice versa. It is this basic atomic arrangement or crystalline structure that gives halite its distinctive cubic crystal form and its characteristic physical properties.

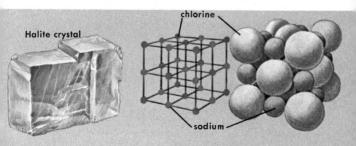

Halite crystal

chlorine

sodium

THE ATOMIC STRUCTURE of each mineral is distinctive but most minerals are more complicated than halite, some because they comprise more elements, others because the ions are linked together in more complex ways. A good example of this is the difference between diamond and graphite. Both have an identical chemical composition (they are both pure carbon) but very different physical properties. Diamond is the hardest mineral known, and graphite is one of the softest. Their different atomic structures reflect their different geologic modes of origin.

DIAMOND, the hardest natural substance known, consists · of pure carbon atoms. Each carbon atom is linked with four others by electron-sharing. The four electrons in the outer shell are shared with four neighboring atoms. Each atom of carbon then has eight electrons in its outer shell. This provides a very strong bond. Its crystal form is a reflection of its structure and of the conditions under which it was formed. Diamond is usually pale yellow or colorless but is found also in shades of red, orange, green, blue, brown, or black. Pure white or blue-white are best for gems.

GRAPHITE, quite different from diamond, is soft and greasy, and widely used as an industrial lubricant. In graphite, carbon atoms are arranged in layers, giving the mineral its flaky form. The atoms within each layer have very strong bonds, but those that hold successive layers together are very weak. Some atoms between layers are held together so poorly that they move freely, giving the graphite its soft, slippery, lubricating properties. Because of its poor bonding, graphite is a good conductor of electricity. Its best-known use is in "lead" pencils.

CRYSTAL FORM of minerals is an important factor in their identification. Grown without obstruction, minerals develop a characteristic crystal form. The outer arrangement of plane surfaces reflects their internal structure. Perfect crystals are rare. Most minerals occur in irregular masses of small crystals because of restricted growth. Since all crystals are three-dimensional, they may be classified on the basis of the intersection of their axes. Axes are imaginary lines passing through the geometric center of a crystal from the middle of its faces and intercepting in a single point.

CUBIC CRYSTALS have three axes of equal length meeting at right angles as in galena, garnet, pyrite, and halite.

TETRAGONAL CRYSTALS have three axes at right angles, two of equal length, as in zircon, rutile, and scapolite.

Galena   Zircon

HEXAGONAL CRYSTALS have three equal horizontal axes with 60° angles and one shorter or longer at right angles, as in quartz and tourmaline.

ORTHORHOMBIC CRYSTALS have three axes at right angles but each is of different length, as in barite and staurolite.

Quartz   Staurolite

MONOCLINIC CRYSTALS have three unequal axes, two forming an oblique angle and one perpendicular, as in augite, orthoclase and epidote.

TRICLINIC CRYSTALS have three axes of unequal lengths, none forming a right angle with others, as in plagioclase felspars.

Epidote   Amazonite feldspar

25

MINERAL IDENTIFICATION involves the use of various chemical and physical tests to determine what minerals are present in rock. There are over 2,000 minerals known, and elaborate laboratory tests (such as X-ray diffraction) are required to identify some of them. But many of the common minerals can be recognized after a few simple tests. Six important physical properties of minerals (hardness, luster, color, specific gravity, cleavage, and fracture) are easily determined. A balance is needed to find specific gravity of crystals or mineral fragments. For the other tests, a hand lens, steel file, knife, and a few other common items are helpful. Specimens can sometimes be recognized by taste, tenacity, tarnish, transparency, iridescence, odor, or the color of their powder streak, especially when these observations are combined with tests for the other physical properties.

MOHS' SCALE OF HARDNESS

10	diamond
9	corundum
8	topaz
7	quartz
steel file — 6	orthoclase
glass — 5	apatite
knife blade — 4	fluorite
penny — 3	calcite
fingernail — 2	gypsum
1	talc

HARDNESS is the resistance of a mineral surface to scratching. Ten well-known minerals have been arranged in a scale of increasing hardness (Mohs' scale). Other minerals are assigned comparable numbers from 1 to 10 to represent relative hardness. A mineral that scratches orthoclase (6) but is scratched by quartz (7) would be assigned a hardness value of 6.5.

LUSTER is the appearance of a mineral when light is reflected from its surface. Quartz is usually glassy; galena, metallic.

Galena crystals

SPECIFIC GRAVITY is the relative weight of a mineral compared with the weight of an equal volume of water. A balance is normally used to determine the two weights. Some minerals are similar superficially but differ in density. Barite may resemble quartz but quartz has a specific gravity of 2.7; barite, 4.5.

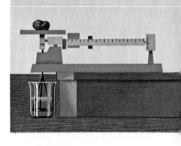

COLOR varies in some minerals. Pigments or impurities may be the cause. Quartz occurs in many hues but is sometimes colorless. Among minerals with a constant color are galena (lead gray), sulfur (yellow), azurite (blue), and malachite (green). A fresh surface is used for identification, as weathering changes the true color.

CLEAVAGE is the tendency of some minerals to split along certain planes that are parallel to their crystal faces. A hammer blow or pressure with a knife blade can cleave a mineral. Galena and halite have cubic cleavage. Mica can be separated so easily that it is said to have perfect basal cleavage. Minerals without an orderly internal arrangement of atoms have no cleavage.

FRACTURE is the way a mineral breaks other than by cleavage. Minerals with little or no cleavage are apt to show good fracture surfaces when shattered by a hammer blow. Quartz has a shell-like fracture surface. Copper has a rough, hackly surface; clay, an earthy fracture.

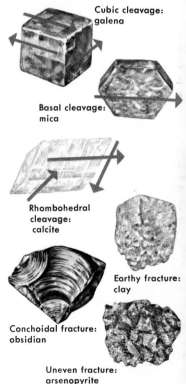

Cubic cleavage: galena

Basal cleavage: mica

Rhombohedral cleavage: calcite

Earthy fracture: clay

Conchoidal fracture: obsidian

Uneven fracture: arsenopyrite

27

COMMON ROCK-FORMING MINERALS include carbonates, sulfates, and other compounds. Many minerals crystallize from molten rock material. A few form in hot springs and geysers, and some during metamorphism. Others are formed by precipitation, by the secretions of organisms, by evaporation of saline waters, and by the action of ground water.

MINERAL CARBONATES, SULFATES, AND OXIDES

LIMONITE is a group name for hydrated ferric oxide minerals, $Fe_2O_3.H_2O$. It is an amorphous mineral that occurs in compact, smooth, rounded masses or in soft, earthy masses. No cleavage. Earthy fracture. Hardness (H) 5 to 5.5; Sp. Gr. 3.5 to 4.0. Rusty or blackish color. Dull, earthy luster gives a yellow-brown streak. Common weathering product of iron minerals.

CALCITE is a calcium carbonate, $CaCO_3$. It has dogtooth or flat hexagonal crystals with excellent cleavages. H. 3; Sp. Gr. 2.72. Colorless or white. Impurities show colors of yellow, or-

GYPSUM is a hydrated calcium sulfate, $CaSO_4.2H_2O$. Tabular or fibrous monoclinic crystals, or massive. Good cleavage. H. 2. Sp. Gr. 2.3. Colorless or white. Vitreous to pearly luster. Streaks are white. Flexible but not elastic flakes. Sometimes fibrous. Found in sedimentary evaporites and as single crystals in black shales. The compact, massive form is known as alabaster.

ange, brown, and green. Transparent to opaque. Vitreous or dull luster. Major constituent of limestone. Common cave and vein deposit. Reacts strongly in dilute hydrochloric acid.

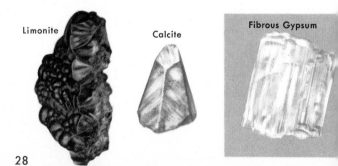

Limonite

Calcite

Fibrous Gypsum

QUARTZ is silicon dioxide, SiO_2. Massive or prismatic. No cleavage. Conchoidal fracture. H. 7; Sp. Gr. 2.65. Commonly colorless or white. Vitreous to greasy luster. Transparent to opaque. Common in acid igneous, metamorphic, and clastic rocks, veins, and geodes. The most common of all minerals.

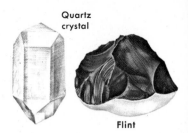

Quartz crystal

Flint

ROCK-FORMING SILICATE MINERALS

FELDSPARS are alumino-silicates of either potassium ($KAlSi_3O_8$ orthoclase, microcline, etc.) or sodium and calcium (plagioclase feldspars $NaAlSi_3O_8$, $CaAl_2Si_2O_8$). Well-formed monoclinic or triclinic crystals, with good cleavage. H. 6 to 6.5; Sp. Gr. 2.5 to 2.7. Orthoclase feldspars are white, gray, or pink, vitreous to pearly luster, and lack surface striations. Plagioclase feldspars are white or gray, have two good cleavages, which produce fine parallel striations on cleavage surfaces. Common in igneous and metamorphic rocks, and arkosic sandstones.

MICAS are silicate minerals. White mica (muscovite) is a potassium alumino-silicate. Black mica (biotite) is a potassium, iron, magnesium aluminosilicate. Both occur in thin, monoclinic, pseudo-hexagonal, scalelike crystals. Superb cleavage gives thin, flexible flakes. Pearly to vitreous luster. Micas are common in igneous, metamorphic, and sedimentary rocks.

Microline

Albite (plagioclase feldspar)

Biotite crystal

Biotite (black mica)

Augite

PYROXENES include a large group of silicates of calcium, magnesium, and iron. Augite, $(CaMgFeAl)_2 \cdot (AlSi)_2O_6$ and hypersthene, $(FeMg)SiO_3$, are the most common. Stubby, eight-sided prismatic, orthorhombic or monoclinic crystals, or massive. Two cleavages meet at 90° (compare amphiboles), but these are not always developed. Gray or green, grading into black. Vitreous to dull luster. H. 5 to 6. Sp. Gr. 3.2 to 3.6. Common in nearly all basic igneous and metamorphic rocks. Sometimes found in meteorites.

Hornblende

AMPHIBOLES are complex hydrated silicates of calcium, magnesium, iron, and aluminum. Hornblende, a common amphibole, has long, slender, prismatic, six-sided orthorhombic or monoclinic crystals; sometimes fibrous. Two good cleavages meeting at 56°. H. 5 to 6; Sp. Gr. 2.9 to 3.2. Black or dark green. Opaque with a vitreous luster. Common in basic igneous and metamorphic rocks. Asbestos is an amphibole.

Olivine

crystal

OLIVINE is a magnesium–iron silicate, $(FeMg)_2SiO_4$. Small, glassy grains. Often found in large, granular masses. Crystals are relatively rare. Poor cleavage. Conchoidal fracture. H. 6.5 to 7; Sp. Gr. 3.2 to 3.6. Various shades of green; sometimes yellowish. Transparent or translucent. Vitreous luster. Common in basic igneous and metamorphic rocks. Olivine alters to a brown color.

COMMON ORE MINERALS

GALENA is a lead sulphide, PbS. Heavy, brittle, granular masses of cubic crystals. Perfect cubic cleavage, H. 2.5; Sp. Gr. 7.3 to 7.6. Silver-gray. Metallic luster. Streaks are lead-gray. Important lead ore. Common vein mineral. Occurs with zinc, copper, and silver.

SPHALERITE is a zinc sulphide, ZnS. Cubic crystals or granular, compact. Six perfect cleavages at 60°. H. 3.5 to 4; Sp. Gr. 3.9 to 4.2. Usually brownish; sometimes yellow or black. Translucent to opaque. Resinous luster. Some specimens are fluorescent. Important zinc ore. Common vein mineral with galena.

PYRITE is an iron sulphide, FeS$_2$. Cubic, brassy crystals with striated faces. May be granular. No cleavage. Uneven fracture. H. 6 to 6.5; Sp. Gr. 4.9 to 5.2. Brassy yellow color. Metallic luster. Opaque and brittle. Also called fool's gold. Common source of sulfur.

Galena

Sphalerite

crystal

Pyrite

Miner in the lead mine Mesters Vig, Greenland

THE CRUST: EROSION AND DEPOSITION

The earth's crust is influenced by three great processes which act together:

Gradation includes the various surface agencies (in contrast to the two internal processes below), which break down the crust (degradation) or build it up (aggradation). Gradation is brought about by running water, winds, ice, and the oceans. Most sediments are finally deposited in the seas.

Diastrophism is the name given to all movements of the solid crust with respect to other parts (p. 106). Sometimes this involves the gentle uplift of the crust. Many rocks that were formed as marine sediments gradually rose until they now stand thousands of feet above sea level. Other diastrophic movements may involve intensive folding and fracture of rocks.

COASTLINES the world over provide evidence of changes in the earth's unstable crust. The photograph shows cliffs made of rocks that were deposited under the seas that covered the area about 130 million years ago. These were uplifted and folded, so their original layers now stand vertical. At present they are undergoing erosion by the sea, typified by the form of the arch. Eroded material is being redeposited as a beach. The rocks of which coastlines are formed are themselves the result of earlier gradational events.

NATURAL ARCH reflects process of erosion, while deposition has produced the beach. Dorset, England.

Eruption of Kapoho, Hawaii, showing paths of molten lava

Vulcanism includes all the processes associated with the movement of molten rock material. This includes not only volcanic eruptions but the deep-seated intrusion of granites and other rocks (p. 83).

These three processes act so that at any time the form and position of the crust is the result of a dynamic equilibrium between them, always reflecting the climate, season, altitude, and geologic environment of particular areas. As an end product of degradation, the continents would be reduced to flat plains, but the balance is restored and the processes of erosion counteracted by the other agencies which tend to build up the earth's crust.

Yosemite valley is the result of interaction of various types of erosional processes.

EROSION involves the breaking down and removal of material by various processes or degradation.

YOSEMITE VALLEY in California is a good example of the complex interplay of gradational processes. A narrow canyon was first carved by the River Merced. This was later deepened and widened by glaciation. Running water is now modifying the resultant hanging

and U-shaped valleys (p. 58), so characteristic of glacial topography. The level of the main valley floor lies 3,000 feet below the upland surface of the Sierras. Differences in topography is partly the result of differences in jointing and resistance of underlying granites. Half Dome and El Capitan are resistant granitic monoliths laid bare by this differential weathering. The region thus shows the effect of many degradational processes. But the 300-ft. thick sediment on the valley floor reveals the continuing aggradational effects that are also at work.

WEATHERING

Weathering is the general name for all the ways in which a rock may be broken down. It takes place because minerals formed in a particular way (say at a high temperature in the case of an igneous rock) are often unstable when exposed to the various conditions affecting the crust of the earth. Because weathering involves interaction of the lithosphere with the atmosphere and hydrosphere, it varies with the climate. But all kinds of weathering ultimately produce broken mineral and rock fragments and other products of decomposition. Some of these remain in one place (clay or laterite, for example) while others are dissolved and removed by running water.

The earth's surface, above the level of the water table (p. 50), is everywhere subject to weathering. The weathered cover of loose rock debris (as opposed to solid bedrock) is known as the *regolith*. The thickness and distribution of the regolith depend upon both the rate of weathering and the rate of removal and transportation of weathered material.

THE EFFECTS of weathering are most strikingly seen in arid and semiarid environments, where bare rocks are exposed without a cover of vegetation. Bryce Canyon, Utah, shows the effects of the bedding and differing resistance of rocks in producing distinctive erosional landforms. Weathering is of great importance to mankind. Soils are the result of weathering processes, and are enriched by the activities of animals and plants. Some important economic resources, such as our ores of iron and aluminum, are the result of residual weathering processes.

FROST SHATTERING is often produced by alternate freezing and thawing of water in rock pores and fissures. Expansion of water during freezing causes the rock to fracture.

SPHEROIDAL WEATHERING occurs in well jointed rocks, because weathering takes place more rapidly at corners and edges (3 and 2 sides) than on single faces.

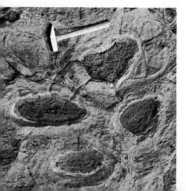

MECHANICAL WEATHERING involves the distintegration of a rock by mechanical processes. These include freezing and thawing of water in rock crevices, disruption by plant roots or burrowing animals, and the changes in volume that result from chemical weathering within the rock. This weathering is especially common in high latitudes and altitudes, that have daily freezing and thawing, and in deserts, where there is little water or vegetation. Rather angular rock forms are produced and little chemical change in the rock is involved. It was once thought that extreme daily temperature changes caused mechanical weathering, but this now seems uncertain.

CHEMICAL WEATHERING involves the decomposition of rock by chemical changes or solution. The chief processes are oxidation, carbonation and hydration, and solution in water above and below the surface. Many iron minerals, for example, are rapidly oxidized ("rusted") and limestone is dissolved by water containing carbon dioxide. Such decomposition is encouraged by warm, wet climatic conditions and is most active in tropical and temperate climates. Blankets of soil or other material are produced which are so thick and extensive that solid rock is rarely seen in the tropics. Chemical weathering is more widespread and common than mechanical weathering, although usually both act together.

SOIL is the most obvious result of weathering. It is the weathered part of the crust capable of supporting plant life. The thickness and character of soil depends upon rock type, relief, climate, and the "age" of a soil as well as the effect of living organisms. Immature soils are little more than broken rock fragments, grading down into solid rock. Mature soils include quantities of humus, formed from decayed plants, so that the upper surface (topsoil) becomes dark. Organic acids and carbon dioxide released during vegetative decay dissolve lime, iron, and other compounds and carry them down into the lighter subsoil.

Residual soils, formed in place from the weathering of underlying rock, include laterites, produced by tropical leaching and oxidizing conditions which consist of iron and aluminum oxides with almost no humus. Transported soils have been carried from the parent rocks from which they formed and deposited elsewhere. Wind-blown loess (p. 77), alluvial deposits (p. 44), and glacial till (p. 59) are common examples of transported soils.

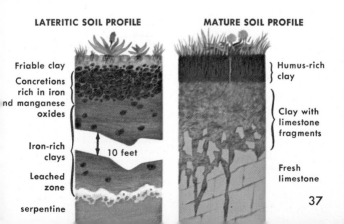

LATERITIC SOIL PROFILE

Friable clay
Concretions rich in iron and manganese oxides
Iron-rich clays — 10 feet
Leached zone
serpentine

MATURE SOIL PROFILE

Humus-rich clay
Clay with limestone fragments
Fresh limestone

37

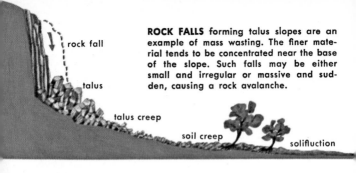

ROCK FALLS forming talus slopes are an example of mass wasting. The finer material tends to be concentrated near the base of the slope. Such falls may be either small and irregular or massive and sudden, causing a rock avalanche.

MASS WASTING is the name given to all downslope movements of regolith under the predominant influence of gravity. Weathered material is transported from its place of origin by gravity, streams ,winds, glaciers, and ocean currents. Each of these agencies is a depositing, as well as a transporting agent and, though they rarely act independently, each produces rather different results.

The prevention of mass wasting of soil is of great importance in all parts of the world. Engineering and mining activities usually require geological advice on slide and subsidence dangers. Some recent tragic dam failures have resulted from slides. The Vaiont reservoir slide in Italy in 1963 claimed 2,600 lives.

EARTH FLOWS may be slow or very rapid. Slow movement (solifluction) takes place in areas where part of the ground is permanently frozen. These areas cover about 20 percent of the earth. On slopes, the thawed upper layer slides on the frozen ground below it. On flat ground, lateral movement gives stone polygons. Sudden flows may follow heavy rains.

SOIL CREEP is the gentle, down-hill movement of the regolith that occurs even on rather moderate, grass-covered slopes. It can often be seen in road cuts.

SLUMPS are slides in soft, unconsolidated sediment. Some are submarine in origin. Fossil slumps are recognizable in some strata. Usually, slumps are on a rather small scale, as when sod breaks off a stream bank.

Hill creep affects fences and trees, as well as bending of vertical strata.

SUBSIDENCE is downward movement of the earth's surface caused by natural means (chemical weathering in limestone areas) or artificial methods (excessive mining or brine pumping). Heavy loading by buildings or engineering structures may also cause subsidence.

LANDSLIDES are mass movements of earth or rock along a definite plane. They occur in areas of high relief where weak planes—bedding, joints, or faults (p. 110)—are steeply inclined; where weak rocks underlie massive ones; where large rocks are undercut; and where water has lubricated slide planes.

Landslides can be of almost any size. Some of the largest involved the movement of millions of cubic meters of rock. Apart from danger to life, these downslope movements cause widespread damage to highways, buildings, and engineering structures. Geologic site investigations can prevent this.

RUNNING WATER

Running water is the most powerful agent of erosion. Wind, glaciers, and ocean waves are all confined to relatively small land areas, but running water acts almost everywhere, even in deserts. One fourth of the 35,000 cubic miles of water falling on the continents each year runs off into rivers, carrying away rock fragments with it. In the United States, this erosion of the land surface takes place at an average rate of about one inch in 750 years. Running water breaks down the crust by the impact of rock debris it carries.

THE HYDROLOGIC CYCLE is a continuous change in the state of water as it passes through a cycle of evaporation, condensation, and precipitation. Of the water that falls on the land, up to 90 percent is evaporated. Some is absorbed by plants and subsequently transpired to the atmosphere, some runs off in streams and rivers, and some soaks into the ground. The relative amounts of water following these paths vary considerably and depend upon the slope of the ground; the character of the soil and rocks; the amount, rate, and distribution of rainfall; the amount and type of plant cover; and the temperature. The hydrosphere is estimated to include over 300,000,000 cubic miles of water, about 97 percent of which is in the oceans.

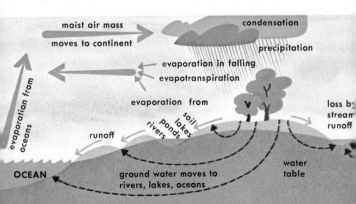

moist air mass moves to continent

condensation

precipitation

evaporation in falling

evapotranspiration

evaporation from soil lakes ponds rivers

evaporation from oceans

loss by stream runoff

runoff

water table

OCEAN

ground water moves to rivers, lakes, oceans

A single shower may involve the downpour of more than a billion tons of water. Each raindrop in the shower becomes important in erosion, especially in areas with sparse vegetation and unconsolidated sediments. Run-off water rarely travels far as a continuous sheet, for it is broken up into rivulets and streams by surface irregularities in rock type and relief.

Running water carries its load of rock debris partly in suspension, partly by rolling and bouncing it along the bottom, and partly in solution. The carrying power of a stream is proportional to the square of its velocity, and so is enormously increased in time of flood.

THE FORM OF RIVERS depends upon many factors. Water runs downhill under the influence of gravity, the flow of the water being characteristically turbulent, with swirls and eddies. The overall long profile of a rivery valley is concave upwards, however much its gradient (its slope or fall in a given distance) may vary. The velocity of the stream increases with the gradient, but also depends on other factors, including the position within the river channel, the degree of turbulence, and the shape and course of the channel, and the stream load (transported materials).

Diagrammatic model of a river system, showing cross sections of channel at three points.

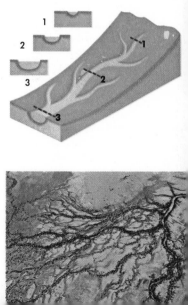

DENDRITIC DRAINAGE PATTERN of Diamantina River, Queensland, Australia is typical of river development in areas where the underlying rocks are relatively uniform in their resistance to erosion. This pattern may be modified by continued downcutting of the river.

Niagara Falls are formed by resistant bed of dolomite.

RIVER CYCLES are stages of development exhibited in rivers. During early river development, changes are reflected by direction and shape of stream courses. Ultimately, river erosion produces an equilibrium between the slope and volume of the river and its erosional and depositional power. This results in a graded profile or profile of equilibrium. Final equilibrium is never reached because of annual and seasonal changes. The downward limit of erosion by a river is the base level, a level below which the river cannot downcut appreciably because it has reached the level of the body of water into which it flows. Sea level is the ultimate base level for all rivers. Larger rivers and lakes into which rivers flow constitute local base levels.

Stages in the cycle of river erosion have been labeled as youth, maturity, and old age. Each stage has certain characteristics that imply no particular age in years, only phases in development. Rivers often show a condition of old age near their mouths, but are mature or youthful in their higher reaches. The old-age stage migrates slowly upstream. The three stages grade into one another without sharp divisions.

THE YOUTHFUL STAGE in development shows rapid downcut of river, with high gradients, steep-sided valleys, irregular courses, waterfalls, and a few well-developed tributaries. The Gunnison River in Colorado is an example of this stage in the development of river erosion.

Longitudinal profile ▶

IN THE MATURE STAGE rivers have a smoother, longer profile, without waterfalls and rapids. The country over which they flow has high relief, but hills and valleys are smooth, not precipitous. Tributaries are well established. The White River in southwestern Missouri is an excellent example.

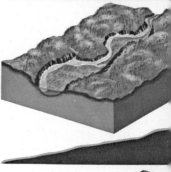

Longitudinal profile ▶

THE OLD-AGE STAGE describes rivers that carry a heavy load and flow sluggishly over rather flat landscapes. Downcutting by the stream is rare, being replaced by horizontal cutting over a very wide valley. The river channel is wide and flat, and meanders along a sinuous, shifting course. Oxbows are abandoned sections of old channels. The lower Amazon and lower Mississippi are examples of old rivers.

Longitudinal profile ▶

43

REJUVENATION or uplift may interrupt the cycle of erosion at any stage to provide new energy for downcutting. The character of the stream is then often a combination of young, recently cut, steep gorges in an old-age meander course. Ancient flood-plains are often left "stranded" as terraces. Uplift and warping may be relatively sudden or slow, frequent or rare, local or regional in extent.

Terraces cut as river swings from one side of valley to other.

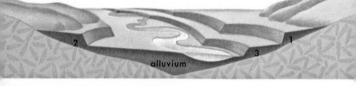

alluvium

WATERFALLS AND RAPIDS are local increases in gradient in the long profile of a river. Most are due to unequal erosion of the stream bed.

◄ **THE FALLS** of the Yellowstone River (the lower of which is twice as high as Niagara Falls) result from resistant lava flows. Niagara Falls is held up by on 80-foot-thick bed of dolomite, which is more resistant to erosion than the underlying shales and thin limestones.

Other falls result from overdeepening of a main valley, often by ice, as in the Bridal Veil Falls in Yosemite, so that the tributaries are left "hanging." Continued erosion by a stream leads to upstream migration and ultimate smoothing out of waterfalls.

UNEQUAL EROSION has already cut Niagara Falls back about 7 miles from the Niagara escarpment, since it began cutting about 9,000 years ago. The weaker shales below the Lockport Dolomite are undercut by the turbulent water in the plunge pool, so that the overlapping dolomite is undermined, and eventually collapses. The Niagara River flows into Lake Ontario from Lake Erie, which will ultimately be drained by upstream migration of the falls.

STREAM PIRACY takes place when the tributaries of one stream erode faster than those of another in the same area. The headwaters of the less active stream are ultimately diverted or cut off. When such "beheaded" streams abandon their path through a ridge, a wind gap results.

DELTAS are masses of sediment deposited where rivers lose their velocity as they enter lakes or seas. Thick, relatively uniform layers of sediment accumulate on the steep outward slope. Deltas of the Mississippi, Ganges, and Po are thousands of square miles in area. Deltas have a characteristic stratification in their deposits.

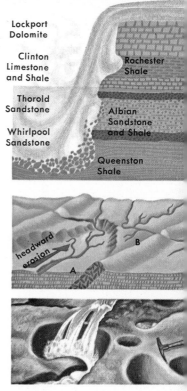

Lockport Dolomite

Clinton Limestone and Shale

Thorold Sandstone

Whirlpool Sandstone

Rochester Shale

Albian Sandstone and Shale

Queenston Shale

headward erosion

A

B

POTHOLES are circular hollows in a stream bed, drilled out by swirling currents of water carrying gravel and pebbles. This "hydraulic drilling," is an important method of down-cutting, even in hard rock.

Coarse-grained sediments

Fine-grained sediments

Fore-set beds

DRAINAGE

CONSEQUENT STREAMS flow in directions determined largely by the original slope and shape of the ground. When their courses are modified by features of the geology, such as valley cutting in soft strata, the adjusted tributaries are known as subsequent streams.

DENDRITIC drainage patterns are those that show treelike branching because the bedrock has a uniform resistance to erosion and does not influence the direction of stream flow.

TRELLIS patterns are characteristic of uniformly dipping or strongly folded rocks. In this rectangular pattern, the tributaries are nearly perpendicular to the main stream.

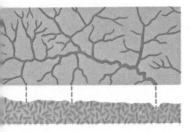

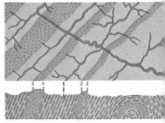

SUPERIMPOSED drainage generally has stream courses that are independent of rock structure. A stream's erosional power may have been strong enough to maintain its antecedent course during uplift and development of a new geological structure. Or it may keep its same course after it cuts through flat, sedimentary rock to an older, irregular rock mass

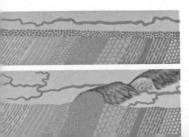

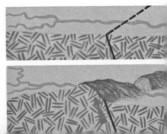

PATTERNS

RADIAL patterns develop on young mountains, such as volcanoes where streams radiate from the high central area.

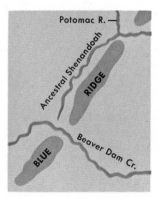

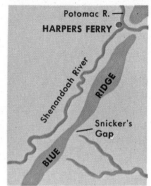

Piracy may cause river diversion. Ancestral Shenandoah River captured headwaters of Beaver Dam, leaving an abandoned water gap.

MODIFIED DRAINAGE may be caused by piracy (p. 45) as well as by glacial or volcanic blocking of stream courses. Glacial diversion results from overdeepening of basins and river valleys by ice, blocking of drainage by ice, morainic deposits, and meltwater, which may produce glacial lakes and new outlets. Changes in sea level may also modify drainage.

Great Lakes basins were carved by ice from soft strata. Original drainage was blocked by ice producing local crustal depressions.

Preglacial drainage systems

Lakes region immediately prior to first known lakes

Ice margin

Modern Great Lakes

EROSIONAL LANDFORMS are produced by running water and other erosional agents. *Mesas* are flat-topped rock mountains, which stand as remnants of a once continuous plateau. *Buttes* are smaller examples of the same thing. *Monuments* describe any isolated rock pinnacle.

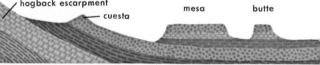

hogback escarpment   cuesta   mesa   butte

HOGBACKS are long ridges formed by steeply dipping resistant strata; cuestas are gently sloping ridges formed in gently dipping strata.

NATURAL BRIDGES are formed of resistant strata, usually sandstone or limestone. Underground erosion has taken place below the original stream bed.

◀ **PINNACLES** at Bryce Canyon, Utah show differential weathering. Erosion has removed the softer, more soluble rocks. Rocks here are of Tertiary (Eocene) age.

GROUNDWATER is found almost everywhere below the earth's surface. Most originates from rain and snow, but small quantities come from water trapped in sediments during their deposition (connate water) or from igneous magmas (juvenile water).

SEPTARIAN NODULE is formed from minerals deposited by groundwater in claylike rocks. Groundwater is an important agent in both deposition and erosion of surface rocks. It can dissolve original cementing materials and deposit new ones. For example, it produces caves and caverns by solution in carbonate rocks.

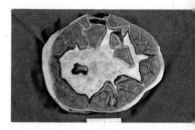

POROSITY, the percentage of pore space to total volume of a rock, depends upon the grain size, shape, packing, and cement of rock particles. The permeability of a rock, or its capacity to transmit or yield water, depends upon the size of pores, rather than their total volume. Pores smaller than 1/20 of a millimeter will not allow water to flow through them.

WELL-SORTED SAND (enlarged view) with high porosity due to sorting, which has removed fine-grained particles.

POORLY SORTED SAND has lower porosity than well-sorted sand, because the pore spaces are filled by fine particles.

LIMESTONES generally hold water in enlarged joints formed by solution; they lack the "pore space" of sandstones.

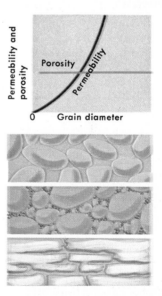

49

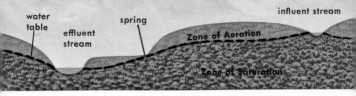

Labels in figure: water table, effluent stream, spring, influent stream, Zone of Aeration, Zone of Saturation

THE WATER TABLE depends on the distribution of groundwater. The open spaces in the rocks of the upper part of the crust are filled mainly with air. This is the zone of aeration. Water moves downward through this zone into the zone of saturation, where openings are filled with water. The upper surface of this saturated zone is the water table. In most areas, the water table is only a few tens of feet below the surface, but in arid regions, it is much deeper. Water-bearing rocks are rarely found below 2,000 feet. Rock pores are closed by pressure at depth, and this determines the lower limit for groundwater. Most rocks will give off water wherever they intersect the water table. But the level of the water table falls after a dry season, so rock formations must be deep enough to penetrate the water table all year round. Sometimes a perched water table results when a pocket of water is held above the normal water table by a saucer of impervious rock. Any water-producing rock formation is called an aquifer.

ARTESIAN WELLS are those where water is confined to a permeable aquifer by impervious beds, and where the catchment or intake area (and thus the water level in the aquifer) is higher than the well head. This allows the water to flow toward the surface under its own internal pressure.

Labels in figure: water table, shale, porous sandstone, impermeable shale

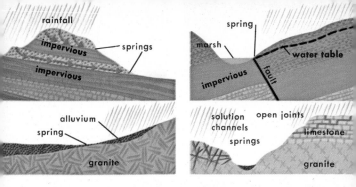

SPRINGS are sources of running water produced by the water table intersecting the ground surface. A few of the many ways they can be formed are shown in the diagrams above. Some springs are dry at seasons when the water table is depressed; others flow without interruption.

HOT SPRINGS are generally confined to areas of recent vulcanism where groundwater is heated at depth by contact with igneous magmas. Such springs are well developed in Yellowstone National Park and North Island, New Zealand. Terrace deposits may be produced when hot spring water deposits dissolved mineral matter. Mammoth Springs of Yellowstone National Park are formed of calcium carbonate (travertine). Geysers, intermittent fountainlike hot springs, often build cones of siliceous geyserite.

FUMAROLES are gentle geysers located in volcanic regions that emit fumes, usually in the form of steam.

Hot Springs, Thermopolis, Wyo.

Norris Geyser Basin, Wyoming.

GEYSERS are thermal springs which periodically discharge their water with explosive violence. All geysers have a long narrow pipe extending down from their vents into their reservoirs. A build-up and sudden release of steam bubbles probably relieves the pressure on the heated water below ground so that it boils and surges upward. The period between eruptions varies from minutes to months in different geysers, depending upon the structure of the geyser, its water supply, and its heat source.

◄ **OLD FAITHFUL** in Yellowstone National Park discharges a column of water and steam up to 170 feet high approximately every 65 minutes.

Typical geyser structure shows complex system of fissures extending down to regions where ground water becomes superheated and finally erupts.
▼

Pudding Basin Geyser, New Zealand shows typical eruption.
▼

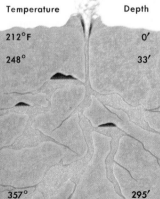

Geyserite (Sinter)

Temperature	Depth
212°F	0'
248°	33'
357°	295'

CAVES reflect the work of groundwater. Limestone is dissolved by circulating water in subsurface joints and fissures. The enlargement gradually produces a cave. Inside a cave, dripping water, rich in calcium bicarbonate and CO_2, often produces precipitates that form stalagmites and stalactites.

GEOLOGICAL WORK OF GROUNDWATER is important in solution and deposition in the rocks through which it passes. It dissolves limestone and other carbonate rocks to form caves and sink holes. Limestone areas are often marked by a karst topography of sinks, few surface streams (they flow underground), and large springs. In caves, the deposition of calcite dissolved in dripping groundwater produces stalactites, icicle-shaped formations hanging from the cave ceilings, and stalagmites, formations that build up from the cave floor. The carrying away of minerals in solution usually occurs above the water table. Below that level, deposition, replacement, and cementation are important. Ball-like masses (concretions), hollow, globular bodies (geodes), and the cement in many sedimentary rocks are the result of the action of groundwater at depth.

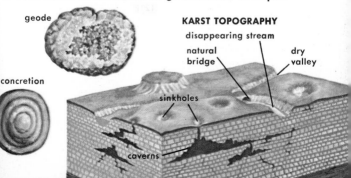

geode

concretion

KARST TOPOGRAPHY

disappearing stream

natural bridge

dry valley

sinkholes

caverns

Cotter Dam supplies water for Australian capital city of Canberra.

THE EARTH'S WATER SUPPLY is one of its most precious natural resources. Although nearly three quarters of the globe is covered by water, over 97 percent of the 326 million cubic miles of earth's water is locked up in the oceans, too salty for drinking or for agriculture. Another 2 percent is frozen in glaciers and ice sheets. The tiny fraction that is available for water supply is very unevenly distributed. One third of the earth's land surface is desert or semiarid. Even in humid areas, water supply and conservation present major problems. The location and development of new industries depend upon adequate water supplies. World demand for water is expected to double in the next twenty years. It requires 600,000 gallons of water to produce one ton of synthetic rubber. The daily consumption of the average household in the United States is 400 gallons.

About three quarters of the water used in most humid industrial areas comes from surface waters (rivers, lakes, artificial reservoirs, etc.). The rest comes from groundwater. Pollution and waste still prevent maximum use of surface waters, on which we depend.

Over one fourth of the earth's land surface is desert, and dam construction can be vital in these areas. The Aswan Dam in Egypt, will bring almost 2.5 million acres of new land into cultivation and generate 10 billion kilowatt-hours of electricity each year. Desalinization of sea water, although used in some arid areas, is still too expensive for general use.

Water conservation is a pressing world need since water supplies, although they are never exhausted but are replenished in the water cycle, can never be increased. They can, however, be more efficiently used and distributed. Pollution of water supplies by domestic and industrial wastes can upset the delicate ecological balance, and has very serious biologic, economic, and recreational effects.

Arid and semi-arid regions cover about 1/3 of the earth's surface. Water hole in Pakistan is typical of local water supplies.

Lake Solitude, Wyoming, a typical area of recent glaciation

GLACIERS AND GLACIATION

We live today in the twilight of a great episode of refrigeration when much of the Northern Hemisphere was covered by continental ice sheets, like those that still cover Antarctica and Greenland. Although the ice itself has now retreated from most of Europe, Asia, and North America, it has left traces of its influence across the whole face of the landscape in jagged mountain peaks, gouged-out upland valleys, swamps, changed river courses, and boulder-strewn, table-flat prairies in the lowlands.

Glaciers are thick masses of slow-moving ice. In the higher lands and polar regions, the annual winter snowfall usually exceeds the summer loss by melting. Permanent snow fields build up, and their lowest boundary is the snow line, the actual height of which varies with latitude and climate. Buried snow recrystallizes to form ice, which moves slowly under its own weight. It moves most rapidly in the middle of the glacier.

GLACIAL EROSION has a powerful effect upon land which has been buried by ice and has done much to shape the mountain ranges of our present world. Both valley and continental glaciers acquire many thousands of boulders and rock fragments, which, frozen into the sole of the glacier, gouge and rasp the rocks over which the glaciers pass. The rocks are slowly abraded down to a smooth, fluted, grooved surface. Glacial meltwater, from periods of daylight or summer thaw, seeps into rock fissures and joints. When it freezes again, it helps to shatter the rocks, some of which may become frozen into the body of the glacier and be carried away as the glacier moves downslope. Avalanches and undercutting of valley sides add to the rock debris.

ROCK SURFACES display fluting, ▶ striation, and polishing effects of glacial erosion. The form and direction of these grooves can be used to show the direction in which the ice moved.

TYPICAL LONGITUDINAL SECTION of a valley glacier shows its structure and its profile of bedrock. Surface ice is brittle, but underlying ice crystals bend, shear, and glide, causing ice to flow by deformation.

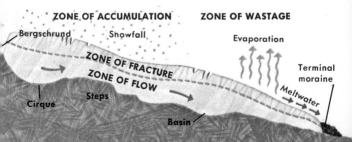

ZONE OF ACCUMULATION   ZONE OF WASTAGE

Bergschrund   Snowfall   Evaporation

ZONE OF FRACTURE
ZONE OF FLOW   Terminal moraine

Cirque   Steps   Meltwater

Basin

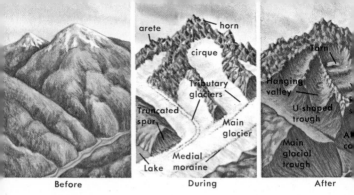

Before • During • After

Labels on image: arete, horn, cirque, Tributary glaciers, Truncated spur, Main glacier, Medial moraine, Lake, Tarn, Hanging valley, U-shaped trough, Main glacial trough

THREE STAGES OF GLACIAL EROSION are illustrated above showing mountain country before, during, and after glaciation. Glaciers cut U-shaped valleys, modifying and deepening the interlocking pattern of earlier meandering river erosion. The valleys are straightened and truncated by ice flow. Tributary hanging valleys develop where the rate of erosion by tributary glaciers is lower than that of the glacier in the main valley. As the ice retreats, waterfalls flow out of them into the main valley.

HORNS, ARETES, AND CIRQUES are all products of glacial erosion. Horns are sharp, pyramidal mountain peaks formed when headward erosion of several glaciers intersect. Aretes are sharp ridges formed by headward glacial erosion. Continental glaciers tend to produce a smoothed-out effect on the landscape, such as that of the Laurentian Shield in Canada. Cirques are bowl-shaped valleys formed at heads of glaciers and below aretes and horned mountains; often contain a small lake, called a tarn.

U-shaped glaciated valley, Clinton Canyon, New Zealand

Horns and aretes in glaciated area, Switzerland.

Labels in image: Retreating ice sheet, Kame, Tunnel, Braided stream, Kettles, Delta, Ice block, Outwash plain, Esker, Icebergs, Marginal lake, Drumlins, Recessional moraine, Terminal moraine

IDEALIZED GLACIAL LANDSCAPES show typical depositional features. They are collectively called till deposits. Glacial deposits of rock fragments are carried by the glacier on its surface within the ice and at its base. This material is deposited either beneath or at the foot of the ice field, forming unsorted and unbedded "till." Meltwater streams flowing from the glacier form sorted, stratified glaciofluvial or outwash deposits. These and other glacial deposits are often described as "drift." Deposits also occur during retreat of ice.

MORAINES are deposits of glacial till formed either as arcuate mounds at the snout of the glacier (terminal moraines) or as sheets of till over considerable areas (boulder clay). Successive terminal moraines often mark retreat stages of glaciers (recessional moraines). Moraines are made up of a variety of unsorted rock fragments in unbedded clay matrix.

ERRATICS are boulders of "foreign" rock carried by glaciers. Some are up to a hundred feet across and most are found

DRUMLINS are low, rounded hills, sometimes reaching a mile in length, found in glaciated areas. Aligned in the direction of ice flow, their steeper, blunter ends point toward the direction from which the ice came. They are formed by plastering of till around some resistant rock mass. They produce a characteristic "basket-of-eggs" topography.

many miles from their points of origin. They often have blunted edges and rather smooth faces, but most lack glacial striations.

KAMES are isolated hills of stratified material formed from debris that fell into openings in retreating or stagnant ice.

Kame terraces are benches of stratified material deposited between the edge of a valley glacier and the wall of the valley

GLACIOFLUVIAL DEPOSITS are all sorted and bedded stream deposits. Outwash deposits, formed by meltwater streams, are flat, interlocking alluvial fans.

ESKERS are long, narrow, and often branching sinuous ridges of poorly sorted gravel and sand formed by deposition from former glacial streams.

KETTLE HOLES are depressions (sometimes filled by lakes) due to melting of large blocks of stagnant ice, found in any typical glacial deposit.

GLACIAL LAKE DEPOSITS are formed either by meltwater or the blocking of river courses. Deltas and beaches mark the levels of many such lakes.

VARVE CLAYS are lake deposits of fine-grained silt, showing regular seasonal alternations of light-colored, thicker bands deposited during wet, summer months and thinner, dark bands representing the finer, often organic, material of winter deposits that settle below the frozen lake surface.

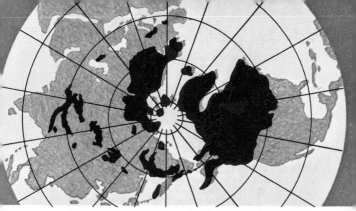

Maximum extent of Pleistocene ice sheets and glaciers

ANCIENT PERIODS OF GLACIATION produced land features still in evidence today. The features already described can be seen in connection with existing glaciers, but older glacial deposits and erosional features prove the occurrence of earlier glacial episodes. The most recent of these is the Pleistocene glaciation which began about two million years ago. It involved four major episodes of glaciation, when continental ice sheets covered about one quarter of the earth's surface, including parts of North America, northern Europe, and northern Asia. Glacial advances were separated by warmer, interglacial periods. In the areas outside those covered by glaciers, especially in the Southern Hemisphere, corresponding pluvial periods of abnormally heavy rainfall marked Pleistocene times, probably caused by changes in the general pattern of wind circulation produced by continental glaciers.

Pleistocene glaciation molded such familiar features of our present landscapes as the jagged peaks of the Rockies and the Alps, the rich farm soils of the northern midwestern states, and the Great Lakes.

61

GLACIATION is important because it has molded the topography of much of the Northern Hemisphere. It also poses a number of basic geologic problems.

CHANGES IN SEA LEVEL of up to 300 feet occurred when much of the ocean's water was locked in continental glaciers. Even today, if present glaciers and ice sheets that cover 10 percent of the earth's surface were to melt, sea level would rise by some 300 feet. The continental margins would be flooded, and many of the world's major ports would be submerged. This may happen again. If it does not, and we are living in an inter-glacial rather than postglacial episode, then continental gla-ciers may again spread across much of the earth.

LOADING THE CRUST by ice caused sags to develop which reached about 1,500 ft. under the thickest ice. With the melt-ing of the glaciers, the crust be-gan to rise again, and the his-tory of this rise can be traced in Scandinavia, North America and Europe. The crust rises about 9 inches per century.

CAUSES OF ICE AGES are still unknown. Possible causes may be changes in the broad pattern of the circulation of the ocean, changes in the relative position of the earth and sun, changes in solar radiation, and the pres-ence of some blanket such as volcanic dust to reduce solar radiation reaching the earth. It has also been suggested that the Pleistocene glaciation of the Northern Hemisphere could have been the result of surges in the Antarctic ice sheet pro-ducing wide ice shelves around the Southern Ocean, which cooled the Northern Hemisphere.

PRE-PLEISTOCENE GLACIA-TIONS are much less easy to detect than the very recent Pleistocene. One major episode of glaciation took place in the Southern Hemisphere in Permo-Carboniferous times, about 230 million years ago. Tillites (in-durated glacial tills) and stri-ated rock pavements show large areas of Australia, South Amer-ica, India, and South Africa to have been glaciated. The char-acter of these glacial deposits suggests that these areas now remote, formed a single mas-sive continent (Gondwanaland) at that time.

There is also evidence of an Ordovician (about 450 million years ago) and a late Pre-Cam-brian glaciation (about 600 million years ago).

UPLIFT,
IN METERS
Since 6800 B.C.

50
150
200
200
150
100
50

Gulf of Bothnia

Gulf of Finland

THE OCEANS

Oceans play a major role in the earth's natural processes because of their production and control of climate, supplying moisture to the atmosphere and providing a vast climatic regulator. They form the ultimate site of deposition of almost all sediment and are the home of many living species of animals and plants.

Although oceans cover over 70 percent of the earth's surface, detailed exploration of this vast area is only beginning. The continents are surrounded by shallow, gently sloping continental shelves. The average ocean depth is almost three miles, but deep trenches associated with volcanic islands are found in the Pacific. The greatest depth yet recorded is 36,198 feet in the Marianas Trench near the Philippines. Although much of the deep ocean floor is a flat plain, some parts are more mountainous than the mountain regions of dry land. A worldwide system of midoceanic ridges includes submarine mountain chains, the site of intense vulcanism and earthquake activity.

California Coast shows force of breaking waves eroding shoreline.

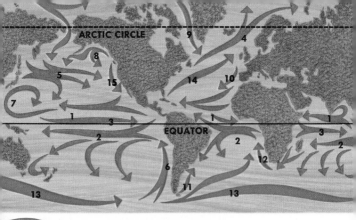

| warm | | |
| cool | | |

OCEANIC CURRENTS AND DRIFTS

1. N. Equatorial	6. Humboldt	11. Falkland
2. S. Equatorial	7. Kuroshia	12. Benguela
3. Eq. countercurrent	8. Alaska	13. West Wind Drift
4. N. Atlantic drift	9. Labrador	14. Florida
5. N. Pacific	10. Canaries	15. California

OCEAN MOTION

CURRENTS have a major influence on world weather patterns. Differences in the density of sea water of varying salinity and differences in temperature produce water circulation in the oceans. The colder, more saline, denser water sinks downward to produce deep ocean currents. Nearer the surface of the sea, the combined influence of winds and the rotation of the earth produce the more familiar surface currents, including the Gulf Stream. These surface currents follow great, swirling routes around the ocean basins and the equator. Some currents move at speeds of over 100 miles a day.

Dissolved chemical salts make up about 3.5 percent of the total sea-water weight. The salts are mostly of the common type with smaller quantities of magnesium chloride, magnesium and calcium sulphates, and traces of about 40 other elements. Salinity is the number of grams of these dissolved salts in 1,000 grams of sea water. Although the proportions of these salts to one another are very similar throughout the oceans of the world, the total salinity of the oceans varies from place to place and with depth. It is low near river mouths, for example, and high in areas of high evaporation.

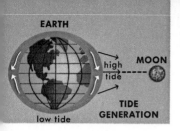

EARTH

high tide

MOON

TIDE GENERATION

low tide

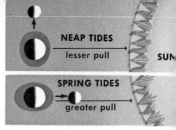

NEAP TIDES
lesser pull

SPRING TIDES
greater pull

SUN

TIDES are twice-daily movements of billions of tons of ocean water influenced by many factors on the surface of the earth as well as from space. Mainly, the gravitational pull of the moon upon the earth causes the waters to bulge toward it twice a day, creating what we call high tides. The corresponding bulge or high tide on the distant side of the earth from the moon is caused by the corresponding lower attraction of the moon at this greater distance, allowing the oceans to "swing" outward. Tides rise only two or three feet on open coastlines, but in restricted channels, can reach fifty feet.

WAVES are produced chiefly by the drag of winds on the surface of water. The water is driven into a circular motion, but only the wave form, not the water itself, moves across the ocean surface. Waves generally affect only the uppermost part of the oceans. Wave base is half the wave length of any particular wave system. When they run into shallow water, waves drag bottom, and the topmost water particles break against the shore. Waves play an important part in the shaping of coastlines, both in sediment transport and in erosion. Some large waves (tsunami) are caused by earthquakes.

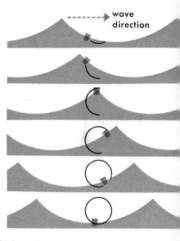

wave direction

Breaker

Beach

wave height increases

wave length decreases

Deep water waves not affected by bottom

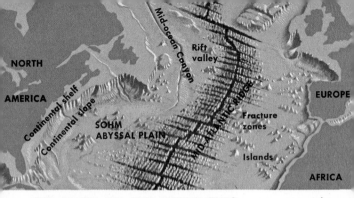

THE EDGES OF THE CONTINENTS are commonly marked by margins of broad, flat shelves which slope gently (at about 1:1000) to a depth of about 450 feet. At this depth, they merge into the steeper continental slope. The width of shelves varies from a few miles to 200 or more miles. Commonly, shelves are about 30 miles wide. The shelves seem to be formed by the deposition and erosion of fairly young sediments, many of them of Pleistocene age. Changes in sea level of some 500 feet have been involved during this period.

THE CONTINENTAL SHELF AND SLOPE rim the continents, the wide shelf dropping off steeply at the slope to the depths of the sea floor. At the base of the continental slope, there is often a convex *rise*, formed from slumped sediments. This area ranges from a few miles to about 100 miles in width. The great vertical exaggeration of the diagram suggests a much steeper profile than really exists. Even so, the slope is almost a hundred times steeper than the shelf.

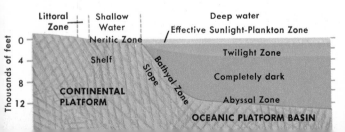

SUBMARINE CANYONS cut through the continental shelves and slopes and are widely distributed along the edges of continents. Some seem to be continuations of rivers on the land, but others show no such relation to drainage and do not extend across the continental shelves. All canyons tend to have a V-shaped profile and to have tributary systems much like those of terrestrial rivers. Their deeper mouths are marked by great deltalike fans of sediment, which gradually build up to form the continental rise.

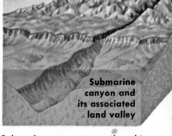

Submarine canyon and its associated land valley

Submarine canyons are thought to be formed by the erosion of turbidity currents, which sometime attain considerable velocity. Heavy with silt, they have a strong scouring and erosive power.

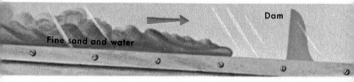

Fine sand and water

Dam

Experimental turbidity current in a laboratory tank.

TURBIDITY CURRENTS are dense, flowing masses of sediment-carrying water flowing at speeds of up to 50 miles per hour. Many are probably triggered by earthquake disturbances of unconsolidated sediment on the continental shelves and slopes. The coincidence of some submarine canyons with river courses, such as those of the Hudson and Congo, has been thought to be the result of river erosion at earlier periods of lower sea level. Probably, it is the result of either the presence of thicker, unstable masses of sediment near river mouths or turbidity flow from river mouths in times of flood.

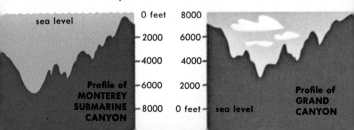

sea level

0 feet
2000
4000
6000
8000

Profile of
MONTEREY
SUBMARINE
CANYON

8000
6000
4000
2000
0 feet

sea level

Profile of
GRAND
CANYON

Coastal view at Hargrave's Lookout, New South Wales, Australia

COASTLINES mark the boundaries of land and sea. Although the great variety of rock types, structures, currents, tides, climate, and fluctuating sea levels produce many different types of coastlines, each can be understood as the product of three simple processes: erosion, deposition, and changing sea level.

Coastal erosion is the result of the twice-daily pounding by the sea, wearing down the margins of the land, creating coastal features, and cutting back the shoreline at a rate of several feet a year.

CLIFFS AND WAVE-CUT PLATFORMS are characteristic of shorelines undergoing erosion. Waves undercut the rocks near sea level.

CAVES are formed by erosion along a conspicuous line of weakness in a cliff, such as along joints and faults. Continuing erosion may form an arch.

BAYS AND HEADLANDS are produced by relative differences in the resistance to erosion of coastal rocks. The more resistant stand out as headlands, but ultimately, the concentration of wave erosion on the headlands and deposition in the bays have a tendency to produce a straight coastline.

Drowned Valley, view from Mt. Wellington, Tasmania

A CHANGING SEA LEVEL is represented by many features around coastlines. Within historic times, established towns have been submerged. Raised beaches and wave-cut platforms are common in many areas, rising many feet above present sea level. Far inland and high on the slopes of mountains, fossils of marine animals give further proof of older and more profound changes in sea level. Submergence and emergence of coastlines modify the general features of erosion and deposition.

EMERGENT COASTLINES are less common than the submerged. They are marked by raised beaches and cliffs, and often by an almost flat coastal plain, sloping gently seaward.

SUBMERGED COASTLINES, due to postglacial rising sea level, are indented coastlines with deep inlets and submerged glacial valleys. The "grain" of the coastline depends upon the character and structure of the rocks. In Atlantic-type coastlines, the structural trends are more or less perpendicular to the coast. In Pacific type, they are parallel to the coast.

"Atlantic" or transverse coastline

"Pacific" or longitudinal coastline

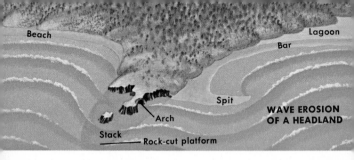

Beach

Lagoon

Bar

Spit

WAVE EROSION OF A HEADLAND

Arch

Stack

Rock-cut platform

MARINE DEPOSITION may be recognized as the dominant process where shorelines are marked by a number of familiar features. Ultimately, the balance of coastal erosion and deposition produces a coastline in equilibrium. Although this is more quickly formed in soft strata, it requires thousands of years in resistant rocks.

BEACHES consist of sediment sorted and transported by waves and currents. Most of the sediment is the size of sand or of gravel, but local cobble and boulder deposits are also common. Beaches vary greatly, depending upon the sediment supply, the form of the coastline, wave and current conditions, and seasonal changes. On irregular coastlines, they tend to be confined to the bays. Oblique waves and longshore currents often produce constant lateral movement of beach material. Beaches thus exist in a state of dynamic equilibrium, as a moving body of wavewashed and sorted sediment.

Interaction of river and marine deposition and erosion, Wales

OFFSHORE BARS are generally separated from the main shoreline by narrow lagoons. They are ancient beach deposits which are characteristic of submerged coasts. In North America, offshore bars are common along the Atlantic and Gulf coasts. They are generally parallel to existing coastlines.

SANDBARS are formed on indented coastlines by longshore drift of sediments parallel with the coast. When sediment is carried into deeper water, as in a bay, the energy of the waves or currents is reduced, and the sediment is deposited as a bar. The slower the current, the more rapidly the sediment is deposited. The bar is an elongation of the adjacent beach, partly or completely cutting off the bay. Spits are bars that extend into open water rather than into a bay. The free ends of many spits are curved landward by wave refraction. In some cases, spit growth may lead to blocking and diversion of rivers that flow into the sea.

Storm beach at Lavernock, Wales

Typical cliff and beach scenery shows balance of erosion and deposition. (Dorset, England)

DELTAS are formed by rapid deposition of material carried by a river when it enters the deep water of a lake or the sea and loses its velocity. All deltas have a similar pattern of deposition and sediment distribution, but their shape and size vary widely, depending upon the local conditions.

STORM BEACHES (or berms) are formed by storms that throw gravel and boulders up above the normal high-tide level.

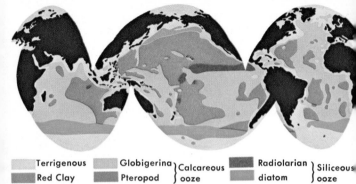

Terrigenous
Red Clay

Globigerina
Pteropod
} Calcareous ooze

Radiolarian
diatom
} Siliceous ooze

MARINE SEDIMENTS are classified in three broad categories: littoral, neritic, and deep-sea sedimentation. Littoral sediments form between high- and low-tide levels; neritic sediments accumulate on the continental shelf. These two groups of shallow-water sediments cover only about 8 percent of the ocean floor. They are made up of a variable mixture of terrigenous or land-derived debris, chemical precipitates, and organic deposits. They differ from place to place due to variations in coastlines, rivers, and changes in sea level.

In general, in shallow-water sediments, there is a direct relationship between the size of a sediment particle and the distance to which a given current will carry it, the larger particles being deposited nearer the source. This pattern is modified by the action of waves, currents, and turbidity currents.

Deep-sea sediments deposited outside the continental shelf form a layer generally less than 2,000 feet thick over the deeper parts of the ocean floor. They are much thinner and younger in age than we should predict from knowledge of present rates of sedimentation. The abyssal parts of the ocean show much more uniform sediments than the continental margins, where most terrestrial debris is deposited. Those of the bathyal zone, deposited on the continental slopes to a depth of about 12,000 feet, include muds of various kinds. The sediments of greater abyssal depths are red clays and various oozes which cover 30 percent and 47 percent of the ocean floor respectively.

CALCAREOUS OOZES are fine-medium-grained sediments that cover almost half the ocean floors. They occur down to a depth of almost 15,000 feet. Below that depth, the calcareous tests of the planktonic foraminifer *Globigerina* and pteropod molluscs, which form most of the sediments, are dissolved.

SILICEOUS OOZES are derived from the remains of surface-living organisms (*diatoms* and *radiolaria*) forming very slowly at great depth in the oceans. Diatom oozes are found chiefly in polar seas where predatory creatures are less common. Radiolarian ooze is most commonly found in the warm, tropical waters.

DARK RED CLAY is formed from meteoric dust and from very fine terrigenous or volcanic particles carried by the wind or in suspension in sea water. It may form as slowly as one inch every 250,000 years. It may include volcanic ash layers. Other sediments, such as manganese nodules, (shown here) are present in some parts of sea floor.

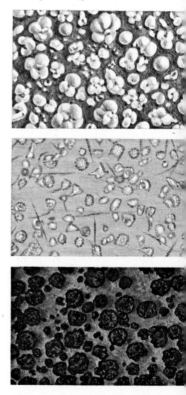

Wind is most effective in transport and deposition in deserts, near shorelines, and in other places where there is a supply of dry, fine-grained, loose sediment with little vegetation to hold it together. The Dust Bowl of the Great Plains in the 1930's was caused by wind transport following prolonged drought.

WINDS

Winds are movements of the atmosphere brought about not only by the rotation of the earth but by unequal temperatures on the earth. The heat of the sun, the chief source of this circulation, is more concentrated in the tropics than in high latitudes. This produces vast atmospheric convection currents, having a broad, constant overall distribution which reflects the earth's rotation. It also shows wide local variations in speed and direction due to differences in topography and other atmospheric conditions.

A major role is played by the wind in the distribution of water from the oceans to the land. Water vapor, in turn, has a blanketing effect which keeps the earth's surface temperature higher than it would otherwise be. Wind is an agent of transport and, to a lesser extent, of erosion. In this, it resembles flowing water, but because of its much lower density (only about 1/800 that of water), it is far less effective and generally transports only the finer dust particles. Dust from volcanic explosions will often give brilliant sunsets in distant lands for many months after the explosion. Winds transport through the atmosphere comparatively large quantities of salt crystals gathered from the ocean's surface.

74

WIND EROSION is very limited in extent and effect. It is largely confined to desert areas, but even there, it is limited to a height of about 18 inches above ground level.

DESERT PLATFORMS are clean, windswept areas where pebbles may have been rolled and bounced along by the force of strong winds. Larger cobbles and boulders were left behind.

VENTIFACTS are pebbles or cobbles found in deserts which have developed polished surfaces and sharp edges under wind abrasion.

Desert Erosion tends to expose bare rock surfaces which may stand up without a cover of vegetation, as in West Pakistan.

Semi-arid landscape has distinctive erosional character.

WIND DEPOSITS consist of transported particles that are effectively sorted according to size because of the limited carrying capacity of the wind. Sand dunes, for example, generally consist of sand grains of more or less uniform size, which are rounded and pitted or frosted by abrasion.

Sand dunes are found in areas where there is a large supply of dry, loose, fine-grained material. Like snowdrifts, they form around local obstructions. They also migrate downwind. Their particular size and form depend upon the sand supply, the presence of vegetation, and the velocity and constancy of direction of the prevailing wind. Dunes may be transverse or longitudinal to the wind direction.

BARCHANS are crescentic dunes that often build up to 400 yards long and 100 feet high, and are formed mostly in deserts with more or less constant wind directions. They may migrate up to 60 feet per year. The crescent points show downwind direction. Winds also produce **giant ripple marks** on sand surfaces. Barchans usually are found in groups, or swarms, and may form long lines, or chains, across a plain.

SAND-DUNE SHAPE typically has gentle windward slope and steep leeward slope, down which sand grains slide or roll. Dotted line shows how continuous movement of sand grains produces migration of whole sand dunes. Dunes take many forms. It would not be easy to compile a complete list of all the varieties. Variations in form include scalloped sides and irregularities in plan of the crest.

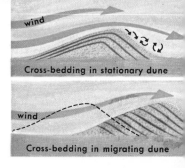

Cross-bedding in stationary dune

Cross-bedding in migrating dune

ANCIENT DUNE DEPOSITS preserved in such sedimentary rocks as those of the Navajo Sandstone in Zion Canyon National Park display aeolian bedding, sorting, and sand grain rounding similar to those of present-day dunes. Careful mapping of bedding directions reveals ancient wind directions. In this way, it has been possible to make a map of the Permian winds of southwestern United States 225 million years ago.

Cross bedding, in wind-deposited sandstone, reflects its formation in ancient sand dunes, east of Echo Cliffs, Arizona

LOESS DEPOSITS, formed of fine-grained silt, lack any bedding but often have vertical joints. Transported by wind from deserts, from dried-up flood plains, from river courses, or from glacial deposits, they are common in midwestern United States, China, Europe, and in many areas surrounding the world's deserts and glacial outwash areas. Loess produces fertile soils, partly because of its very high porosity. Loess is yellow or buff in color and often forms vertical cliffs. Artificial caves in easily worked loess may provide homes.

PRODUCTS OF DEPOSITION

Sedimentary rocks are generally formed from the breakdown of older rocks by weathering and the agents of erosion described on pp. 34-76. A few are chemical precipitates, or organic debris. Sedimentary rocks cover about 75 percent of the earth's surface.

CLASTIC OR DETRITAL SEDIMENTARY ROCKS are formed from the debris of pre-existing rocks or organisms. The weathered rock material is generally transported before it is deposited. This movement often gives round grains. The debris is eventually laid down in horizontal layers, usually as marine deposits but sometimes as deposits from rivers, lakes, glaciers, or wind. Clastic rocks are solidified sediments.

CONGLOMERATE consists of rounded pebbles or boulders held tightly in a finer-grained matrix. The pebbles are usually of quartz at least ¼ inch or more in diameter.

SANDSTONE consists of sand-size particles, usually of quartz. It may show considerable variation in cementing minerals, in rounding and sorting of particles, and in forms of bedding.

ARKOSE is a quartz-feldspar sandstone usually formed in desert areas by rapid erosion and deposition of feldspar-rich igneous rocks.

CALCARENITE consists of broken shells or other organic material and fragments from older limestones. It is deposited as sedimentary debris.

GRAYWACKE is a poorly sorted mixture of rock-fragments, quartz, and feldspar fragments in a clay matrix. Often formed by turbidite flows (p. 67), graywacke always indicates rapid erosion and deposition under unstable conditions.

SHALE consists of very fine-grained particles of quartz and clay minerals. It is consolidated mud that has been deposited in lakes, seas, and similar environments. About 45 percent of all exposed sedimentary rocks are shales.

ORGANIC SEDIMENTARY ROCKS are formed from organic debris—the deposits or remains of once-living organisms (shells, corals, calcareous algae, wood, plants, bones, etc.). Although they are a form of clastic rock, organic rocks may contain more and better-preserved fossils, as they are laid down near the place where the animal or plant once lived.

CHEMICALLY FORMED SEDIMENTARY ROCKS consist of interlocking crystals precipitated from solution. They, therefore, lack the debris-cement composition of other sedimentary rocks. A decrease in pressure, an increase in temperature, or contact with new materials may cause minerals to precipitate from solution.

LIMESTONE consists chiefly of calcite from concentrated shell, coral, algae, and other debris. It may grade into dolomite, characterized by the presence of calcium and magnesium carbonate (p. 28). Chalk is a fine-grained limestone of minute coccoliths. Travertine is limestone precipitated by springs.

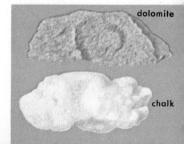

dolomite

chalk

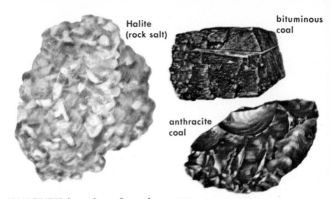

Halite (rock salt)

bituminous coal

anthracite coal

EVAPORITES have been formed by evaporation from solution, usually in shallow, land-locked basins of sea water. They vary greatly in texture and composition. Rocksalt, gypsum, anhydrite, and potassium salts are the most common.

COAL is consolidated peat, formed by the decomposition of woody plant debris (p. 98). It is an organic rock, and plant structures may still be preserved in it. Coals grade from lignite to anthracite, which has about 95 percent carbon in it.

SEDIMENTARY ROCKS are important natural resources. Shales and limestones are used for cement, clays for ceramics; other rocks are used for road metal. Sedimentary iron ores, bauxite, and coal form the basis of much heavy industry; soil is the ultimate basis of all our food supplies.

A typical coal mine operation

THE SIZE, SHAPE, AND SORTING of sedimentary structures within rocks may provide clues to the depositional environment that existed during their formation. Rounded, frosted, well-sorted grains, for example, indicate wind-deposited sand.

CROSS-BEDDING is a term applied to sweeping, arclike beds that lie at an acute angle to the general horizontal stratification. It is common in stream and deltaic deposits, in deeper marine waters, and in sand dunes. Cross-bedding reflects the direction of current flow.

GRADED BEDDING is due to differential settling of mineral grains, and is useful for determining the correct "way up" in folded strata. The layers of coarse rock have a sharp base and gradually grade upward into finer-grained materials.

VARVED BEDDING is a type of thin, graded bedding that has alternate laminations of coarse and fine-grained material. Especially common in glacial lake deposits, it is characteristic of seasonal deposition, each pair of varves representing a year. (See page 60.)

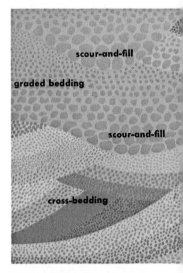

scour-and-fill

graded bedding

scour-and-fill

cross-bedding

SCOUR AND FILL structures are formed by erosion and subsequent filling of valleys and channels in a river bed.

MUD CRACKS form where lake and mud deposits are dried by the sun and are preserved by burial under mud.

RIPPLE MARKS were produced by wind in desert sand deposits and by waves or current in various aqueous areas.

81

THE CRUST: SUBSURFACE CHANGES

Running water, ice, wind, and other agents of erosion slowly wear down the surface of the continents. Over the earth as a whole, some 8,000,000,000 tons of sediment is carried by rivers into the sea every year, equivalent to some 200 tons per square mile of land surface. This represents an average lowering of the rivers' drainage areas by approximately one foot every 9,000 years.

The ultimate effect of this erosion would be to reduce the continents to a flat surface, but there are two earth processes which tend to restore the balance: the tectonic uplift of areas of both the existing continental and offshore areas of sedimentation (diastrophism), and the broadly related process of igneous activity (p. 83). Most of these forces act slowly, over long periods of time, and the earth's crust is always in a state of dynamic equilibrium, though continuously changing, as a result of their interaction.

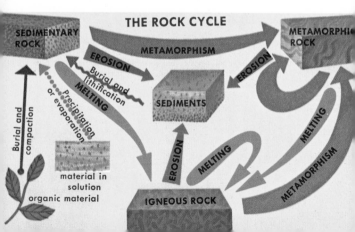

THE ROCK CYCLE

SEDIMENTARY ROCK

METAMORPHIC ROCK

METAMORPHISM

EROSION

Burial and lithification

MELTING

SEDIMENTS

EROSION

Precipitation or evaporation

Burial and compaction

material in solution
organic material

EROSION

MELTING

MELTING

METAMORPHISM

IGNEOUS ROCK

Volcanic cones stand out as hills near Springville, Arizona.

Igneous rocks form the foundations of the continents, but most of the surface of the continents is made up of sedimentary rocks of various ages. These layers have been deposited on and around ancient continental cores or shields and are made chiefly of granitic igneous and metamorphic rocks. The cores of mountain chains generally reveal the same rocks. These igneous rocks were generally formed at great depths and later uplifted, eroded, and covered with a relatively thin veneer of sediments.

VOLCANOES

Volcanoes are mountains or hills, ranging from small conical hills to peaks with 14,000-foot reliefs, formed by lava and rock debris ejected from within the earth's crust. Of the more than 500 active volcanoes, some extrude molten lava, others erupt ash and solid (pyroclastic) fragments. Still others eject both, and all emit large quantities of steam and various gases. Some eruptions are relatively "quiet," others explosive.

83

VOLCANIC ACTION results in the formation of five basic types of volcanoes; but no two are ever quite alike. The kind of materials that erupt from a volcano largely determine the shape of its cone. Fluid streams of lava travel far and usually produce wide-based mountains; thick lavas usually build up steep cones.

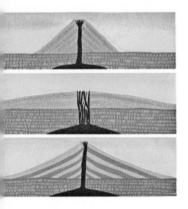

CINDER CONES are steep-sided, symmetrical cones, such as Vesuvius, formed by the eruption of cinders, ash, and other pyroclastic products.

SHIELD VOLCANOES are relatively broad, gentle domes formed by lava flows from a central vent or from fissures and parasitic vents on the flanks.

COMPOSITE CONES are formed from interbedded lava flows and pyroclastic debris. They are intermediate in form between cinder and shield volcanoes.

CALDERAS are formed by the collapse of the top of a volcano following an explosion. New cones may be born in the caldera. Crater Lake in Oregon is an example of this type of volcano.

PLATEAU BASALTS cover great areas in the Columbia River Valley, Iceland, and India, and are apparently extruded, to spread in thin sheets, not from central vents but from cracks or fissures.

VOLCANIC PRODUCTS include bombs, cinders, ash, and dust, as well as lava and gases. Most lava has a basaltic composition (p. 93) consisting of plagioclase feldspars, pyroxene, and olivine. Erupted at temperatures of between 900 and 1,200 C, it can flow for great distances at considerable speeds.

THE TYPES OF LAVA differ in form and texture. Pillow lava (left) is formed by submarine volcanoes. Blocky lava has a jagged surface and is produced by sudden gas escape. Ropy lava (right) forms at a higher temperature than blocky lava.

VOLCANIC BOMB shows spindle-shaped form.

VOLCANIC TUFF is a fine-grained, pyroclastic rock.

DISTRIBUTION OF VOLCANOES follows a definite pattern, concentrated in narrow belts and areas. Many lie in a "ring of fire" around the Pacific Ocean. Others are formed in such areas of recent tectonic activity as the Mediterranean or the African Rift Valleys. Most oceanic islands are volcanic.

WORLD DISTRIBUTION OF VOLCANIC AREAS

INTRUSIVE IGNEOUS ROCKS are formed from magma rising within the earth's crust. Unlike the extrusive rocks, intrusive rocks crystallize below the earth's surface, and their presence becomes obvious only after the country rock into which they were intruded has been removed by erosion.

Intrusions show great variation in form. Some cut across bedding planes (discordant), while others run parallel with them (concordant). They range in size from dikes measuring a few inches wide to batholiths hundreds of miles across.

Intrusive rocks are often associated with important metallic mineral deposits, such as copper or nickel.

FORMS OF IGNEOUS INTRUSIONS

PLUTONIC, INTRUSIVE ROCKS, similar to granite, are identified by having a coarser crystal texture, produced by slower cooling than that in extrusive rocks. In general, rocks formed at shallow depths in the crust have an intermediate texture.

DIKES are usually vertical intrusive sheets, often discordant. They may occur in vast dike swarms, associated with central volcanic neck or intrusive centers. Dikes and sills frequently have fine-grained, chilled contact margins.

Dikes, such as on left, show chilled margins of fine-grained texture, where in contact with the country rock, as on right.

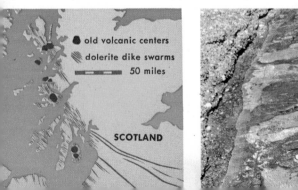

old volcanic centers
dolerite dike swarms
50 miles

SCOTLAND

Old volcanic neck at Shiprock, New Mexico, is circular in outline and fed a radiating series of once molten dikes.

VOLCANIC PLUGS or necks are more or less cylindrical, vertical-walled intrusions, generally of porphyritic rock. Whether or not they pass upward into lavas, or breccias, depends to a great extent upon the depth of local weathering.

SILLS are horizontal intrusive sheets, either concordant or discordant. Such sills as the Palisades on the Hudson River show vertical texture layering because of gravitational crystalization differentiation. Some sills and dikes are only a few feet in thickness; some develop good columnar jointing similar to that of lava flows. As illustrated, sills (A) are distinguished from lava flows (B) by the baking of overlying adjacent country rock by sills.

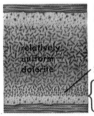

fine-grained chilled zone 1% olivine

PALISADES SILL

relatively uniform dolerite

25% olivine

fine-grained chilled zone 1% olivine

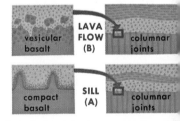

vesicular basalt — **LAVA FLOW (B)** — columnar joints

compact basalt — **SILL (A)** — columnar joints

LACCOLITHS are dome-shaped intrusions having a flat base but an arched concordant roof, formed by intrusive pressure, and a rather flat floor. They may show differentiation.

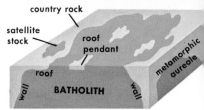

country rock

satellite stock

roof pendant

roof

wall   BATHOLITH   wall

metamorphic aureole

BATHOLITHS or plutons are major, complex, intrusive masses, generally granitic and often several hundred miles in extent. They are the largest intrusions and are found in areas of major tectonic deformation as in the Idaho Batholith and in the continental shields. Although many plutonic granites show sharp contacts with older rocks, and are, therefore, intrusive in a strict sense, others show complete transition with surrounding country rocks and seem to result from the metamorphism or granitization of older sedimentary and metamorphic structures.

Coast Range Batholith

500 miles

Idaho Batholith

Sierra Nevada Batholith

Stock and associated laccolith, Henry Mountains, Utah

stock

STOCKS are discordant, intrusive masses, a few miles in diameter. Some are plutonic, but others pass upward into ancient volcanic plugs. They differ from batholiths in that they are smaller in size.

LOPOLITHS AND LAYERED INTRUSIONS are saucer-like intrusions up to one or two hundred miles across. These intrusions have rather complex geologic histories. Distinct mineralogical layering is present, the more basic minerals generally being in the lower layers, as in the Bushveld complex in South Africa and the Sudbury, Ontario lopolith. Gravity settling and convection currents seem largely responsible for this layering.

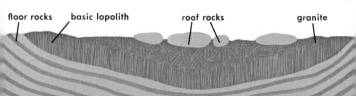

floor rocks   basic lopolith   roof rocks   granite

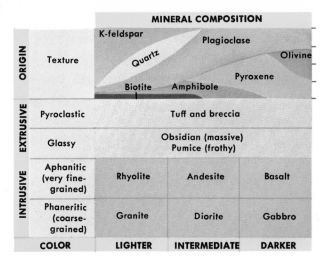

		MINERAL COMPOSITION		
ORIGIN	Texture	K-feldspar Quartz Biotite	Plagioclase Amphibole	Olivine Pyroxene
EXTRUSIVE	Pyroclastic	Tuff and breccia		
	Glassy	Obsidian (massive) Pumice (frothy)		
INTRUSIVE	Aphanitic (very fine-grained)	Rhyolite	Andesite	Basalt
	Phaneritic (coarse-grained)	Granite	Diorite	Gabbro
	COLOR	**LIGHTER**	**INTERMEDIATE**	**DARKER**

CLASSIFICATION OF IGNEOUS ROCKS

We have already seen that igneous rocks vary in their occurrence, which tends to produce differences in texture (crystal size, shape, and arrangement). They also vary greatly in mineral content, and thus in chemical composition. Acid rocks (those containing quartz) make up the bulk of plutonic intrusions but seem to be confined to the continents, whereas basaltic rocks account for most of the volcanic rock of both the continents and the oceans.

Igneous rocks are commonly classified by their texture (the size, shape, and variation in their crystalline form) and their chemical composition (represented by their constituent minerals). These two factors reflect their rate of cooling and original magma composition.

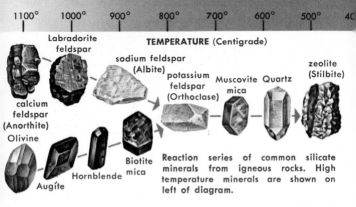

Reaction series of common silicate minerals from igneous rocks. High temperature minerals are shown on left of diagram.

MAGMA is the molten silicate source material from which igneous rocks are derived. Although lava provides a surface sample of magma, the increased pressures and temperatures of deeper magmas permit a higher gas and water content than at the surface.

Igneous rocks show great variation in chemical composition, but this does not mean that each of the many types has crystallized from a different kind of magma. It seems probable that a single kind of basaltic magma is the parent of all varieties of igneous rocks, and that different chemical compositions result from crystallization differentiation.

Field and laboratory studies of igneous rocks show that igneous minerals have a definite sequence of crystallization: Iron, magnesium, and calc-silicate minerals (such as olivine, pyroxene, and calcium-plagioclase feldspars) form before sodium and potassium feldspars and quartz. This sequence is seen in differentiated intrusions.

Although crystallization of a basaltic magma would normally give a basalt (if the early-formed minerals are separated from the bulk of the magma by gravity settling or tectonic pressure), the remaining magma would be acid relatively rich in both silica and potassium and in sodium alumino-silicates. Continued crystallization and separation would then produce a rhyolitic magma. About 90% of the original magma would remain as crystalline rocks of basic composition.

The hypothesis of a single parent basaltic magma explains many otherwise puzzling features of igneous rocks, including the preponderance of basalt lavas and the frequent small and late rhyolitic flows in basaltic volcanic eruptions. Undisturbed cooling would produce granites, which would overlie basic rocks.

But the abundance of granites in mountain ranges, and their apparent continuity with metamorphic rocks, implies that many granites are formed by the "granitization" of deeply buried sedimentary rocks in the roots of mountain chains. This metamorphic origin of granitic, plutonic rocks might then provide "intrusive magmas" at higher levels in the crust. It seems unlikely that such huge masses of granites could have formed by differentiation of basic lavas.

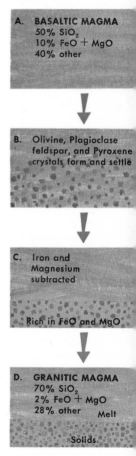

CRYSTAL SETTLING

Evolution of Granitic magma from Basaltic magma

A. **BASALTIC MAGMA**
50% SiO_2
10% $FeO + MgO$
40% other

B. Olivine, Plagioclase feldspar, and Pyroxene crystals form and settle

C. Iron and Magnesium subtracted

Rich in FeO and MgO

D. **GRANITIC MAGMA**
70% SiO_2
2% $FeO + MgO$
28% other   Melt

Solids

Granite landscape in Sierra Nevada shows sheetlike weathering.

THE FORM AND TEXTURE of igneous rocks differ greatly in details of appearance and in the gross forms of the entire rock bodies. In contrast to volcanic lavas, which are extrusive igneous rocks, those formed at great depth are known as intrusive or plutonic. These tend to crystallize more slowly and, therefore, have larger crystals than extrusive rocks. The texture of an igneous rock depends upon its rate of cooling, and thus on its geologic mode of formation (p. 89). The chemical and mineral content of igneous rocks depends upon the composition of the magmas from which they were formed. Magmas (or melts) rich in silica produce granitic (acid) type rocks. Those rich in iron and magnesium tend to be more mobile, and these produce basaltic (basic) type rocks. Because of their durability, many igneous rocks are used as road material. Large, specially cut blocks are used as ornamental building stones.

The color of an igneous rock is related to its composition. Acid rocks generally tend to be lighter in color than basic ones.

92

COMMON INTRUSIVE IGNEOUS ROCKS

GRANITE, usually light-colored and coarse-grained, contains about 30 percent quartz and 60 percent potash feldspar. It may be pinkish red or black-spotted. Granite is common in many large intrusions and often associated with mineral deposits.

GRANITE PORPHYRY is a granitic type ground mass with longer crystals (phenocrysts) of feldspar, quartz, or mica. Very coarse-grained acidic rocks (pegmatites) have crystals over 40 feet long. This porphyritic structure is also found in lavas.

GABBRO is dark-colored and ▶ has a coarse, granitic-type texture consisting of plagioclase feldspar and pyroxene with traces of other minerals, but it contains no quartz.

COMMON EXTRUSIVE IGNEOUS ROCKS

RHYOLITE is a light-colored, ▶ fine-grained volcanic rock, often porphyritic, with phenocrysts of quartz and orthoclase. It is similar in composition to granite.

OBSIDIAN AND PUMICE have similar composition to rhyolite. Both are rapidly cooled. Obsidian is a translucent glass. Pumice is a rhyolitic froth characterized by cavities left by the release of gas.

▼

BASALT, the most common lava, is dark, fine-grained, and rather heavy. It consists of pyroxene and a plagioclase feldspar. Cindery basalt (scoria) may have secondary minerals within the cavities formed by gas.

▼

93

METAMORPHISM

Metamorphism is the process of change that rocks undergo when exposed to increasing temperatures and pressures within the earth at which their mineral components are no longer stable. Rocks of any kind may undergo metamorphism. But the preservation of "ghost" structures (relics of the parent rock as bedding, or even fossils) implies that metamorphic change takes place in a solid, rather than a molten, state.

Effects of metamorphism depend upon the composition, texture, and shearing strength of the original rock, and on the temperature and pressure under which metamorphism takes place. Metamorphosed rocks may differ in texture, mineral content, and total chemical composition from the parent rock.

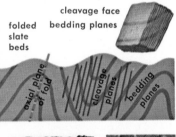

folded slate beds / cleavage face / bedding planes / axial plane of fold / cleavage planes / bedding planes

TEXTURAL CHANGES are shown by most metamorphic rocks. Cleavage in slates (their fissility along definite planes) is produced by parallel realignment of such flaky minerals as mica, and is often inclined sharply to original bedding in the rocks. Cleavage is mainly the result of the increased pressure of dynamic metamorphism.

FOLIATION is the development of wavey or contorted layers under more intense metamorphism. It involves structural and mineralogical changes. Schists have closely spaced foliation.

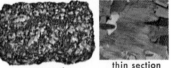

gneiss / thin section

PHYLLITES have a rather glossy, slaty appearance caused by recrystallization of flaky minerals along cleavage planes. Characteristics are in between schists and slates.

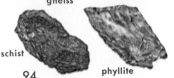

schist / phyllite

GROWTH OF NEW MINERALS results from intensive metamorphism, such as regional metamorphism involved in mountain building. Loss of some chemical components and addition of others may produce changes in total chemical composition of the original rock. Such flaky minerals as mica are unstable under these conditions, and high-grade metamorphic rocks often have a granular appearance, developing whole new suites of metamorphic minerals. The particular assemblage depends upon the composition of the parent rock and the metamorphic environment. This has lead to a concept of metamorphic facies.

MARBLE, fine to coarsely granular, is composed chiefly of calcite or dolomite. It derives from metamorphosed limestone.

QUARTZITE is a tough rock of metamorphosed quartz sandstone with a sugary texture. Its color is white to pink-brown.

GARNETIFEROUS SCHIST shows foliation in parallel arrangement of platy micas, and growth of garnet as a new mineral.

ECLOGITES are red-green-colored rocks, formed from basic rocks; origin obscure.

metamorphosed sedimentary rock

aureole, zone of contact metamorphism

STOCK (granitic intrusion)

RECRYSTALLIZATION of some minerals and the conversion of others is a feature common to many metamorphic rocks, especially those formed at high temperatures, such as those around intrusions (thermal metamorphism). Rocks around intrusions often display this as a result of contact metamorphism.

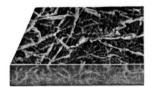

Black Marble

Quartzite

Garnetiferous schist

Eclogite

Off-shore drilling rig symbolizes man's search for petroleum.

MINERALS AND MAN

The foundation of 20th-century civilization is industrial, and the basis for industry is fuels and metal ores. The things which form the basis of life in the Western world—clean water supply, buildings, highways, automobiles, hardware, tools, fertilizers, plastics, fuels, chemicals, and more—ultimately come from the crust of the tiny planet on which we live.

Economic minerals are very unevenly distributed. Although most minerals themselves are widely scattered, deposits sufficiently rich to mine depend upon rare combinations of geologic processes. They are often found in isolated areas, and long geologic study may be needed to locate and exploit them. Almost 90 percent of the world's nickel supply, for example, comes from a single intrusion near Sudbury, Ontario

New industrial processes and inventions bring demands for new minerals and fuels. The need for radio active minerals spurred development of new tech-

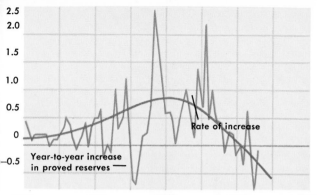

Rate of increase of proved reserves of crude oil in the U. S., exclusive of Alaska (after M. King Hubbert)

niques and dimensions in geologic surveys after World War II. The discovery of new mineral deposits can rapidly revolutionize the civilization of whole nations, as it has in the Middle East where some of the world's largest petroleum resources have brought great wealth to Arab countries.

All mineral deposits are exhaustible. Once we have mined a vein of silver or a bed of coal, there is no way of replenishing it. This demands careful conservation of mineral deposits as well as long-term exploration and planning for new supplies.

Depletion of some essential minerals now poses serious long-term problems. It is estimated by some that 80 percent of the world's economically recoverable supplies of petroleum will be exhausted within a century. Some metals, including lead and copper, have comparably limited reserves. These estimates are based upon present rates of consumption, but an exploding world population could quadruple our mineral needs by the year 2000.

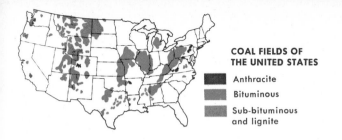

COAL FIELDS OF
THE UNITED STATES

■ Anthracite

■ Bituminous

■ Sub-bituminous
and lignite

MINERAL FUELS are basic to an industrial economy not only for heating, lighting, and transport but also for the industrial power needed in mineral processing, mining, and in manufacturing. Hydroelectricity, though of great importance in some areas, provides only a small fraction (less than 2 percent) of the world's power. Mineral fuels (oil, coal, and gas) provide about 98 percent. Coal and petroleum are fossil fuels.

Bituminous coal

Carnotite, a uranium mineral

COAL is a sedimentary rock formed from the remains of fossil plants. Buried peat, under pressure, loses water and volatiles and achieves a relatively high carbon content. Peat has about 80 percent moisture; lignite (an intermediate step between peat and coal), about 40 percent; bituminous coal, only about 5 percent. Anthracite, formed under conditions of extreme pressure, contains 95 percent carbon compared with bituminous coal, which has only about 80 percent. Most great coal deposits are in rocks of Pennsylvanian or Permian age.

ATOMIC FUELS at present supply only a fraction of the world's resources, but they will become more important. Mineral fuels used are ores of uranium.

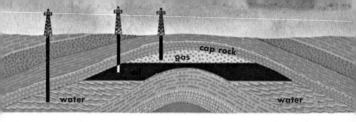

Cross section of oil field shows subsurface structure; petroleum is trapped in crest of an anticline sealed by impervious cap rock.

PETROLEUM is a general term for a mixture of gaseous, liquid, and solid hydrocarbons. When burned, this fossil fuel releases solar energy stored millions of years ago. Petroleum migrates from the source rock, where it forms, to other rocks. Most petroleum remains dispersed in rock pores and much escapes at the surface of the earth. But in commercial fields, it is trapped between an impermeable cap rock and a permeable reservoir rock often floating on water, as illustrated.

OIL SHALE is carbonaceous shale that yields hydrocarbons when distilled. At present, the cost of oil and gas production from it is too high to make it economically important, but it may be used in the future.

PETROLEUM EXPLORATION involves both geological and geophysical studies. Since most of the more obvious surface traps have now been discovered, seismic and other surveys are increasingly used to discover subsurface and submarine structures, such as those beneath the North Sea.

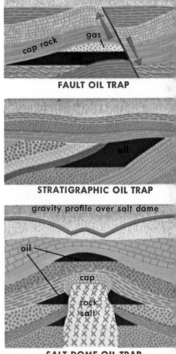

FAULT OIL TRAP

STRATIGRAPHIC OIL TRAP

gravity profile over salt dome

oil

cap

rock salt

SALT DOME OIL TRAP

ORE DEPOSITS are natural concentrations of metallic minerals in sufficient quantity to make their exploitation commercially worthwhile. Most industrial metals, other than iron, aluminum, and magnesium, are present as only a fraction of one percent in the average igneous rocks of the earth's crust. Platinum, for example, has an abundance of .000,000,5 percent by weight; silver and mercury, .000,01 percent. An ore with 1 percent antimony contains 10,000 times as much as the average igneous rock. There are several geological processes by which ore-bearing minerals are concentrated in the crust.

MAGMATIC ORES are concentrated from molten rock where crystals settle during cooling. Some of the world's greatest ore bodies were formed in this way.

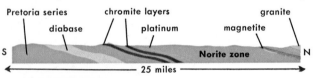

THE BUSHVELD magnetite and chromite deposits of South Africa occur in a series of layered lopoliths of norite (gabbro with hypersthene pyroxene).

THE SUDBURY nickel deposits of Ontario occur as stringers in a norite intrusive complex.

DIAMONDS are formed deep in volcanic pipes, crystallizing from a distinctive ultrabasic rock, kimberlite. Exposure by weathering may subsequently concentrate diamonds in river placer deposits.

METAMORPHIC ORES are formed around some intrusions by contact metamorphism of the country rocks. Asbestos, used for insulation and fireproofing, is a common nonmetallic metamorphic mineral.

HYDROTHERMAL ORES include many of the largest deposits of lead, zinc, copper, and silver. Deposited from hot, aqueous solutions, their distribution is usually controlled by joints, faults, bedding, and lithology of the country rocks. The mineralizing solutions arise from magmatic sources, although the parent igneous rock may not always be exposed. The copper deposits of Butte, Montana, and Utah, silver of Comstock Lode, Nevada, and gold of Cripple Creek, Colorado, are all hydrothermal deposits. A large portion of the world's gold is mined from deposits that originated from hydrothermal solutions.

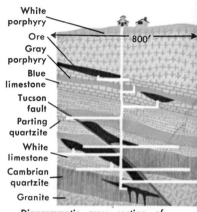

Diagrammatic cross section of structural ore control in lead and zinc mine, Leadville, Colorado. (After Argall)

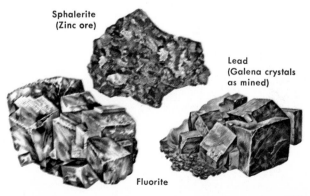

Sphalerite (Zinc ore)

Lead (Galena crystals as mined)

Fluorite

Drilling in taconite iron ore rocks requires special equipment.

METALLIC ORES, such as the iron around Birmingham, Alabama, and Northamptonshire, England, are sedimentary rocks rich in original hematite. Carnotite, a sedimentary uranium ore, is found in sandstones of the Colorado Plateau.

SEDIMENTARY ORES form in a variety of different ways. Some are formed as direct sedimentary deposits or by evaporation; others have an igneous origin and are concentrated by sedimentary processes.

EVAPORITES are mineral salts (halite, gypsum, potash, etc.) formed by evaporation of restricted bodies of water. The great salt deposits of Germany, Utah, and New Mexico are examples. Evaporites may be impure, containing clay, sand, or carbonates.

RESIDUAL MINERAL DEPOSITS are formed by weathering and leaching with corresponding enrichment of low-grade ore deposits, many of sedimentary ori-

PLACER DEPOSITS are formed by concentration of fragments in stream deposits. Such heavy minerals as gold, diamonds, magnetite, and tin oxide are often concentrated in this way. Examples are the tin deposits of Malaysia and the goldfields of California and Australia.

gin. The great iron deposits of the Great Lakes and the aluminum (bauxite) deposits of Arkansas have been concentrated in situ by this process.

Iron ore pit, Virginia, Minn.; rocks are Precambrian.

CONSTRUCTIONAL AND INDUSTRIAL MINERALS, although more abundant than ore minerals, are used in much greater quantities. They are generally quarried, rather than mined.

BUILDING MATERIALS are extracted from the earth, whether brick, stone, steel girders, or glass. Building stones must be durable, easily quarried, and easily worked. The particular stones selected often depend upon the local weathering conditions (determined by amounts of industrial gases), and local availability of stones.

Other industrial minerals, such as sulphur, salt, potash, gypsum, asbestos are not so widely distributed, but are used in many industrial processes. They occur in very different geologic settings.

CLAYS are used for brick-making, in chemical industries, in ceramics, and in the manufacture of many other products. Each use demands slightly different qualities. Many varieties of clay are known and mined.

SAND AND GRAVEL are widely used in concrete construction. Most supplies come from glacial and river deposits. Reserves are plentiful, but distribution is patchy.

STONE AGGREGATE for highway, airfield, and dam construction is also used in great quantities. It is resistant and cheaply quarried. In some tropical areas, it has to be imported.

LIMESTONE is used in the manufacture of cement, as a metallurgical flux, as an aggregate, and in agriculture. Limestones are widely distributed, and over 500 million tons are quarried annually in North America alone.

▼

THE CHANGING EARTH

If the processes of erosion and deposition were counteracted only by igneous activity, we should expect the continents to be featureless plains, broken only by active volcanoes or plateaus of lava. But there are considerable movements of the earth's crust.

Ancient caves, high above present beach, indicate former position of sea level, N. Ireland.

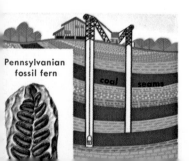

Pennsylvanian fossil fern

coal seams

EARTHQUAKES provide dramatic evidence of crustal movements. Small relative movements of the crust can very often be measured after earthquakes have taken place (p. 126).

RAISED BEACHES and buried forests (p. 150) often involve warping rather than simple uplift. Raised beaches show a rise in the California coastline over the past years, but on the other hand, parts of Denmark are sinking.

OTHER COASTAL FEATURES such as wavecut platforms indicate relative uplift of the land; drowned valleys indicate relative sinking (p. 69). Raised coral reefs often show uplift, tilting, and even reversal of movement.

FOSSILS of marine animals in land areas indicate relative uplift of the land. The presence of coal seams with land plants thousands of feet below present ground level shows that sinking has also taken place. Lake sediments are often interbedded with sediments that were deposited in the sea.

Crustal movement is a common feature of the earth. It is found throughout the world, in rocks ranging in age from the oldest to the youngest. It involves various kinds of movement: gentle, slow uplift or sinking, regional warping, rapid earthquake movements, and regional stresses strong enough to buckle and break great masses of rock.

INCISED MEANDERS of rivers are thought to result from relative uplift of the land surface (p. 44). The Grand Canyon, which measures more than a mile deep, is an example.

RECENT MOVEMENT of the crust is indicated by famous temple ruins near Naples. The pillars, erected on land, were bored by marine molluscs, indicating submergence by the sea and the subsequent uplift of the land.

Roman temple, build on dry land, is now flooded.

UNCONFORMITIES (p.114) represent breaks in the deposition of sediments, sometimes indicating periods of significant crustal disturbance.

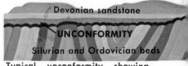

Devonian sandstone

UNCONFORMITY

Silurian and Ordovician beds

Typical unconformity showing effects of uplift in pre Devonian.

FOLDS in ancient strata range from small warps, only one or two feet in height, to great domes, miles across. In areas where rocks have responded in a brittle manner, breaks (faults) have developed.

Folding in limestone, Victoria, Australia ▼

FAULTS involve fracture and relative movement of rock units (p. 111). In nearly all cases, the rocks involved were originally in a horizontal position.

ROCK DEFORMATION

Although sedimentary rocks are generally deposited in almost horizontal beds, we generally find them distorted and tilted, if we follow them over any considerable distance. Such structures are the result of large-scale crustal deformation which produces corresponding changes in volume, shape, and sometimes chemical composition of the rocks themselves. The intensity of the changes is proportional to the intensity of deformation and the depth of burial (see Metamorphism, p. 94). Under some stress conditions, rocks behave as though they were elastic, but as stress increases, they undergo permanent (plastic) deformation and may ultimately fracture. The most intense zones of deformation are associated with mountain chains.

DIP of a bed is a measure of its slope or tilt. The *direction of dip* is the direction of maximum slope, or the direction a ball would run over the bed if its surface were perfectly flat. The *angle of dip* is the acute angle this direction makes with a horizontal plane. The *strike* of a rock bed is the direction of the intersection of its dip direction with a horizontal plane. It is expressed as a compass bearing and lies at right angles to the direction of dip. Dip-strike symbols are used on most geologic maps.

Clinometers are elaborate instruments used by geologists to measure dip. A simple instrument, however, may be made from a plastic protractor fixed to a flat base with a weighted thread to measure the maximum dip. The strike of the dip is then measured with a compass.

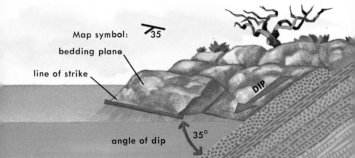

Map symbol: 35

bedding plane

line of strike

DIP

angle of dip 35°

Sheep Mountain, Wyoming, is a fine example of pitching anticline.

FOLDS are wrinkles or flexures in stratified rocks. They range from microscopic sizes in metamorphic rocks to great structures hundreds of miles across. They sometimes occur in isolation, but more often, they are packed together, especially in mountain ranges. Up-folds are called *anticlines*, and downfolds are called *synclines*. Folds with one limb more or less horizontal are called *monoclines*. All folds tend to die out as they are traced along their lengths.

FORMATION OF FOLDS shown in stages. In Stage 1, the rocks are deposited. In Stage 2, they are folded. In Stage 3, they are up-lifted and their tops eroded, with only their dipping limbs remaining. The oldest beds (1) are always in the core of an anticline, but on the flanks of a syncline.

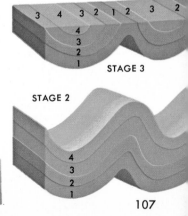

STAGE 3

STAGE 2

STAGE 1

107

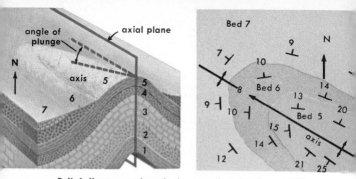

Relief diagram and geologic map of a plunging anticline.

THE STRUCTURE OF FOLDS (above) shows that the axial plane is drawn so that it bisects the angle of the fold. The axis is its trace on a bedding plane. If the axis is not horizontal, the fold is said to pitch.

ANTICLINES can be spotted on geologic maps by the dip arrows pointing away from the axis. A pitching fold gives a

SYNCLINES occur where the beds dip toward the axis. They can pitch and be either symmetrical or asymmetrical. A structural basin is a basin-shaped syncline where dips converge on a central point or area.

"closing" outcrop pattern. A dome is an anticline that has dips pointing in all directions from a central point or area.

KINDS OF FOLDS

SYMMETRICAL FOLDS (a) have limbs dipping in opposite directions at the same inclinations. The axial plane (ap) is vertical.

ASYMMETRICAL FOLDS (b) are those having an inclined axial plane and, like symmetrical folds, have limbs dipping in opposite directions, but at different inclinations.

OVERTURNED FOLDS (c) have an inclined axial plane and limbs dipping in the same direction. One limb is inverted.

ISOCLINAL FOLDS (d) have equal dips of two limbs; axial plane dips in same direction.

RECUMBENT FOLDS (e) have horizontal axial planes.

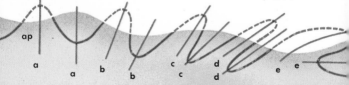

Folded rocks form cliffs 1500 feet above San Juan River, Utah.

FOLD PATTERNS are rarely as simple as idealized ones shown on these pages. They often pass into faults. Some beds yield to strain more readily than others. Such incompetent rocks as shale and rock salt, for example, often yield by flowing and slipping in folds. Flowage of salt may produce structural domes, leading to petroleum reservoirs. Such incompetent rock movements are sometimes so strong that, as in some Middle East oilfields, major folds at depth are not reflected at the surface. Folds that do reach the surface are best exposed in arid and semi-arid areas and in rock faces and cliffs, but regional mapping of other vegetation-covered areas, such as the Appalachians, often shows folding over great areas. Anticlinal fold structures sometimes provide petroleum accumulations.

Section across southern Appalachian Mountains.

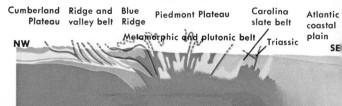

Cumberland Plateau   Ridge and valley belt   Blue Ridge   Piedmont Plateau   Carolina slate belt   Atlantic coastal plain

Metamorphic and plutonic belt   Triassic

NW   SE

ROCK FRACTURES

Rock fractures are another major way in which rocks yield to stress.

JOINTS are fractures or cracks in which the rocks on either side of the fracture have not undergone relative movement. Common in sedimentary rocks, they are usually caused by release of burial pressure or by diastrophism. They play an important part in rock weathering as zones of weakness and water movement.

◀**JOINTS IN SEDIMENTARY ROCKS** occur in parallel sets at right angles to the bedding. Tensional, compressional, and torsional stresses all produce distinctive joints.

JOINTS IN IGNEOUS ROCKS may result from shrinkage during cooling. In fine-grained rocks, there is a characteristic polygonal arrangement. Granite masses may show sheet jointing.

Giant's Causeway, Northern Ireland, shows hexagonal columns formed by cooling of basalt lavas.

FAULTS are fractures where once continuous rocks suffered relative displacement. The amount of movement may vary from less than an inch to many thousands of feet vertically and to more than a hundred miles horizontally. Different types of faults are produced by different compressional and tensional stresses, and they also depend upon the rock type and geological setting.

Faults are the cause of earthquakes, which suggests that repeated small movements rather than one "catastrophic" break characterize faults. Distinctive, large-scale fracture zones displace the mid-oceanic ridges in several areas (p. 136).

KINDS OF FAULTS

NORMAL, GRAVITY, OR "TENSIONAL" FAULTS are not necessarily the most common fault type, nor are they necessarily formed by tension. They are faults in which relative downward movement has taken place down the upper face or hanging wall of the fault plane. (We cannot generally prove whether both beds have moved, or only one.) The throw of the fault is the vertical displacement of the bed (ac); the heave is the horizontal displacement (bc). The angle abc is the dip of the fault plane, and the complement of this is the hade. The dip is usually steep. Sometimes there may be more than one episode of movement along the fault plane.

Block diagram of normal fault before weathering.

Block diagram of normal fault after weathering.

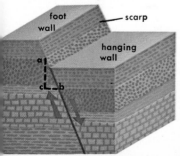

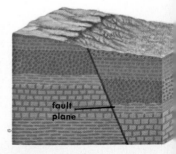

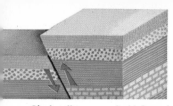

Block diagram of high-angle reverse fault.

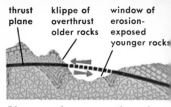

thrust plane   klippe of overthrust older rocks   window of erosion-exposed younger rocks

Diagrammatic cross section of eroded low-angle thrust fault.

REVERSE OR THRUST FAULTS have relative upward movement of the hanging wall of the fault plane. They often occur in areas of intense folding such as mountain belts. Lateral displacement may be many miles. Reverse faults often have a low dip and result in repetition and apparent reversal of stratigraphic order in a vertical sequence that a borehole through the fault would penetrate. Chief Mountain Montana, is an eroded remnant of a large thrust.

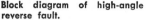

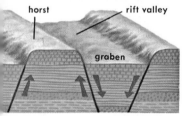

horst   rift valley

graben

Topographic Depression marking San Andreas Fault is occupied by a lagoon, Bolinas Bay.

A GRABEN is a block that has been dropped down between two normal faults. An uplifted fault block is a *horst. Rift valleys* are graben structures hundreds of miles in length. The most spectacular is that along the Red Sea, but they are also found in East Africa, the Rhine, and California, and they also occur beneath the oceans along the crests of the mid-oceanic ridges.

TEAR FAULTS or strike-slip faults are those in which the predominant movement is horizontal. The displacement may exceed 100 miles. The San Andreas Fault in California is 600 miles long and has a displacement of over 600 kilometers. The 1906 San Francisco earthquake was caused by the movement of the San Andreas fault, which is still active!

FAULTS IN THE FIELD as shown are all diagrammatic. Rotational movements often complicate the simple vertical and horizontal movements, and the throw and hade of a fault may change along its length. The fault plane is often poorly defined, and is represented by a fault zone made up of broken and distorted rocks. Faults often occur in groups (fault zones) made up of many individual faults. Except in desert areas, cliff faces, and quarries, faults are rarely seen at the surface, but their presence is indicated by one or more of the following features:

FAULT BRECCIA occurs where the rocks of the fault zone are shattered into angular, irregularly sized fragments. Some may be reduced to a gritty clay.

TOPOGRAPHIC EFFECTS occur when faults bring together rocks of differing hardness. Denudation may indicate the faulting by showing sharp, "unnatural" topographic contact. The Grand Teton mountains in Wyoming are an example, where resistant Pre-Cambrian igneous rocks are faulted against softer Tertiary sediments (p. 118). Other topographic effects. bays or valleys, for example, may result from the weakness of a fault zone, which itself may undergo strong differential weathering.

SPRINGS may be produced by faults when pervious and impervious strata are brought into contact (p. 51). Lines of springs often indicate the existence of a fault.

SLICKENSIDES, polished striations or flutings, are often found in the fault plane or zone. They may indicate the direction of relative movement.

DISPLACEMENT OF OUTCROP is another indication of a fault. As well as displacing rocks vertically, faults in dipping beds will displace their outcrop patterns. In geologic mapping, faults are often inferred from outcrops which "won't match."

Small-scale faulting in limestone

UNCONFORMITIES are ancient erosion surfaces in which an older group of rocks has been uplifted, eroded, and subsequently buried by a group of younger rocks. Unconformities can be used to date periods of crustal movement in the reconstruction of earth history. The time span represented by the erosion surface (absence of deposits) may vary from very long to very short periods. A "break" in fossil sequence, often a characteristic feature of unconformities, can be measured by comparing the fossils with those of uninterrupted rock sequences. Unconformities vary in form, and in the erosional intervals they represent.

DISCONFORMITIES occur where the beds above and below the erosion surface are parallel. If the older group of rocks has been folded and eroded before the deposition of the younger group, their beds will not be parallel, and they represent an *angular unconformity*.

The *eroded upper surface* of the underlying group of rocks may be flat or have considerable relief. Old soils are sometimes preserved. The lowest overlying beds are often *conglomerates* made up of eroded fragments of the underlying group of rocks.

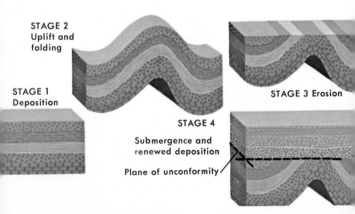

STAGE 2
Uplift and folding

STAGE 1
Deposition

STAGE 3 Erosion

STAGE 4
Submergence and renewed deposition

Plane of unconformity

The Matterhorn, Switzerland, shows sharp outline formed by glacial erosion typical of many mountains.

MOUNTAIN BUILDING

Mountains are among the most conspicuous features of the earth's surface. Although they are formed in various ways and are of various ages, they are usually concentrated in great curved belts that run along the continental margins. Not all are confined to the land. The Mid-Atlantic Ridge stretches thousands of miles, rising almost 10,000 feet above the ocean floor. Similar ridges are found in other oceans (p. 136).

Any isolated, upstanding mass may be called a mountain. There is no minimum height or particular shape involved. Some of the ways in which mountains may be produced are shown on the following pages.

VOLCANIC MOUNTAINS include some of the world's most beautiful and famous mountains. Mt. Fujiyama in Japan, Mt. Vesuvius in Italy, Mt. Hood in Oregon, and Mt. Rainier in Washington are all classic examples of strato volcanic mountains. All are characteristically steep and symmetrical. Other volcanic mountains, such as Mauna Loa in Hawaii, are formed by shield volcanoes (p. 84). They tend to be rounded and flattened, but may still be high and large. Mauna Loa rises almost 14,000 feet above sea level and about 32,000 feet above the sea floor. With its diameter of 60 miles, it is the world's largest mountain in terms of volume.

Volcanic mountains may form very rapidly. Mt. Paracutin, Mexico, began to grow in February, 1943. Within a week, its cone was 500 feet high, and within two years it had reached 1,500 feet.

Some volcanic mountains occur as isolated structures, but others form parts of extensive volcanic chains. Volcanic islands may form great island arcs, of which the 1,000-mile Aleutian chain is an example.

Mt. Fujiyama, Japan's sacred mountain, is a volcano.

Blue Mountains, New South Wales, Australia, are erosional in origin consisting chiefly of horizontal Permian and Triassic strata.

EROSIONAL MOUNTAINS are found in regions of crustal uplift. These are wide areas where crustal uplift (epeirogeny) has produced elevated plateaus, and thereby provided new erosional energy to rivers. The steep gorges with precipitous edges of "Grand Canyon type" topography, for example, are generally thought of as a dissected plateau, rather than a mountain. Some well-known mountains, such as the Blue Mountains of New South Wales, Australia, are formed in this way. If erosion continues long enough, huge isolated, resistant remnants are left. An example is Mt. Monadnock in New Hampshire which rises 1,800 feet above a "peneplane" and gives its name to such isolated structures (monadnocks). These structures are thus outliers of younger rock, resting on an exposed basement of older rocks.

DOME MOUNTAINS are the simplest kind of structural mountains. They tend to be relatively small, isolated, structural domes, uplifted without intense faulting. They may be associated with such igneous intrusions as laccoliths. The Black Hills of South Dakota are an example.

STRUCTURAL MOUNTAIN RANGES are by far the most numerous and extensive mountain ranges and differ from volcanic and erosional mountains. Their biggest difference lies in the structural deformation (diastrophism) they have undergone. Some of them are unimpressive as high mountains go (the Appalachians, for example), but they share certain common structural characteristics with other mountain chains. It is these, more than just height, that are a clue to an understanding of the nature of structural mountains.

FAULT BLOCK MOUNTAINS may be formed in any type of rock. They are often, though not always, structurally undeformed where differential vertical displacement or tilting by steep normal faults give relatively uplifted and downsunk blocks. Rift valleys are often associated with the mountain scarps, which tend to run parallel with the faulting. Such mountains may be very large. The Sierra Nevada represents the uptilted edge of a block of granite 400 miles long and 100 miles wide, with an eastern scarp 13,000 feet above sea level. There are several such ranges from Oregon to Arizona.

Tertiary volcanics

Paleozoic strata

Mount Moran

Jackson Ho

Quaternary

Tertiary sediments

PRE- CAMBRIAN

0 1 2 3 4 5 miles

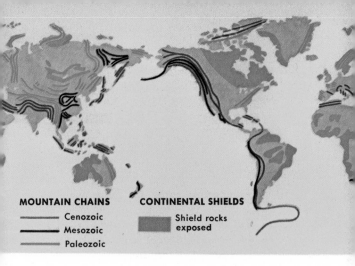

MOUNTAIN CHAINS

———— Cenozoic

———— Mesozoic

———— Paleozoic

CONTINENTAL SHIELDS

Shield rocks exposed

FOLDED MOUNTAIN RANGES all have similar characteristics. Most of the world's great mountain chains, such as the Himalayas, Alps, Rocky, Appalachian, Andes, and Atlas, belong to none of the groups so far discussed. In spite of many individual differences, all are fundamentally folded ranges and share these six important characteristics:

1. Linear Distribution of mountain ranges indicates they are not haphazardly scattered across the earth's surface; they are found in long, narrow belts. The Appalachians, for example, stretch 1,500 miles from Newfoundland to Alabama and are up to 350 miles wide. The Rockies are 3,000 miles long and continue southward for another 5,000 miles in the Andes of South America. The location of most mountain ranges near the margins, or former margins, of continents is a major clue to their origin.

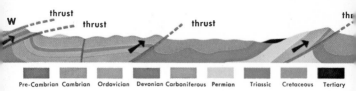

W   thrust   thrust   thrust   thr

Pre-Cambrian   Cambrian   Ordovician   Devonian   Carboniferous   Permian   Triassic   Cretaceous   Tertiary

Generalized section across the Rockies from eastern Idaho to western Wyoming.

2. Thick, sedimentary rocks that are found in all the world's major mountain chains are generally 30,000 to 40,000 feet (6-8 miles) in thickness. Fossils and structures show many of them to be deposits of shallow seas; others accumulated at greater depths. Some were formed above sea level. They are usually clastic sediments, with subordinate carbonates. Bordering strata of equivalent age are often only a tenth of this thickness and generally have a higher proportion of carbonates.

These thick deposits accumulated in long, down-warps (geosynclines), often associated with volcanoes, in which long-continued subsidence kept pace with sedimentation. The continuous incoming of detritus indicates that the neighboring land source area must have been undergoing more or less continuous uplift.

3. Distinctive igneous rocks are found in mountain chains. Clastic sediments are often interbedded with great thicknesses of volcanic lava, and eroded cores of mountain chains include vast granitic batholiths, as well as migmatites. The batholiths and migmatites were probably formed from the effect of depth and heat on deeply buried sediments.

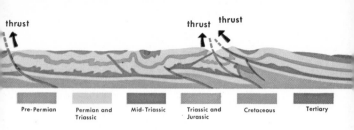

Generalized section across the Swiss Alps showing influence of thrusting (After Aubert).

4. Intense folding and faulting found along major mountain chains often involves thrusting onto the neighboring continental margin, with displacements of many miles. It implies great shortening of the crust. In the Alps, this shortening may be as much as 100 miles.

5. Mountains have roots. They are not simply lumps of rock resting on a uniform surface. They have roots of light material extending far down below their normal depths. This is suggested by the gravity anomaly of mountains, by the paths of earthquake waves through them, and by high heat flow associated with mountains. Since mountains deflect a plumb line *less* than the mere attraction of their surface mass resting on a "normal" basement, they must be underlain by a larger amount of light material.

0 milligals

actual measured gravity

—50

folded sedimentary rock

CRUSTAL ROCK

MANTLE ROCK

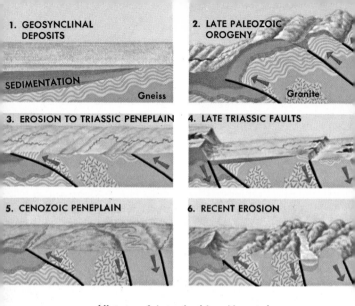

1. GEOSYNCLINAL DEPOSITS

SEDIMENTATION
Gneiss

2. LATE PALEOZOIC OROGENY

Granite

3. EROSION TO TRIASSIC PENEPLAIN

4. LATE TRIASSIC FAULTS

5. CENOZOIC PENEPLAIN

6. RECENT EROSION

History of Appalachian Mountains

6. Repeated uplift and elevation have taken place
in folded mountains. Unconformities and conglomerates
in the strata of mountains show that uplift took place
during sedimentation both during and after folding.
Many older mountain ranges have been eroded down
to peneplanes before being uplifted again by subsequent earth movement. The flat surface below the
Cretaceous rocks bordering the Appalachians is an
example of such erosion. The present 6,000-foot elevation of the Appalachians results from Tertiary movements. Some areas may have no great surface relief
but still have the structure of ancient mountains. The
Continental Shields are an example. The Laurentian
Canadian Shield has six mountain belts, which are now
almost completely eroded away.

122

OROGENY is the name given to the processes of mountain-building. By studying several orogenic belts, we can reconstruct the various typical stages through which folded mountains have passed. Not all mountain ranges have a similar history, but most of the following stages can usually be recognized.

1. Geosynclinal sedimentation, a regional downwarp of very thick sedimentation, develops near continental margins. There is often associated volcanic activity. Sediments deposited in shallow shell seas include limestone and well-sorted sandstones. Dark shales and turbidites are characteristic of deeper water deposits.

2. Folding, together with faulting, uplift, and erosion, gives local unconformities and coarse, clastic sediments, generally in outer volcanic (eugeosynclinal) belts. Island arcs may form. These movements continue over long periods of time, and gradually move towards the ancient land masses.

3. Continued subsidence, with lateral extension of the geosyncline (metamorphism in eugeosyncline), renewed crustal compression. Deltaic sediments are formed over extensive areas.

4. Thrusting and folding of the entire belt, with metamorphism and mobility of roots at depth, giving migmatites and granite batholithic intrusions. Repeated uplift. Continental sediments formed.

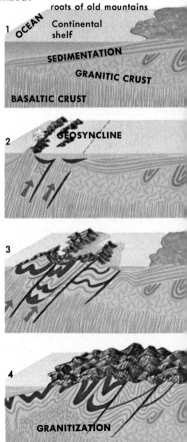

roots of old mountains

1 OCEAN   Continental shelf

SEDIMENTATION

GRANITIC CRUST

BASALTIC CRUST

2   GEOSYNCLINE

3

4

GRANITIZATION

THE SEARCH FOR A MECHANISM of mountain-building is one of the major tasks of earth science. Although surface processes play some part in the growth of mountains (by providing sediments for geosynclines, for example), the chief processes must operate within the earth's interior. These forces must account for the position and down-sinking of geosynclines, for the tectonic, magmatic, and metamorphic events associated with mountain-building, and for the post-orogenic history of mountain chains.

To discover such a mechanism, we need information on the internal structure of the earth. Most of this is obtained by the analysis of earthquake data.

EARTHQUAKES

Earthquakes are rapid movements of the earth's crust which result from natural causes. About 150,000 take place each year and as many others occur that are so weak they may be detected only by very sensitive recording instruments (seismographs). About 90 percent of all earthquakes seem to originate at a *focus,* the point of maximum intensity of the earthquake in the outer 40 miles of the crust. A few deep-focus earthquakes originate at depths as great as 400 miles.

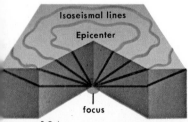

TYPICAL EARTHQUAKE EFFECTS are shown on block diagram. Earthquake waves radiate outwards. Those that travel direct to the surface are shown. Isoseismal lines join at places where the earthquake is recorded with the same intensity. These generally form approximate circles or ovals of decreasing intensity around the epicenter, which is directly above the focus.

Earthquake destruction of State Highway 287 in Montana, 1959.

EARTHQUAKE DESTRUCTION occurs when shock waves are absorbed by buildings. Those on thick soil or rock debris are most affected. Steel-frame buildings on solid rock are more likely to survive. Violent earth movements may be accompanied by earth flows and slumps, cracks, small faults (with horizontal or vertical movement up to about 30 feet), and temporary fountains. Fires often result from broken gas lines.

Tsunamis are gravity waves in the oceans which result from earthquakes. Movement of a part of the ocean floor disturbs the water and leads to huge oscillatory waves, often over a hundred miles long. Moving at speeds of up to 500 mph, they pile up along shores, often causing great destruction.

EARTHQUAKE BELTS encircle the earth. About 4/5 of all earthquakes occur in a belt around the Pacific. A less active belt runs through the Himalayas and Alps.

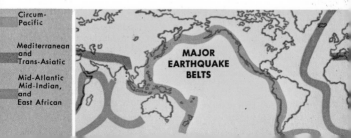

Circum-Pacific

Mediterranean and Trans-Asiatic

Mid-Atlantic Mid-Indian, and East African

MAJOR EARTHQUAKE BELTS

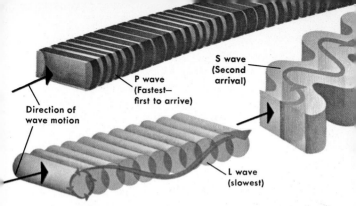

Direction of wave motion

P wave (Fastest—first to arrive)

S wave (Second arrival)

L wave (slowest)

EARTHQUAKE RECORDS or seismograms show that various types of earthquake waves travel through the earth by different paths. There are two types of waves which travel *through* the earth—P (push-pull) waves that are compressional and travel by moving the particles backward and forward through any material, and S (shake) waves that pass only through solids. S-waves shake the particles perpendicularly to the direction of their movement, like waves made in a rope by holding one end still and shaking the other up and down. L (surface) waves travel around the

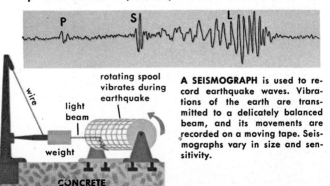

P   S   L

rotating spool vibrates during earthquake

light beam

wire

weight

CONCRETE

A SEISMOGRAPH is used to record earthquake waves. Vibrations of the earth are transmitted to a delicately balanced beam, and its movements are recorded on a moving tape. Seismographs vary in size and sensitivity.

surface of the earth and can pass through any material. From many observations, it has been shown that when recording stations are more than 7,000 miles away from an earthquake epicenter, the otherwise very regular travel times of P-waves is reduced. They arrive later than calculated, and S-waves are eliminated completely. This occurs because changes of composition within the earth's interior influence the paths and speeds of the various waves.

By using a world-wide seismograph network and studying the paths and travel times of these waves, it is possible not only to locate an earthquake at its source but also to build up a model or picture of the nature of the earth's interior.

EARTHQUAKE WAVES passing through the earth are illustrated below, showing the effect of refraction on P-waves. S-waves are completely eliminated by the core. P-waves are indicated by red lines; S-waves by the blue lines.

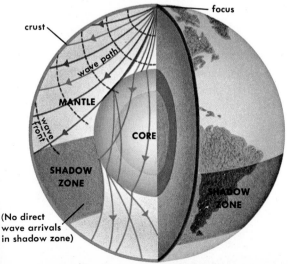

crust
wave path
MANTLE
wave front
CORE
SHADOW ZONE
SHADOW ZONE
focus
(No direct wave arrivals in shadow zone)

THE EARTH'S INTERIOR

The earth's interior is not homogeneous but is made up of a series of thick, concentric shells of different composition. This seems to be the best explanation for the behavior of earthquake waves.

Using data from seismographs, a hypothetical model of the interior shells can be constructed. We have no direct method of testing its accuracy, but there are several lines of indirect evidence which seem to support it (p. 126). The three main layers are called crust, mantle, and core. The boundary between the crust and the mantle is called the Mohorovicic discontinuity, commonly called the Moho.

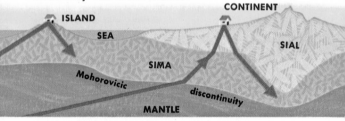

THE CRUST, 10-25 miles thick below the continents, consists of solid rock. Beneath the continents, P- and S-wave speeds suggest that there is an upper layer 10-15 miles thick of granitic type composition, called the *SIALIC* layer because silicon and aluminum are its most abundant elements. This layer appears to be underlain by a denser one of similar thickness of basalt composition, called *SIMA* because silicon and magnesium are its most characteristic elements. Below the oceans, this Sialic layer is thin or absent, and the Simatic layer below the sediments is only about 3 miles thick.

The andesite line is the boundary between the continental and oceanic provinces. It separates the ocean floors, largely basalt, from the marginal areas in which the islands have characteristically folded "continental" structure and lavas, intermediate between rhyolitic and basaltic. The thickness and composition of the crust vary.

THE MANTLE, lying below the crust, is where P- and S-wave velocities show a sharp increase, which suggests a change in composition. This is the outer limit of the mantle, or the Mohorovicic discontinuity, which seems to be a solid of rather basic composition, rich in iron magnesium minerals. The wave velocity increases further with depth, suggesting that the mantle may become more rigid. A sharp discontinuity occurs at a depth of 300 miles. The mantle extends downward to a depth of 1,800 miles and overlies the earth's central core.

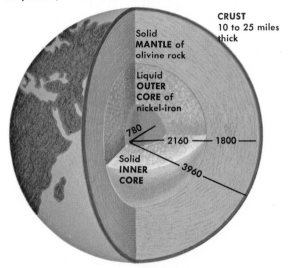

CRUST
10 to 25 miles thick

Solid **MANTLE** of olivine rock

Liquid **OUTER CORE** of nickel-iron

780

2160 — 1800

3960

Solid **INNER CORE**

THE CORE, just below the mantle, is recognized where the S-waves are eliminated and P-wave velocity is slowed down. This indicates that the outer core is not a solid. It is probably a "liquid," but the fact that P-waves speed up again at a depth of 3,160 miles from the surface suggests that the "core of the core" (the inner core) is solid. Most geologists believe it has an iron-nickel composition because of its high density (15 for the inner core), and by analogy with meteorites, which probably formed at the same time. It may, however, be a similar composition to the mantle, its differences arising from variations created under very high pressure. Little is known of the behavior of materials at extreme pressures.

MODERN GEOPHYSICAL MEASUREMENTS provide additional information about the earth's interior and mountain-building processes. Artificial earthquakes, produced by explosions used in seismic studies of subsurface structure, reveal the nature and boundaries of interior earth layers. Measurements of gravity and magnetic variations are useful in subsurface studies, both "deep" as those beneath mountain roots and "shallow" as in the location of petroleum traps or mineral deposits. Heat-flow studies are used to analyze deep structures. Radar mapping is of potential importance. Continuous, rapid geophysical survey measurements are now being made from aircraft and ships.

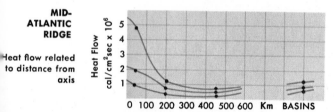

MID-ATLANTIC RIDGE

Heat flow related to distance from axis

Heat Flow cal/cm^{2}sec x 10^6

0 100 200 300 400 500 600 Km BASINS

HEAT-FLOW STUDIES in mines and boreholes show that the temperature of the earth's crust increases by an average of 30° C per kilometer of depth, although there are wide local variations caused by the geological setting and the thermal conductivity of the rocks involved. Over the continents, most of the background heat seems to originate from radioactivity in the crust. Where the crust is thick, as in mountain ranges, values tend to be high.

Seismic shot explosion produces a plume of soil.

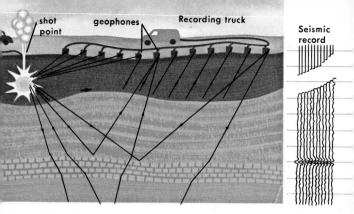

Seismic record

GEOPHYSICAL EXPLORATION is widely used in the location of mineral deposits, petroleum traps, and in geologic mapping. The diagram shows how seismic studies provide a structural profile of an anticlinal oil trap. Geophones placed at measured intervals record the trace and time of P-waves.

ELECTRIC LOGGING of the resistivity and self-potential of rock penetrated by boreholes is measured and plotted. Electric logging is an aid in subsurface correlation of oil wells. (Landes)

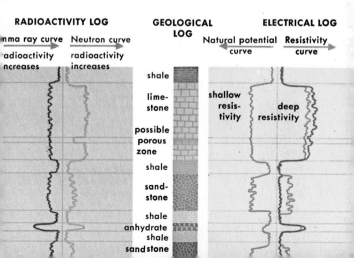

RADIOACTIVITY LOG

Gamma ray curve →   Neutron curve →

radioactivity increases   radioactivity increases

GEOLOGICAL LOG

shale

limestone

possible porous zone

shale

sandstone

shale

anhydrate shale

sandstone

ELECTRICAL LOG

← Natural potential curve   Resistivity curve →

shallow resistivity   deep resistivity

THE FORCE OF GRAVITY is present in every part of the universe, from the smallest particle to the largest star. The earth attracts everything around it with a pull towards its center. The sun holds its planets in their orbits by gravitational attraction. The force (F) involved is not constant but varies inversely with the square of the distance between the two bodies involved (D), and directly with their masses (M_1 and M_2). We can calculate it by using the equation developed by Newton, $F = \dfrac{G M_1 M_2}{D^2}$, where G is the earth's gravity constant (6.67×10^{-11} cubic meters per kilogram second^2).

The force of gravity is not the same at every place on the earth. It is lower on high mountain tops, and shows a general decrease of about one-half of one percent from the poles toward the equator.

Gravity influences almost all geological processes. Weathering and erosion, patterns of sediment distribution, the form of mountains, and even the cooling of igneous rock, all reflect the influence of gravity.

Principle of gravity is shown by spring balance; relative extension of spring is proportional to density of underlying rock.

A GRAVIMETER is used to make rapid and accurate determinations of relative differences in the earth's gravity field. It is a very sensitive spring balance, an increase in gravity being recorded by the stretching of the spring. Gravimeters employ optical and electrical methods to "magnify" the minute increase in spring length that have to be measured.

GRAVITY PROFILE may show also low gravity (negative anomaly) due to presence of light-weight salt in a salt plug, invisible from the surface.

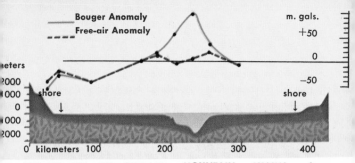

	m. gals.
Bouger Anomaly	+50
Free-air Anomaly	0
	-50

THE RED SEA AND GULF OF ADEN, unlike other rift valleys, have positive gravity anomalies. They are underlain by basic rocks and are bounded by wrench faults. This suggests they were formed by the crustal separation of Arabia and Africa, the "gap" between them being filled by rising basic material from the mantle.

MOUNTAIN CHAINS often have a major negative gravity anomaly caused by a root of light-weight granitic material. Negative anomalies across rift valleys are partly explicable by thick sediments within the valleys themselves, and may result from the concentration of light-weight alkaline magmas and volcanoes in rift areas.

ISOSTASY is the state of equilibrium that exists in the earth's crust. Because mountains have roots and also stand above the average level of the generally similar rocks of surrounding areas, some kind of balance must exist between them and the denser material on which

they "float." As erosion reduces the mass of the mountain, uplift takes place below it as plastic material flows under it—just as unloading cargo from a ship causes it to rise in the water. The postglacial uplift of Scandinavia is an example of isostatic adjustment.

Airy's isostatic hypothesis (1) suggested equilibrium results if crustal blocks of similar density have different heights; Pratt's hypothesis (2): blocks of different density have a uniform level of compensation. Modern hypotheses suggest variation in density in and between columns.

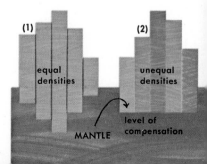

(1) equal densities

(2) unequal densities

MANTLE

level of compensation

GEOMAGNETIC BEHAVIOR tells geologists the earth behaves as though it were a giant bar magnet surrounded by a magnetic field. The force causes a compass to rotate so that it points toward the magnetic north pole. The earth's magnetic field may be due to convection currents in the outer core.

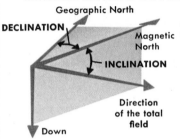

MAGNETIC DECLINATION is the angle between geographic ("true") north and magnetic north. The vertical angle between the horizontal and a freely dipping magnetic needle is the *inclination*. The declination shows daily changes and also slow, measurable changes over long periods of time. The magnetic poles change position relative to the geographic poles at a present rate of about four miles every year, although the deviation is never large.

MAGNETIC DATA achieved with the development of new instruments has permitted geophysicists to measure quantities with a precision considered impossible only a few decades ago.

A MAGNETOMETER is used to measure the intensity of the earth's magnetic field at any point on its surface. Distortions of the earth's magnetic field by rocks of varying magnetic susceptibility are measured also. Traverses are made on the ground or by using an airborne magnetometer which gives continuous and rapid readings.

MAGNETIC SURVEYS are often used in the exploration of minerals. These surveys are carried out so that buried rocks and ore bodies of different magnetic properties can be located and mapped.

Airborne magnetometer

THE MAGNETIC FIELD of the earth has been measured and mapped. The lines of force, marked by arrows, show its direction at various places. It also varies in intensity (being twice as great at the poles as at the equator), and the inclination ranges from zero degrees at the magnetic equator to 90° at the magetic poles. Local anomalies are often produced by distinctive magnetic properties of some rock bodies.

MAGNETIC STORMS are sudden fluctuations in the earth's magnetic field caused by charged particles from the sun (the solar wind). Magnetic storms often precede aurora displays.

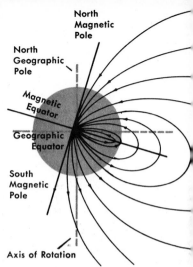

PALEOMAGNETIC MEASUREMENTS show that cooling igneous rock bodies and settling sedimentary particles may reflect the ancient magnetic fields in which they were formed. Magnetic sedimentary particles, for example, are oriented just like compass needles, so they indicate the "fossil" magnetic field at the time of their formation. This remnant magnetism has made it possible to construct paleomagnetic maps of earlier periods of geologic time.

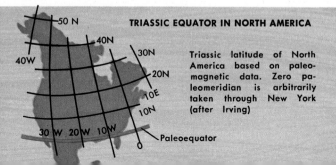

TRIASSIC EQUATOR IN NORTH AMERICA

Triassic latitude of North America based on paleomagnetic data. Zero paleomeridian is arbitrarily taken through New York (after Irving)

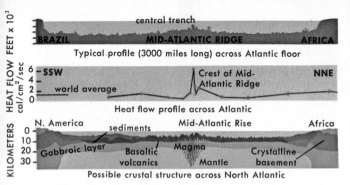

Typical profile (3000 miles long) across Atlantic floor

Heat flow profile across Atlantic

Possible crustal structure across North Atlantic

STRUCTURE OF THE OCEAN FLOOR

MID-OCEAN RIDGES form a great network of mountain chains linking the various oceans. They range up to 1,500 miles in width and reach a height of 18,000 feet above the adjacent floor of the abyssal plain; most are about 10,000 feet above it. The crests are marked by elongated trenches or rift valleys up to 12,000 feet deep and 30 miles wide. Ridges are of volcanic origin, emerging above sea level in places.

RIFT VALLEYS occur in places where the ridges are laterally offset by major transform faults. Profiles of typical mid-oceanic ridges are marked by intense earthquake activity and very high heat flow. Seismic studies show the ridge to typically consist of a thin layer of sediment overlying less than 2 miles of rock with characteristics of basalt, overlying a substratum of rock intermediate between basic oceanic rocks and the mantle.

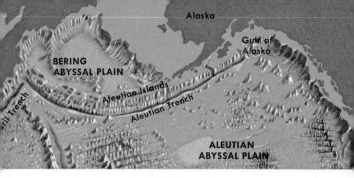

ABYSSAL PLAINS form the real floors of the oceans, covering over 60 percent of the total area. They are flat basins, hundreds of miles across, with surfaces generally broken only by ocean ridges, rises, or seamounts. They lie at depths below 15,000 feet. Geophysical studies show that they have a thin cover of sediments, which merge with those of the continental rise. In places, the abyssal plains are cut by relatively wide, shallow canyon systems, probably cut by the same turbidity currents that deposit the sediments.

SEAMOUNTS are steepsided, conical hills rising up to 12,000 feet above the abyssal plain.

GUYOTS are similar to seamounts but have flat tops. These are the remains of submarine volcanoes whose peaks have been eroded by waves to a flat surface and then submerged by subsidence of the sea floor. Most lie at 3,000-5,000 feet below present sea level.

RISES are broad, regional uplifts a few hundred miles wide, that are partly volcanic in origin, as in the Bermuda and Hawaiian rises.

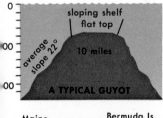

VOLCANIC ISLAND ARCS, common around the basin of the Pacific, are also found in the Caribbean. The Aleutians and the Philippines are examples. They are generally bordered on their convex oceanic side by elongated, narrow trenches, which exceed 36,000 feet in depth. Sites of vulcanism and earthquake activity, these are also areas of great crustal instability. Pleistocene coral reefs in Indonesia now stand 4,000 feet above sea level.

Lavas from volcanoes on island arcs are invariably andesitic, being intermediate in composition between the granitic continental rocks and the basaltic lavas of the oceanic islands. Island arcs are also marked by large negative gravity anomalies (p. 133). Nearly all deep-focus earthquakes occur in these arcs, which may mark a major fracture zone between the continents and the oceans (pp. 140, 147).

TRENCHES OF THE PACIFIC BASIN

1. Aleutian
2. Kurile
3. Japan
4. Nansei Shoto
5. Mariana
6. Palau
7. Philippine
8. Weber
9. Java
10. New Britain
11. New Hebrides
12. Tonga-Kermadec
13. Peru-Chile
14. Acapulco-Guatemala
15. Cedros

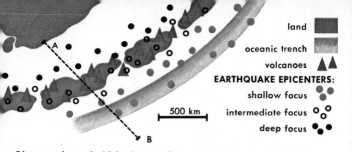

land

oceanic trench

volcanoes ▲▲

EARTHQUAKE EPICENTERS:

shallow focus

intermediate focus ○ ○

deep focus ● ●

500 km

Diagram of a typical island arc and trench structure, showing relative position of volcanoes; shallow-, intermediate-, and deep-focus earthquakes; and oceanic trench. **AB** represents line of sections below: length about 1,200 kilometers.

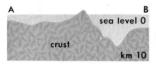

TOPOGRAPHIC PROFILE shows very steep sides of typical island-arc trench.

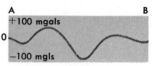

GRAVITY PROFILE shows island-arc trench areas as belts of strong negative anomalies.

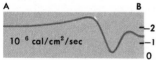

HEAT FLOW very high on landward side in volcanic areas but very low across trenches implies an occurrence of differing processes below the sea floor.

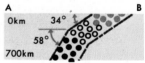

EARTHQUAKE EPICENTER PLOT shows planes of foci dipping toward the continents at 30-60°. This may be a major oceanic-continental fracture zone.

PROBABLE GEOLOGIC STRUCTURE shows the relationship of a fracture to crustal structure below an island arc.

MANTLE CONVECTION CURRENTS may produce trenches and volcanic arcs. Theoretically, this explains the gravity profile.

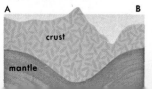

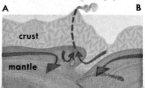

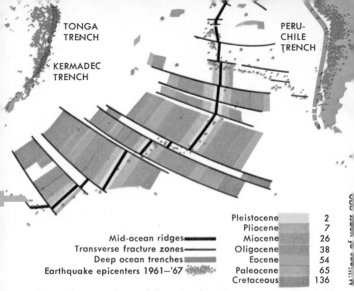

Pleistocene		2
Pliocene		7
Mid-ocean ridges	Miocene	26
Transverse fracture zones	Oligocene	38
Deep ocean trenches	Eocene	54
Earthquake epicenters 1961–'67	Paleocene	65
	Cretaceous	136

Magnetic anomalies, existing as mirror images across the Pacific mid-oceanic ridge, strongly suggest sea floor spreading.

SEA-FLOOR SPREADING accounts for many oceanic features, such as its enormous relief and complexity, with variations ranging from the depths of 35,000 feet in the Mariana Trench to heights of 32,024 feet above the ocean floor of the volcanic mountains of Hawaii. Geophysical studies indicate that the ocean floor is similar to the lower "basaltic" layer of the crust below the continents. There is no trace over most of the oceans of the sial layer, although it is present below some ridges and islands. The oceanic crust is covered by a thin layer of sediment, all less than 150 million years old.

Some transcurrent faults of the Eastern Pacific are 1,000 miles long, and produce submarine scarps 10,-000 feet high. Magnetic surveys over these faults indicate horizontal displacement of over 600 miles. Such faults as these and the Alpine Fault of New Zealand prove continental movement (or drift) of hundreds of miles. The San Andreas Fault is still undergoing horizontal movement of some 2 inches per year, and suggests a general relative dextral movement.

The structure of the trenches around the Pacific basin seems to imply underriding of the continent by the ocean floor. If so, new oceanic crust must be rising somewhere to replace that "lost" under the continents.

ANOMALIES in the remnant magnetism of the oceanic crust show reversals, reflecting changes in the magnetic field at the various times of crust formation. Studies of lava flows have given a time scale of magnetic reversals for the past 4 million years, and this is confirmed in deep-sea cores. Similar anomalies exist in symmetrical bands, parallel to the mid-oceanic ridges. This suggests that new crust is being formed and spreading at rates up to 6 centimeters per year.

THE SHORES of the western Pacific are still rising at measurable rates.

VOLCANIC ACTIVITY in ocean areas may indicate upwelling and renewal of the crust.

YOUNG SEDIMENT on the Pacific floor suggests that oceans are not permanent features. Older sediments may have been "swept under" the continents. Other oceans may lack thick sediments because they are young.

PROFILE OF SEAMOUNTS in the Gulf of Alaska (Pratt-Welker range) shows that mounts farthest from the Aleutian Trench are 6,000 feet higher than those which lie within it (p. 142). Other Pacific islands show how migration of volcanic centers away from an area is accompanied by subsidence. This could imply the lateral and vertical migration of ocean floors. Other facts about volcanoes and coral reefs also seem to support this hypothesis.

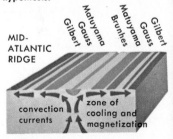

Model shows possible rise of new sea floor, "imprinted" with reversals of successive magnetic **periods.**

CORAL REEFS AND VOLCANOES provide major clues to the history of the oceans. The depth and stage of development may be used to trace the changing pattern of volcanic activity.

THE PRATT-WELKER chain of guyots runs from the Gulf of Alaska toward the Aleutian Trench (p. 137). Guyot GA-1 has a surface lying almost 6,000 feet below the general level of all the other guyots. It must have been carried down by the subsidence that produced the Aleutian Trench.

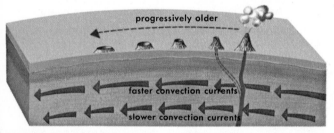

MIGRATION of the center of volcanic activity, in a broad southeasterly direction, is seen in many Pacific volcanic islands, such as the Tahiti Chain with atolls or even seamounts in the northwest, grading into active volcanoes in the southeast.

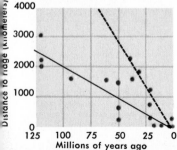

THE OLDEST AGES of lavas from Atlantic volcanic islands have a broad relationship to their distance from the Mid-Atlantic Ridge. This seems to imply that the volcanoes may have originated on the ridge and then moved away from it, perhaps implying a migration of the islands, and presumably of the whole ocean floor, away from the mid-ocean ridge.

Volcanic island with fringing reef | **Island sinking, barrier reef** | **Atoll**

OTHER CORAL REEFS develop around islands, especially the volcanic islands of the Pacific, where they may form *fringing reefs* (growing on the fringe of the island), *barrier reefs* (separated from the island by a lagoon), or *atolls* (ringlike ramparts of lagoons with no main island core). Charles Darwin suggested these three types of reefs represented three stages in the sinking of the ocean floor around a volcanic island, the coral growth at sea level keeping pace with the sinking of the floor.

Geophysical surveys and borings on Pacific atolls confirm this theory. On Eniwetok, 4,000 feet of coral sediments were found to be underlain by olivine basalt. It may not be a complete explanation, however, because of the generally uniform depth of lagoons (from 150 feet for the smaller ones to 270 feet for the larger ones). Although they have been partly filled by sediment, it seems probable that this, their broadly uniform depth, may be the result of Pleistocene erosion of older reefs during periods of lower sea level. Many theories have been proposed, but no one theory can account for the varied types of coral reef structure.

		atoll
Sea level C	**lagoon**	
Sea level B	**lagoon** **sediments**	**Barrier reef**
Sea level A	**Subsiding Volcanic Island**	**Fringing reef**

CONTINENTAL DRIFT is not demonstrated by paleomagnetic reconstructions of Pliocene and Quaternary rocks, but differences of up to 90° are known from older rocks. A curve showing the course of polar wandering for each continent implies not only polar wandering but also relative movement of continents.

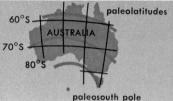

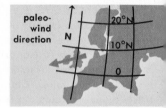

PALEOMAGNETIC RECONSTRUCTIONS generally agree with other geologic data, a few of which are shown above.

DIRECTIONS OF ANCIENT WINDS that deposited sedimentary rocks agree well with former continental positions.

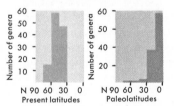

Present latitudes   Paleolatitudes

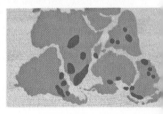

▲
PERMO-CARBONIFEROUS glacial deposits (brown) are more easily explained by a reconstruction of continental drift, than by present geography.

DISTRIBUTION of late Paleozoic amphibians is better explained by paleomagnetic reconstruction of former continental positions than by present ones.

SOME MOUNTAIN CHAINS and rock formations, as well as the continental blocks themselves, fit together when the continents are reassembled.

THE POWER necessary for continental drift is still unknown, but it may come from heat convection currents in the upper mantle.

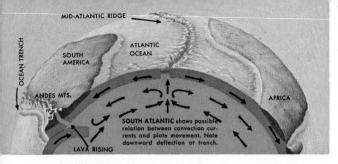

Diagram showing MID-ATLANTIC RIDGE, OCEAN TRENCH, SOUTH AMERICA, ATLANTIC OCEAN, ANDES MTS., AFRICA, LAVA RISING. **SOUTH ATLANTIC** shows possible relation between convection currents and plate movement. Note downward deflection at trench.

PLATE TECTONICS relates sea floor spreading to continental drift. Six major rigid plates, and several minor ones, each about 100 Km thick, appear to be carried by sub-crustal convection currents at rates of a few centimeters a year away from mid-oceanic ridges, where new crustal material is generated (p. 140). Plates "converge" at trenches, where one plate is deflected beneath another (p. 139). Plates may also slide laterally with respect to one another at transform faults (p. 137, 147). Continuation of existing plate movements would lead to further opening of the Atlantic Ocean, closure of the Mediterranean Sea, and the impingement of Australia on the Asian mainland.

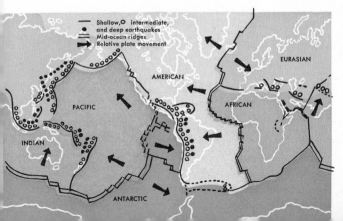

Shallow, O intermediate, • and deep earthquakes; Mid-ocean ridges; Relative plate movement. Plates labeled: PACIFIC, INDIAN, AMERICAN, AFRICAN, EURASIAN, ANTARCTIC.

CONVECTION CURRENTS in the mantle have been suggested (p. 139) as an explanation for the complex features of island arcs and trenches. Might they also explain other features and earth processes?

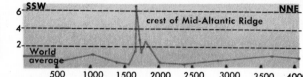

Heat flow pattern shows increase across typical mid-oceanic ridge.

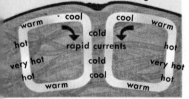

STAGE 2-Root formation and mountain building

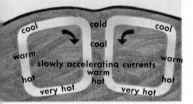

STAGE 3-Emergence of mountains

HEAT FLOW traversing across the oceans shows sharp rises over the mid-oceanic ridges. The relatively low radioactive content of basic rocks makes radioactivity very improbable as a source. It is believed that up-rising convection currents in the mantle could best explain this heat pattern, and that the low heat values on the seaward side of island arcs represent the downturning of such currents, which "sweep" the ocean floor toward the continents.

MOUNTAIN-BUILDING involves the development, uplift, and compression of geosynclines, in which up to 40,000 feet of sediments were deposited. The continuous sinking of the crust in geosynclines cannot be caused by the weight of sediment itself. This is too light to have any major effect in the underlying sima. Convection currents seem the most probable downwarping mechanism. Three stages of a hypothetical cycle are illustrated at the left.

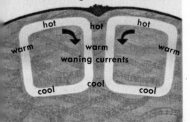

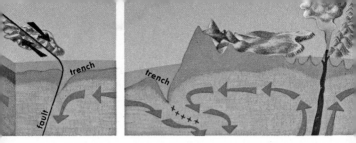

MOVEMENT OF CONTINENTAL BLOCKS is now clearly proved by such faulted areas as New Zealand, where the western part of South Island has been completely moved some 300 miles northward relative to the eastern part. Paleomagnetic data suggest major movement of the continents in the past and also sea-floor spreading (p. 140). The diagram shows one possible mechanism for such movement. Horizontal movement may take place in an upper zone of the mantle characterized by low seismic velocity, lying above an average depth of about 60 kilometers which is probably characterized by Rheid flow and partial melting.

CONVECTION CURRENTS still remain hypothetical. They cannot be directly observed, but studies of the physical properties of the mantle give strong support to their existence. It has been calculated that the mantle would have to be 10,000 times more viscous than post glacial rebound suggests to prevent convection currents. Experimental studies using earth models and the wide variety of earth processes provide the only tenable explanation. Currents would probably move at only a few millimeters a year, and may be confined to the upper mantle. The source of heat could come from the core or from the mantle, or from both.

AN INTEGRATED EXPLANATION of all these complex processes is still lacking. We know little of the precise causes and effects of convection currents (assuming they exist) or of the detailed relationship between orogeny and continental drift. We know even less about the origin of the continental masses and the early state and origin of the earth. But patient observation and experiment, mapping and measuring, and charting and correlation have already provided enough information for us to be optimistic.

THE EARTH'S HISTORY

The age of the earth has been a subject of speculation since man's early days, but only in the last century have attempts been made to measure it. Geologists studying earth processes are concerned with the sequence of rocks and structures in time, and thus with the history of the earth itself.

RATE OF COOLING was once thought to show the earth was only 20-40 million years old. Discovery of heat produced by radioactivity provides new data that invalidate this conclusion.

TOTAL AVERAGE THICKNESS of sediment over the earth, if regularly deposited, was thought to provide the earth's age, if divided by the average annual addition to new sediments. While this method may be acceptable for a few local deposits, there are far too many variables and unknowns (such as redeposition of sediment) to allow its use for determining the age of the earth.

SALT CONTENT OF THE OCEANS is presumed to have come from weathering of rocks and was divided by the annual increment to give an age for the oceans of about 90,000,000 years. The same limitations apply to this factor as to sediment-thickness calculations. Both figures involve corrections which would increase their value.

RADIOACTIVE DECAY provides the best present method of measuring the age of rocks. Radioactive elements undergo spontaneous breakdown by loss of alpha and beta particles into stable elements. The rate of breakdown, which can be accurately measured, is independent of any environmental conditions, such as temperature or pressure. The ratio of decayed to parent elements thus provides an indication of the age of the mineral in which it is found. Different elements have very different decay rates.

◀ Thickness of sedimentary rocks in Grand Canyon, Arizona, gives rough indication of relative geologic time.

URANIUM (U238) is a commonly used element, going through 15 disintegrations before it becomes the stable element lead (Pb206). Different elements have different rates of disintegration. U238 has a half-life (the time taken for half its atoms to disintegrate) of 4,500 million years. Some other elements commonly used in age studies are thorium, potassium, and rubidium.

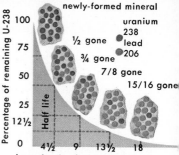

Increasing time (in billions of years)

THE OLDEST ROCKS measured by radioactive methods have an age of about 3,500 million years. This is younger than the earth itself, which is probably about 4,500 million years old. Studies of meteorites, which are samples of the planetary material from which the earth probably originated, also indicate an age of about 4,500 million years. The oldest known fossils are about 2,800 million years old, but common fossils are found only in rocks younger than 600 million years old.

Radio carbon dating is useful for rocks that contain woody fragments and are younger than about 30,000 years. C14 from the atmosphere is incorporated in plant tissues and disintegrates to N14 with a half life of 5,570 years.

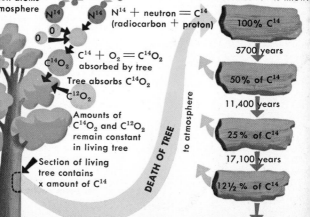

Neutrons bombard nitrogen atoms in atmosphere

cosmic rays

N^{14} + neutron = C^{14} (radiocarbon + proton)

C^{14} + O_2 = $C^{14}O_2$ absorbed by tree

Tree absorbs $C^{14}O_2$

Amounts of $C^{14}O_2$ and $C^{12}O_2$ remain constant in living tree

Section of living tree contains x amount of C^{14}

DEATH OF TREE

to atmosphere

Rate at which C^{14} decays and becomes N^{14} is known

100% C^{14}

5700 years

50% of C^{14}

11,400 years

25 % of C^{14}

17,100 years

12½% of C^{14}

UNDERSTANDING THE EARTH involves the study of the development of animals and plants and of the continuously changing ancient geographies. In general, the study of earth history involves the detailed dating of sedimentary rocks by various methods, which are then related to a geologic time scale. This is difficult because most radioactive minerals used for age determinations occur in igneous rocks, although glauconite is a mineral used for age studies of sedimentary rocks.

SUPERPOSITION of sedimentary rocks indicates their relative ages. In undisturbed sections, younger rocks overlie older.

STRATIGRAPHIC CORRELATION of strata in one place with those of the same age, deposited at the same period of time in another place, is fundamental in the interpretation of geologic history.

FOSSILS are the most important single method of correlation. Fossils are the remains of, or direct indication of, prehistoric animals and plants. Although they are influenced by environment of deposition, similar assemblages of fossils generally indicate similarity of age in the rocks that contain them.

ROCK FACIES, the sum total of the characteristics of a rock's depositional environment, are independent of geological time. An awareness of them, however, is important in correlation. Figure shows how a shallow sea transgressed over a deltaic and near-shore environment.

LITHOLOGICAL CORRELATION uses the similarity of mineralogy, sorting, structure, bedding, sequence, and other features as indications of similar ages of rocks. It is of limited value, since rocks of different lithology often are deposited at the same time in adjacent areas.

GEOPHYSICAL CORRELATION makes use of similarity of physical rock properties (electrical resistivity and self-potential, for example) as an indication of similar age. Widely used in boreholes, this method is limited by the same factors as lithological methods.

STANDARD GEOLOGIC COLUMN, gradually built up by combining rock sequences from different areas, provides a rock succession that represents a time scale relative to the history of fossil organisms the rocks contain. This is like a master motion picture film in which local rock sequences each represent a few single frames.

ROCK SYSTEMS in the geologic column are major divisions of rocks deposited during a particular period of geologic time. Names of systems are taken from areas where rocks were first described, such as Devonian from Devonshire, or from their characteristics, as Cretaceous from the chalk, which is found in many strata of this age.

World Wars	Renaissance			Roman Empire		Assyrian Empire		Egyptian Middle Kingdom
2000	1500	1000		A.D.	B.C.	1000		

Geologic time in millions of years (below) compared with last 4000 years

C M Pale. | Precambrian

| | 500 | 1000 | 2000 | 3000 | 4000 |

Age of layers in millions of years

Sandstone
Limestone
Shale
Limestone and sandstone
Sandstone and shale
Limestone, sandstone and shale

BRYCE CANYON — 60

ZION CANYON — 135
— 166
— 181

The Earth's total history is pieced together by comparison of rocks from many areas.

GRAND CANYON

— 230
— 280
— 300
— 345
— 600

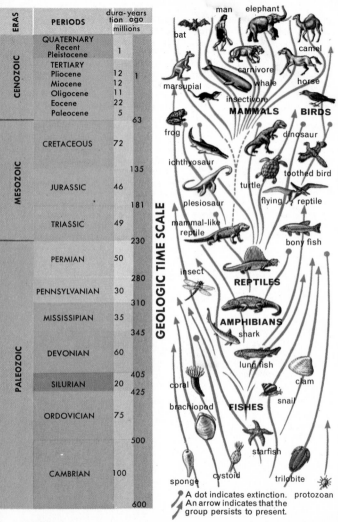

ERAS	PERIODS	duration millions	years ago millions
CENOZOIC	QUATERNARY Recent Pleistocene	1	
	TERTIARY Pliocene	12	1
	Miocene	12	
	Oligocene	11	
	Eocene	22	
	Paleocene	5	
			63
MESOZOIC	CRETACEOUS	72	
			135
	JURASSIC	46	
			181
	TRIASSIC	49	
			230
PALEOZOIC	PERMIAN	50	
			280
	PENNSYLVANIAN	30	
			310
	MISSISSIPIAN	35	
			345
	DEVONIAN	60	
			405
	SILURIAN	20	425
	ORDOVICIAN	75	
			500
	CAMBRIAN	100	
			600

GEOLOGIC TIME SCALE

man elephant
bat camel
carnivore horse
marsupial whale
insectivore
MAMMALS **BIRDS**
frog dinosaur
ichthyosaur toothed bird
turtle
plesiosaur flying reptile
mammal-like reptile bony fish
insect
REPTILES
AMPHIBIANS
shark
lung fish
coral clam
brachiopod snail
FISHES
starfish
sponge cystoid trilobite
protozoan

A dot indicates extinction.
An arrow indicates that the group persists to present.

152

PALEOGRAPHIC MAPS are reconstructions of the geography of particular periods of the geologic past. Maps of present-day geography involve fairly simple surveying and cartographic plotting of visible coastlines and other features. Past geographies are available to us only by their indirect representation in rocks and fossils. Unraveling and interpreting these clues to the past is the basic task of historical geology. Methods used are illustrated on page 150.

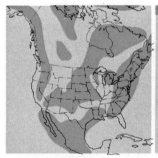

1. ORDOVICIAN
about 450 million years ago

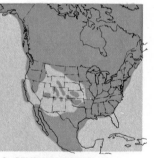

2. PENNSYLVANIAN
about 280 million years ago

3. CRETACEOUS
about 100 million years ago

4. MIOCENE
about 20 million years ago

153

GEOLOGIC MAP OF

QUATERNARY
Rocks and unconsolidated deposits of Pleistocene and Recent age

TERTIARY
Rocks of Paleocene, Eocene, Oligocene, Miocene, and Pliocene age

MESOZOIC
Rocks of Triassic, Jurassic, and Cretaceous age

LATE PALEOZOIC
Rocks of Devonian, Mississippian, Pennsylvanian, and Permian age

EARLY PALEOZOIC
Rocks of Cambrian, Ordovician, and Silurian age

PRECAMBRIAN
A variety of igneous, metamorphic, and sedimentary rocks (includes some metamorphosed Paleozoic loca

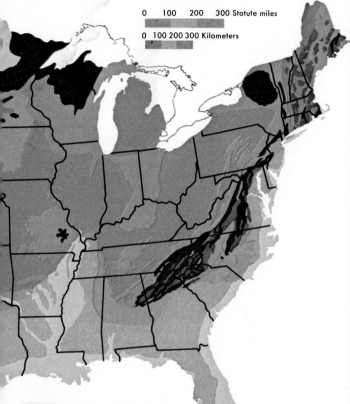

0   100   200   300 Statute miles

0   100 200 300 Kilometers

EXTRUSIVE IGNEOUS ROCKS
Chiefly lava flows of
Tertiary and Quaternary
age

INTRUSIVE IGNEOUS ROCKS
(includes some metamorphic
rocks) Granitoid rocks of
various ages

FOR MORE INFORMATION

MUSEUMS AND EXHIBITS provide excellent displays of general geologic topics and of regional geology. Many universities and most large cities have museums with geologic exhibits.

STATE GEOLOGICAL SURVEYS publish maps, guide books, and elementary introductions to geology. The U.S. Geological Survey, Washington, D.C. 20242 and the Geologic Survey of Canada also publish many useful reports and maps.

NATIONAL PARKS AND MONUMENTS are generally areas of great geologic interest. They provide guided tours, talks, museums, and pamphlets.

FURTHER READING

BOOKS will help you develop your interest in earth science. Here are a few useful titles:

Bertin, Leon, *Larousse Encyclopedia of the Earth*, Prometheus Press, New York, 1965. Useful introduction to earth science.

Cailleux, Andre, *Anatomy of the Earth*, McGraw Hill, New York, 1968. Well-illustrated general guide in paperback.

Clark, Thomas H., and Stearn, Colin W., *Geological Evolution of North America*, Second Edition, Ronald Press Company, New York, 1968. College level introduction to historical geology.

Gilluly, James; Waters, Aaron C.; and Woodford, A. O., *Principles of Geology*, Third Edition, W. H. Freeman and Company, San Francisco, 1968. College level introduction to physical geology.

Investigating the Earth, E. S. C. P., Houghton Mifflin Company, Boston, 1967. Junior and senior high school level introduction.

Rhodes, F. H. T., *The Evolution of Life*, Penguin Books, Baltimore, Md., 1962. A paperback account of the history of life.

Rhodes, F. H. T.; Zim, Herbert S.; and Shaffer, Paul R., *Fossils*, Golden Press, New York, 1962. A paperback guide to fossils.

Zim, Herbert S., and Shaffer, Paul R., *Rocks and Minerals*, Golden Press, New York, 1957. A paperback guide to rocks and minerals.

PHOTO CREDITS: Unless otherwise credited photographs are by the author. p. 4 R. Wenkam, p. 15 Am. Museum of Natural History, p. 31 E. Moench/Photo-Researchers, p. 33 R. Wenkam, p. 34 top Kai Curry-Lindahl, bot., Douglass Hubbard, p. 52 bot., New Zealand Geological Survey, p. 58 M. Rosalsky, p. 60 top J. Wyckoff, p. 63 C. Trautwein, p. 64 Luray Caves, p. 68 top, M. Rosalsky, p. 69 top, E. Druce, p. 75 J. Wyckoff, p. 76 J. Wyckoff, p. 80 H. Schlenker/Photo-Researchers, p. 83 M. Rosalsky, p. 85 J. Muench, p. 96 E. Druce, p. 102 L. Carlson, p. 103 top J. J. Witkind, p. 105 M. Rosalsky, p. 112 California Geology, p. 115 M. Rosalsky, p. 116 H. Bristol, p. 125 J. J. Witkind, p. 134 Airborne Geophysics Division, Lockwood, Kessler & Barlett, Inc.

INDEX

D   E